PRAISE FOR A
MARY BALOGH

"Once you start a Mary Balogh book, you won't be able to stop reading."
—*New York Times* bestselling author
Susan Elizabeth Phillips

"Mary Balogh has the gift of making a relationship seem utterly real and utterly compelling." —Mary Jo Putney

"Winning, witty, and engaging . . . fulfilled all of my romantic fantasies."
—*New York Times* bestselling author
Teresa Medeiros

"Mary Balogh just keeps getting better and better . . . interesting characters and great stories to tell . . . well worth your time." —*The Atlanta Journal-Constitution*

"Mary Balogh is a superb author whose narrative voice comments on the characters and events of her novel in an ironic tone reminiscent of Jane Austen."
—*Milwaukee Journal Sentinel*

"Mary Balogh reaches deep and touches the heart."
—*New York Times* bestselling author
Joan Johnston

"This is Mary Balogh at her riveting best."
—#1 *New York Times* bestselling author
Debbie Macomber

continued . . .

"[Mary Balogh] writes with wit and wisdom.... *The Proposal* is both moving and entertaining and the beginning of what promises to be an outstanding series."

—Romance Reviews Today

"This sexy, touching book revisits the marriage-of-convenience plot, joining two heroic, conflicted characters who are navigating their own versions of darkness and delivering them to the redemptive power of love. Regency bestseller Balogh once again takes a standard romance trope and imbues it with heart, emotional intelligence, and flawless authenticity."

—*Kirkus Reviews* (starred review)

"This touching, totally enthralling story overflows with subtle humor, brilliant dialog, breathtaking sensuality, and supporting characters you want to know better."

—*Library Journal* (starred review)

"Balogh can always be depended on to deliver a beautifully written Regency romance with appealing, unusual characters, and the second in her new Survivors' Club series is no exception.... Future series installments promise more compellingly tormented heroes."

—*Publishers Weekly*

"[A] poignant and thoughtful romance."   —*Booklist*

"A compassionate love story with a unique hero and heroine.... The dialogue is snappy, and the climax ... is exciting and helps bring about the blissful ending.... *The Arrangement* [is] a must read."   —Fresh Fiction

PRAISE FOR THE NOVELS
OF MARY BALOGH

Longing

"Balogh capture[s] the allure of the land and the culture of the proud people of Wales . . . a very different sort of historical romance. Ms. Balogh's writing has a very lyrical quality to it which draws out the feelings of yearning so that the reader can palpably sense them . . . pretty powerful." —The Hope Chest Reviews

"A particular favorite of mine." —The Romance Reader

Beyond the Sunrise

"Thoroughly enjoyable."
  —*New York Times* bestselling author Janelle Taylor

"Balogh's . . . epic love story is a winner . . . absorbing reading right up until the end." —*Publishers Weekly*

"High intrigue, daring exploits, a passionate love affair, what more could you want in a romance? Balogh gives us a humdinger of a tale set during the Napoleonic Wars. Great fun. Highly recommended."—*Manderley Magazine*

"*Beyond the Sunrise* is an utterly absorbing, powerful tale of a love that was once doomed and yet blooms again amidst the intrigue and ordeal of war. With infinite care and deft plotting, Ms. Balogh spins an intricate tale with the skill of a master weaver. She draws you into the era by evoking the aura of the war and the passionate emotions of her characters. If you have never read another book by Mary Balogh, then *Beyond the Sunrise* will be your introduction to a writer of remarkable talents." —*RT Reviews*

ALSO BY MARY BALOGH

ONLY A PROMISE

A SURVIVORS' CLUB NOVEL

Mary Balogh

A SIGNET BOOK

SIGNET
Published by the Penguin Group
Penguin Group (USA) LLC, 375 Hudson Street,
New York, New York 10014

USA | Canada | UK | Ireland | Australia | New Zealand | India | South Africa | China
penguin.com
A Penguin Random House Company

First published by Signet, an imprint of New American Library,
a division of Penguin Group (USA) LLC

First Printing, June 2015

 REGISTERED TRADEMARK — MARCA REGISTRADA

ISBN 978-0-451-46967-0

Printed in the United States of America
10 9 8 7 6 5 4 3 2 1

I

$\mathcal{T}$here could surely be nothing worse than having been born a woman, Chloe Muirhead thought with unabashed self-pity as she sucked a globule of blood off her left forefinger and looked to see if any more was about to bubble up and threaten to ruin the strip of delicate lace she was sewing back onto one of the Duchess of Worthingham's best afternoon caps. Unless, perhaps, one had the good fortune to be a duchess. Or else a single lady in possession of forty thousand pounds a year and the freedom to set up one's own independent establishment.

She, alas, was not a duchess. Or in sole possession of even forty *pence* a year apart from her allowance from her father. Besides, she did not *want* to set up somewhere independently. It sounded suspiciously lonely. She could not really claim to be lonely now. The duchess was kind to her. So was the duke in his gruff way. And whenever Her Grace entertained afternoon visitors or went visiting herself, she always invited Chloe to join her.

It was not the duchess's fault that she was eighty-two years old to Chloe's twenty-seven. Or that the neighbors with whom she consorted most frequently must all be upward of sixty. In some cases they were very much upward. Mrs. Booth, for example, who always carried a large ear trumpet and let out a loud, querulous "Eh?" every time someone so much as opened her mouth to speak, was ninety-three.

If she had been born male, Chloe thought, rubbing her thumb briskly over her forefinger to make sure the bleeding had stopped and it was safe to pick up her needle again, she might have done all sorts of interesting, adventurous things when she had felt it imperative to leave home. As it was, all *she* had been able to think of to do was write to the Duchess of Worthingham, who was her mother's godmother and had been her late grandmother's dearest friend, and offer her services as a companion. An *unpaid* companion, she had been careful to explain.

A kind and gracious letter had come back within days, as well as a sealed note for Chloe's father. The duchess would be delighted to welcome dear Chloe to Manville Court, but as a guest, *not* as an employee—the *not* had been capitalized and heavily underlined. And Chloe might stay as long as she wished—forever, if the duchess had her way. She could not think of anything more delightful than to have someone young to brighten her days and make *her* feel young again. She only hoped Sir Kevin Muirhead could spare his daughter for a prolonged visit. She showed wonderful tact in adding that, of course; as she had in writing separately to him, for Chloe had explained in her own letter just why living at home had become intolerable to her, at least for a while, much as she loved her father and hated to upset him.

So she had come. She would be forever grateful to the

duchess, who treated her more like a favored grand-daughter than a virtual stranger and basically self-invited guest. But oh, she *was* lonely too. One could be lonely and unhappy while being grateful at the same time, could one not?

And, ah, yes. She was unhappy too.

Her world had been turned completely upside down *twice* within the past six years, which ought to have meant, if life proceeded along logical lines, as it most certainly did not, that the second time it was turned right side up again. She had lost everything any young woman could ever ask for the first time—hopes and dreams, the promise of love and marriage and happily-ever-after, the prospect of security and her own place in society. Hope had revived last year, though in a more muted and mod-est form. But that had been dashed too, and her very identity had hung in the balance. In the four years be-tween the two disasters her mother had died. Was it any wonder she was unhappy?

She gave the delicate needlework her full attention again. If she allowed herself to wallow in self-pity, she would be in danger of becoming one of those habitual moaners and complainers everyone avoided.

It was still only very early in May. A largish mass of clouds covered the sun and did not look as if it planned to move off anytime soon, and a brisk breeze was gusting along the east side of the house, directly across the ter-race outside the morning room, where Chloe sat sewing. It had not been a sensible idea to come outside, but it had rained quite unrelentingly for the past three days, and she had been desperate to escape the confines of the house and breathe in some fresh air.

She ought to have brought her shawl out with her, even her cloak and gloves, she thought, though then of course she would not have been able to sew, and she had promised to have the cap ready before the duchess awoke from her afternoon sleep. Dratted cap and dratted lace. But that was quite unfair, for she had volunteered to do it even when the duchess had made a mild protest.

"Are you quite sure it will be no trouble, my dear?" she had asked. "Bunker is perfectly competent with a needle."

Miss Bunker was her personal maid.

"Of course I am," Chloe had assured her. "It will be my pleasure."

The duchess always had that effect upon her. For all the obvious sincerity of her welcome and kindness of her manner, Chloe felt the obligation, if not to earn her living, then at least to make herself useful whenever she was able.

She was shivering by the time she completed her task and cut the thread with fingers that felt stiff from the cold. She held out the cap, draped over her right fist. The stitches were invisible. No one would be able to tell that a repair had been made.

She did not want to go back inside despite the cold. The duchess would probably be up from her sleep and would be in the drawing room bright with happy anticipation of the expected arrival of her grandson. She would be eager to extol his many virtues yet again though he had not been to Manville since Christmas. Chloe was tired of hearing of his virtues. She doubted he had any.

Not that she had ever met him in person to judge for

herself, it was true. But she did know him by reputation. He and her brother, Graham, had been at school together. Ralph Stockwood, who had since assumed his father's courtesy title of Earl of Berwick, had been a charismatic leader there. He had been liked and admired and emulated by almost all the other boys, even though he had also been one of a close-knit group of four handsome, athletic, clever boys. Graham had spoken critically and disapprovingly of Ralph Stockwood, though Chloe had always suspected that he envied that favored inner circle.

After school, the four friends all took up commissions in the same prestigious cavalry regiment and went off to the Peninsula to fight the forces of Napoleon Bonaparte, while Graham went to Oxford to study theology and become a clergyman. He had arrived home from the final term at school upset because Ralph Stockwood had called him a sniveling prig and lily-livered coward. Chloe did not know the context in which the insult had been hurled, but she had not felt kindly disposed toward Graham's erstwhile schoolmate ever since. And she never had liked the sound of him. She did not like boys, or men, who lorded it arrogantly over others and accepted their homage as a right.

Not many months after they had embarked for the Peninsula, Lieutenant Stockwood's three friends had been killed in the same battle, and he had been carried off the field and then home to England so severely wounded that he had not been expected to survive.

Chloe had felt sorry for him at the time, but her sympathies had soon been alienated again. Graham, in his capacity as a clergyman, had called upon him in London a day or two after he had been brought home from Portugal. Graham had been admitted to the sickroom, but the wounded man had sworn foully at him and ordered him to get out and never come back.

Chloe did not expect to like the Earl of Berwick, then, even if he *was* the Duke of Worthingham's heir and the duchess's beloved only grandson. She had not forgiven his description of her brother as a lily-livered coward. Graham was a *pacifist*. That did not make him a coward. Indeed, it took a great deal of courage to stand up for peace against men who were in love with war. And she had not forgiven the earl for cursing Graham after he had been injured without even listening to what Graham had come to say. The fact that he had undoubtedly been in great pain at the time did not excuse such rudeness to an old school friend. She had decided long ago that the earl was brash, arrogant, self-centered, even heartless.

And he was on his way to Manville Court. He was coming at the duchess's behest, it must be added, not because he had chosen of his own free will to visit the grandparents who doted on him. Chloe suspected that the summons had something to do with the duke's health, which had been causing Her Grace some concern for the past couple of months. She fancied that he was coughing more than usual and that his habit of covering his heart with one hand when he did so was a bad sign. He did not complain of feeling unwell—not, at least, in Chloe's hearing—and he saw his physician only when the duchess insisted. Afterward he called the doctor an old quack who knew no better than to prescribe pills and potions that served only to make the duke feel ill.

Chloe did not know what the true state of the duke's

health was, but she did know that he had celebrated his eighty-fifth birthday last autumn, and eighty-five was an awfully advanced age to be.

However it was, the Earl of Berwick had been summoned and he was expected today. Chloe did not want to meet him. She knew she would not like him. More important, perhaps, she admitted reluctantly to herself, she did not want him to meet *her,* a sort of charity guest of his grandmother's, an aging, twenty-seven-year-old spinster with a doubtful reputation and no prospects. A pathetic creature, in fact.

But the thought finally triggered laughter—at her own expense. She had whipped herself into a thoroughly cross and disagreeable mood, and it just would not do. She got determinedly to her feet. She must go up to her room without delay and change her dress and make sure her hair was tidy. She might be a poor aging spinster with no prospects, but there was no point in being an abject one who was worthy only of pity or scorn. That would be too excruciatingly humiliating.

She hurried on her way upstairs, shaking herself free of the self-pity in which she had languished for too long. Goodness, if she hated her life so much, then it was high time she *did* something about it. The only question was *what*? Was there anything she *could* do? A woman had so few options. Sometimes, indeed, it seemed she had none at all, especially when she had a *past,* even if she was in no way to blame for any of it.

When he found his grandmother's letter beside his plate at breakfast one morning along with a small pile of invitations, Ralph Stockwood, Earl of Berwick, had only recently returned to London from a three-week stay in the country.

He had come to town because at least it offered the promise of some diversion for body and mind, even if he did not expect to be vastly entertained. He would no doubt lounge about at his usual haunts in his usual aimless way for the duration of the spring Season. The whole of the beau monde had moved here too for the parliamentary session and for the frenzy of social entertainments with which it amused itself with unrelenting vigor for those few months. Ralph did not have a seat in the House of Lords, his title being a mere courtesy one, while procuring a seat in the House of Commons had never held any real appeal for him. But he always came anyway and attended as many parties and balls and concerts and the like as would alleviate the boredom of his evenings. He whiled away his days at White's Club and frequented Tattersall's to look over the horses and Jackson's boxing saloon to exercise his body and Manton's shooting gallery to maintain the steadiness of eye and hand. He spent as many hours with his tailor and his boot maker and hatmaker as were necessary to keep himself well turned out, though he had never aspired to the dandy set. He did whatever he needed to do to keep himself busy.

And he always yearned for . . .

Well, that was the trouble. He *yearned,* but could name no object of his yearning. He had a home, Elmwood Manor, in Wiltshire, where he had grown up and that he had inherited with his title from his father. He had also inherited a perfectly competent steward who had been there forever, and therefore he did not need to spend a great deal of time there himself. He had almost sole use of his grandfather's lavish town house, since his grandparents scarcely came to London any longer and his mother preferred to keep her own establishment. He had fond relatives—paternal grandparents, a maternal grandmother, a mother, three married sisters and their offspring, and some aunts, uncles, and cousins, all on his mother's side. He had more money than he could decently spend in one lifetime. He had . . . What else did he have?

Well, he had his life. Many did not. Many who would have been his own age, that is, or younger. He was twenty-six and sometimes felt seventy. He enjoyed decent health despite the numerous scars of battle he would carry to the grave, including the one across his face. He had friends. Though that was not strictly accurate. He had numerous friendly acquaintances, but deliberately avoided forming close friendships.

Strangely, he did not usually think of his fellow Survivors as friends. They called themselves the Survivors' Club, seven of them, six men and one woman. They had all been variously and severely wounded by the Napoleonic Wars, and they had spent a three-year period together at Penderris Hall in Cornwall, country home of George, Duke of Stanbrook, one of their number. George had not been to war himself, but his only son had died in Portugal. The duchess, the boy's mother, had died a few months later when she threw herself over the high cliffs at the edge of their property. George, as damaged as any of the rest of them, had opened his home as a hospital and then as a convalescent home to a group of officers. And the seven of them had stayed longer than any of the others and had formed a bond that went deeper than family, deeper even than friendship.

It was they, though, his fellow Survivors, who had caused the worse-than-usual restlessness bordering on depression he was feeling this spring. He almost welcomed his grandmother's letter, then. It suggested, in that way his grandmother had of making an order sound like a request, that he present himself at Manville Court without delay. He had not been there since Christmas, though he wrote dutifully every two weeks, as he did to his other grandmother. His grandfather had not been actively unwell over the holiday, but it had been apparent to Ralph that he had crossed an invisible line between elderliness and frail old age.

He guessed what the summons was all about, of course, even if his grandfather was not actually ill. The duke had no brothers, only one deceased son, and only one live grandson. Short of tracking back a few generations and searching along another, more fruitful branch of the family tree, there was a remarkable dearth of heirs to the dukedom. Ralph was it, in fact. And he had no sons of his own. No daughters either.

And no wife.

His grandmother had no doubt sent for him in order to remind him of that last fact. He could not get sons—not legitimate heirs anyway—if he did not first get a young and fertile wife and then do his duty with her. Her Grace had delivered herself of a speech along those lines over Christmas, and he had promised to begin looking about him for a suitable candidate.

He had not yet got around to keeping that promise. He could use as an excuse, of course, the fact that the

Season had only just begun in earnest and that he had had no real opportunity to meet this year's crop of marriageable young ladies. He had already attended one ball, however, since the hostess was a friend of his mother's. He had danced with two ladies, one of them married, one not, though the announcement of her betrothal to a gentleman of Ralph's acquaintance was expected daily. Then, his obligation to his mother fulfilled, he had withdrawn to the card room for the rest of the evening.

The duchess would want to know what progress he was making in his search. She would expect that by now he would at the very least have compiled some sort of list. And making such a list would not be difficult, he had to admit, if he just set his mind to the task, for he was eminently eligible, despite his ruined looks. It was not a thought designed to lift Ralph's spirits. Duty, however, must be done sooner rather than later, and his grandmother had clearly decided that he needed reminding before the Season advanced any further.

The memory of the precious three weeks he had recently spent with his fellow Survivors at Middlebury Park in Gloucestershire, home of Vincent Hunt, Viscount Darleigh, only added to Ralph's sense of gloom. All seven of them had been both single and unattached just a little over a year ago during their last annual reunion at Penderris Hall. Without giving the matter any conscious thought, Ralph had assumed they would remain that way forever. As if *anything* remained the same forever. If he had learned one thing in his twenty-six years, surely it was that everything changed, not always or even usually for the better.

Hugo, Baron Trentham, had been the first to succumb

while they were still at Penderris, after he had carried Lady Muir up from the beach, where she had sprained an already lame ankle. They had promptly fallen in love and married a scant few months later. Then Vincent, the youngest of their number, the blind one, had fled one bride chosen by his family and then had narrowly missed being snared by another. He had been prompted by gallantry to offer for the girl who had come to his rescue that second time when she had thwarted the schemer, but ended up being chucked out of her home as a result. They had married a few days after Hugo and in the same church in London. Meanwhile Ben—Sir Benedict Harper—had been staying with his sister in the north of England when he met a widow who was being treated shabbily by her in-laws. He had chivalrously accompanied her when she fled to Wales and had ended up marrying her as well as running her grandfather's Welsh coal mines and ironworks. Bizarre, that! And now this year, during their reunion in Gloucestershire, Flavian, Viscount Ponsonby, had suddenly and unexpectedly married the widowed sister of the village music teacher and borne her off to London to meet his family.

Four of them married in little more than a year.

Ralph did not resent any of the marriages. He liked all four of the wives and thought it probable that each marriage would turn out well. Although in truth, he knew he must reserve judgment upon Flavian's, since it had happened so recently and so abruptly, and Flave was a bit unstable at the best of times, having suffered head injuries and memory loss during battle.

What Ralph did resent was change—a foolish resentment, but one he could not seem to help. He certainly did not resent his friends' happiness. Quite the contrary. What he did resent, perhaps—though *resentment* might be the wrong word—was that he had been left behind. Not that he wanted to be married. And not that he believed in happiness, marital or otherwise. Not for himself, anyway. But he had been left behind. Four of the others had found their way forward. Soon *he* would be married too—there was going to be no escaping that fate. It was his duty to marry and produce heirs. But he could not expect the happiness or even the contentment his friends had found.

He was incapable of love—of feeling it or giving it or wanting it.

Whenever he said as much to the Survivors, one or another of them would remind him quite emphatically that he loved *them,* and it was true, much as he shied away from using that exact word. He loved his family too. But the word *love* had so many meanings that it was in fact virtually meaningless. He had deep attachments to certain people, but he knew he was incapable of *love*, that something special that held together a good marriage and sometimes even made it a happy one.

There were a few social commitments he was forced to break after his grandmother's letter arrived, though none that caused him any deep regret. He sent his apologies to the relevant people, wrote a brief letter to his mother, who was in town and might expect him to call, and set out for Sussex and Manville Court in his curricle despite the fact that it was a brisk day in early May and there was even the threat of rain. He never traveled by closed carriage when he could help it. His baggage followed in a coach with his valet, though he doubted he would have much need of either. His grandmother would be too eager to say her piece and quickly send him back to London with all its parties and balls and eligible brides.

Unless Grandpapa really was ill, that was.

Ralph felt an uncomfortable lurching of the stomach at the thought. The duke was a very old man, and everyone must die at some time, but he could not face the prospect of losing his grandfather. Not yet. He did not want to be the head of his family, with no one above him and no one below. There was a horrible premonition of loneliness in the thought.

As if life was not an inherently lonely business.

He arrived in the middle of the afternoon, having stopped only once to change horses and partake of refreshments, and having been fortunate enough not to get held up at any toll booths or to get behind any slow-moving vehicles on narrow stretches of road. The front doors of Manville stood open despite the fact that the afternoon was not much warmer than the morning had been. Obviously he was expected, and there was Weller, his grandfather's elderly butler, standing in the doorway and bowing from the waist when Ralph glanced up at him. He was not looking particularly anxious—not that Weller ever displayed extreme emotions. But surely he would have done if Grandpapa were at his last gasp.

And then his grandfather himself appeared behind Weller's shoulder and the butler stepped smartly aside.

"Harrumph," the duke said—a characteristic sound that fell somewhere between a word and throat clearing— as Ralph relinquished the ribbons to a groom and took the steps up to the doors two at a time. "Making a filial visit just as the London Season is swinging into action, are you, Berwick? Because you could not go another day without a sight of Her Grace's face, I daresay?"

"Good to see you, sir." Ralph grinned at him and took the duke's bony, arthritic hand in his own. "How are you?"

"I suppose Her Grace wrote to tell you I was at death's door," the old man said. "I daresay I am, but I have not knocked upon it or set a toe over the doorsill yet, Berwick. Just a bit of a cough and a bit of gout, both the results of good living. Well, if you were sent for, you will be expected upstairs. We had better not keep the duchess waiting."

He led the way up to the drawing room. The butler was already stationed outside the double doors when they got there, and he flung them open so that the two men could enter together.

The duchess, who looked more like a little bird—a fierce little bird—every time Ralph saw her, was seated beside the fire. She nodded graciously as Ralph strode across the room to bend over her and kiss her offered cheek.

"Grandmama," he said. "I trust you are well?"

She glanced at the duke. "This is a pleasant surprise, Ralph," she said.

"Quite so," he agreed. "I thought I would run down for a day or two to see how you did. And Grandpapa too, of course."

"I must have the tea tray brought up," she said, looking vaguely about her as though expecting it to materialize from thin air.

"Allow me to ring the bell, Your Grace," a lady who

was sitting farther back from the fire said, getting to her feet and moving toward the bell rope.

"Oh, thank you, my dear," the duchess said. "You are always most thoughtful. This is my grandson, the Earl of Berwick. Miss Muirhead, Ralph. She is staying with me for a while, and very thankful I am for her company."

It was said graciously, and for one startled moment Ralph thought that perhaps he had been brought here to consider the guest as his prospective bride. But he could see that she was no young girl. She might even be older than he. She was not dressed in the first stare of fashion either. She was tall and on the slender side with a pale complexion and what looked like a dusting of freckles across her nose. She might have looked like a faded thing, or at least a fading thing, if it had not been for her hair, which was thick and plentiful and as bright a red as Ralph had ever seen on a human head.

"My lord." She curtsied without either looking at him or smiling, and he bowed and murmured her name.

His grandmother did not actually ignore her. Neither did she draw her any more to Ralph's attention, however, and he relaxed. Obviously she was of no particular account. Some sort of companion, he supposed, an aging, impecunious spinster upon whom Her Grace had taken pity.

"Now, tell me, Ralph," his grandmother said, patting the seat of the chair beside her, "who is in town this year for the Season? And who is new?"

Ralph sat and prepared to be interrogated.

2

The Earl of Berwick was really quite different from what Chloe had expected.

There were his looks, for one thing. He was not the handsome boy she had always imagined, frozen in time, arrogant and magnetically attractive, riding roughshod over the feelings of others. Well, of course he was no longer that boy. It had been eight years since he and Graham left school, and during those years he had been to war, lost his three friends, been desperately wounded himself, and made a slow recovery—perhaps. Perhaps he had recovered, that was. She had never really wondered what war did to a man apart from killing him or wounding him or allowing him to return home when it was over, mercifully unscathed. She had considered only the physical effects, in fact.

Lord Berwick fell into the second category—wounded and recovered. That should have been the end of it. He had been left with scars, however. One of them was horribly visible on his face, a nasty cut that slashed from his left temple, past the outer corner of his eye, across his cheek and the corner of his mouth to his jaw, and pulled both eye and mouth slightly out of shape. It must have been a very deep cut. Bone deep. The old scar was slightly ridged and dark in color and made Chloe wince at the thought of what his face must have looked like when it was first incurred. That it had missed taking out his eye was nothing short of a miracle. There must have been some permanent nerve damage, though. That side of his face was not as mobile as the other when he talked.

And if there was that one visible scar, there were surely others hidden beneath his clothes.

It was not just his scarred face, though, and the possibly scarred body that made him very different from the person she had expected and made her wonder more than she had before about what war did to a man. There were his eyes and his whole demeanor. There was something about his eyes, attractively blue though they were in a face that was somehow handsome despite the scar. Something . . . dead. Oh, no, not quite that. She could not explain to herself quite what she saw in their depths, unless it was that she saw no depths. They were chilly, empty eyes. And his manner, though perfectly correct and courteous, even affectionate toward his grandparents, seemed somehow . . . detached. As though his words and his behavior were a veneer behind which lived a man who was not feeling anything at all.

Chloe had gained this chilly impression of her brother's former schoolmate at their first meeting and realized how foolish she had been to expect him to be exactly as Graham had described him all those years ago. He was not that boy any longer, and had probably never been exactly as she had imagined him anyway. She had only ever seen him, after all, through the biased eyes of her brother, who was very different from him and had always both envied and resented him.

Chloe found this man, this stranger, disturbing, a cold, brooding, detached, controlled man it would surely be impossible to know. And a man who seemed largely unaware of her existence despite the fact that they had been introduced. Although he did not pointedly ignore her during dinner, neither did he initiate any conversation with her or show any particular interest in anything she had to say, though truth to tell she did not say a great deal. She was just a little bit intimidated by him.

She wished he were the man she had expected him to be. She could have felt open scorn at his arrogant assumption that he was God's gift to the human race instead of allowing him to make her feel somehow . . . diminished. Oh, dear, *did* she feel diminished? Again? If she allowed herself to feel any more so, she would surely disappear altogether and become just an easily forgotten memory to those who had known her. She almost chuckled aloud at the thought.

The duchess was a knitter. She made blankets and bonnets and booties and mittens for the babies born on the vast ducal estates scattered about England. She loved doing the actual knitting, she had once explained to Chloe. She found it soothing. But she hated the accompanying tasks of rolling the skeins of wool into balls before she started and sewing together the little garments when she was finished.

Chloe, of course, had immediately volunteered to perform both tasks.

After they had all drunk tea in the drawing room following dinner, the duke as usual got to his feet to bid the ladies good night and withdraw to the book room, his own domain. He invited his grandson to accompany him, but the earl glanced at the duchess, whose head was bent over her knitting, and professed his intention of remaining to keep her company for a while longer.

As though she had no one else to do that.

The duke made his way from the room with the aid of his cane while his grandson held the door open for him. Chloe moved away from the fireplace, where the coals had been piled high against the chill of the evening, so that she could use the conveniently spaced knobs of the sideboard cupboards over which to stretch a skein of the pale blue wool the duchess was currently using while she rolled it over her fingers into a soft ball. She sat down to the task, her back to the room, thankful that she had something to do while Her Grace settled into a conversation with the earl.

"You will have noticed a difference in your grandfather since Christmas," the duchess said after the door was closed.

"He seems to be doing well enough," the Earl of Berwick said.

"That is because he has put on a good show for you today," she told him, "as he does for everyone when he is outside his book room and his private apartments."

"And when he is *not*?" the earl asked.

"Your grandfather's heart is weakening," she told him. "Dr. Gregg says so. But of course he will not give up either his pipe or his port."

"They are indulgences that give him pleasure," the earl said. "Being deprived of them would perhaps make him miserable and neither improve his health nor prolong his life."

"That is exactly what Dr. Gregg says." The duchess sighed. "It would not surprise me at all, Ralph, if Worthingham does not survive another winter. He had a chill after Christmas and was a long time recovering from it, if he has recovered fully, that is. I doubt he could fight off another."

"Perhaps, Grandmama," the earl said, "you are being overpessimistic."

"And perhaps," she said, sharply, "I am not. The fact is, Ralph, that at some time in the not-too-distant future you are going to be the Duke of Worthingham yourself with all the duties that go along with the title."

Chloe heard the slow intake of the earl's breath. The ticking of the clock on the mantel seemed louder than usual.

"I shall be ready when the time comes, Grandmama," he said. "But I do not *want* the time to come. I want Grandpapa to live forever."

"Forever is not granted to any of us," the duchess said. "Even tomorrow is not granted as by right. Any of us can go at any moment."

"Yes," he said. "I know."

There was a whole universe of bleakness in his voice. Chloe's hands stilled as she turned her head to look at him. He was standing to one side of the fire, his elbow propped on the mantelpiece. There was a stillness about him that chilled her. Yes, he must know as well as anyone how quickly and suddenly life could be snuffed out. She wondered why he had been allowed to purchase a military commission when he was heir to a dukedom and had no brothers to provide spares in case of his demise.

She shivered slightly and wished she had brought her shawl over here with her instead of leaving it draped over the arm of the chair on which she had been sitting earlier. But she would not get up now to fetch it and draw attention to herself. She resumed her self-appointed task.

"Even you," Her Grace added unnecessarily.

"Yes, I know."

Chloe wound the wool more slowly during the silence that ensued. She was halfway through this particular skein and did not want to finish it too soon. She would have to return to her chair or else sit here idle, staring at the sideboard cupboards. Either way she would risk drawing attention to herself. She wished now she had made some excuse and left the room with the duke.

"It is time you married, Ralph," the duchess said bluntly into the silence.

"Yes, I know."

"You *knew* at Christmastime when we spoke on the same subject," she said. "Yet I have not heard that you are courting any particular lady, Ralph, despite the fact that I have my sources of information. Tell me that you *do* have someone in mind—someone young and eligible, someone both ready and willing to do her duty."

"I do not, I must confess," he said. "I have met no one with whom I can imagine spending the rest of my life. I know I must marry, but I do not *want* to marry, you see. I have nothing to offer. I am fully aware, however, that *must* will have to take precedence over *want*. I shall start looking, Grandmama, as soon as I return to London. I shall start looking in earnest. I shall make my choice before the end of the Season—well before. There. It is a promise. Are you reassured?"

"You have *nothing to offer*?" the duchess said, her tone incredulous. "*Nothing to offer,* Ralph? I doubt there is a more eligible bachelor in England."

"Nothing of myself to offer, I meant," he told her, his voice quieter than it had been so that Chloe had to still her hands again in order to concentrate upon hearing him. "There is nothing, Grandmama. Nothing in here."

Presumably he was tapping his chest.

"Nonsense," she said briskly. "You had a nasty time of it during the wars, Ralph, as did thousands of other men who fought that monster Bonaparte. You were one of the fortunate ones, however. You lived. You have all your limbs as well as the use of them, and you have both eyes and a sound mind. Why you had to spend all of three years in Cornwall I do not understand, but your prolonged stay there seems to have done you more harm than good. It prevented you from returning to your rightful place in society and to yourself as you were. It made you despondent and self-pitying, an attitude that does not become you. It is time you shook it off. You have everything in the world to offer some very fortunate young lady. Choose someone fresh from the schoolroom, someone who can be molded to the role she must play. But someone of impeccably good birth and breeding. Enlist your mother's help. The countess has a good head upon her shoulders despite our differences."

The Earl of Berwick chuckled, a sound so devoid of amusement that it could hardly be categorized as a chuckle at all.

"You are right, Grandmama," he said. "I am not likely to be rejected by anyone upon whom I fix my interest, am I? Poor girl, whoever she turns out to be. I shall *not* consult Mama. She will have a list longer than both my arms within a day, and all of the candidates will be trotted out for my inspection within a week. It will come to a matter of closing my eyes and sticking a pin in the list. I would prefer to choose for myself. And I *will* choose. I have promised. Shall I go back to town tomorrow?"

"His Grace will be disappointed," she said. "He was disappointed tonight when you chose to stay with me rather than go down to drink port with him in the book room."

"Shall I go down now?" he asked.

"He will be snoring in his chair by now," she told him. "Leave it until tomorrow. But return to town within the week, Ralph. It is already May and soon all the very brightest matrimonial prospects will have been laid claim to by men who have far less to offer than you do."

"It will be done," he said. "And the sooner the better. Life in town becomes tedious. When I have a wife, I will go home to Elmwood with her and stay there. Perhaps life in the country will suit me better. Perhaps I will settle down at last."

He sounded almost wistful.

"That would be a relief to everyone who loves you," she said. "Oh, dear, I have come to the end of my ball of wool and have no other ready to go."

Chloe, who had just wound the last strand onto the ball, got to her feet.

"I have one here ready for you, Your Grace," she said, crossing the room with it held out in the palm of her hand.

"Oh, how very thoughtful of you, dear," Her Grace said. "And you have been sitting far from the fire to wind it, have you? Come closer and have another cup of tea to warm you up. Though I fear what is left in the pot must be cold. I wish it were not. I would not mind another cup myself."

"I shall ring for a fresh pot," Chloe offered, moving toward the bell rope and having to pass very close to the earl on her way there.

He was looking at her, she saw when she raised her eyes briefly to his. He appeared slightly surprised, as though he were only just realizing that he was not alone in the drawing room with his grandmother.

Just thus must all ladies' companions, paid and unpaid and unacknowledged, waft through their lives, she thought ruefully—unnoticed, invisible for all intents and purposes. But she was not going to sink into the dismals again over *that* sad fact.

And if she did not like her life as it was, she had thought this afternoon, then she must simply change it.

Ha! *Simply.*

Her life had seemed impossible to change this afternoon. It still did this evening.

But nothing, surely, was impossible.

Apart from all the things that were.

The sun was showing its face from behind a receding bank of clouds the next morning when Ralph's valet drew back the curtains from the window of his bedchamber before disappearing into his dressing room. Two fine days in a row and this one perhaps even sunny? Though it was early yet. It might still rain.

Before it could or did, though, he shaved and dressed and went downstairs. There was no sign of either of his grandparents. He had not expected there would be. He was not hungry. He would wait for them. In the meanwhile, he wandered into the morning room, which was flooded with sunshine, facing east as it was. He found the French windows already unlocked and ajar, a fact that ought to have alerted him. He pulled one of them open, stepped through onto the terrace, and stood looking across the freshly scythed expanse of the east lawn to the river in the distance. He drew in a deep breath of fresh air and released it slowly.

He had not slept well. He had kept waking himself up from dreams that were not exactly nightmares but were bizarre nonetheless. He could remember only one of them, one of the more coherent. He had been in a ballroom he did not recognize, a room so long that even with a telescope he doubted he would have been able to see the far end of it. Along its full length, stretching to infinity, was a line of young ladies, all dressed in ballroom finery, and all of them plying a fan, though they were otherwise motionless. And he was marching with slow deliberation along the line, clad in his scarlet, gold-faced officer's dress uniform, inspecting them, his mother on one side, Graham Muirhead in full clerical robes on the other. It was *not* one of those dreams that defied interpretation, though why Muirhead of all people should have popped into it he could not imagine.

Ah. And then he could.

He became suddenly aware of a flutter of movement off to his right and turned his head sharply to see Miss Muirhead standing a short distance away, bonnetless and clutching the corners of a shawl to her bosom, presumably to prevent it from blowing away in the nonexistent wind. He felt instant irritation. She had overheard that very personal conversation he had had with his grandmother last evening and had not had the decency either to clear her throat to remind them of her presence or to leave the room. He had been quite unaware of her, as one tended to be unaware of servants. Though she was not a servant, was she? She was a *guest* of his grandmother's— one who ran and fetched for her and effaced herself in a most unguestlike manner. A woman seemingly without character or personality or conversation.

Was she related to Graham Muirhead by any chance? It was not a common name—*Muirhead*. His irritation only increased at the possibility that there was a connection.

"My lord," she murmured.

"Good morning." He inclined his head curtly to her and stepped off the terrace in order to stroll out across the lawn where he could be alone again.

What he must do now, he decided as he approached an old oak tree and set a hand upon its sturdy, familiar trunk, was spend as much of today as he could with his grandfather and then return to town tomorrow. He could make the excuse of a pressing engagement, and he would not be lying. He had an urgent appointment with his own destiny. And there must be at least one ball and half a dozen other parties of varying sorts to choose among for tomorrow evening, and of course he had been invited to all of them. There were always myriad entertainments every evening during the Season. He must simply find his invitations, make his choice, and go.

He was quite resigned to what his immediate future

had in store for him. He had had enough time to think about it, after all. His grandmother had talked openly about it at Christmastime. His mother had been hinting for at least the past year. He had been procrastinating. That must stop.

He would persuade his grandfather to talk about his boyhood and young manhood today. Grandpapa enjoyed telling the old, oft-repeated stories, and who knew if Ralph would be hearing them for the last time? *Was* his grandfather ailing? Or could he go on as he was now for another ten years or so? The answer to that question, impossible to know, did not affect the central issue, though, did it? The duke had an heir, but that heir himself did not. And life, as Ralph's grandmother had observed last evening, was always uncertain, even for the young. He could die at any moment.

Indeed, there had been times when he had wanted to die and had even tried to help the process along . . . But he would not be drawn into remembering those dark days. Now was the time to think of life. Though what sensible man would wish to be responsible for bringing yet another human life into this world?

He shook his head. Such thinking must not be pursued.

"How old do you think it is?" a voice asked from behind him, and he turned in amazement to discover that Miss Muirhead had followed him across the lawn and was standing just a short distance away. "The oak, I mean."

He gazed at her without smiling. Had he *asked* for company? Did he look like the sort of man who would feel lonely and pathetic if left to stroll alone? But he looked at the trunk beneath his hand and up into the spreading branches when perhaps he ought to have ignored her question and her entirely.

"Several hundred years," he said. "Perhaps even more than a thousand. The second duke, who had the house built more than a century ago, had the good sense to leave the oak standing and to build farther back from the river."

"It looks like a child's paradise," she said. "Did you climb it as a boy?"

"It is too visible from the house," he said. "My grandmother had me spanked after she caught me up there one day when I was five or six. Even then she must have been afraid that I would fall and kill myself and my father would beget no more sons."

"And did she have you spanked when you chose to become a military officer?" she asked. "You did *choose* to be one, I suppose?"

He looked back at her, all amazement again, and had to remind himself that she was *not* a servant. She was standing out in the sunshine, and the sunlight was gleaming off her hair and making it appear even more startlingly red than it had looked yesterday. With her pale complexion and freckles, she must have to be very careful about exposure to the sun. Her skin would surely burn horribly. Yet she was wearing no bonnet.

He was surprised to notice now that he was looking fully at her that she was rather good looking, even beautiful in a unique sort of way. Her eyes were large and decidedly green. Her nose was straight and the perfect length to fit her oval face. Her cheekbones were well defined, her lips full and well shaped, her mouth on the wide side. With her hair down . . .

But she had asked him a question—an impertinent, intrusively personal question. He answered it nevertheless.

"I begged and pleaded with my father to no avail," he told her, "and my mother was firmly and tearfully on his side. My grandmother threatened to have me whipped—*horse*whipped, to use her exact words. I suppose she thought I had outgrown spankings. But my grandfather surprised us all and incensed everyone but me. It had been his boyhood dream, it seemed, to be a military officer, a *general* no less, but of course it had not been allowed because he was a duke's heir and had no brothers. His own son had been a disappointment to him—yes, he said it in the hearing of my father, who was the epitome of the dutiful heir. Let the boy have his way, then, he said of me. Let him follow his dream of glory. I was eighteen years old and just getting finished with school. I was as innocent and as ignorant as a newborn babe. But the word of the Duke of Worthingham was law to his family. And so he purchased my commission in the very best regiment as well as all the finest trappings money could buy."

"But your dream was soon shattered," she said softly.

What did she know about it? He looked stonily at her before turning his head away sharply. Should he stride off toward the river and trust she would not come trotting after him to offer her company and her conversation again? Or should he stride back to the house and rely upon outpacing her?

He hesitated a moment too long.

"I could not help but overhear your conversation with Her Grace last evening," she said. "I was not deliberately eavesdropping."

His eyes returned to hers. He removed his hand from the trunk and leaned his shoulder against it. She must think a gale was blowing. She had a death grip on the corners of her shawl.

"I understand," she said, "that you do not wish to marry but that you must."

He crossed his arms over his chest and raised one eyebrow. Her impertinence knew no bounds. Though she was quite correct—she had not been eavesdropping. She had been in the drawing room by right of the fact that she was a guest here.

"I do not believe it is *just* your youth, is it?" she asked.

He raised the other eyebrow to join the first.

"That makes you reluctant, I mean," she said. "It is not just that you are young and wish for more time to sow some wild oats before you settle down. It is not, is it?"

He felt a curious mixture of urges. One part of him wanted to bellow with laughter. Another part wanted to explode with fury.

"I believe," she continued when he remained silent, "it is as you told the duchess. You have nothing to offer beyond what almost every single girl in the land and her mama want. I am not expressing myself very well, am I? But I know what I mean, and you know. There is nothing left inside you to offer, is there? Something has taken it all away. War, perhaps. And you are empty."

He had turned cold. It was still quite early morning,

of course, and he was standing in the shade of the tree away from what heat there was in the sun. But it was not that. It was not an outer coldness.

"You presume to know me inside and out, do you, Miss Muirhead," he said, his voice matching his feelings, "after . . . what is it? An eighteen-hour acquaintance?"

"I do not know you at all," she said. "I believe you have made yourself unknowable."

"But you have concluded that I am empty." He looked contemptuously at her. She did not even have the decency to look uncomfortable, apart from those gripping hands. "Therefore you believe you must know all there is to know of me."

"How inadequate words are," she said, shaking her head slightly. "However it is, Lord Berwick, you need a wife and you are dreading the thought of going back to London to search for one in the ballrooms and other haunts of the *ton*."

"Dreading." He laughed. "How foolish I would be if that were true, Miss Muirhead. I am, without exaggeration and without conceit, one of the most eligible men in the land. Young ladies—beautiful, rich, well-born young ladies—already cluster hopefully in my vicinity. They will positively swarm when it becomes clear that I am ready to make my choice among them."

"*Young* ladies," she said. "I suppose you mean straight from the schoolroom. Poor girls—as you yourself observed last night. The one you choose is not likely to remain happy for long, is she?"

"Because I look like this?" He flicked the fingers of one hand in the direction of his scarred cheek. "Or because I have an empty soul?"

He did not know why he was enduring this conversation.

"Because you have nothing to offer," she said. "Nothing that would make a young, hopeful, innocent girl happy after the euphoria of the wedding is over."

"A countess's title, with the prospect of a duchess's to follow, will not make her eternally ecstatic?" he asked. "And taking precedence over almost every other lady in England for the rest of her life? Having wealth untold at her fingertips? And all the clothes and carriages and jewels and other faradiddle she could ever dream of?"

"I know by the tone of your voice that you agree with me," she told him.

He laughed again. "You think I will be a cruel husband, Miss Muirhead?"

"Probably not knowingly," she said.

Well, he thought irritably, it was nice to be known, to be understood. He wondered idly if anything ever shook her calm, if she ever lived up to the promise of that red hair.

"You would do better to marry me," she said.

What?

He stood where he was, his arms folded, his eyes riveted upon hers.

"I am older," she said, "and well past the age of innocence. I am twenty-seven years old. However, I still have many childbearing years left and have no reason to believe I may be barren. My father is the sixth baronet of his line, and my mother was the daughter of a viscount. I have no illusions about marital happiness and would be quite willing to accept the marriage for what it would be. I would not interfere with your life. I would live mine in a way that would never publicly embarrass you or pri-

vately inconvenience you. If you were to agree to marry
me, you would be saved from all the bother of making
your choice among the many eligible young ladies in
whom you have no interest whatsoever."

He found his voice at last.

"I have no interest in *you*, Miss Muirhead." It was
brutal, but he felt savage—and cold to the heart.

"Of course you do not," she said, looking unmoved,
though a downward glance showed him that her knuck-
les had whitened against her shawl. "I would not expect
it, or desire it. I am suggesting a mutual . . . *bargain,* Lord
Berwick. Something that would suit us both without
hurting either. You need a wife though you do not wish
for one. I want a husband but have little chance of finding one. You are not looking for love. Neither am I. I had
it once, but it proved deceptive and ridiculously painful.
I want marriage because the alternative for a woman is
dreary in the extreme. I want my own home and a place
in society. I want children—and upon them I *will* lavish
love. You will not disappoint me. I would expect nothing
from you beyond what duty would dictate. And I would
not disappoint you. You would not expect anything from
me beyond duty, and that you would have without question or complaint. You wish to remove to your home in
the country after your marriage. Such a retired existence
would suit me admirably. I would not be forever begging
you to take me to town and all its entertainments."

The hair was an illusion, he thought. She was as cold
a fish as he had ever encountered.

Marry her?

But being married to her would be the next best thing
to remaining single. He could not remain single, how-

ever. He must marry. She was twenty-seven years old, older than he. She had grown past both youth and innocence. She had loved once. Did that mean . . . ?

"Are you a virgin, Miss Muirhead?" he asked. Again it was a brutal question. It was also an unnecessarily impertinent one. He was not seriously considering her outrageous proposal, after all. Was he?

"Yes," she said, "I am."

They stood and stared at each other.

"Are you related to Graham Muirhead?" he asked her abruptly.

"He is my brother," she told him.

Ah. His eyes strayed to her hair and back to her green eyes. Graham was dark haired and dark eyed, but he was her brother. It was hardly a recommendation in her favor.

She must have read his thoughts.

"I am suggesting that you marry *me*, Lord Berwick," she said, "not my brother."

3

There was an uncomfortably long silence during which the Earl of Berwick stood where he was, his shoulder propped against the ancient oak, his arms folded over his chest, his booted feet crossed at the ankles. He looked rather menacingly large and . . . dark. He looked dark, of course, because he was in the shadow of the tree, but rather than muting the effect of the scar across his cheek, the dimness accentuated it—and it was the cheek turned more fully toward her.

There was not a glimmering of humor or any other emotion on his face or in his blank eyes.

Whatever had made her think she could marry him? Or that he would marry her? He was all brooding, dark emptiness. Even dangerous, though she had not thought *that* until this moment. For one did not know, would probably never know, what emotions were buried deep inside him, ready to erupt at any moment.

She wondered what she would do if the silence stretched much longer. Perhaps he had no intention of moving or saying anything. Should she turn and walk away, then? From her last chance? But chance for what?

Perhaps marrying him would not after all be more desirable than living the rest of her life as she was, in dreary but independent spinsterhood.

He spoke at last.

"Tell me something, Miss Muirhead," he said. "If marriage is of such importance to you, even the poor apology for a marriage into which you are proposing to enter with me, why are you still unwed at the age of twenty-seven?"

Ah.

Because no one has asked me? It was true. But the answer was not nearly as simple as that.

"I am ineligible," she told him, lifting her chin. An understatement if ever she had spoken one.

"Yet you expect me to marry you?" His eyebrows soared again and he looked more the way she had expected him to look from the start—arrogant and supercilious. "In what way are you ineligible, pray? You have just told me your father is a baronet with a solid lineage and that your mother was the daughter of a viscount. Birth surely counts for something in the marriage mart. And you do not exactly look like a gargoyle."

Was that a compliment?

She drew a slow breath.

"My sister ran off with a married man six years ago," she told him. "He married her a year later, a scant three months after his wife died and one month before her confinement, but their marriage restored only a very limited degree of respectability to what had been a very public scandal. She will never be received by any of the highest sticklers in polite society, and we have not been entirely forgiven either, for my father refused to cast her off even when for a few months her seducer abandoned her to return to his dying wife."

"We," he said. "Why, pray, did the scandalous behavior of your sister and the socially unwise reaction of your father make you a pariah, Miss Muirhead?"

"Well." She looked down at her fingers, which she had spread out before her as though she were examining her manicure. "The man was the darling of society at the time, wild and eccentric though he was, a playwright of flamboyant appearance and smoldering good looks to rival those of Lord Byron. And his wife was the daughter of a government minister. It could not have been worse. Lucy was seventeen. She had not even made her debut in society. She was in London only because I was making my come-out at the grand age of twenty-one and she had persuaded our mother that she would expire of boredom if she were forced to remain behind in the country with her governess. She met Mr. Nelson in Hyde Park when she dropped her reticule and its contents spilled at his feet while she was walking there one morning with Mama's maid. His wife's family made a dreadful fuss after he had run off with her. Her father had Papa expelled from one of his clubs. Her brother forced a quarrel upon *my* brother in a public place and challenged him to a duel. Graham refused to fight."

The earl interrupted the ghastly narrative.

"Did he, by Jove?" he said. "But, yes, I suppose he would."

"Oh, he kept the appointment," she said, looking up at him with a frown, "but he would not take up one of the pistols. He walked off the paces at the signal and turned and stood, his arms at his sides. Apparently he did not even stand sideways to offer a narrower target. His adversary bent his arm at the elbow and shot into the air, and everyone jeered at Graham for his cowardice, though I still think it was the bravest thing I have ever heard of. My mother insisted that we try to weather the storm while Papa went in pursuit of the runaways and Graham tried in vain to apologize to Mrs. Nelson and her family. We attended those entertainments to which we had already been invited, but new invitations stopped coming. When Mama took me calling upon ladies who had always welcomed us, they were suddenly not at home even if other people's carriages were drawn up outside their doors to give the lie to their words. When we arrived at Almack's one evening for the weekly ball, it was to the discovery that our vouchers had been revoked."

There was a brief silence. "Why were you twenty-one when you made your come-out?"

"My grandmother died when I was eighteen," she explained, "and Mama insisted we go into strict mourning, though Papa said it surely was not necessary to ruin the plans that had been made for me. My mother was very ill for a couple of years after that. It was the illness that finally killed her, though she did rally to take me to London for my long-overdue debut into society."

"And you never went back to London after that first time?" he asked. "Not in six years? Memories are notoriously short among the beau monde. Yesterday's scandal is soon swallowed up by today's indiscretion and that by tomorrow's catastrophe. And it was not *you* who had eloped. Who was the man you loved?"

His eyes raked over her from head to toe and she clutched the ends of her shawl again.

"What?"

"You told me you had known love once," he reminded her, "but that it had proved deceptive and painful."

Ah.

"He was wealthy and titled and handsome," she said without really answering his question, "and attentive from the moment of our introduction at my very first ball. He seemed like a dream come true, and of course I tumbled into love with him as though I did not have a brain in my head. But why would I not have done? Mama encouraged the connection. We danced at almost every ball and sat beside each other at concerts. We conversed at soirees and strolled together at picnics. I was in theater parties that included him. He paid me lavish compliments and even declared a lasting affection for me. My head was thoroughly turned. I expected every day that he would speak formally with my father and I would be the happiest girl in the world. I call myself a *girl* because that was what I was then even though I was twenty-one years of age. I thought he loved me. And indeed I was the envy of many other young ladies of my acquaintance."

She paused to draw a deep breath and let it out on a sigh.

"There was a ball a week or so after Lucy ran away with Mr. Nelson. Mama and I went despite everything. I was engaged to dance the opening set with the man who had so recently paid court to me. He approached as expected when the time came and smiled dazzlingly as he made a flourishing bow and held out his hand toward . . . the lady standing next to me. It was a very deliberate cut, and of course every eye in the ballroom was upon me.

Everyone saw me smile with happy relief after such a distressing week and step forward and begin to stretch out my own hand."

She had to stop for a moment to draw a steadying breath.

"We packed our bags that night, Mama and I," she said, "and went home the next day. Love is a strange phenomenon, my lord. It can die so abruptly and so completely that one sees it immediately for the empty illusion it is."

"But painful," he reminded her.

"At the time," she admitted. "But I got over it. I survived. And it was a lesson well learned. You need not be afraid that I will ever turn sentimental and imagine myself in love with you—if you should choose to accept my bargain, that is."

"A survivor," he said softly. "You did not ever go back?"

"Yes, I did." She half smiled. "Last year. I went at the persuasion of my aunt, Lady Easterly, who was feeling lonely with all her daughters, my cousins, married and scattered about the country. She told me exactly what you just told me, that the collective memory of the *ton* is short. And five years had gone by. I attended a few concerts and soirees with her. I had agreed to accompany her to some parties and even one ball that was being given by a cousin of my uncle's. But suddenly the gossip began, strange whisperings and significant glances my way. I thought at first it must be the old scandal rearing its head, but it was something else. Something totally unexpected and terribly silly. Aunt Julia told me what it was about one morning when I was getting ready to go out to the library. And Graham arrived soon after to confirm what she had said."

She clasped her hands behind her back. She closed her eyes for a moment before opening them and continuing.

"I daresay," she said, "that if you were in London last spring you met Lady Angela Allandale, daughter of the Marquess of Hitching? She had come from the north of England to make her debut and took the *ton* by storm."

She risked a glance at him.

"I remember hearing she was a diamond of the first water," he said, "with half the bachelor population of England dangling after her. I never saw her. I made sure not to. At that time I was still avoiding all possible danger of being trapped into marriage."

"She had hair and eyes the exact color and shade of mine," she said. "She had my pale complexion too. When a few people began to remark upon the likeness between us, there were those among the older members of the *ton* who remembered the handsome, red-haired marquess, her father, as a young man in London, paying court to the lovely Miss West, *my mother,* before financial distress caused him to change his affections and propose marriage to the heiress of a vast fortune who is now the Marchioness of Hitching."

The Earl of Berwick offered no comment when she paused.

"My mother and father married before the end of that Season," she said. "Mama always spoke of their whirlwind courtship as a great love story. I did not believe any of the gossip that was soon in full flight last year. I still do not. I tried to brazen it out, just as I had five years before.

But at a picnic I attended with my aunt, I had the misfortune of coming face to face with Lord— I came face to face with my former beau and greeted him by name. He raised his quizzing glass to his eye, looked pointedly through it at my hair, made me a slight and distant bow, and walked away, making sure I heard the remark he made to the gentleman who was with him. The word *bastard* was part of it. I went home the next day."

She had been standing too long in the same position, she realized. There was a buzzing in her ears, a coldness about her head and in her nostrils, and she feared she was close to fainting. She drew breath, shook her head, looked about, dug her fingers into her palms, and willed herself not to do anything so utterly humiliating.

"And you confronted your father?" Lord Berwick asked.

"No," she admitted. "I told him a few weeks in London had been enough, that I had been bored and homesick. The gossip followed me eventually, however. Some people who were staying with our neighbors over Christmas recognized me at a local assembly, and the story spread like wildfire until it reached Papa's ears. He was incensed. He . . . made a *scene*. He was stopped only just in time from challenging one of the visitors to a duel. We went home early, and *then* I asked him. He would not give me a direct answer. He told me he had loved my mother from the time he first set eyes upon her and that she had loved him. He told me he had always loved me, before my birth and every day after. I was his firstborn, his beloved elder daughter, he said. He told me there were some redheads among his ancestors. But he was vague about exactly *when* he had married Mama—I did not know the date, I realized—and I did not press the point or make any attempt to find out another way. I was born the February after that Season. I do not *believe* the gossip. But you ought to be aware of it, I suppose. If you are considering my proposed bargain, that is. Which I do not suppose you are."

She moved at last, turning to face the house. She had really not thought this through carefully enough last night, had she? She had thought only of proposing her bargain in a lucid and dispassionate way. It had seemed a real possibility, a marriage that would be of equal benefit to them both. She had not really considered the personal baggage she brought with her, all of which would deter any sane man from wanting any connection whatsoever with her. And now she had spilled it all out, and she felt drained and humiliated. And appalled at her own temerity.

"I understand," she said, "that marrying me would be no bargain at all for you, Lord Berwick, even if it *would* save you the bother of having to choose a bride in London. Please forget that I suggested it."

"I do not believe I add a poor memory to my other shortcomings, Miss Muirhead," he said. "And it would have to be *very* poor."

Indeed.

Suddenly the sun seemed very hot even though it must still be quite early morning. Her cheeks were burning. He was not going to say anything more, she realized, and she had nothing further to say. If she could have stepped straight into oblivion at that moment, she would gladly have done it. As it was, the house seemed an impossible distance away.

She made her way toward it on legs that felt a bit like stilts without knee joints. She could almost feel his eyes — those cold, blank eyes — on her back.

Ralph had breakfast with his grandfather. Fortunately there was no one else in the breakfast parlor. It was Her Grace's habit, he knew from past experience, to rise at eleven after partaking of a cup of chocolate in bed.

The two of them spent the rest of the morning in the duke's study, talking on a variety of topics until the old gentleman nodded off over a cup of coffee. Ralph sat silently watching him and remembering the vigorous, half-fearsome figure of his grandfather as he had been years ago, full of barks and fury at any sign of misbehavior, but with eyes that twinkled incongruously. One of his waistcoat pockets had always slightly bulged out of shape with the sweetmeats he carried there.

Ralph went riding after luncheon. He went to see his grandfather's physician and found him just returning from a distant farm, to which he had been summoned to set the broken arm of a laborer who had tumbled from a barn loft.

His Grace was not suffering from any particular malady, Dr. Gregg assured the Earl of Berwick. Except old age, of course. His heart was not as strong as it had once been, as was to be expected, and he had a tendency to fall victim to any chill that happened to be lurking in the neighborhood. He suffered from the rheumatics and a touch of gout and indigestion and many of the other ills age was prey to. He was frail when compared with a younger man. But he might outlive them all for anything the physician could say to the contrary.

Ralph thanked him, shook him by the hand, and took his leave.

His grandmother was unnecessarily fearful, then. Grandpapa was not at death's door. However, no matter how close the duke was to his end, the fact remained that there was only the one heir. It was that heir's clear duty to marry and produce sons of his own, preferably while his grandfather was still alive.

Ralph determinedly kept his mind off the peculiar events of the early morning. It was made easier by the fact that Miss Muirhead did not put in an appearance for the rest of the day, and when the duke remarked upon her absence during dinner, Her Grace explained that the poor young lady was feeling under the weather and was keeping to her own room for fear of infecting either of Their Graces.

"She really is kindness itself," Her Grace remarked.

After that Ralph was more determined than ever to leave in the morning. He spent the evening with both grandparents and ended up reading aloud to them while his grandmother knitted and his grandfather rested his head against the chair back and closed his eyes. The duchess looked speakingly at Ralph when he began to snore softly. Ralph read on.

He took his leave the next morning and drove back to London in his curricle under heavy clouds that again threatened rain at every moment but did not actually shed any. The weather exactly matched Ralph's mood. His future course had been set for him, and there was no longer any possibility of procrastinating. The days of his freedom—if he ever had been free—were effectively over. What if no one was ever free, though? What if everything was preordained? But only deeper depression could come from thinking thus, and he shrugged off those thoughts and turned to others.

Yesterday morning.

Was she just a fortune hunter? A gold digger? A cold fish?

I am ineligible.

To be fair, perhaps, it had sounded as if none of the disasters that had befallen her was her fault. She was enjoying the pleasures of her first Season when her sister ran off with that stupid ass Freddie Nelson—at least, he assumed that was the playwright she had spoken of—who seemed to believe that a flamboyant lifestyle was a good substitute for brains and talent. She was not the one who had made a prize spectacle of herself during the resulting affair of honor. How *exactly* like Graham Muirhead, though, to turn up for a duel and then refuse to take up a pistol or make as small a target of himself as he could.

Nor was it her fault that the man who had made her the object of his gallantries—she had not named him beyond starting to call him *Lord* Somebody-or-other—had turned out to be a cad of the first order. And it was not her fault that her mother had once been shockingly indiscreet with a man with hair of a distinctive shade of red or that he had passed on that feature to the child she had borne less than nine months after her hasty marriage to Muirhead.

Ralph felt little doubt that the gossips—for once—had the right of it. Miss Muirhead probably felt little doubt either, though she denied it.

As much as none of these crimes was her fault, she

was indeed ineligible. She must have been mad—or just desperate—to expect that he would marry her simply to save himself the bother of courting someone else. His grandmother had received her as a guest into her home, it was true, despite her notoriety, but she would surely have forty fits of the vapors if he should suddenly announce his intention of marrying the woman. And he could only imagine the reaction of his mother and sisters.

He shook off the thought of Miss Muirhead. He had other, more pressing and even more dreary things to consider.

He ought to have begun his campaign that evening. He had even found an invitation to a ball that would be attended by all the cream of the *ton* and its daughters. He went instead, after dining alone at home, to Stanbrook House on Grosvenor Square, to call upon George, Duke of Stanbrook, if by some chance he was at home.

George was both friend and father figure, having opened his home all those years ago to wounded soldiers and given them the time and space in which to heal. And healing, George had recognized, as so few people did, did not consist just in a mending of broken bones and a knitting together of cuts and gashes, but in a restoration of peace and sanity to troubled, shattered minds. True healing was a slow business, perhaps a lifelong one. George had always had the gift of making each of the six of them who had stayed the longest feel that he or she was special to him.

Ralph had often wondered if any of them had lavished nearly as much attention upon George, who had been as deeply wounded as any of them by war even though he had not been on any of the Napoleonic battlefields.

He *was* at home, and by some miracle had no plans to go out. Ralph found him sitting by the fire in his drawing room, a glass of port at his elbow, an open book in his hand. He closed the latter and set it aside with a welcoming smile, and for the first time it occurred to Ralph that perhaps it had been selfish of him to come thus, unannounced. Perhaps George had been looking forward to a quiet evening at home.

"Ralph." He got to his feet and stretched out a hand. "Come and warm yourself by the fire while I pour you a drink."

They talked about inconsequential matters for a few minutes, and Ralph felt himself begin to relax.

"I have just come up from Sussex," he said at last. "I was summoned there by my grandmother. But I was not kept. I was sent scurrying back to choose a bride, soon if not sooner. And to get her with child on our wedding night unless I want to incur Her Grace's undying wrath."

George regarded him with quiet sympathy.

"Your grandfather is poorly?" he asked.

"He is well into his eighties," Ralph said by way of explanation.

"You are not regretting," George asked, "that you let Miss Courtney go?"

Ralph winced and looked down into the contents of his glass while he twirled it slowly. Miss Courtney was the younger sister of Max Courtney, one of his best friends—one of his *dead* best friends. Ralph had known her since he was a boy and she was just a child. He had used to tease her whenever he went to stay with Max during a school holiday and, when they were a bit older, flirt just a little with her. After his return to town from his three years in Cornwall, he had run into her more than once at a social entertainment, and she had glowed with happiness and explained that being with him brought her closer again to her beloved brother. She had started to write to him, indiscreet as it was for a single lady to communicate privately with a single gentleman. Ralph had feared that she was developing a tendre for him. He had avoided her whenever he could, and had ignored a few of her letters and written only brief, dispassionate replies to the others. While he was at Middlebury Park this spring, she had written to inform him that she was about to marry a clergyman from the north of England. He had felt guilty then about having offered her so little consolation after Max's death, about ignoring the affection she had tried to give him. He had shared his feelings with his fellow Survivors.

"I had nothing to offer her, George," he said. "I would have made her life a misery. I was too fond of her to encourage her to attach herself to me."

George said nothing. He sipped from his glass and leaned back, crossing one leg over the other and draping his free arm along the arm of his chair. He was the picture of elegant relaxation. His eyes rested upon Ralph without in any way staring at him. It was his gift, that pose, that silence, that attention. Waiting. Inviting. Not in any way threatening or judging.

Ralph set down his own glass, rested his elbows on the arms of his chair, and steepled his fingers beneath his chin. He settled his gaze on the fire.

"I will make any woman's life a misery," he said. "I can choose a lady and marry her, George. I can give her all the security of my name and wealth and prospects. I can bed her and impregnate her. That is all, though. And it is not enough."

"Many women would call it paradise," George said gently.

"I think not," Ralph said.

"No," George agreed softly after the silence had stretched awhile. "It is not."

Ralph's eyes moved to his. George agreed that a marriage devoid of all feeling, even affection, would be hell on earth. He had never talked of his own marriage, which had begun at a very young age and ended when his wife committed suicide after the death of their son in the Peninsula.

"There are all those young ladies out there," Ralph said, "eager to find husbands at the great marriage mart. Eligible husbands. I am as eligible as anyone could possibly be. Any one of them would be ecstatic to net me, even if I *do* look like this." He freed one hand in order to gesture toward his scarred cheek.

"Some say the scar makes you more dashing," George said.

"I have to marry one of those girls," Ralph said harshly. "Soon. And then I will shatter her dreams and ruin her life."

"And yet," George said, "the very fact that you know it and pity the young lady you will choose demonstrates that you care. You *do* care. You just have not fully understood that yet."

Ralph gazed broodingly at him.

"I should hate you," he said.

George raised his eyebrows.

"For saving my life," Ralph told him. "More than once."

It was something they had not spoken of for a long time—those occasions when Ralph had tried to take his own life, the further occasions when he had wanted to do it but had talked about it instead until he had been persuaded out of it.

"And do you?" George asked. "Hate me?"

Ralph did not answer him. He transferred his gaze back to the fire.

"There is one woman," he said, and stopped.

He did not want to *think* about that one woman.

George was silent again.

"Did you ever meet Lady Angela Allandale last year?" Ralph asked.

"The Incomparable?" George asked. "She had an army of young bucks and a few older ones dangling after her, but would settle for none of them. Is she back this year? Is *she* this one woman?"

"And did you hear," Ralph asked, "any scandal about a young lady who looked exactly like her and was almost certainly a by-blow of the Marquess of Hitching?"

"I did, yes," George said, "and thought how unfortunate it was that the poor lady had inherited his very distinctive coloring and looked so exactly like his legitimate daughter that she was almost bound to arouse gossip. She was not strictly illegitimate though, if I remember correctly. She was the acknowledged daughter of some baronet. Hmm. Muirhead, I believe?"

"Yes," Ralph said.

"Is *she* the one woman?" George asked.

"She is staying with my grandmother at Manville Court," Ralph explained. "Her mother, now deceased, was Her Grace's goddaughter. Miss Muirhead is there, I believe, because she feels uncomfortable at home with her father, who insists that the gossip is so much nonsense yet almost came to public blows with someone who brought that gossip into his neighborhood. She suggested a mutually beneficial bargain to me yesterday. She wants a husband but no emotional tie. She knows that I need a wife but have no emotional tie to offer."

"A match made in heaven, then," George said softly.

"Perhaps," Ralph agreed.

There was a lengthy, rather heavy silence during which a log shifted and crackled in the fire, sending a shower of sparks up the chimney.

"Tell me why you are considering making what would appear to be an unwise connection with this unfortunate lady," George said. "Is it perhaps because you believe you will end up hurting her less than you would one of the innocents just out of the schoolroom? Be careful if that is so, Ralph. We can all be hurt. Even ladies who have become social pariahs. Even you. But *tell* me."

Ralph gazed broodingly into the fire before he spoke again.

We can all be hurt.

4

It was her last chance, Chloe had thought yesterday when she made her proposition to the Earl of Berwick. *Her last chance.* Well, if that was what it had been, then it was gone today. Just as he was.

The excuse she had made for the rest of yesterday of feeling under the weather had hardly been a lie. The thought of having to face him again had made her stomach churn with threatened nausea. So had the thought of facing anyone else. Or even herself for that matter. She felt she had somehow abused the duchess's hospitality. Her Grace would be *horrified* if she knew what Chloe had suggested to her precious grandson.

Chloe had sat cross-legged on her bed for hours on end staring straight ahead, the curtains pulled across her window, her shawl hugged about her shoulders and across her bosom. If she got to her feet, she had thought once or twice when she had been tempted, she might see herself in the dressing table mirror. And if she got to her feet, she would have to admit that life went on and that she had no choice but to go on with it, day after dreary day until the end, which doubtless would be far distant just to spite her. She would probably live to the age of ninety.

Her life since the age of eighteen had been one disappointment and disaster after another, culminating in last year's ghastly suggestion that everything in her life so far had been based on a lie. For of course she *had* suspected—and still did—that perhaps her papa was not her real father. The Marquess of Hitching! The very name could turn her cold to the very core. Yet she had still dared to hope this morning that the future might yet hold *something* for her. The dashing of that hope had caused her to hit the rock bottom of despair.

Again.

It was beginning to feel like an almost familiar place to be. But perhaps hitting this new low had something to be said for it, she thought now, this morning, after she had awoken and realized in some surprise that she had slept for several hours. At least now there was no further down to go. And at least she would not have to fear coming face-to-face with the Earl of Berwick again, not for a long while, anyway. The maid who had brought up her pitcher of hot water when she rang for it was able to assure her that his lordship had already left Manville, taking his curricle and his baggage coach and his valet with him.

And so, because she had little choice in the matter anyway, Chloe went downstairs. She deliberately counted off all her many blessings as she made her way to the breakfast parlor despite a total lack of appetite. There was much for which to be grateful, not least of which was the fact that she was not an employee at Manville Court but a guest, and Her Grace was invariably kind to her.

She had the freedom to wander where she would, the park about the house being extensive and beautifully landscaped. And summer was coming. Everything looked better in the sunshine and heat. Oh, yes, there were many blessings. There were thousands of women who would give a right arm for her life.

Her thoughts touched upon her father, who had been very upset before she left home and even more so when she did leave, but she shied away from those particular memories. She had had to leave. She had needed to put some distance between them while she sorted out a few things in her mind, though she could not quite name what those things were. Either she believed him or she did not.

Why was she here if she believed him?

Four days after the Earl of Berwick had returned to London, Chloe went for a longer-than-usual walk. The weather seemed to have turned a corner from the chill of late spring to the warmth of approaching summer, and the sun was shining. The duchess had gone visiting but had said with a twinkling smile at luncheon that she did not expect Chloe to accompany her, since Mrs. Booth had grown very deaf and would surely be happier with the company of just one very old friend.

Chloe walked across the east lawn, taking care to give the old oak tree a wide berth, until she came to the river and the humpbacked stone bridge that led across to the meadow, which was an integral part of the park though it was made to look half wild rather than cultivated. It looked very inviting in the sunshine, its waving grass liberally dotted with daisies and buttercups and clover. Even from this side of the river she could see butterflies fluttering among them. But she was not in the mood to-day for sunshine or gaiety. Perhaps some other day . . .

She followed the path along the near bank instead and was soon in the deep shade of the trees that grew in a dense band on both sides of the river. The water was dark green here until it quickened its pace into small eddies with white bubbles of foam as it approached the downward slope to the west and the rapids and the series of falls that would take it plunging into the large natural lake below. She slowed her steps and reveled in the smells of water and greenery, in the sights of the myriad shades of green and the occasional shaft of sunlight, in the sounds of rushing water and shrill birdsong.

She picked her way carefully on the natural stepping stones of the rough path, though fortunately they were dry and posed no real danger. And then she was down and came out into full sunlight on the bank of the lake. Shade and the sound of the falls fell away behind her.

She was still determinedly counting her blessings. How very fortunate she was to have this park to walk in whenever she chose to step beyond the confines of the house, and how fortunate to have the house itself to live in for as long as she wished. She did not know how long she *would* stay. Surely eventually she would return home. She knew her papa had always loved her as dearly as he loved Graham and Lucy, who were undoubtedly his. She knew that the gossip and her questions had caused him a great deal of distress. She did not know if he had told her the truth. Perhaps she never would. And perhaps it did not matter. She loved him anyway. She knew *that,* at least.

But if she only knew without any doubt what the truth *was* . . .

It was dreadful indeed—only someone who had experienced what she was going through could possibly understand—to discover at the age of twenty-six that one's very identity was in question, that one's father, one's beloved *papa,* might not be one's real father at all. One of her reasons for leaving London in a great hurry last spring had been her horror at the possibility that she might run into the Marquess of Hitching somewhere and somehow feel a connection to him. It had been worse than horror, in fact. It had been mindless panic. If there was one person in this world she *never* wanted to meet or even glimpse in passing, it was the man who had known her mother nine months before *her* birth.

She shook off the unwelcome, plaguing thoughts yet again and tried very hard to rejoice in the peaceful beauty of her surroundings. She stooped to pick up a few flat stones and leaned back against the slender trunk of a willow tree that bowed its branches over the water on either side, enclosing her in what seemed like her own private world. The water was blue here and sparkled in the sunshine. The fronds of the willow were very green. The air was loud with birdsong.

She took one of the stones in her right hand, positioned it carefully with her thumb, and tossed it across the water in the way her father had taught her with endless patience when she was a child. But she was out of practice. It hit the surface and sank from sight without bouncing even once.

Well, one must not give in to defeat after just one try, or even, perhaps, after twenty. Her second stone bounced five times—an all-time record—and was halfway across the lake before it finally sank from view. Chloe smiled smugly. Even her father had never done better than that.

Oh, Papa. Suddenly she felt like weeping.

She should have been content with the triumph of those five bounces, she thought ruefully a short while later when the fifth stone, and the third in a row, bounced once halfheartedly before sinking. Though perhaps her attempts had accomplished something. She was feeling a little more cheerful.

"It is all in the flick of the wrist," a voice said from so close by that Chloe jumped with alarm and dropped the three remaining stones.

She peered through the fronds of the willow to her left. But she had not mistaken the voice. It was not one of the gardeners. The Earl of Berwick was standing out on the grass a mere few yards from the tree. He must have walked the direct route down from the house. He was dressed for riding, complete with long drab coat worn open and tall hat that cast his face in shadow but did not quite mask the menace of his scar. He was flicking a riding crop against the supple leather of his boots. Her heart felt as though it had leapt into her throat and was beating wildly there like a bird trying to escape.

"If you had been here a few moments ago," she said, "you would have seen one of my stones bounce five times."

"Braggart," he said. "Or fibber."

"It is true," she protested.

What *on earth* was he doing back at Manville? And not just at the house but down here at the lake? She felt a little ridiculous standing where she was, as if she were cowering behind the willow fronds, hoping not to be seen. She pushed her way through and stepped out onto the grass.

He looked her over unhurriedly, a slight frown between his brows, his eyes cool and unreadable. Chloe clasped her hands behind her back and stopped herself from apologizing for being here when perhaps he had been seeking some solitude. He could have avoided talking to her, after all. It must have been obvious to him that she had not seen him come.

But why would he seek solitude in the park when he must have just arrived? His boots were covered with a film of dust, which suggested that he had ridden this time, not driven his curricle. Had he ridden all the way from London? Why?

She said something very foolish instead of waiting for him to break the silence.

"I am not going to apologize for the other morning," she said. "I have had time to reflect upon what I suggested, and I have changed my mind. It was nothing but foolish impulse. I have forgotten it. I hope for the duchess's sake you have brought her happy news from London."

"Changed your mind?" he said after a few moments, during which his riding crop tapped rhythmically against one boot. "That is a pity. I came back here to offer you marriage, Miss Muirhead."

The duke was dozing in his study, Weller had informed Ralph on his arrival, and Her Grace had gone to pay an afternoon call on Mrs. Booth. Miss Muirhead had not accompanied her. He regretted that he did not know where she was.

She was not in either the drawing room or the morning room. Ralph had looked in both. Nor was she on the eastern terrace. A gardener he had hailed had seen her walking across the east lawn in the direction of the river an hour or so ago. But she was neither down on the riverbank nor in the meadow on the other side of the bridge. Ralph looked to his right when he reached the bridge, but going that way would have brought her to the driveway and on out through the gates to the village. He would surely have seen her if that had been her destination. Besides, if she had been going to the village, why take such a circuitous route? The path to the left led in among trees and around the bend in the river to the rapids and then the falls. If she had gone that way and kept going, she would have ended up at the lake. It seemed a likely destination on such a lovely day.

Ralph took the short route to the lake past the house again and down the steep west lawn. He almost missed seeing her when he got there. The bank of the lake seemed deserted. But then a stone arced out from behind the nearer fronds of the weeping willow and bounced once at far too sharp an angle to allow for a second bounce. It sank from sight. It could only have been thrown by a human hand—a not-very-skilled one. Another followed it, and then another, with the same result.

And then he saw her, standing with her back to the slender trunk of the tree, her green dress an almost perfect camouflage against her surroundings. Except that she wore no bonnet and that red hair of hers gave her away if she was indeed hoping to stay hidden. Did she never wear a bonnet?

She had not seen him approach, and, stupidly, he almost turned back before she did. But what the devil? He had come all this way, on horseback, ahead of his baggage coach and his valet, with the sole purpose of seeking her out privately. Good fortune had been with him—he had seen neither of his grandparents first.

He had attended a ball the evening after he called upon George. There had been nothing unusual about that, of course. He often attended balls. He usually danced a few sets with ladies of his acquaintance. It would be impolite to his hostess not to dance at all. What he did *not* often do, though, was allow that hostess— Lady Livermere in this case—to latch on to his arm as though she had been presented with a prize trophy and parade him about, introducing him to what had seemed like an endless stream of young ladies he had not seen before. And their mamas too, of course. No self-respecting young lady attended a ball without her mother at her elbow every moment when she was not dancing.

He had wondered if his mother had been having a word with Lady Livermere. The two ladies enjoyed more than just a passing acquaintance.

He had become aware of a buzz of sharpening interest around him as the evening proceeded. He was quite sure he had not imagined it. For of course he had been obliged to reserve a set of dances with as many of those young ladies as could be fitted into a long evening of dancing. He ought to have been glad. Without any real effort on his part he had been presented with a number of the Season's eligible hopefuls, and at the same time signaled that this year he was in search of a bride. He might, if he had really wanted to avoid the bother of a protracted search, have made his choice before the evening ended, presented himself to the young lady's father the following day, and made his offer before another evening came along. His betrothal might have been announced in all the morning papers the day after that. All the uncertainties of his existence might have become certainties.

It was *not* vanity that made him believe it would have been that easy. He had an earl's title and fortune, after all. More than that, though, he was heir to a dukedom, and the incumbent was an old man well into his eighties. Ducal properties, all of them extensive and prosperous, were spread across large swaths of England.

Most of his dancing partners had been pretty. All had been young and graceful, with polished, pleasing manners. A few had been vivacious. One or two had appeared intelligent and had had some conversation—as far as one could judge in the distracting setting of a ballroom. All were eminently eligible. Only one had looked noticeably repelled by his facial scar.

As soon as the final set drew to a close, he had gone home to bed. How had his fellow Survivors done it—Hugo and Vincent first, and then Ben and Flavian? How had they been able to give up everything to take on a lifetime commitment that might well bring them nothing but misery, and, equally important if not more so, that might bring misery to their wives? How could they *know*? Or did they not? Did they merely hope for happiness and gamble the rest of their lives on a risky possibility?

None of them, as far as Ralph knew, had been forced into marrying out of any sense of duty. Well, Vincent had, perhaps. But none of them had stood in a ballroom, knowing that within its walls he must find his lifetime partner.

There had not been much of the night remaining after he returned home from the ball. He had spent it staring upward at the intricately ruched satin canopy over his bed thinking, not about any of the very real candidates for his hand that he had met in the course of the evening, but about the very ineligible Miss Muirhead.

Ineligible by her own admission. She was not technically illegitimate, of course, even if the rumors were true, since Sir Kevin Muirhead must have acknowledged her as his own at her birth, but she had the misfortune to have the distinctive coloring shared by Hitching and his legitimate daughter, which fact made it difficult *not* to believe what the gossips had said last year. And there was the other baggage she carried about too. Her sister, at the age of seventeen, had eloped with Freddie Nelson while his wife still lived, and then Graham Muirhead had got himself embroiled in a farce of a duel. Her father, instead of disowning his wayward daughter, had taken her back and then presumably paid the newly widowed Nelson a fortune to marry her before her child was born. Miss Muirhead meanwhile had been publicly humiliated and jilted and equally publicly denied admittance to Almack's.

To call her ineligible was to understate the case. Ralph's duty was to marry. And since he expected no personal satisfaction from marriage and therefore did not much care *whom* he married, it behooved him to please his grandparents and his mother by choosing a young lady who was both eligible and accomplished, someone who would adjust smoothly to her future role, someone over whose name not a whisper of scandal breathed.

He had met at least half a dozen perfect candidates at the ball. Yet he had lain awake thinking of Miss Muirhead and her absurd, impertinent suggestion that they agree to . . . What had she called it? A bargain.

Some bargain.

He had called on his mother the following day. Obviously she *had* spoken to Lady Livermere, though she had not been at the ball herself. She had heard of his triumph, of the buzz of interest and excitement he had caused, of the partners with whom he had danced. She had drawn up a select list of young ladies with whom it would be unexceptionable for him to strike up an acquaintance, soon to become a courtship. There was a neat dozen. He had danced last evening with four of them. She would invite four more, with their mamas, to tea one afternoon soon, along with some other ladies so that her purpose would not be vulgarly obvious, and Ralph would happen to call in upon her on that particular afternoon. The remaining four . . .

Ralph had stopped listening.

Four days after leaving Manville Court, he had found himself on his way back there to seek out Miss Muirhead. Suddenly her so-called bargain had looked like the best of his options. At least neither of them would be hurt by it. How could one suffer disappointment when there were no expectations? She wanted a husband and a home and family, a perfectly understandable ambition for any woman. He needed a wife and family. Neither of them expected or even wanted love or romance or any of those finer sensibilities some people of a romantic disposition deemed necessary for a good marriage. He had nothing whatsoever to offer along those lines, and she did not want anything. She was done with love.

He carefully kept his mind away from what George had had to say on the topic.

She was ineligible, yes. But unfairly so. In all the admittedly unsavory events in which she had been involved during the past six years, she appeared to have been quite blameless. And, he had recalled as a final point in her favor, she wanted to live a quiet life in the country. She wanted nothing more to do with London and its myriad entertainments. Neither did he.

However it was, no matter how much he was rationalizing instead of using plain common sense, he had come. He had sought her out, and he had told her quite baldly *why* he had come.

I came back here to offer you marriage, Miss Muirhead.

But he had said it only after she had had her own say on the subject.

I have had time to reflect upon what I suggested, and I have changed my mind. It was nothing but foolish impulse. I have forgotten it.

He liked her the better for her spirited words, for thumbing her nose at him to all intents and purposes. He liked her better for the fact that her chin had jutted upward and an almost martial gleam had lit her eyes.

"Why?" she asked him now.

It sounded like a challenge.

5

*C*hloe's hands were still clasped behind her back. Tightly. For some reason the third finger of each hand was crossed over the forefinger.

"I have to marry," he said in answer to her question. "Given that fact, I would rather it be to someone who neither expects nor craves what I cannot give. I *can* give my name with all it entails at the present and promises for the future, and I can offer security and respectability and protection. I can give a home and children. Indeed, the latter is what I will work most diligently to give. But you know all this. I can offer all the material benefits of my wealth and position. I will allow you freedom within the bounds of respectability. I will *not*, however, give love or romance or even a feigned affection I do not feel, though I *will* show unwavering respect and courtesy. You informed me a few mornings ago that you wish to be married, to have a secure home of your own, to have children of your own. You informed me that you have no wish for any emotional bond within marriage. Is this correct, Miss Muirhead?"

His eyes and his voice were quite devoid of emotion.

Yet he was speaking of marriage—his own and hers. He could not have made it sound more impersonal if he had tried. But of course she was the one who had started it all. She had overheard what he said to his grandmother, and, remembering his words during the night that followed, she had seen the faint chance of improving her situation.

Improving?

I will not, *however, give love or romance or even a feigned affection I do not feel.*

What had happened to him? He had not been like this when he was a boy at school. Graham had always described him as a vibrant, charismatic figure, as a passionate leader everyone wanted to follow.

"Yes," she said, matching the tone of her voice to his, "it is correct."

"Then I offer you marriage," he said.

Just like that. With a simple *yes* she could be a wife and mother. She could have a home of her own, the security and respectability of being a married lady. Never again, even if he predeceased her, would she feel essentially homeless and rootless and without identity. She would be Chloe Stockwood, Countess of Berwick. She would discover what it felt like to be with a man. For years she had wondered and ached with the secret and very unladylike longing to find out.

Then I offer you marriage.

She closed her eyes and wondered if being married under such bleak circumstances would actually be worse than remaining as she was. But how *could* it? Nothing could be worse . . .

I will allow you freedom within the bounds of respectability.

Did that mean what she thought it meant? And did it presuppose that he would take a similar freedom for himself? Would she be able to bear it?

She thought briefly of the dreams of romance and love and marriage with which she had embarked upon her come-out Season at the advanced age of twenty-one. And of the ghastly awakening that had killed those dreams. Reality was preferable. With this marriage she would at least know ahead of time just what to expect—and what not to expect. There would be no surprises and therefore no emotional ups and downs. There were always far more downs than ups when one allowed oneself to be caught up in emotion.

"A home?" she said, opening her eyes to look at him again. "In the country?"

"Elmwood Manor in Wiltshire is mine," he said. "It is a sizable manor surrounded by a pleasingly landscaped park. I have not spent a great deal of time there since my boyhood, but I intend to change that—after my marriage."

"You would live there in the spring?" she asked. "As well as in the summer and winter?"

"Neither London itself nor the spring Season holds any great appeal for me," he told her. "I would be happy to avoid both. Once I am married I will be able to do just that. I wish for a wife for my home and a mother for my children, not for a hostess for my social life. I would never compel you to go where you had no wish to go."

She almost asked him to promise. But a gentleman's word was promise enough.

"Very well, then." She gazed steadily at him while her fourth and little fingers crossed behind her back too. "I accept."

He did not smile or toss his hat exuberantly skyward. Indeed, he looked almost menacing, with his hat's brim shading his eyes and the scar slashing diagonally across his face. And he looked very large, perhaps because he was standing slightly higher on the slope of the lawn than she. Had she really just agreed *to marry* this morose stranger?

"I have brought a special license with me," he said.

If he had closed one hand into a fist and driven it into her stomach she could not have felt more robbed of breath. She could not possibly be ready . . .

But what was there to wait or prepare for?

"My father?" she said. "Your mother?"

Oh, and a million other persons and considerations. A wedding outfit. Bride clothes. A church and invitations. A wedding breakfast. Betrothal notices. Time to *think*. None of which was essential. This was to be a marriage of necessity for him, a marriage of great convenience to her. It was not a match to be celebrated with family and friends and feasting and dancing. It was not an occasion a bride might be expected to look back upon for the next half century as the happiest day of her life. Their nuptials would be a mere formality, the sealing of a business arrangement to which they had mutually agreed.

"You are of age," he said. "I assume you do not need your father's consent. My mother may learn of our marriage after it has been solemnized. She would want a hand in the proceedings if she knew in advance. I would prefer to marry you without fuss or further ado."

"Before you can change your mind?" she asked.

"I will not change my mind," he assured her. "Why should I? If it is not you, Miss Muirhead, it will have to be someone else. At least I can be sure of not hurting you."

Yes. He could be sure of that. Illogically, she felt hurt.

His eyes were very steady on hers and saw perhaps deeper than she had intended.

"I will *not* hurt you, Miss Muirhead," he said. "It is a promise. After we are married, I will treat you with all the deference and respect due my wife and my countess. I have already drawn up a written agreement, which I will present to your father for discussion after our nuptials. It will give you all the future security you could possibly ask for, even in the perfectly likely event that I should predecease you. You suggested our bargain to me and I have accepted it on your own terms since they so nearly match my own. You are certain this *is* what you want?"

She uncrossed her fingers and moved her hands to the front in order to smooth out the skirt of her dress. For the first time she realized she was without either bonnet or gloves—just as she had been a few mornings ago.

She would have a husband, a quiet, secluded home in the country, children, security. Whatever else could she possibly ask for, when just a few days ago, even an hour ago, she had been looking forward to a bleak life of dreary dependence? And it had indeed been she who had suggested their very bloodless bargain.

"I am quite certain," she said, looking up into his eyes.

"Good." He nodded briskly. "Now we have only the hurdle of informing my grandparents to clear before I go to make arrangements with the vicar. For . . . tomorrow, I hope."

Tomorrow?

She felt that somersaulting in her stomach again.

"They will not like it," she said. "They will hate it. And they will despise me and see me as nothing but a fortune hunter. Perhaps they will even be right."

His riding crop had been tapping against his boot again until it stopped abruptly and he looked around.

"Walk with me, Miss Muirhead," he said, and he turned to stride across the grass in the direction of the falls and the steep stepping-stones beside them that she had descended earlier. He did not look back to see if she was following him, and that inherent arrogance, that assumption that he would lead and others follow, was more as she had expected him to be when she first met him.

She went after him and fell into step beside him. He made no attempt to offer his arm or engage her in any sort of conversation.

Climbing the steep path was very much more strenuous than going down. She had never done it in this direction before. She ignored the hand the Earl of Berwick offered to help her up the steeper, more perilous parts, pretending not to notice it. He did not press the point but went on ahead of her until they were up the steepest part and had only the rapids to pass before coming to level land. He had stopped walking to look back down, and Chloe stood beside him, the sound of rushing water half deafening her again.

"This was my favorite spot in the park when I was a boy," he said, his voice raised. "I was strictly forbidden to come here alone, so of course I came all the time."

She almost laughed. "It *is* dangerous for a child," she said.

"Of course," he agreed. "And for adults too. But children are far more surefooted than adults give them credit for, and the world was made for them to explore and challenge."

"And for them to harm themselves in? Perhaps kill themselves in?" she said.

"Accidents happen." He shrugged.

She looked at him. His eyes were squinting as he looked at something out in the fast-flowing river. His good profile was to her, and it struck her how very handsome he was. And it was not just his face and his dark hair. He had the perfect physique for his height and wore his riding clothes with casual elegance despite the dust that dulled the sheen of his boots. He looked restless, she thought, as though there were some power, some energy within just awaiting the opportunity to break free. It struck her that she scarcely knew him. And even that was an overstatement. She did not know him at all. Yet this time tomorrow it was altogether possible she would be married to him.

He turned abruptly toward her and held out his riding crop.

"Take this," he said imperiously. And when she took it, looking at him in some surprise, he pulled off his riding gloves and thrust them at her too. "Take these."

And he stepped out into the river, his right foot on a submerged stone while his left foot reached ahead to another.

The riverbed was sloping here. The water was flowing fast over a rocky bed. The falls began only a few yards away. If he missed his footing . . .

Chloe bit her lower lip and refrained from calling out

a warning to him to be careful. Or from demanding to know what on earth he thought he was doing.

He stopped halfway across and bent over a group of stones that poked above the surface of the river. She could not see what he was doing, though his hand went once to the pocket of his coat. After that he turned and picked his way back toward the bank.

"Whatever were you *thinking*?" she cried when he was safe beside her again. She had no choice but to speak loudly in order to be heard over the din of the falls. "You could have *killed* yourself."

He looked at her with blank eyes, though she had the disturbing sensation that there was something hovering in their depths, something almost . . . mischievous? He took his crop and gloves back with one hand and reached into his pocket with the other. He came out with a single stone—a flat, thin, smooth, almost round pebble.

"Perhaps," he said, holding it out to her, "the next time you are at the lake you can make this one bounce *six* times."

She took the perfect stone and stared at him.

"You risked your life," she asked him, "for a stone I may well pitch into the water without achieving even a single bounce?"

"Or," he said, "for a stone that may bounce *seven* times."

What . . . ? She closed her fingers about the pebble and knew in a flash that she would never throw it anywhere, certainly not into the depths of any lake. She knew she would keep it. One day perhaps she would show her grandchildren what their grandfather had given her on the day he asked her to marry him. Not diamonds or gold, but ... a stone. And she would tell them that he had risked his life quite, quite idiotically in order to obtain it.

Her own little touch of romance lay safely clasped in her hand.

"If we ever bring children to Manville," she said, "I shall tie one end of a ribbon about their wrists and the other about my own whenever they step outdoors and not let them out of my sight for a single moment."

His expression was totally blank.

"A simple thank-you would have sufficed, Miss Muir-head," he said, and with a certain sense of shock she realized that he was actually enjoying himself.

And that perhaps she was too.

He turned abruptly and resumed the climb toward level ground. The sound of rushing water receded behind them, and Chloe could hear her labored breathing as the water became calm and dark green again. Through the treetops she could see blue sky and sunshine. They would be back at the bridge soon and turning in the direction of the house.

She stopped walking.

"What are you going to say?" she asked. "Both the duke and the duchess must surely know by now that you have come back but are nowhere in the house."

"I shall say that I have been walking in the park with you," he said, turning toward her, "and that I have been proposing marriage to you. I shall tell them you have accepted. I have always found that the truth is the wisest thing to speak when there is no reason on earth *not* to tell it."

She drew a slow, ragged breath.

"I have agreed, Miss Muirhead," he explained to her, "that it is my duty to marry. I have allowed my grandparents, or at least my grandmother, to urge matrimony upon me because it is no less than I must urge upon myself. I will not, however, allow anyone else except the lady to whom I have proposed marriage to influence my choice of bride. I have chosen you for the reasons of which you are aware. If the members of my family do not like that choice, that is their concern, not mine."

"Her Grace has been kind to me," she said.

"You will not persuade me to change my mind, Miss Muirhead," he told her. "Have you changed yours? Because you do not have the courage to marry me, perhaps?"

He was not even trying to press reassurances upon her. She rather liked that. *Did* she have the courage to marry him? More to the point, perhaps, did she have the courage *not* to? She would never have a chance like this again. Or *any* chance, in all likelihood. She rubbed her fingers over the stone she clutched in one palm.

"I have not changed my mind," she told him.

She would have liked nothing better as they approached the house than to go up to her room while he broke the news to his grandparents. But then the moment would come when she would have to come back down and face them. Better to do it now before she lost her nerve entirely.

Things did not proceed according to plan, however. They discovered the butler in the hall, looking unusually distracted, while a footman was shifting awkwardly from one foot to the other as though awaiting instructions before dashing off somewhere. The door to the duke's book room was wide open and the mingled voices of the duke, the duchess, and His Grace's valet came from within.

Her Grace appeared in the doorway, still dressed in the carriage clothes she had worn to visit Mrs. Booth, and addressed herself to the butler.

"He will not have the physician, Weller," she said. "He says he will not see him even if he comes. You might as well forget about sending for him."

"I don't need any damned quack," the duke's voice rumbled from within. "Can a man not sleep and snore in his own private room in his own private house without everyone assuming he has one foot through death's door? Bentley, you villain, stop *hovering* or I shall send you packing without notice or a character."

The duchess had seen the earl, who was striding across the hallway toward her.

"Ah, Ralph," she said, without commenting on his sudden and unexpected appearance, "just the man I need. Come and talk some sense into your grandfather. He was moaning and clutching his chest and fighting to breathe when I peeped in on him a short while ago after returning from Mrs. Booth's. Yet now he declares himself to be in the best of good health. He will drive *me* into the grave before I am one hour older."

The Earl of Berwick had been transformed before Chloe's eyes. He had changed into a commanding presence, and it was very easy to see him as the military officer he had been. He was striding toward the study even before his grandmother started speaking, his boot heels ringing on the marble floor. He squeezed her shoulder in passing and disappeared inside the room.

"Berwick," the duke said. "The world has gone mad."

"How are you, sir?" The earl's voice was crisp. "You look hale and hearty, I must say. But Grandmama has been upset and needs to have her mind put at rest. Allow me, for her sake, to summon Dr. Gregg, and after he has found nothing whatsoever wrong with you, you will have all the satisfaction of saying *I told you so.*"

"Damned quack," the duke grumbled again, but Chloe could tell he was about to give in.

"Bentley," the earl said, "kindly have Weller send someone to fetch the doctor. And when you have done that, bring a glass of brandy. You may be feeling perfectly healthy, sir, but why waste the excuse to enjoy some hard liquor during the daytime?"

The duke's valet was already brushing past Chloe in the doorway. He was on an unnecessary errand, however. The butler had signaled to the footman, who was already darting out through the front doors to fetch the doctor.

"He is *so* stubborn," Her Grace complained to Chloe. "He always was. I do not know how I have put up with him all these years."

"It was on account of my handsome face," the duke said, coughing and covering his heart with one hand.

"Ha!" And then the duchess looked at her grandson and frowned. "*Ralph?* Whatever are *you* doing here? Never tell me you have good news already? Or, rather, *do* tell me you have. *Have* you?"

He was standing before the duke's chair, frowning down at him. But he turned at her words and looked first at her and then at Chloe.

"I do," he said, "if by good news you mean the announcement of my engagement, Grandmama. I am betrothed, very *newly* betrothed. Miss Muirhead has just done me the honor of accepting my hand in marriage."

Chloe clasped her hands tightly in front of her.

"I trust you will wish us happy," he added.

Ralph had told Miss Muirhead that his choice of bride was his alone, that what his relatives thought of that choice would be their concern, not his. Even so, he had felt some anxiety over how his grandparents would react when the moment came. For though Her Grace had taken in the granddaughter of the dearest friend of her youth out of the kindness of her heart, she could not necessarily be expected to look favorably upon a marriage between that lady and her only grandson. Indeed, it had seemed very probable that she would be as horrified as Miss Muirhead had predicted she would be. He was not going to regret his choice even if that proved to be the case. But he would regret disappointing his grandparents.

Now he had something else to think about other than their simple reaction to his betrothal. For his grandfather certainly looked unwell. There was a suggestion of grayness about his mouth and the creases on either side of his nose. And his grandmother was agitated and deeply concerned about him. For one moment Ralph had thought of answering her question a different way and putting off the announcement until later. But he had made the split-second decision to answer with the truth.

An immediate reaction proved impossible, for Bentley was hurrying back into the study, a glass of brandy in one hand, while Weller hovered just outside the door, his usual impassive demeanor replaced by very obvious anxiety.

Bentley tried to hold the glass to the duke's lips, got bellowed and rumbled at for his pains, and relinquished it into the hands of his employer, who took two generous sips before lowering it.

"You will shut the door behind you on the way out, Bentley," he said. "Your Friday face and Weller's are enough to make me feel ill."

The rest of them had been standing in a silent tableau and continued to do so until the door clicked shut.

The duchess was the first to speak.

"Chloe?" she said, sounding more puzzled than outraged. "You are going to marry *Chloe*, Ralph?"

Chloe. The funny thing was that it was the first time he remembered hearing her given name. She was still standing just inside the door, her hands clasped at her waist, looking like someone's governess.

"I am," he said. "My interest was aroused when I was here a few days ago. I returned today to make her an offer, having realized in the meanwhile that I had already met the lady I wished to marry and did not need or desire to look in the ballrooms of London."

The duke had taken another sip of brandy and was already looking more himself.

"You are considering marriage, then, are you, Berwick?" he said. "At the age of what? Twenty-five?"

"Twenty-six," Ralph said. "And yes, sir. With Father gone and no brothers, I have considered marrying the responsible thing to do."

"Helped along by a little encouragement from your mother and your grandmother, no doubt," the duke said.

"I suppose that is why you came here a few days ago and stayed only long enough to blink. You were read a lecture on my extreme old age and sent on your way to do your duty, were you?"

"It so happens, sir," Ralph said, "that my duty has also become my pleasure."

His grandfather harrumphed.

"Chloe," his grandmother said again, a note of wonder in her voice. "My dearest Clementine's granddaughter and my grandson. Why on earth did I not think of it for myself? Oh that Clemmie had lived to see this day with me."

Ralph raised his eyebrows. Miss Muirhead turned her head sharply in his grandmother's direction.

"Chloe, my dear," the duchess said, spreading her arms wide. "Come and give me a hug."

"You are not . . . angry with me, Your Grace?" Miss Muirhead asked as she moved toward her.

"Oh, perhaps I ought to be," the duchess said as she hugged the younger lady and then held her at arm's length to look at her. "Certainly the countess, Ralph's mother, will expect me to be furious, as will all the highest sticklers of the *ton,* stuffy lot as they all are. But why should I be swayed by vulgar gossip? Or by the naughtiness of your sister? You have the look of Clementine, your grandmother, you know, even though your coloring is quite different. She had hair of the darkest, most lustrous brown and blue eyes and a rose-petal complexion. She was the most dazzling beauty of our day and I would have hated her with a passion if I had not loved her so dearly. Does not Chloe look like Clemmie, Worthingham?"

"How would I know?" the duke asked with deliberate meekness as he prepared to drink the last drop of his brandy. "You forbade me to look at her ever again when you and she were both eighteen and I complimented her on the beauty patch she had placed so artfully next to her mouth. I never did look again after that."

Her Grace clucked her tongue and tossed her glance at the ceiling.

"Now tell me, Chloe," she said, "do you love this rogue of a grandson of mine? He claims that all his ability to love was left behind on the battlefield when he almost lost his life too, but I say that is so much nonsense and all he needed was to meet the right woman."

"I am deeply honored by Lord Berwick's offer, Your Grace," Miss Muirhead said. "I shall do my very best to make him comfortable and . . . and h-happy."

The duchess patted her hand, which she had taken in both her own.

"Of course you are honored," she said. "What girl would not be when a future duchess's title is dangled before her? I can remember how *I* felt. I would have had to be *very* averse to His Grace's person to have found the courage to say no. Fortunately I was not averse at all. Quite the contrary. You are right, though, to avoid answering my question about loving Ralph. That is a private admission to be made when the two of you are alone together."

The duke harrumphed again. "I think the occasion calls for champagne," he said. "Have Weller send some up to the drawing room, Berwick. And have him send Bentley to help up there. No, forget that. You can give me *your* arm since I daresay your betrothed can get herself up the stairs without needing to lean upon you. And tell Weller that if that quack should come within the hour, he can wait and kick his heels in the hall."

"Yes, champagne in the drawing room," the duchess agreed. "We have a betrothal to celebrate and a *wedding* to discuss. Give me your arm, Chloe, if you please. And Ralph, tell Weller that he is to come and inform *me* the very minute Dr. Gregg arrives."

No, Ralph thought, he had not made a mistake. His announcement had distracted his grandmother in a positive way. And it had taken some of the focus of attention away from his grandfather, who had rallied, though he still looked far from well.

6

The first fence had been cleared without mishap. Ralph was less hopeful about the second. Weller had brought the champagne to the drawing room and poured them each a glass before withdrawing. Ralph broached the subject of the wedding before his grandfather could propose a toast.

"I think it best that we marry as soon as possible and with no fuss," he said. "I have brought a special license with me."

"A special license?" The duke was clearly outraged. His bushy white eyebrows met above the bridge of his nose. "You are suggesting a havey-cavey wedding for the Earl of Berwick, boy? It is out of the question. The eldest male of the line has always had the grandest of grand weddings in London at St. George's, Hanover Square, with the whole of the *ton* in attendance. Even some of the royals usually put in an appearance."

"And a grand wedding breakfast always follows at Stockwood House," the duchess added. "It is what *we* had, and it is what your mother and father had, Ralph. However . . ."

Miss Muirhead's pale complexion had turned paler, Ralph saw when he glanced at her. His grandmother's eyes were resting upon His Grace, and she looked troubled again.

"It would take a month for the banns to be called," she continued. "It would mean a move to London and endless visits to dressmakers and tailors. It would mean dinners and parties and the prewedding ball we had and your father had, Ralph. And Stockwood House would be turned topsy-turvy for the ball and then for the wedding breakfast. I am not sure I would be able to summon the energy to do it all."

As though, Ralph thought, she would be the one called upon to do the planning and the hosting, not to mention the scrubbing and polishing and cooking. As though she and His Grace could not simply arrive in London the day before the wedding and leave again the day after. But he understood what she was up to and held his peace. Miss Muirhead was holding the sides of her dress. The folds of her skirt failed to disguise the fact that two fingers on each hand were crossed for luck.

"Eh?" his grandfather said inelegantly. "A ball? And a wedding breakfast? Both at Stockwood House?"

"They always have been held there," Her Grace said. "It would be expected of us. It would be considered not at all the thing if we broke with tradition."

"Harrumph. I'll not have you bothered with all that fuss and faradiddle," His Grace said. "It is out of the question, Berwick. You will have to be married here."

As though it were his own original idea.

"During the month of the banns," Her Grace said, one finger tapping against her lips as she frowned in thought—and glanced once, sharply, at the duke—"there will be time to send out invitations to every relative and friend and acquaintance in England. Every guest room here will be filled and every room at every inn for miles around. There will be all those mouths to feed for several days and all those people to be entertained. And there will still be the expectation of a ball and a wedding breakfast."

Ralph sat back in his chair and did not even try to contribute to the conversation. It seemed to him that his grandmother had it well in hand. He caught the eye of Miss Muirhead—Miss *Chloe* Muirhead. He did consider for a moment winking at her and was sorry he had not done so a moment later when she pursed her lips slightly and he realized that she understood too. Her hands had disappeared from sight and he could not tell if she had uncrossed her fingers.

He thought of her as she had looked on the bank of the river earlier while he had picked his way to the middle of it to find her a stone that would be a good bouncer—though, come to think of it, what the devil had possessed him to do something so impulsive? He would have felt like a prize ass if he had slipped and got a thorough dunking, especially if he had also gone sailing away over the falls. She had looked anxious and prunish. She had been almost vibrating with the urge to scold him. And he had found himself almost liking her.

And why, after all, should he *not*? He had no strong feelings for her and never would. But if she was to be his wife, if they were to spend the rest of their days, not to mention their nights, in almost constant proximity to each other, if they were to share children and their upbringing, then surely it would be better to like her than not.

"If Berwick has brought a special license with him," the duke said, "why wait a whole month? Why wait a week? Why go to the bother of inviting a houseful of guests merely so that they can keep us awake at night with their dancing and carousing and eat us out of house and home? Why wait a *day*?"

"You think Ralph should speak to the Reverend Marlowe as soon as we have done with the toasts, then, Worthingham?" the duchess said. "I do think that is a very good idea. And Ralph can surely be persuaded or he would not have gone to the trouble of bringing a license. Chloe, my dear, what do *you* think? Perhaps a wedding outfit and bride clothes and parties and guests are important to you, and you, after all, are the bride."

Ralph watched his betrothed close her eyes for a moment, the only sign that she was not fully composed. Her hands, all fingers uncrossed, had moved to her lap and looked perfectly relaxed.

"I have no wish for any of those things, Your Grace," she said. "I will be perfectly happy to marry the Earl of Berwick tomorrow if it can be arranged."

And her eyes came to rest upon him and widened slightly as though the reality of it all was only beginning to hit her.

As it was him.

Soon she was going to be almost as familiar to him as his own image in the glass. What was it going to feel like—not being alone? It was his essential aloneness that had been the worst of his afflictions after he had been brought home from the Peninsula, for he had not been alone since before he went off to school at the age of twelve, and even then there had been his sisters and his parents. Gradually over the years following his return, of course, he had formed the deep attachment to his six fellow Survivors. He loved and trusted them totally. But he had never made the mistake of believing that they could fill the emptiness at the core of his being.

He was alone and would forever be so. Somehow he had made a friend of his aloneness. Now marriage was going to threaten that. There was going to be a woman— *this* woman—always in his life, even in his bed. He did, as it happened, find her sexually appealing, but that might be small consolation for the loss of privacy he was going to have to endure.

The prospect was chilling.

And tomorrow it would begin.

His grandfather cleared his throat and raised his glass to propose a toast.

Chloe had one outfit that was both new and reasonably fashionable, since she had bought it just last year in London. She had never worn it. It was a walking dress of pale spring green with long, close-fitting sleeves, a deep ruff for a collar, a high waist, and a slightly flared skirt. There was a matching small-brimmed bonnet, which curved high at the back to accommodate the bulk of her hair. It was unadorned except for the dull gold satin ribbon that secured it beneath her chin. She had soft shoes and gloves to match the ribbon.

She had almost not brought the outfit with her to Manville Court, but she had reminded herself that she was going to be staying indefinitely with a duchess and might possibly find herself attending an event requiring a greater-than-usual formality of dress. She had not expected that event to be her wedding.

She was a bride, she thought as she checked her appearance in the long mirror in her room. She was satisfied with what she saw. The duchess had insisted upon sending her own maid to assist her, and Miss Bunker had created intricate curls at the back of her head before placing the bonnet just so over them. She had tied the ribbon in a soft bow close to Chloe's left ear. The dress looked both pretty and elegant and surely showed off her slender figure to advantage.

All of which satisfactory facts did not still the butterflies that fluttered in her stomach. The next time she stood here, perhaps an hour or two from now, to remove her bonnet before luncheon, she would be a married lady. She would be Chloe Stockwood, Countess of Berwick — if something disastrous did not happen to stop the proceedings, that was. If someone did not dash into the chapel to declare an insurmountable impediment to their marriage during that dreaded pause in every wedding service after the clergyman had posed the question.

Butterflies were all very pretty in a meadow. They were altogether less comfortable in her stomach. She wished suddenly, with a great stabbing of longing, that her father was here. Or Lucy or Graham. Or Aunt Julia. Oh, she wished they were *all* here. She had never expected to be so all alone on her wedding day. But then she had never expected a wedding day at all, had she? Not in the past six years anyway. And *certainly* not since last year.

Someone tapped on the bedchamber door behind her

and opened it without waiting to be summoned—the duchess. She was dressed in royal blue and wore a large, old-fashioned bonnet with tall plumes.

"Bunker was quite right," she said. "You look very fine, Chloe, considering the fact that we have not had time to shop for bride clothes. Forgive me, my dear, for backing up Ralph's wish to marry today by persuading His Grace that it was his suggestion. I regretted being obliged to do so, for it is not what any bride dreams of. Ralph, of course, decided that the time had come when he must marry and therefore, to him, the logical thing to do is simply to marry. He probably gave not a single thought to all the trappings of a wedding that his bride and both families and the whole of the fashionable would both want and expect. As for Worthingham—well, he has been spoiled all his life and does not have the imagination to understand that when some grand event happens, it does not simply materialize out of thin air without causing endless work and great anxiety and discomfort to all sorts of people. Even so, we could have—"

"I understand perfectly, Your Grace," Chloe assured her.

"Do you?" The duchess sat down on the edge of the bed and looked a little lost suddenly. "Yes, I believe you do. I suspected the truth even before Dr. Gregg confirmed it yesterday, of course. Worthingham had a slight heart attack, though I do not know quite what can be slight about it. It seems something of a contradiction in terms to me. He should be fine as long as he takes things easy and does not eat or drink to excess. At least, that is what Dr. Gregg assured His Grace and me. What he said to Ralph afterward when they went into the village together I do not know. I have been afraid to ask. But I feared the results of protracted wedding plans and drawn-out celebrations. It seemed best to dispense with both. I was very selfish."

"Perhaps," Chloe said, "we ought to have waited, Your Grace. Perhaps we still could. Perhaps—"

But the duchess interrupted her.

"Oh, you must not misunderstand me, my dear," she said. "I want to see Ralph married, and the sooner the better. And the more I think of it, the better pleased I am with his choice. You are older and more experienced than any of the young girls he would have met in the ballrooms of London. And you have a great deal of good sense. He is a troubled man, Chloe. If you had known him as he used to be, you would understand. And I do not mean just his appearance. He left something behind on that battlefield, and he has not found it again since. But at least he is no longer suicidal. All he could seem to say when he was first brought back was that he wanted to die, that he wanted to put an end to it all. He even tried it once, or once that I heard of. His medication had been left within his reach—not just the next dose, but all of it. He almost . . . Well, never mind. It did not happen. But it was what decided my son, his father, who was still alive at the time, to send him with the Duke of Stanbrook to Cornwall, where there was a physician who dealt with cases like Ralph's. Head cases, that is. He stayed there for three years until we wondered if he would ever come home. But why am I talking like this on your wedding day when we should be in a festive mood and making our way to the chapel?"

Chloe felt chilled. He had wanted to die? He had actually tried to kill himself? And he had spent three years in Cornwall before he was deemed well enough to return home? With empty eyes and empty soul and the inability to love?

Head cases, that is.

What was she *doing*?

But it was too late now to do anything but what had been set in motion yesterday. The vicar had been engaged to marry them in half an hour's time. They were not going to the village church. He was coming to the chapel behind the house, nestled among the trees not far from the riverbank where it began to slope downward over the rapids toward the falls. The chapel was used for family christenings, Chloe knew, and for other private family occasions. It had never before, though, been the scene of a wedding.

She offered her arm for the duchess to lean upon.

They made their slow way out to the chapel, the four of them, past the herb garden, between the vegetable patch on the one side and the neat rows of the flower garden on the other. And on out toward the trees.

The vicar would be awaiting them.

There would be no other guests.

Ralph was quite sure that neither of his grandparents was entirely happy about this wedding with its absence of pomp and noble guests. Even his mother and sisters were not here. Neither was his bride's father or brother and sister. But the wedding was important to them nonetheless. His grandfather, Ralph suspected, had been more shaken by yesterday's mild heart attack than he cared to admit. Though he did not speak much about the succession, Ralph believed he would be easier in his mind if he could see his grandson and only immediate heir married. His grandmother too was worried, even though Ralph had not told her what Dr. Gregg said yesterday as the two of them made their way into the village. A heart attack of the sort His Grace had suffered, though mild, he had warned, could be merely the first in a series of such attacks. Any one of them, or a culmination of a series of them, could prove fatal.

Grandmama was afraid the fuss of a large wedding would be beyond the duke's strength. More important, Ralph suspected, was her fear that he would die before the wedding could be solemnized and thus force its postponement just at a time when the need for Ralph's marrying would be more urgent than ever.

Ralph had purchased the license and suggested today as the wedding day merely because he wanted to get it over with before he could think of excuses for procrastinating. But his grandfather's episode yesterday had convinced him it was the best course.

And Miss Muirhead? What were *her* thoughts and feelings?

If this were a normal wedding, he would be in the chapel now, anxiously awaiting her arrival, and she would approach him from the door on her father's arm while admiring family and friends looked on. Some people even believed it was bad luck for the groom to see the bride before the wedding. But they were walking to the chapel together. At least, he was walking with his grandfather on his arm while she provided the like service for his grandmother.

She was looking neat and composed. She was dressed

with understated elegance in a dress that flattered her slender figure. Her bonnet—yes, she was wearing one today—was pretty though simple of design. Her bright hair was elaborately curled at her neck.

It was impossible to know what she thought or how she felt. And he was not really curious to know. He had spoken the truth to her yesterday when he had pledged always to treat her with respect. He would, of course, inevitably get to know her better during the course of their marriage, but he had no desire to *know* her. He would take her at her word and believe that she wished for no emotional tie with him. He wanted none with her.

His grandfather did not make any conversation. Ralph suspected he needed all his breath and all his energy just to walk the short distance from the house to the chapel. Ralph would nonetheless have welcomed some kind of chitchat. He was remembering two other weddings he had attended this year, though it was still only May, and two he had attended last year—each of them for one of his fellow Survivors. Only Ben and Vincent had missed Hugo's last year and Ben had also missed Vincent's. Only Vincent had missed Ben's in faraway Wales this past January. All of them had been at Flavian's wedding at Middlebury Park just a few weeks ago. Ralph was to be the first of them to marry without even one of the others in attendance. It caused him a surprising pang of regret and loneliness.

But at least he had his grandparents here. Miss Muirhead had no one. He would *not* pursue that thought, however. She wished to be married. And she had agreed upon today. He was not going to allow the barrenness of this wedding to place yet another burden of guilt on his shoulders.

They reached the open doors of the chapel, and Ralph was aware of candlelight flickering within. The vicar was here, then, and ready for them.

And suddenly he wished . . .

For what? His mind would never take him to the conclusion of these unexpected yearnings. He could never see what it was he longed for. But such moments always left him with a faint ache of near despair.

They changed partners, and the duke led Her Grace inside to the padded front pew. Ralph looked at his bride, and she looked back, her eyes calm and unreadable. He knew a twinge of something that might have been panic before inclining his head and offering his arm, formally, as he would to a dancing partner, a stranger, at a ball. She set her gloved fingers half on his hand, half on his wrist, and he led her inside to be married.

There was no music. There was no long nave to be processed along slowly while the solemnity of the coming nuptials built into pleasurable anticipation. And the marriage service itself, stripped of all its pomp, was brief and dispassionate. He had remembered to buy a ring—he had had to guess her size. He spoke his vows and she spoke hers. He slid the ring onto her finger. He had guessed well enough, though perhaps the ring was one size too large. And then the vicar was pronouncing them man and wife and leading them into the tiny cupboard of a vestry to sign the register while his grandparents came along more slowly behind to sign as witnesses.

Stone buildings were always cold inside, especially

when they had been built among trees and very little sunlight ever penetrated their small windows. And especially when it was a cloudy day in May. But surely the chapel was colder than other stone buildings of its kind, though he had not noticed it before. He felt chilled through to the very heart.

His grandparents were clearly delighted. In the congested confines of the vestry, while the vicar effaced himself and squeezed out through the door, his grandfather boomed out his congratulations, pumped Ralph's hand and slapped him on the shoulder, and then folded Miss Muirhead—the Countess of Berwick—in a bear hug and planted a smacking kiss on one of her cheeks. His grandmother framed his face with both hands and, when he bent his head downward, kissed him on the lips and beamed happily. She hugged his bride tightly and complained crossly that Bunker had not had the good sense to put more than one small handkerchief into her reticule. The duke produced one from his coat pocket that looked more like the sail of a small boat and handed it to her.

Miss Muirhead—the Countess of Berwick—his *wife*, was smiling and biting her lower lip and looking suspiciously bright-eyed and . . . Well, by God she was beautiful. There was no denying it. There were two spots of warm color in her cheeks.

They walked back to the house as they had come, the duke wheezing slightly on Ralph's arm, the duchess chirping cheerfully as she walked ahead with . . . his wife. Ralph wondered how long it would take him to get used to thinking of her as such. She was his *wife*. What would he call her? It was a foolish thought, one he had not considered until now. What would she call him? He had never heard his grandparents call each other by their given names, though he knew they were exceedingly fond of each other. Perhaps in the privacy of their own apartments . . .

The servants all knew about the wedding, of course, though Ralph did not believe any formal announcement had been made to them. The butler and the housekeeper had every last one of them lined up on either side of the back hallway, including Ralph's valet and the coachman who had driven his baggage coach, the menservants on one side, the maidservants on the other. They all curtsied or bowed when the small entourage stepped inside, and Weller made a stiff, pompous little speech before leading the staff in three self-conscious cheers.

The duke harrumphed, Ralph made an impromptu little speech of thanks, which he feared sounded every bit as pompous as Weller's, the duchess looked both regal and benevolent, and the Countess of Berwick smiled and glowed and thanked everyone for their kind good wishes and for the lovely surprise of their welcome, all without sounding even the tiniest little bit pompous.

Ralph drew her hand through his arm and patted it.

The wedding breakfast, Weller announced with a bow, would be served in the dining room at the convenience of His Grace and Her Grace and his lordship and her ladyship.

The wedding breakfast?

"It may be served in half an hour's time," the duchess said, nodding graciously to all her servants again and leading the way to the front of the house.

Ralph looked down at his bride when they had left the back hallway and the servants behind.

"I fear," he said, "the ring may be a little large." It was hidden beneath her glove at the moment.

"Just a little, perhaps," she agreed. "But it can be put right. Most things can."

Could they? *Could* they?

"That was unplanned," he said, jerking his head in the direction of the back hall. "So, I believe, was the breakfast, though perhaps it is just Weller's grand name for luncheon today. I hope you have not been made to feel uncomfortable."

He felt dashed uncomfortable for no reason he could explain to himself. Except that, good Lord, this was his *wedding* day. He had a sudden memory of Flavian and his bride driving away from the village church in Gloucestershire a few weeks ago, Flave kissing her while the guests spilling out of the church and the villagers gathered outside cheered and whistled and the church bells pealed joyfully. Ralph felt a little ashamed of the shabby apology for a wedding to which he had subjected *his* bride. He had not even offered a token kiss.

"Not at all," she said, smiling up at him. "I was having a hard time believing in the reality of our wedding until I saw the servants waiting to greet us. But I think we really are married, my lord."

"Ralph," he said, frowning. "You had better call me that since, yes, we really are married."

It was too late now to go back and do things differently.

"Then you must call me Chloe," she said.

"Chloe." And now what the devil? His eyes swept over her. "You will need to change?"

It struck him belatedly that he could have told her,

quite truthfully, how pretty she looked. He still could raise her hand to his lips.

"Yes," she said, withdrawing her arm from his before he could put his thought into action. "I shall be back down within the half hour, my l— Ralph."

He watched her climb the stairs. She looked the same as ever from behind—slim, neat, a near stranger. But within the past hour everything had changed. She was his *wife*. She was *Chloe*. And he did not have any idea how to deal with her or how to deal with married life. He did not want to have to deal with either.

Tonight there would be the consummation.

He strode off in the direction of the book room to make sure the exertions of the past hour had not been too much for his grandfather.

7

Chloe sat on the side of her bed, her hands clasped in her lap. She felt restless and self-conscious, though she was still alone. She was wearing the nightgown she had made a little over a year ago before she went to London to stay with her aunt. She had appliquéd yellow-centered daisies about the hem of the fine white linen and at the edges of the sleeves. She had always liked it, but she did not suppose it was very bridelike.

She had braided her hair and wound it about her head beneath the frilled cap she had made to match the nightgown but had never worn before tonight. She had hesitated about wearing it now, and about braiding her hair and putting it up. Perhaps she ought to have left it down and uncovered. It was just that it was so very . . . well, *red*.

She felt mortifyingly skittish, as though this were a wedding night that really mattered. It *did* matter, of course, for perhaps tonight or tomorrow night or some other night soon she would conceive. Yes, tonight meant a great deal except in any personal way. It really was not important what she did with her hair or what she wore. Or how she felt.

She unclasped her hands and gazed down at her palms. She was married, yet Papa did not know, or Graham, or Lucy. *His* mother did not know or any of his sisters. Tomorrow they were going to leave here and start changing all that. They had decided they were going first to Hampshire to break the news to Papa. The Earl of Berwick—*Ralph*—would discuss the marriage settlement with him even though the nuptials had already taken place. Then they would go home to Elmwood Manor in nearby Wiltshire and write to their other relatives. So many letters to be written, so many people to be surprised. And a marriage announcement would have to be sent off to all the London papers for the information of other acquaintances and the *ton* in general.

When informed of their plans during the wedding breakfast, the duchess had expressed disappointment. In her opinion they ought to proceed to London immediately after calling upon Chloe's papa. There they would be able to call in person upon the Dowager Countess of Berwick, Ralph's mother; upon Lady Keilly, Ralph's youngest sister, who was in town for the Season with Viscount Keilly, her husband; upon the Reverend Graham Muirhead and Mrs. Nelson, Chloe's sister—all within one day. They would also be able to make a round of social appearances while the whole of the beau monde was gathered in London. They would be able to host a ball at Stockwood House in celebration of their marriage. It would be one of the grand squeezes of the Season.

"For you were the subject of gossip and speculation last spring, Chloe, before you fled London," she had explained. "Everyone will wish to set eyes upon you now that you have made the most brilliant match of the Season. And, fickle as the *ton* invariably is, all who looked askance at you last year will embrace you this year—*if* you have the courage to face them, that is, your head held high. You are the daughter of a baronet, remember, and the granddaughter of a viscount. You will have all the consequence of Ralph's title behind you. And you will have all the grandeur of the ducal power behind you too on the night of the ball, for Worthingham and I will surely travel up to town for the occasion."

She had warmed to her theme. The duke had harrumphed but not said anything to contradict her.

"And for the ball, Chloe," she had continued, "you must wear emerald green, and special care must be taken over the dressing of your hair. It must remain uncovered since it needs no adornment. And since you cannot hide its color, which fact caused you so much embarrassment last year, then you must flaunt it instead."

Chloe, sitting on her bed now, several hours later, rubbed the fingers of her left hand in a circle about her right palm, and then reversed hands. Was the duchess right? Was that what they ought to do? But she felt sick at the thought and was very glad that Ralph had refused his grandmother's suggestion.

"We are not going to London, Grandmama," he had said, "despite the good sense of your arguments. Chloe has no wish to mingle with the very society that has quite unjustly rejected her *twice*. And, frankly, I am tired of the tedium and artificiality of life in town. We are going to Elmwood. It is high time I settled there and took an active hand in the running of the estate, and it is where my wife will be most comfortable."

Chloe had glanced at him with silent gratitude. One thing that had taken her completely by surprise during the day was her own happiness. It was a quite inappropriate mood under the circumstances and was likely to cause her pain if she did not check it. It would certainly bring her embarrassment if her husband should suspect. Though it was not as though it were the happiness of love or the expectation of romance. It was just . . .

Well, it was just that she was *married*.

It had been the strangest, most subdued of wedding days. It ought to have felt dreary and anticlimactic and anything but happy. Who, after all, would want a quiet wedding in a tiny chapel to a man who had no personal feelings for her and for whom she had almost none? It ought to have chilled her to the bone, despite the touching scene with the servants when they arrived back at the house and the festive little wedding breakfast, complete with flowers and ribbons and candles and even a small wedding cake, all of which the servants had planned and prepared without even Her Grace's knowledge. Chloe ought to have been outraged or at least upset when her new husband chose to spend the evening alone with the duke while she sat in the drawing room with the duchess.

She ought to be feeling as flat as the flattest of pancakes now. Instead, apart from a certain nervousness, she was *happy*. She was a *married lady*. Her new title was unimportant to her, for she would be just as happy to be plain Mrs. Stockwood. The fact that she was married meant everything.

She clasped her hands again and consciously stopped herself from twiddling her thumbs. But despite her restlessness—what was it going to *feel* like?—she waited in happy anticipation of the arrival of her bridegroom and the consummation of her marriage. Soon she would be a married lady in every sense of the word. What a blessing it was that her courses had finished just two days ago.

She wondered if she would stay happy. There was not necessarily a link between happiness and love, was there? One did not have to be in love with one's husband in order to be happy with him, did one?

Would she be happy with the Earl of Berwick? He had once wanted to be dead. He had even tried to kill himself. He had been taken to Cornwall to heal and recuperate, but even now he was a man who could not love, a man with cold, empty eyes. He was very different from the boy he had been. Even the duchess said so. It was as though a large part of him, all that was brightest and best, really had died. Chloe shut her eyes tightly and bent her head forward. How would she be able to live with him . . .

There was a firm knock on the door of her bedchamber. She lifted her head sharply and looked toward the door, but it did not open.

"Come in," she called.

He was wearing a long dressing robe of dark blue satin. It might have looked almost effeminate, but it somehow emphasized both his muscularity and his masculinity. Or perhaps it seemed that way merely because he was in her bedchamber and he had come to assert his marital rights.

She ought to have prepared something to say, she thought too late. She said nothing and tried not to clutch her hands too tightly. He closed the door behind his back, and she could see his eyes take in the bed turned down on both sides for the night, the branch of candles burning on the dressing table, her bare feet, her modest nightgown, her cap. His eyes paused on that last item.

"I hope I have not kept you waiting," he said.

"No."

There was a brief silence, and she felt her breath quicken.

"I shall try not to hurt you," he told her. "After tonight you should find it more comfortable."

It.

"Yes."

His voice and manner were quite matter-of-fact, even brisk. He appeared to share none of her embarrassment.

Now what? Too late it occurred to her that she might have had some wine brought up. She could have poured them each a glass now and begun some easy, relaxed conversation about . . . well, about something. Instead, she was as skittish as a young girl. Perhaps more so. Her age and inexperience embarrassed her.

He came toward her and held out a hand for one of hers.

"Come," he said. "Pain or not, I believe you will be more comfortable *afterward,* will you not?"

"Oh." She allowed him to draw her to her feet. "Yes, I believe I will. I am so sorry. I am nervous. I do not know quite what to . . . do."

"It would be strange if you did," he said, "since you have admitted to never having done this before. Lie down while I extinguish the candles."

He drew the covers farther back on the near side of the bed so that she could lie down, but he turned away before she actually did so. She was thankful for that. She lay down on her back and closed her eyes. Then, against her eyelids, she saw sudden darkness. She could hear him coming around the foot of the bed to the other side. There was a coolness as he drew the covers farther back, and then she felt the mattress beside her depress beneath his weight.

Tomorrow night, she thought, and the next night and the night after that this would be a growingly familiar ritual, without embarrassment or awkwardness. Perhaps it would be something to which she would look forward. She hoped so. There had been those nameless and unladylike yearnings that had often plagued her through the last ten years or so, and she hoped it was *this* for which she had yearned, that it would live up to her hopes.

It was one of those nights that was almost as bright as twilight. She could see as well as feel that he had turned onto his side and raised himself on one elbow to lean over her. His hand moved flat down her side from her waist to her hips and on down the outside of her leg until he reached even lower and grasped the hem of her nightgown and drew it upward. She had to half lift herself until it was bunched about her waist.

He came on top of her then and she realized in some shock that he had shed his robe and was wearing nothing beneath it. His legs pressed between hers and pushed them wide, and his hands slid beneath her buttocks to lift her and tilt her. Her hands came reflexively to his shoulders, which seemed massive and hard with muscle. She was aware of the hard ridge of what must be a scar curving from the front of his right shoulder over to the back.

And then he was pressed against her and she told herself not to hold her breath but to relax and breathe normally while he came inside her. She waited for the pain and schooled herself not to flinch. But there was only the unfamiliar feeling of being stretched and filled until, after the merest twinge of what threatened to be pain but was not, he came deeper in and she feared there would not be enough room.

He held still in her while his hands slid free and he half raised himself on his elbows. It was only then she realized how heavy he had been on her. She kept her eyes closed and slid her hands partway down his back. The scar extended downward to the edge of his shoulder blade—on the opposite side of his body from his facial scar. That particular cut must have come close to taking off half his face and his arm with half his shoulder as it slashed down across him.

He withdrew almost completely from her and pressed inward again before repeating the action, slowly at first, almost tentatively, as though he was being careful not to give her too much pain, and then with firmer, swifter strokes that had her squeezing her eyes more tightly closed and knowing that nothing in her yearnings had quite matched this.

She lay still beneath him and let it happen. He was her husband and he was making her his wife. Perhaps he was also impregnating her. There *was* some pain, a growing soreness that she guessed would remain with her for the rest of tonight and probably into tomorrow. But it was a lovely pain. And this was lovely. She was no longer embarrassed or apprehensive.

His weight descended full on her again after a while, and his hands slid beneath her again, and the thrusting of his body was harder and deeper until she felt him releasing his breath against the side of her face on what was almost a sigh, and he held deep and she felt a gushing of heat inside.

It was absurd to feel that this was the happiest day of her life. It was a chill bargain into which they had entered today. What had just happened was merely a part of it. Even in her inexperience she could not convince herself that they had just made love. There had not been any love involved with anything that had taken place today. He had married a breeder for his heir, and she had got a husband and home so that she would not live out her life as a dependent spinster. That was all, according to their bargain.

Oh, but it *was* the happiest day of her life nonetheless.

After a minute or two, he lifted himself off her and moved to her side. He lowered her nightgown and pulled the bedcovers up over her. She wondered if he would return to his own room now, but he lay down and pulled the covers over himself too.

"Thank you, Chloe," he said.

She turned her head his way and only just stopped herself from thanking him too.

"I hope it was not too painful for you," he said.

"No," she said. "No, it was not."

"I will try to see to it," he said, "that you do not regret today."

"A wedding without guests or any pomp?" she said. "I rather liked our wedding."

"I meant our marriage," he said. "I will try to see to it that you do not regret marrying me."

"I will not," she assured him. "It is all I have ever

wanted, you see—a respectable marriage and a home and a family. I will not regret our marriage."

She thought of the emptiness of his eyes and hoped she spoke the truth.

"I will try to see to it that *you* do not regret it either," she added.

"I will not," he told her. "It is over."

He did not explain what he meant. But it was a chilling little phrase—*it is over*. As though, once he had begotten an heir and perhaps another son to provide a spare, his duty would be done and there would be nothing further for which to live.

Surely he had not meant that.

She wished the duchess had not told her that he had once been suicidal. It had been many years ago, after all, and his injuries had probably been such that the pain had come near to driving him out of his mind. But *three years* to heal? And an empty soul afterward?

Head cases, that is.

She waited for him to say more or to decide after all to return to his own room. But she became aware after a while of the evenness of his breathing and realized that he had fallen asleep.

It is over. Perhaps all he had meant was that now he was married he would no longer have his relatives and his own sense of responsibility constantly pestering him to do his duty and choose a bride. No doubt that was all he had meant.

Or perhaps he had merely meant that today was over.

Had she just imagined that his voice as he spoke the words had been utterly bleak?

Chloe closed her eyes and concentrated upon the soreness—the lovely soreness—he had left behind inside her.

She was married. In every way.

She hugged happiness to herself as she fell asleep.

Ralph was staring up at the canopy over the bed. He guessed he had slept for an hour or two. He rarely slept longer at a stretch and often had a hard time going back to sleep after he woke. He was wide awake now and feeling a bit claustrophobic. Although this was not a small bedchamber, it was considerably smaller than his own. And the canopy seemed lower and the bedposts heftier.

It was not those facts that made him feel closed in, though, he knew. It was the fact that he was sharing the room, sharing the bed. He was not touching her, but he could feel her body heat along his right side, and he could hear her soft breathing.

He fought the desire to get up and return to his own room. He had decided that for a while, until she was pregnant, he would spend the nights in her bed so that he could have her more than once. His reason for marrying, after all, had been the need to produce heirs, and he meant to do the job diligently. He would not take her again tonight, however, not even once, not even in the morning before getting up. She must be sore, even though she had said it had not been painful. He could only imagine what losing one's virginity must feel like for a woman.

He could have allowed himself one more night in his own bed and the privacy of his own room, then, but he had decided to stay here, to start his marriage as he meant to continue with it. He hoped she did not mind. He had not consulted her. But she had known and accepted his reason for marrying her—his only reason.

He had been a little disconcerted by her appearance when he came to her room. Not so much the nightgown. It was pretty even if rather excessively modest. But the cap . . . Again, it was pretty. But he had been imagining to himself what her hair was going to look like. He had wondered if it would be braided or left loose. He had certainly not expected that it would be all but invisible.

Perhaps it was just as well. He must, and did, feel some sort of sexual attraction to her, but he did not want there to be more than that. And he suspected very strongly that she did not either. She had lain passive and quiescent beneath him. It was a bit chilling to know that the pattern of his sex life had been set tonight.

She murmured something unintelligible and rolled onto her side, facing him. He turned his head to look at her, but she was not awake. Her forehead almost touched his shoulder. The frill of her cap, he could see in the near darkness, framed her cheek and forehead and gave her a look of innocence.

He was surprised by a stirring of desire. He would not act upon it, however. He had the feeling she would not resist him, but it would be callous . . .

He turned away from her, closed his eyes, and willed himself to go back to sleep. He almost succeeded. He was actually drifting off when a brisk knock on the bedchamber door brought him back to full consciousness with a start.

"My lord." The door had opened a crack. It was his valet's voice, low but urgent. "You are to come."

Chloe sat bolt upright. Ralph swung his legs over the side of the bed and reached for his robe.

"His Grace?" he asked.

"He has taken a nasty turn, my lord," his valet confirmed. "Her Grace says you are to come."

Chloe was on her feet too. Ralph strode around the foot of the bed, belting his robe as he went.

"Stay here," he told her. "You might as well go back to sleep."

"What foolishness," she said as he hurried from the room and along the corridor to his grandfather's room, which was bright with candlelight.

He took in the scene at a glance. His grandfather was lying on the bed, his head and shoulders propped up by a bank of pillows. Even in the flickering light of the candles it was obvious that his complexion was a livid gray. His eyes were closed, his fingers clenched on the sheet that covered him. His valet was bent over him, one hand to his brow. The duchess, very upright beside the bed, clutched the edges of a heavy dressing gown to herself.

"Dr. Gregg has been sent for?" Ralph asked, striding into the room.

It spoke volumes that his grandfather did not even open his eyes to protest.

"He has, my lord," the valet said. "Weller has gone to wake Robert. He is the swiftest and most reliable of the footmen."

The duke opened his eyes and looked around at the group.

"How are you, sir?" Ralph asked foolishly.

His grandfather's eyes found him, and for a moment

there seemed to be a glimmer of humor in them—and of affection.

"Dying, my boy," he said. "A foot and a half through the door at last. And not before time. I have long outlived my allotted three score years and ten."

Ralph would have moved around the bed to his grandmother's side, but Chloe was already there, he saw when he looked up. She had an arm about the duchess's shoulders.

The valet was dabbing a wet cloth to the duke's face. The housekeeper had appeared at the door, where she stood beside Weller. Ralph's own valet hovered just outside the door with a cluster of other servants.

The duke had closed his eyes again. Her Grace had taken his hand in both of hers and raised it to her cheek. Chloe stood with her hands clasped at her waist, her eyes upon the duke's face.

"The physician needs to hurry," the duke's valet said, straightening up and looking imploringly at Ralph, anguish in his eyes.

"He will come as fast as he can." Ralph moved up beside him and squeezed his shoulder, and the man stepped away to wash off the cloth in the basin and squeeze it out until it must have been nearly dry.

Ralph touched his grandfather's shoulder and gazed down into his face.

Don't die, he begged silently. *Don't die. Please don't die.*

But everything died just as surely as love did.

The old, dying eyes opened again and found the duchess.

"Emmy," he said.

"Ned. My dearest."

Ralph looked away. His eyes met Chloe's across the bed and she half smiled at him. Strangely, it did not seem an inappropriate expression, only an apparent acknowledgement that she knew his mind was repeating the same words over and over — *Don't die. Please don't die.*

He heard himself swallow, and then, only a moment or two later, it seemed, he heard his grandmother's voice again, very quiet, very calm.

"He is gone."

And he was indeed. He was lying as before, his eyes closed, his gray face peaceful. But something had changed. *Everything* had changed. There was no one there.

He was gone.

8

The duchess and Ralph, on either side of the bed, were gazing numbly down upon the duke's dead body. Chloe glanced from one to the other of them, wondering which she should try to comfort first. But of course there *was* no comfort. She remembered that very well indeed from the night her mother died.

A hushed voice close to her ear broke the silence.

"What ought I to do, Your Grace?" It was the housekeeper. "What ought we all to do? We can hardly just go back to bed."

Chloe turned to beg the woman not to disturb the duchess at such a moment, only to realize in some shock that Mrs. Loftus was addressing her. *She* was the Duchess of Worthingham. Ralph was the duke. It was a nasty shock that made her feel as though she was about to buckle at the knees.

Mrs. Loftus and Mr. Weller normally kept Manville Court running with smooth precision and absolute authority. But both were rather elderly. They had probably occupied their positions for many years and had grown deeply attached to their employers. They ought, of course, to be prepared for this moment, since the old duke had been in precarious health for some time, but clearly they were not. Both were looking lost and helpless and had turned to Chloe for guidance.

She was, after all, now the mistress of Manville Court—shocking, ghastly thought. But *someone* had to take charge. She stepped out into the corridor beyond the bedchamber door with Mr. Weller and Mrs. Loftus and spoke with lowered voice to the servants gathered there—and there was a fair crowd of them. Chloe doubted anyone was still in bed.

"It will be best if Mr. Weller remains up here," she said. "His services will almost certainly be required. Perhaps you will choose one of the footmen to remain with you, Mr. Weller. You will wish to stay too, of course, Mr. Bentley." She looked with sympathy at the haggard face of the duke's elderly valet, who was hovering in the doorway. "You will definitely be needed. None more so."

"Yes, Your Grace," he murmured.

Chloe led everyone else down to the kitchen. There she found a couple of kitchen maids and one young boy clustered forlornly about the cook. All of them curtsied to her and fell silent, looking to her for direction. They must all know far better than she what needed doing, of course, but for the moment they were collectively stunned and helpless.

Only a matter of hours ago, they had all been lined up in the back hall, beaming with pleasure at the sight of a new bride and groom . . .

Chloe instructed the cook to get the fire going in the big range and sent a maid to fill the large kettle and the boy to work the pump for her. She suggested an early breakfast for all the servants who were not otherwise employed, as the day ahead was likely to be a busy one and different from the usual routine, and none of them could be certain when they would next be at leisure to partake of a good meal. She directed that a tea tray be prepared and the kettle kept at the boil so that tea or coffee could be made at a moment's notice. She suggested that a batch of scones be baked as soon as possible and that one of the footmen should check the liquor decanters in the drawing room to make sure they had been filled last night. She assigned another footman to make sure the coal scuttle in the drawing room was full and sent a maid up with him to light the fire and start warming the room. Mrs. Loftus would supervise everything else that needed doing, Chloe told them all, since Mr. Weller was otherwise occupied, at least for now.

But in the meanwhile, she said at last, and before doing anything else, they must all take a few moments to return to their rooms to dress. Goodness knew when they would have another chance, and any visitors who arrived later might consider it odd to say the least if they found all the servants and other residents of the house in their nightgowns and nightcaps.

She was suddenly acutely aware of her own nightgown and old dressing gown and of her frilled cap—and of the fact that this had been her wedding night and the servants were all fully aware of the fact.

Her words drew a weak laugh from everyone as they dispersed.

In the absence of a black dress—it had not occurred to her to bring any of her old mourning clothes to Manville with her—Chloe donned a dark blue one. It would have to do for now. She left her hair braided about her head.

By the time she came back downstairs, she had thought of a few other things that needed to be done without delay. Robert had just returned with the physician only to learn that they had arrived too late. Chloe comforted him with the assurance that Dr. Gregg could not have saved the duke's life anyway, and she sent the footman back to the village to fetch the vicar even though it was still night. The presence of a clergyman was needed, and the Reverend Marlowe would not mind the hour. Indeed, he would probably be hurt if he was not summoned until after daybreak. It was not often he was called to the deathbed of a Duke of Worthingham.

She sent the footman who was on duty in the hallway to fetch something with which to muffle the sound of the door knocker, black crepe if possible.

And then there was nothing left to do that she could think of. She stood in the hall for a few moments and glanced up the stairs. Ought she to go back up there? Was that where her place was, at her husband's side? But there was nothing she could do, and the thought of going back into that room with its silent, empty presence was daunting. If she had not left at all, it would be different. But she had.

She could not go back.

She went into the drawing room instead and pulled Her Grace's chair closer to the fireplace. She picked up the fire tongs and heaped a few more coals onto the fire. The room still felt chilly. But she was too restless to sit. She went back down to the kitchen instead, to make sure everything was proceeding smoothly. It was. Mrs. Loftus had recovered both her poise and her authority and was instructing the chambermaid who had already finished her breakfast to check all the rooms to make sure the curtains were drawn across every window. As soon as the others were finished, she assured Chloe, they would be sent to dust and polish in the main rooms, though they had all been done just three days ago. The footmen were being sent back to their rooms to change into their best livery. Miss Bunker had volunteered to make black armbands for them.

Chloe arrived back in the hall just as the vicar was coming through the door. He strode toward her, both hands outstretched.

"My dear duchess," he said, squeezing hers tightly. "Under what sadly different circumstances we meet today. Please accept my deepest sympathies and those of my dear wife. But the Lord is merciful, you know. Yesterday it was very clear that His Grace was happy he had lived long enough to witness the nuptials of his only grandson."

She led the way upstairs, but she was glad to relinquish him to the care of Weller, who was waiting on the upper landing, all stiff, formal dignity.

She sat in the drawing room after that, waiting, and gradually dawn grayed the room through the curtains. It struck her fully then. The duke, that gruff but kindly old gentleman of whom the duchess was so very fond, was dead. Gone. Leaving a heavy emptiness behind, even for her. She could only imagine what Her Grace and Ralph were feeling. And indeed she *could* imagine it. Her mother's death still felt recent.

When the drawing room doors finally opened, Chloe

got to her feet and pulled the bell rope before turning. It was a moment she had been dreading.

Ralph had his grandmother on his arm. Both were fully dressed, both in black. Her Grace was straight backed and regal, her face looking as though it had been sculpted of marble. Ralph's was ashen, stern, and forbidding. Dr. Gregg and the Reverend Marlowe came behind them.

Choosing which one to comfort was instinctive. Chloe hurried across the room and drew Her Grace into her arms. They clung wordlessly together for several moments before Chloe led her to her chair by the fire and spread a lap robe over her knees.

"The tea tray will be here in a moment," she said, "and a plate of scones."

"I could not eat or drink a thing, Chloe," Her Grace said, "but Dr. Gregg and the vicar will be glad of some refreshments, I daresay. I regret that they were dragged from their beds at such an hour. Perhaps they would prefer something stronger than tea, though?"

Both men held up staying hands and shook their heads. Dr. Gregg assured Her Grace that a cup of tea would be much appreciated.

"And you will drink too, Grandmama," Chloe told Her Grace firmly, "and have a bite to eat. You must."

The duchess smiled wanly.

"I just asked Weller how the servants are faring," she said. "He told me they have been under your direction and that everything is running smoothly. Thank you, my dear. I might have guessed you would take charge without any fuss or panic. I will drink tea since you insist. And I will try half a scone."

Ralph meanwhile had crossed the room without a word to anyone and stood now at the window. He had opened the curtains back a few inches and was staring out at the gray dawn, his hands clasped at his back.

A tray on which there was both a coffeepot and a teapot was carried in almost immediately. Chloe busied herself pouring and carrying around the cups and saucers and then the freshly baked scones. The Reverend Marlowe had seated himself close to the duchess and was speaking quietly to her. Dr. Gregg stood at his shoulder, listening and looking down at the duchess with obvious concern.

Chloe crossed the room to her husband, set a cup of coffee down on a table close by, and rested a light hand on his sleeve. She felt his arm stiffen, though he did not flinch quite away from her.

"Ralph," she said softly.

"Everyone," he said without turning his head, "keeps calling me *Your Grace.*"

"I have poured you some coffee," she said. "And there are fresh scones."

"I want nothing," he said.

"He went peacefully," she told him. An utterly foolish thing to say, of course. But what *did* one say?

"You became a countess yesterday," he said, "a duchess today. It is the stuff dreams are made of."

Her hand tightened a little on his arm before she removed it. Did he mean . . . ? But of course he did not.

"I beg your pardon." He turned his head sharply to frown at her. "I do beg your pardon, Chloe. I did not mean that the way it sounded."

For once there was something in his eyes more than the usual blankness. There was apology there, and pain.

"Oh, I know," she said. "But it is the truth nevertheless, and I wish it were not so. Drink your coffee, or I will bring you tea if you prefer. And try to eat a scone. I shall fetch some for both of us, though I have no appetite either."

Such mundane matters when there were worlds of emotions to feel and realities of which to think and speak! One of the most horrible realities about the death of someone closely related, she remembered, was the necessity of going on almost immediately with the triv-ialities of living. As though nothing of any real signifi-cance had changed.

"Coffee will be fine," he said, his eyes straying to the cup. "I'll share a scone with you."

She went to fetch it and to pour herself some tea, and then she returned to stand beside him again. They ate half a scone each from the same plate before he took up his coffee. Last night, just a few hours ago really, they had consummated their marriage. It seemed an eon ago. She was suddenly terribly glad they had married in time.

"Weller and Mrs. Loftus have ruled Manville with an iron thumb apiece for longer than I can remember," he said. "I understand they came close to falling apart last night, however. They were quite devoted to the duke, of course. But you held them together and now, I under-stand, all is running smoothly again."

"They would have done very well without me," she said.

"They would have managed, of course," he agreed, "but they looked to you for leadership and you gave it."

She set down the empty plate, pleased at his approval, and picked up her cup and saucer. "I am your wife," she said. And she was. In every way.

"You are my *duchess*." He frowned at her. "Which fact makes me the duke. Hell and damnation."

He did not apologize for his shocking words. Perhaps he did not even realize he had spoken them aloud.

"I had better start behaving like one," he said, setting down his empty cup and saucer. "Come."

And he moved toward the fireplace and waited for Chloe to seat herself before speaking.

"Gentlemen," he said, addressing the physician and the vicar, "I thank you for coming out so promptly in the middle of the night and for the words of comfort you have offered to Her Grace, my grandmother, and to my wife and me. We are indeed grateful. We will need to discuss the funeral, Reverend Marlowe. Not now, though. I will be sending my grandmother and my wife to bed soon. They both need to sleep or at least to rest if sleep is not possible. Perhaps you will return later."

Both men recognized their cue to leave. Ralph saw them on their way, and Chloe was alone with his grandmother for a few minutes. Her Grace was staring into the fire, but both the cup and the plate beside her were empty.

"It is the strangest feeling in the world," she said. "One moment someone is there, speaking one's name. The next moment his body is still there but he is not. And never will be again. There is no calling him back. What was not said before he went will never be said now. His body is still upstairs. It looks like him and yet does not. He is not there."

Chloe clasped her hands and refrained from offering words of meaningless comfort.

Her Grace turned her head and smiled at her.

"But we celebrated your wedding yesterday," she said, "and we were both happy, Worthingham and I. Perhaps it was selfish of us not to persuade the two of you to wait and marry with all the proper pomp and formality in London. But I cannot feel sorry we *were* selfish. Somehow it felt like the loveliest wedding I have ever attended, with the possible exception of my own. And you cannot know the comfort it is to me today, Chloe, to know that Ralph is married and has a wife to see him through this difficult time. And to know that you are no longer just my guest, my dear Clemmie's granddaughter, but my *own* granddaughter by marriage. I could not bear to be the duchess any longer, you know. I am *so* glad that your position as Ralph's wife has relegated me to the position of dowager duchess. Oh, Chloe, my love."

Her eyes welled with tears, and Chloe hurried over to perch on the arm of Her Grace's chair and wrap an arm about her shoulders.

"How am I to go on without him?" Her Grace asked, tipping her head sideways to rest on Chloe's shoulder. "Oh, the selfishness of the man to go before me." She laughed shakily and fumbled for a handkerchief. "But in some ways I am glad he did. I shall do better without him than he would have done without me. He would have been lost . . . I just wish we could have gone together."

Ralph came back into the room as she was blowing her nose. His eyes met Chloe's and he came toward them and went down on his haunches before his grandmother's chair. He held out his hands to her as she tucked away her handkerchief.

"Grandmama," he said when she took them. "I will send you up to your room now and have Bunker summoned. Chloe will accompany you and then go to her room. You must both lie down and try to sleep."

His voice was quiet, even gentle, but there was a thread of implacable will in it, and Chloe guessed that he might be somehow transformed by his new role, that he would take his responsibilities very seriously. Perhaps, she thought, they would even be his salvation, though she did not know quite what she meant by that.

He drew his grandmother to her feet and Chloe stood too and offered her arm.

"But perhaps you would be more comfortable in one of the guest rooms, Grandmama," Ralph suggested.

"Because only our dressing rooms stand between my room and your grandfather's, do you mean?" she asked. "But I am not afraid. He would never have harmed a hair on my head while he lived. Why would he harm me now that he is dead? Besides, he is no longer there, you know. No one is."

He looked bleakly at her as she took Chloe's arm and they went upstairs together. Chloe was back down no more than five minutes later, however. He was still in the drawing room, gazing into the fire, one arm propped on the mantel above his shoulder. He turned his head and raised his eyebrows at sight of her.

"What are *you* going to do?" she asked him.

"No one knows anything of what has happened here in the last twenty-four hours," he said. "No one knows of our marriage. No one knows of the duke's passing. It is a dizzying thought, is it not? There were no guests at our wedding. We chose not to wait. Now, for the next big event, we *must* wait, for there are all sorts of people who will want to be here for the funeral. He was the *Duke of*

Worthingham. There are family members to inform—about both events—and friends and his closest associates as well as some dignitaries to inform of my grandfather's passing. There must be no delay if they are to have the chance to travel here in time. Notices must be put in the papers. And there are all sorts of other details to attend to, some of which I have probably not even thought of yet. I have summoned my grandfather's secretary to meet me in the study. He is my own secretary now, I suppose. He is probably waiting for me there already."

Something inside Chloe turned cold and still.

. . . for there are all sorts of people who will want to be here for the funeral.

Of course. Oh, of course.

There would be no setting out today or tomorrow for Hampshire and then, after a visit with Papa, for Elmwood Manor and home. There would be no setting out until after the funeral, which would be attended by all sorts of people. *There are family members to inform and friends and his closest associates as well as some dignitaries.* And perhaps—even probably—there would be no setting out even then. For surely Elmwood would no longer be their principal home. Manville Court would be.

She felt a moment's dizziness and shook it off. This was not a time to think of herself.

"There will be letters to write, then," she said briskly. "Many of them and not all of them identical. And the notices to the papers will need to be composed and copied several times. That is a great deal for two men to do with so little time. I shall come with you."

He turned fully away from the fire and frowned at her.

"You need not concern yourself," he said, his tone almost chilly. "You have been up half the night, and you have been busy. Go and rest."

"You have been up just as long," she pointed out. "There is a great deal to do, and I shall help you do it."

He looked as if he was going to argue or perhaps issue orders. He appeared suddenly haughty and autocratic. And then an expression almost like a smile flitted across his face before it was gone.

"I am reminded," he said, "that I really do not know you at all, Chloe. You intend to be more than just the mother of my children, do you?"

"What I agreed to be," she told him, "and what I promised to be yesterday in church, was your *wife*. Having your children is just one of my obligations."

"Obligations," he said softly.

"They are not always negative things." She smiled at him suddenly. "I *like* writing letters."

But she felt as though something cold was clutching her heart. She had not been expecting any of this. How foolish of her. Despite all the signs and warnings that had stared her in the face since she arrived at Manville Court, she had not even thought of this happening in the near future. And now the future had become the present.

"Come, then." He strode past her to the door and then stopped and looked back at her, still frowning. "I suppose trotting along at my heels is another obligation, is it? Take my arm."

Arthur Lloyd, the late duke's secretary, already had lists drawn up of people he considered needed to be informed and things that had to be done. Chloe sat down beside him and Ralph looked over their shoulders, though the secretary had tried to relinquish his own chair to His Grace. And together they completed the lists and divided up the tasks.

Chloe had made it clear that she was not going to simply go away. She undertook to write to her brother and sister and aunt and uncle—Lord and Lady Easterly. She also wrote a letter to her father to be included with the more formal note Ralph composed. She made several copies in an elegant sloping hand of the wedding announcement and the death notice that Lloyd had drafted and Ralph had approved after Chloe had suggested a few minor adjustments to the wording. Ralph wrote to his mother and sisters and his six fellow Survivors, while Chloe and Lloyd dealt with the formidable number of more formal notes that needed to be sent to various other people of importance for whom the announcement in the papers would not be sufficient.

When Ralph and Lloyd began to discuss what needed to be done to prepare the house for the arrival of family members and close friends for the funeral, Chloe looked up from the letter she was writing and told them quite firmly that they need not concern themselves with domestic matters. That was her domain, and she would confer with Mrs. Loftus. Ralph exchanged a straight-faced stare with the secretary before saying that in that case he would start jotting down ideas for the funeral to discuss with the vicar.

Somewhat later, just before the Reverend Marlowe returned, Ralph mentioned the necessity of acquiring some mourning clothes, especially for Chloe, who apparently had nothing black. He would send to London for some ready-made garments and hope they would fit well enough. But again Chloe looked up from what she was doing and told him he need not worry. She had considered sending home for the old mourning clothes she had had for her mother, but there was a better solution. A skilled dressmaker lived no more than eight miles away. Chloe would ask her to come and to bring an assistant and fabrics and all her sewing needs with her so that she could stay for a few days. Ralph's grandmother would perhaps wish to avail herself of her services too.

Ralph found himself growing increasingly irritated. He was accustomed to command, though he had not done a great deal of it in the last seven years, it was true. But he was certainly accustomed to independence, to making his own decisions, to having servants follow his orders without question or interference. Chloe, of course, was not a servant. What irritated him most about her, perhaps, was that she really was a help—an invaluable help, in fact. And that she did it all cheerfully and efficiently. And that she could—and did—think and act independently.

It fairly set his teeth on edge—until he remembered how unabashedly happy his grandfather had been yesterday. And his grandmother too. And how his grandmother had been leaning into Chloe earlier on in the drawing room after he had seen the doctor and the vicar on their way. And how he himself needed a wife, and how now more than ever he needed an heir.

And what type of wife would he prefer? Someone helpless and timid and vaporish? Someone he could bed at night and ignore by day? Or someone . . . like Chloe?

His irritation, he admitted to himself, was unreasonable. And then suddenly, out of the blue, he thought of someone else who had always had a similar effect upon him—someone for whom he had felt respect and annoyance in equal measure. Someone he could never either dominate or quite dismiss from his notice.

Graham Muirhead. Her brother, for the love of God.

They were *nothing* alike. They looked as different as night and day. Of course, it was possible, even probable, that they were only *half* siblings, was it not?

He was relieved when Weller appeared at the study door to inform him that the vicar awaited his pleasure in the small salon. Chloe's red head with its bright coronet of braids was bent over a letter when he left. She was gone when he returned. Her Grace, the dowager duchess, had awoken and asked for her, the secretary informed him.

Ralph was tired and dispirited when she appeared at the door sometime later. There were still letters to write, but his mind was addled and a certain numbness he had held within since last night was beginning to give place to the full realization that his grandfather was gone forever. Yesterday they had walked out to the chapel and back together. They had spent the evening together, reminiscing about Ralph's boyhood. Today he was gone.

"It is time to change for dinner," Chloe told him.

He frowned at her with undisguised annoyance.

"I have no appetite," he said. "I will have something later on a tray if I am hungry." And he bent his head to continue writing.

"Neither is your grandmother hungry," she said. "But it is of the utmost importance that she eat and keep up her strength. I have no appetite either. It is up to you and me, though, especially you, to set the example. And you had no luncheon."

He dropped his pen and spattered small blots across his half-written letter, ruining it. He could feel irritation escalate to anger. He opened his mouth to give her some sort of blistering setdown, but he paused and shut his mouth again while he passed a hand over his eyes. She was quite right, damn it.

"I will go up now," he said, getting to his feet. "I'll escort you."

She must be just as tired as he. And it must be as difficult for her to adjust to his ways as it was for him to adjust to hers. More so. She was not frowning and scowling at him at every turn. She was just quietly going about her business.

Ralph was forced to admit to himself over the next few days that he did not know how he would have managed without her help. Though even that admission was an irritant. He had spent three years at Penderris Hall and four years since learning to live alone, learning to be dependent upon no one—especially not emotionally dependent.

Not that he was growing *emotionally* dependent upon his wife. Sex, after all, was not an emotion. Which was a very good thing. For he came near to becoming dependent upon it during those days leading up to the funeral, or, rather, during the nights. Tired though he was each night, he went to her bed and found some relief from the stresses of the day in her body. It was never an overly erotic experience. She always wore her nightgown to bed, and he never tried to remove it. She always wore a nightcap too, the glory of her hair all but hidden beneath it.

But he took her twice each night, three times on one occasion, and he did not even pretend to himself that it was all out of duty and the need to beget an heir, though that was his justification for taking pleasure when his grandfather's body was still in the house, laid out downstairs in the state rooms.

He had no idea if it was a pleasure for her too. She always lay quietly beneath him, her body warm and relaxed and moist within, prepared to welcome him. But her arms almost always came about him when he was on her, the fingers of one hand running lightly over the worst of his scars, the saber cut that had almost severed both his arm and his shoulder after first opening up his face. She never commented on the ugliness of it, though she had seen it in the mornings when he got up from her bed, naked, as he always slept. His body was not a pretty sight, he knew. She never flinched from it, though.

He had the feeling she was going to be a good wife. She would probably be a good mother too. He was not sure if he was more pleased than annoyed. His whole life felt . . . invaded.

And his very identity had changed yet again. Earl of Berwick five years ago when his father died suddenly while Ralph was still at Penderris; now Duke of Worthingham. And a married man.

He sometimes wondered where Ralph Stockwood had gone, if anywhere. Perhaps he was still there, lurking and lowering somewhere deep inside. But he was not sure he wanted to search for him. Sometimes sleeping dogs really were best left lying.

9

Chloe was kept very busy during the days following the old duke's passing and had little time to reflect upon the trials that were facing her, though they were many. Even the original situation had been daunting enough, when she was merely the new Countess of Berwick and had only to face her own relatives and in-laws with the fact of her sudden marriage.

Merely. And only.

Now, in addition, she was the Duchess of Worthingham and must welcome to her home—and yes, that really was Manville Court, no longer the far more modest Elmwood Manor—as many relatives and as many of the crème de la crème of society as cared to make the journey into Sussex for the funeral. Ralph and his grandmother believed that a large number of people would wish to pay their last respects.

These were the same people who had turned their collective back upon Chloe six years ago after Lucy had run away with Mr. Nelson and again last year when it had become painfully apparent that she, Chloe Muirhead, bore a striking resemblance to the daughter of a man once a beau of her mother's.

She had little time during those days to reflect upon the state of her marriage, which was, admittedly, in its very early stages and was progressing under very different circumstances from what either of them had anticipated. She did not know if her husband liked her or not. She did not know whether she liked him. She supposed it did not matter much either way, though. They were married and would just have to make the best of it. It was not as though either of them had any romantic illusions.

The days were difficult. She threw herself into her new role because she knew she was needed and because she knew too she must begin as she meant to go on—a false step now might forever alienate her servants and mar future relations with her neighbors. But she felt like a usurper, especially as the dowager duchess was still very much in residence. And Ralph seemed to resent her energy and efficiency because, she suspected, he had never had to share leadership with anyone. Not that he ever complained. On the contrary, he frequently thanked her and even complimented her, but he did so in a stiff, cool manner that suggested what he would really like to do was snarl at her at the very least. And she resented his resentment, for she believed he would despise her if she settled into being the timid mouse of a wife he had probably expected.

The whole point of her wishing to be married had been that she would never again have to efface herself and pretend to be placid and bland. Provided she did not have to face the beau monde again, that was. Yet that was precisely what was about to happen, albeit in a limited way. Oh, life was not easy. And what an earth-shatteringly original observation that was.

But she had to admit to herself that the nights made up for the trials of the days. She liked his regular, dispassionate lovemaking, for want of a more appropriate word. She liked it very much indeed and tried her very best not to want more—fond words and tender touches, for example, and . . . Well, and a great deal more to which she could not even put a name because of her lamentable inexperience. But none of that, whatever it was, was a part of their bargain. Indeed, their very absence was a part of it.

No emotional ties.

The Dowager Countess of Berwick, Ralph's mother, arrived two days before the funeral in company with Viscount Keilly and his wife, Nora, Ralph's youngest sister. Ralph went downstairs to meet the carriage as soon as he was made aware of its approach, and Chloe proceeded more slowly behind, his grandmother leaning heavily on her arm. The travelers were out of the carriage and standing on the terrace by the time the two of them emerged from the house and descended the steps. The younger lady was in Ralph's arms, sobbing against his shoulder. The older lady came hurrying across the terrace to hug the dowager and express her sorrow.

Chloe took a step back and clasped her hands at her waist—like the perfect companion, she thought, fading into the background—and wished fervently that that was just what she was.

The gentleman was shaking hands with Ralph and offering words of sympathy.

And then they all seemed to be finished at the same time with that first outpouring of grief and mutual condolences. Everyone turned in a body to look at her. Her first foolish thought was that she was very thankful Miss Rush really was a skilled seamstress and that she worked fast and efficiently. Chloe was wearing a simply designed but well-fitting black dress that covered her from the neck to the wrists to the ankles. She had brushed her hair smooth over her head and dressed it in a tight coil of braids at her neck. It was the best she could do to subdue the inappropriate brightness of its color. She probably looked even more like someone's governess than she did a duchess's companion.

"Mama," Ralph said. "Nora and Keilly, may I have the pleasure of presenting my wife? My mother, my sister, and my brother-in-law, Chloe."

At least he had not called her his duchess.

The dowager countess was a handsome lady and looked much younger than Chloe had expected. Her daughter was a younger version of her. Ralph resembled them both.

The dowager looked at her with colder eyes even than her son's and inclined her head with almost exaggerated graciousness. Viscount Keilly made her a graceful bow, and Lady Keilly looked her over from head to foot before raising her eyebrows and looking away.

Chloe was the only one of them to curtsy, and she was left with the feeling that she had somehow committed a social blunder. Of course, she did outrank them all, a thought that caused her an inward grimace. And she could not think of a thing to say. How could she welcome them to her home, after all, when they must know it so well as the home of the late duke and the dowager duchess? How could they not see her as the most obnoxious of gold diggers and intruders, especially at this time of family sorrow?

"Ah, there is the housekeeper," her mother-in-law said, glancing up to the open doors of the house and reaching out a hand to take Ralph's arm. "You may show us to our rooms, Mrs. Loftus. The usual ones, it is to be hoped? And Weller will see to it that our bags are brought up. We will join you shortly for tea in the drawing room, Mother."

The dowager duchess had taken Lady Keilly's offered arm.

"I am quite sure dear Chloe will have made all the arrangements to everyone's satisfaction," Her Grace said. "I absolutely do not know how either Ralph or I would have coped with the trials of the past few days without her."

Lord Keilly was following his wife up the steps into the house, his hands clasped at his back.

Chloe trailed along in their wake. Asserting herself with the servants had been the easy part of her new role, she realized. They had made it easy. This was not an auspicious start to her acquaintance with her in-laws. But at least it had begun. Sometimes waiting and imagining were far worse than actually doing.

The situation improved with the next arrival a mere half hour later.

Lady Ormsby, Her Grace's widowed sister, came in a carriage so old and so ornate that it would not have looked out of place in a museum. It was so hedged about with servants—a maid, liveried footmen, stout outriders, an ancient coachman—and so loaded down with baggage that Chloe fully expected six persons to emerge from the interior, not one.

"Emily," the lady said after looking sharply about the terrace, and she folded Her Grace to her ample bosom. "Emily, my sweet one. And so ends one of the great love stories of the century—this century and the last. I cannot begin to imagine what your life will be like without Edward. How did he die? Peacefully, I hope, which is more than I can say for my poor Hubert. You must ply me with tea, which Ralph will lace with a drop of brandy, and tell me all about it. There, there. I suppose you have not had a good weep. You never were a watering pot, unlike Caroline, God rest her soul, who used to drown us as well as Mama and Papa with floods of tears at the merest provocation. Even the sight of a dead field mouse would set her off. Do you remember that mouse and the burial she insisted upon arranging for it? You look very somber and very delicious in black, I must say, Ralph. And quite like a pirate with that scar. And what is this about your marrying without inviting a soul? I would be as cross as a bear with you if your poor grandpapa had not turned up his toes the very next day and ensured that all my sensibilities must be devoted to my poor dear sister. Is this the bride?"

And she raised a long-handled lorgnette to her eyes and turned them, hugely magnified, upon Chloe.

"Great-aunt Mary," Ralph said, making her a bow, "may I present my wife? Lady Ormsby, Chloe, Grandmama's elder sister."

"My lady." Chloe decided to curtsy again, whether it was the correct thing to do or not, and the lorgnette remained trained upon her for a few moments before being snapped downward.

"Your grandmama was Clementine West," Lady Ormsby told her, "or at least she was after her marriage. I cannot remember who she was before that. She was Emmy's bosom bow, however. She was a great beauty, a fact I would have resented to the point of tantrums if I had not already been married to Ormsby. But her beauty did not outdo yours, girl, though where you got your coloring from the Lord only knows unless the gossips have the right of it, which they very rarely do. You may thumb your nose at the lot of them now, however. No one is going to give the cut direct to a duchess with fiery red hair, especially when she looks so dramatic in black and has married a pirate. You may kiss my cheek, but be careful not to smear my rouge or my maid will sulk for a week."

She declined the offer to be shown to her room. She linked her arm through her sister's instead and led the way to the drawing room, instructing the housekeeper as she passed to send up a large pot of tea without delay.

"If you will pardon me for the familiarity, Duchess," she threw over her shoulder at Chloe.

Ralph looked sidelong at Chloe as they followed behind.

"Most families seem to have at least one eccentric among their number," he murmured. "Usually someone's aunt."

Chloe smiled. It was the closest he had come to joking with her.

The next morning brought some neighbors, as the previous days had done, come to pay their respects. Chloe welcomed each one, for though all regarded her with open curiosity, none appeared hostile. And of course they had not come primarily to meet her. They had, after all, seen her in church with the duchess on a number of occasions. They had come to commiserate with Ralph's grandmother and with her daughter-in-law and grandchildren.

The day also brought word of posting inns for miles around filling up with persons of high rank come to attend tomorrow's solemn rituals.

The afternoon brought more travelers. Lady Ormsby, who insisted that Chloe call her Great-Aunt Mary, spotted the carriage approaching along the drive and drew Ralph's attention to it.

"There is a crest on the side panel," she said. "I would recognize it in a moment if I were a quarter of a mile closer to it or if these eyes were fifty years younger. Lorgnettes are perfectly useless for anything more practical than intimidating the presumptuous. Whose carriage is it, Ralph?"

"The Duke of Stanbrook's," he said, after moving up beside her.

"I suppose," his mother said, "he will expect to stay here. You must have him informed, Mother, that only family is to stay. Or I shall do it if you find it difficult. I have never warmed to the man."

"I shall go down and meet him," Ralph said, and he turned to Chloe with a curious light in his eyes. "Come with me?"

The Duke of Stanbrook, he explained briefly as they made their way down to the terrace, was the owner of Penderris Hall in Cornwall, where he had spent three years recovering from his wounds.

Chloe held back while Ralph strode across the terrace to open the carriage door himself and set down the steps. The duke was considerably older than her husband, tall and handsome in an austere sort of way, with dark hair silvering at the temples. He came quickly and wordlessly down the steps and caught Ralph up in a tight hug. She saw both their faces before they broke apart and was startled to see raw emotion in both.

Then they turned back to the carriage and Ralph held out a hand to help someone else alight—a lady. She was small and blond and very pretty, and she set her hands on his shoulders and stood on tiptoe to kiss him on his good cheek and murmur something Chloe could not hear.

Another person followed her down, a great giant of a man with close-cropped dark hair and a face that was all frowns and ferocity as he caught Ralph up in a hug even tighter than the duke's.

"Ah, lad," he said after a few silent moments, "we came with George as soon as we heard."

Chloe found them even more intimidating than her in-laws for some inexplicable reason. For she sensed immediately that they were of a world shared by her husband, a world from which she was excluded. Ralph had been transformed before her. The deadness had gone from his eyes. And instantly, unreasonably, she resented these people. She was his *wife*, yet she had never until this moment glimpsed any of this . . . *animation* in him.

They all turned together, rather as his family had done yesterday, suddenly aware, it seemed, of her silent presence a short distance away. Ralph extended one arm toward her, his fingers slightly beckoning, putting her somehow in the wrong for not having approached of her own volition. His eyes held hers, and they were blank and unreadable again.

"Chloe," he said, "let me present the Duke of Stanbrook and Lord and Lady Trentham. My wife, the Duchess of Worthingham."

The two men regarded her gravely. *The outsider,* they seemed to be thinking. Lady Trentham smiled with unaffected warmth, however, and she came limping toward Chloe and took both of Chloe's hands in hers.

"Duchess," she said, "what a wretched honeymoon you are having, you poor thing. And how sad that we cannot celebrate your new marriage with you just yet. I am delighted for you both, nevertheless. All the Survivors are dearly fond of one another, as I am sure you know, but they have opened their close circle to welcome each of the newly acquired wives. Hugo and I have been married for not quite a year, and there have been four other marriages since, counting yours. I do hope you will be as happy as the rest of us once this very sad occasion is behind you."

The survivors? But Chloe did not ask.

"Thank you," she said, smiling back and then looking from one to the other of the men. "And welcome to Manville Court."

The Duke of Stanbrook was holding out a hand for hers. "Duchess," he said, taking it in both his own as he looked directly into her eyes, "I strongly suspected when Ralph left London a few days ago that I would be meeting you soon, though I did *not* suspect it would be under such sad circumstances. I am sorry about that. But I am glad Ralph has you to bring him some comfort."

"Let me look at you, lass," Lord Trentham said, his amiable voice at variance with the fierceness of his facial expression. He took her right hand in his large one. "Someone said you had the reddest hair of anyone else they had ever seen, and I can see they did not exaggerate. Ralph has found himself a rare beauty. Have I said something wrong, Gwendoline?"

But his wife merely shook her head slightly and laughed as she linked an arm through his.

Ralph gestured toward the steps and the main doors. "You will, of course, be staying here," he said. "All the guest rooms have been prepared."

"We would not dream of imposing," the duke said. "We will stay in the village or wherever there is room for us."

"But we would not dream of allowing you to stay anywhere else but here," Chloe said. "You are my husband's friends."

And it was not so much resentment she felt against them, she realized, as jealousy pure and simple, for clearly they *were* his friends while she was not. She was merely his wife, to whom he had promised respect but never affection.

She led the way inside and paused to have a word with Mrs. Loftus before following them upstairs.

And then, less than an hour later, Graham arrived with Lucy and Mr. Nelson. Ralph accompanied her downstairs again to greet them.

Lucy came tumbling out of the carriage first, squealing with a quite inappropriate display of high spirits. She rushed into Chloe's arms.

"Chlow," she cried, "you are *married*. To a *duke*. But

why did you not wait to have a grand wedding and invite us to it, you horrid thing? I will never forgive you. You do look fine in black, I must say. But I remember remarking on that fact after Mama died. You have the coloring to carry it. Does she not, Freddie? I look a perfect fright in black myself. I simply fade away behind dark, dreary colors. But I ought not to run on so, ought I? You have suffered a *bereavement,* and I daresay you are quite sad about it even if the duke was an old man."

"My dear sister," Frederick Nelson said, making Chloe a flourishing bow as though he were on stage, playing to the highest gallery, "or my dear *duchess,* ought I to say? I suppose you will have to observe a bit of a mourning period, but as soon as you can, before the end of the Season, it is to be hoped, I shall be imploring you to set up your own salon in London and cut a dash entertaining all the best wits and artists and poets and, dare I say, *playwrights?*"

Chloe gave him a speaking glance. These two never changed. They absolutely deserved one other. Mr. Nelson inhabited his own eccentric world, seemingly unaware of the real one, while what had begun as mere youthful, impulsive exuberance in Lucy had become, with the removal of the refining influence of her father and mother, an amiable near vulgarity. But at least she *was* amiable. And family.

"Lucy, Mr. Nelson," she said, "allow me to introduce you to my husband. My sister and brother-in-law, Ralph."

"Ah, but the Duke of Worthingham and I have a long-standing acquaintance," Mr. Nelson said effusively.

Ralph acknowledged him with a polite inclination of the head and bowed over Lucy's hand. He had been shaking hands with and exchanging some pleasantries with Graham, though they had both been looking a bit stiff and awkward about it.

Graham hugged her. "Chloe," he said for her ears only, "whatever have you done? And without a word to anyone?"

"There was no time to let anyone know," she told him. "The duke was ailing, and the duchess was eager for us to marry without either fuss or delay. I am glad we did, but I am sorry there was no time for our two families to gather here."

Mr. Nelson was delivering what sounded like a bombastic speech of condolence and Lucy was gazing at Ralph in some awe when someone else descended the steps of the carriage more slowly and hesitantly than the others. He looked at Chloe and raised his eyebrows, as though he was not sure of his welcome.

She looked back at him and felt as though her heart was breaking.

"Papa," she whispered, and then she hurried forward and was in his arms, held tight to all his comforting bulk and the familiar smell of his snuff. "I am so sorry."

He held her away from him and looked inquiringly down at her.

"There was no time to ask for your permission," she explained.

"You are of age, Chloe," he reminded her.

"For your blessing, then," she said. "The duke was ill, and the duchess feared the excitement of grand wedding preparations or even the delay for more modest ones would prove too much for him."

"It is a brilliant match you have made, Chloe," he said.

"But will you be happy? It was all so very sudden. Was it because you had persuaded yourself you had no home of your own to which to return?"

But there was no time to answer him. Mr. Nelson had finished his monologue and Lucy for once was speechless. Chloe turned. "This is my husband, Papa. The Duke of Worthingham. My father, Ralph."

The two men shook hands, sizing each other up. Neither smiled.

"I hope to make amends later, sir," Ralph said, "for not having consulted you before I married your daughter. I thank you for undertaking such a long journey. It will be a comfort to my wife to have her family with her during the next few days."

"I was in London when Chloe's letter to my son was delivered," her father said. "I was there to spend a couple of weeks or so with him and my younger daughter and grandchildren and my sister. I was glad to be able to avail myself of the opportunity to come here to offer my condolences."

"Do come inside, sir," Ralph said.

"I will have you taken up to some guest rooms," Chloe said, slipping a hand through her father's arm, "and then you must come back down to the drawing room for tea. I am sure you will wish to pay your respects to Her Grace."

"*You* are Her Grace, Chlow," Lucy said. "But I know who you mean. You mean the old duchess. I daresay I shall be awed speechless when I meet her. We are not received by many of the highest sticklers of the *ton*, you know, but everyone will have to be polite to us for the

next few days, will they not? And to you too, Chlow. After last year, I expect—"

"I believe it would be wiser, Lucy," Graham said, "to
hold your tongue."

"Oh, you are *so* stuffy, Gray," she said, rolling her eyes.
But mercifully, she obeyed him.

10

The rest of the day proceeded in a bit of a whirl for Ralph. In a way he was thankful. For the past few days he had gone more than once to spend time with his grandfather, laid out in state for those who wished to pay their respects, and more and more each time he felt his loss. For his grandmother had been right on the morning of his death. His body was there, but he was not. Only memories of him remained.

Most of Ralph's memories of his paternal grandparents were of pure, unconditional love, not unmingled with some pretty firm discipline when it had been necessary. His father had always been bookish and reserved in manner. His mother had always been distracted by her social obligations. Not that either parent had been cruel or unloving or even neglectful. But they had lacked a certain warmth that Ralph had found in his grandparents.

Which fact made him wonder what sort of father he would make to his own children. Chloe, he was almost certain, would be a good mother. She had told him on the morning she suggested her bargain that she would love any children they might have, and he believed her. The servants loved her. He did not believe that was an exaggeration. Servants had only ever respected him. Though maybe that was not strictly accurate. A number of the older ones had been party to some sort of conspiracy to protect him from his grandparents' wrath whenever as a boy he had got himself into one of his frequent scrapes.

There were other arrivals later in the day—his eldest sister, Amelia, and her husband, an aunt and uncle, a few cousins, a few particular friends of his grandparents. And then three unexpected guests.

Flavian, Viscount Ponsonby, a fellow Survivor, came with his wife from Candlebury Abbey, their country home some distance away though also in Sussex, where they had been hiding away on their honeymoon. And, very late in the evening, Vincent, Viscount Darleigh, the blind one of their number, arrived, having traveled all the way from Gloucestershire with his valet and his guide dog. They could not have lingered anywhere on the road to have arrived in time. Ralph was more deeply moved than he could say. The only two of their number who had not come were Ben, who lived in the farthest reaches of West Wales, and Imogen, who was in Cornwall.

Ralph was late going up to bed that night. Very late, in fact. Everyone had wanted to sit up and talk, as invariably seemed to happen in the face of a recent death. It was as though the living needed to assert their vitality against the great silencer. But his grandmother and his great-aunt had finally gone to bed, and almost everyone else retired soon after. Chloe, Lady Ponsonby, and Lady

Trentham went up together, Ralph was pleased to see. They seemed all to like one another. Finally only he and his fellow Survivors remained in the drawing room—and Graham Muirhead. It was an annoyance to Ralph at first that Muirhead chose to intrude upon the closeness of their group, but it was unreasonable of him, for this was not a gathering of the Survivors' Club. Graham was as much a guest in his house as the others were.

Ralph had always had a complicated relationship with Graham Muirhead, if it could be called by that name. At school Graham had always hovered on the edge of Ralph's inner circle of four friends, but he had never become part of it. Ralph had liked him. Sometimes he had believed he would enjoy a closer, meaningful friendship with him, for Graham was intelligent and sensible and well read. At other times Ralph had found him so irritating that even his worst enemy would be a preferable companion, for Graham had a mind of his own and did not scruple to disagree with any idea or scheme that ran contrary to his beliefs. To be fair, Ralph had the feeling that Graham had felt the same way about him. Perhaps it was because they were both strong willed. But while Ralph's strong will had made him a leader, someone other boys emulated and followed, Graham's had shown itself in a quiet stubbornness, a total disregard for popularity or the approval of others. They had often clashed heads, even if only metaphorically. They had never recovered from the last time it had happened.

Graham was a clergyman now, but not just *any* clergyman. Not for him the quiet, respectable living he might have found in a country parish, with a wife to make the parsonage cozy and children about his knees, a wealthy patron to offer him security until he inherited his father's title and modest fortune. And not for him the sort of ambition that would have sent him clawing his way up the ladder of the church hierarchy until he became a bishop or even an archbishop. Oh, no. Graham Muirhead had attached himself, by personal choice, to a poor parish in the very least desirable area of London, his parishioners being the slum dwellers, pickpockets, whores, drunks, moneylenders, ragged orphans, and other undesirables who filled its confines to overflowing. Not to mention the filth and stench of the streets.

And he had done it, he explained to an avidly interested George, Hugo, Flavian, and Vincent, not from any saintly sort of notion that he was going to bring the masses to the church pews, where they would fall to their knees in tearful penitence, but from his conviction that if his Lord had been born in early-nineteenth-century London instead of in Roman Palestine, then it was in that precise part of London he would have been found most often, consorting with the lowest of the low, healing them, eating with them, accepting them as they were, treating with dignity, and rarely if ever preaching at them. Simply *loving* them, in other words.

"For that is what my religion is," he explained without any suggestion of pious pomposity, "and what it impels me to do with my life. Simply to love and accept without judgment."

Faradiddle, Ralph had wanted to say with great irritability at the same time as there was an ache of something—*tears?*—in his throat. For the words were not self-righteously spoken or designed to impress. They were merely Graham being Graham.

"Damnation!" Hugo exclaimed, slapping one large hand on his knee. "But you are right, Muirhead."

"I would rather you than me," Flavian said. "But you have my d-deepest admiration."

"Is love enough, though?" George asked. "Love does not find homes for those orphans or respectable employment for those whores or comfort for those who are robbed."

"No man can do everything," Graham explained. "Each of us can do only what is within his power. If we dwell upon our inability to solve the world's problems, our only possible recourse is to despair. Despair accomplishes nothing."

A spirited debate followed, in which Ralph did not participate, though he listened and watched with interest — and with something he recognized as resentment. For these men all liked one another. Graham Muirhead fit right in as though he were one of them.

What was Ralph's problem, then? Did he want to keep his friends to himself, unwilling to share? The possibility that that might be the case was embarrassing, to say the least. And childish.

"Ralph." George's eyes were resting upon him, and the others turned to look at him too, even Vincent. "We are keeping you up. And you need rest. One has only to look at your face to see that. You were very deeply attached to your grandfather. Tomorrow will be difficult for you."

"I actually find it rather soothing," Ralph said, "just to sit here and listen to you all talk. Thank you for coming. I really did not expect it. You too, Graham. It means a great deal to Chloe to have her family here with her."

Hugo got to his feet, rubbing his hands together.

"Well, I am for my bed," he said, a signal to them all, including Vince's dog.

It was well past midnight when Ralph let himself into his wife's room without tapping on the door, as he usually did. He expected that she would be asleep. He had even considered staying in his own bed tonight, but he found the prospect cheerless. He would not wake her, though, he had decided. Tomorrow was going to be busy for her too.

There was a small coal fire burning in the fireplace. That was unusual. But then he saw she was seated in an armchair beside it, her arms wrapped about her legs, her bare heels resting on the edge of the seat. Her nightgown covered her to the ankles and to the wrists. Her nightcap allowed a mere glimpse of her hair. Even so, she looked more inviting than any courtesan he had ever encountered—a rather absurd thought, surely. Firelight flickered warmly off her person and off one side of her face when she turned it toward him.

He set his back against the door and crossed his arms over his chest. He had a strange, and strangely disturbing, sense of homecoming.

Chloe turned to look at him. She had not been sure he would come. She ought not to have waited up. But she had been unable to go to bed. If she had, she would not have slept.

"I thought you would be sleeping," he said.

"No."

"I am sorry," he said, "that my mother and Nora and Amelia are still virtually ignoring you. They will come around if you are willing to give them time. It is just that my sudden marriage took them completely by surprise and they are quite unjustly punishing *you*. I should perhaps have told my mother about you before I left London."

She had not expected his mother and sisters to welcome her with open arms. At least they had not been openly unkind. But she did not want to think about them tonight.

"At least Lucy has been unusually quiet," she said. "She is awestruck, and long may she remain so. She is speechless with admiration of your great-aunt. Have you noticed how she seats herself as close to her as possible and takes note of her every word and gesture? I suspect she will be begging Mr. Nelson to buy her a lorgnette when they return to London."

"She is fond of you," he said. "So are your father and your brother."

"Yes."

She did not want to think of Papa either tonight.

"Come to bed?" he suggested, but she did not move.

"Tell me about the survivors," she said. "It is a word Lady Trentham used this afternoon regarding your friends, and she sounded as though it ought perhaps to be written with a capital *S*. They were all with you in Cornwall? They were all wounded? I did not realize, you know, when you introduced Viscount Darleigh to me that he was blind. As soon as I spoke to him, he looked so directly at me that I assumed he could *see* me. I wondered why he had brought the dog, but then I suddenly understood when he did not take my outstretched hand. Were you all in Cornwall for three years? It is an awfully long time."

She could almost sense him sighing inwardly as he uncrossed his arms and came closer. She ought not to have asked. They had agreed to show no real interest in each other's lives, had they not? They had agreed to no emotional involvement. But surely they needed to know some things about each other?

He sat down on the low ottoman beside her chair.

"Penderris Hall in Cornwall is George's home—the Duke of Stanbrook's," he told her. "He set it up as a hospital for wounded officers toward the end of the wars. He persuaded an excellent doctor of his acquaintance to work there and hired extra staff. A number of wounded men were there for a while and then left. A few died, one at Penderris and two after they had returned home. But there were six of us who stayed for all of three years. I suppose we were the ones whose wounds were not just physical, or in some cases not physical at all. We stayed to heal and then to convalesce, to put ourselves as well as our bodies back together. The doctor was very skilled at that former aspect of his work. He believed that war often wounds the soul as deeply as it does the body, sometimes more so. And we formed a deep bond, the six of us, seven counting George. He had not been to war himself, but his only son died in the Peninsula, and a few months later his wife threw herself to her death over the cliffs that border their estate."

"Oh," she said on a gasp of horror.

"He was as broken as the rest of us," he said. "One day one of us—I believe it was Flavian, though it might have been me—called our group the Survivors' Club as a sort of joke. And the name stuck. The two who are not here now are Ben—Sir Benedict Harper—who lives in

West Wales with his wife, and Imogen, Lady Barclay, who lives in Cornwall. Ben's legs were crushed in a cavalry charge and he has never recovered the full use of them despite Herculean efforts on his part. Imogen's husband died under torture in the Peninsula, and she was made to watch some of it as well as his death. We all left Penderris at the same time four years ago. It was probably the hardest thing any of us has ever had to do, though it was absolutely necessary, of course. We could not live out our lives in an artificial bubble. Now we get together for three weeks each year in the early spring, usually at Penderris, though this year we went to Middlebury Park in Gloucestershire, Vincent's home, instead. He did not want to leave his wife so soon after her confinement."

"He speaks with great pride and affection of his son," she said. "How sad it is that he cannot see the baby."

"It would be a mistake to pity Vince," he said. "He very rarely pities himself. He considers himself well blessed and happy."

"They mean more to you than anyone else in the world," she said, "your fellow Survivors."

"Yes, in a way." He looked up at her and reached for her hand. She wondered if he had intended to do so, but he did not release it. "It is a special bond that we share, but it does not preclude other bonds. Five of us have married, all within the past year, incredible as that sounds. Three of the wives came to Middlebury Park this year. Flavian married while we were there. And now I have had my turn. Marriage creates a different sort of bond, Chloe. It is not necessarily inferior to what I have with the Survivors. Indeed, it is *not*."

He set one of his hands palm to palm against hers and spread his fingers along her own.

"Do you feel threatened by them?" he asked her.

"No." She shook her head, not sure she spoke the truth. "I have seen evidence of your physical hurts, Ralph, and I realize they were dreadful indeed. What were your other hurts? Why were you at Penderris for three years?"

Why did you leave there so changed?
And with such lifeless eyes and empty soul?
And believing yourself incapable of love?

Chloe did not ask those questions out loud.

She was terribly aware of Ralph's hand pressed to hers, large, long fingered, darker skinned than her own, very masculine. And of his head just below the level of her own, bent over their hands. In the firelight there appeared to be gold strands in his dark hair.

Despite her initial reaction, she liked his friends, his fellow Survivors—and yes, it was a word that would need a capital *S* if written. The rather austere bearing of the Duke of Stanbrook was explained by his history, by the loss of his only son in battle and the suicide of his wife shortly after. But instead of allowing those two deaths to embitter or destroy him, he had concentrated his resources upon bringing healing to others who had suffered.

There was no outer sign of the injuries Lord Trentham must have sustained. He was large and seemed powerfully strong, and his face beneath the close-cropped hair looked rather forbidding, as though frowns came more easily to him than smiles. Yet when he spoke he was kindly, and it was clear he loved the small, dainty Lady

Trentham, and she him. Yet he had been damaged enough by the wars to have spent three years with the others at Penderris Hall.

Viscount Darleigh's injuries were more obvious. He was a very young man even now, perhaps even younger than Ralph. How old must he have been when . . . ? It did not bear thinking of. He had a sweet, sunny-natured temperament. And Viscount Ponsonby stammered very slightly, but that might have nothing to do with what had happened to keep him at Penderris for so long a time. He was suave and charming and witty and seemed outwardly undamaged by war or life. He was obviously very much in love with his new wife.

She liked Ralph's friends, but . . . Ah, yes, she *had* felt threatened by them, for there was something quite extraordinary about the way the five men related to one another. She had even resented the fact that Lady Trentham and Lady Ponsonby did *not* seem to feel threatened.

Everyone now gathered at Manville Court, with the exception of her father and Lucy and Mr. Nelson, knew Ralph better than she did. Even Graham. She knew almost nothing. And so she had asked her questions even though it was late and she ought perhaps to have gone to bed instead of waiting up for him. And she ought to have allowed *him* to go to bed. Tomorrow was going to be both busy and emotionally draining.

He held his hand against hers and laced their fingers tightly. He kept his eyes on their hands.

Why were you at Penderris for three years? she had asked.

"I wanted to die," he said, his voice without inflection. "It was why my father sent me to Penderris. I ranted and raved and talked of nothing else except putting an end to it all. I tried to swallow all my medication. I reached for anything that looked sharp enough to let blood. When my hands were tied to my bed with bandages, I fought like a demon to prevent my wounds from healing."

"Your physician could give you nothing to control the pain?" she asked.

He had lowered their hands to the seat of the chair, their fingers still laced.

"I almost welcomed the physical pain," he told her. "I lashed myself with it. I thought perhaps if it was bad enough I could atone with it."

"Atone?" She felt a chill crawl along her spine.

"For causing death," he said, "and untold suffering. For surviving."

"But was it not your duty as an officer to lead your men into battle?" she asked him. "Were you not under orders yourself from superior officers? Do men not die in battle?"

He raised his eyes to hers. She expected them to be full of pain. Instead they were expressionless. Empty.

"I took three men to war with me," he said. "They did not want to go. They would not even have thought of going for themselves. And none of them was designated by his family for a military career. Quite the contrary. Their families fought their determination to go with me. But my power and influence over them was greater than that of family. I convinced them and they came. And died."

"Your three friends from school, do you mean?" she asked.

"Thomas Reynolds, son of Viscount Harding," he said.

"Maxwell Courtney, son of Sir Marvin Courtney, and Rowland Hickman, son of Baron Janes."

She remembered their names from a long-ago past, though Graham had not talked about them as often as he had of Ralph Stockwood.

"But the decision was theirs," she said.

He was still looking with chilling blankness into her eyes.

"It was," he agreed. "That is what I learned to accept during those three years. What degree of blame must we share for the decisions and actions of others? All of it? Some? None? It is an interesting question, and everyone concerned would no doubt answer it in a different way depending upon the perspective each brought to bear on it. In three years I learned to change my answer from *all* to *some*. I never progressed to *none*. But I stopped trying to kill myself. I stopped boring everyone silly by talking about it ceaselessly and alarming them by threatening it. I was healed and I went home."

She gazed at him, appalled.

"But did you stop wishing you were dead?" she asked and could have bitten out her tongue as soon as the words were out.

He half smiled, though it was perhaps more grimace than smile.

"Fate played a cruel joke on me," he said. "Instead of killing me and assigning me to hell, where I no doubt belonged, it saved me and gave me hell on earth instead. But all things can be endured, given time. One adjusts to the circumstances in which one finds oneself—one's own small revenge upon fate, perhaps. We all adjusted, the seven of us. We are all living our lives in a more or less productive manner. And I must apologize for speaking so depressingly and so self-pityingly. It will not happen again, I assure you."

"Do their families blame you?" she asked.

He released her hand and stood up abruptly.

"I do not doubt it," he said, extending a hand to help her to her feet. "You need not concern yourself."

But she could not leave it alone. Not yet.

"Have you *asked* them?" She slid her hand free of his when she was on her feet.

He startled her by leaning forward and setting his mouth to hers. Hard. She had no time to decide if it was a kiss—or if it was merely a way of silencing her. She stared mute and wide-eyed at him when he lifted his head again.

If it had been a kiss, it was her first. How utterly absurd! She was twenty-seven years old and she had been married for almost a week. But she did not believe it *had* been a kiss. It had silenced her, though.

He was frowning. Then he raised both hands, removed her cap, and dropped it to the chair behind her.

"Have you always worn a nightcap?" he asked her.

"No."

"Have you *ever* worn one before this past week?"

"No."

"Why now, then?"

She could not think of any reason to give except the truth. "I did not want you to think I was trying to . . . to entice you."

His eyes, which had been directed at her braid, were suddenly focused upon hers.

"You were hoping I would merely go away?" he asked her.

"Oh, not at all," she said. "I would have hated that. But I did not want you to think . . ." How could she complete the sentence?

"That you are beautiful?" he said. "And desirable? But I *had* thought both and still *do* think them. Is your hair a dreadful trial to you?"

Baron Cornell, her beau during her first Season, had once laughingly told her that with her hair she could pass any day for the most luscious and flamboyant of courtesans, and the highest paid to boot. He had apologized when he realized that he had deeply shocked her, but she had never forgotten. And then, last year . . .

"Yes."

It was the simplest answer she could think to give. Every woman wants to be thought beautiful, and she was no exception. But she did not want to be looked upon with . . . with lascivious hunger, as she had been looked upon too many times for comfort.

His hands were drawing out the pins that held the coils of her braid to her head. When it fell, like a heavy pendulum against her back, he reached behind her, removed the ribbon that bound the end, and unraveled the braid. He pushed his fingers through the hair and brought two locks of it over her shoulders.

"We made our bargain," he said. "We each know what to expect of the other and what *not* to expect. We did not speak of desire, however. I hope I do not offend you by desiring you and by admiring your beauty and the glory of your hair. And indeed, I hope you desire me, that the marriage bed is not in any way repugnant to you."

"It is not," she assured him.

... *the glory of your hair.*

He drew a breath and let it out audibly.

"Why are we up so late?" he asked her. "Tomorrow is going to be busy, and you will be exhausted. May I weary you a little longer, though?"

A smile flitted across his face like a shadow and was gone.

She ached within, longing for him. "Yes," she said.

II

Yes, she had said when he asked if he could weary her a little while longer. Yet when he set his mouth to hers, she did not kiss him back. And when he mounted her on the bed a few minutes later, she lay quiet beneath him, as she always did. The dutiful wife, upholding her end of their bargain. Wanting a child as much as he did, he supposed, if for different reasons. She *would* love any children they had. He did not doubt that—just as he did not doubt that she would keep her promise and never love him. Had she spoken merely to reassure him, then?

He lay beside her on the bed, as he usually did after sex. But, *not* as usual, he had slid his arm beneath her shoulders as he moved off her and had brought her with him, so that she was on her side against him, his arm about her. Her nightgown was still bunched about her waist. Her legs, smooth and slim, were against his. Her head was resting on his shoulder, her hair over his arm and down his chest. He could not see its color in the darkness, but he could feel its silkiness and smell the faint fragrance of the soap she used to wash it. He did not think she was sleeping. Her breathing was too quiet.

Was this more than she had bargained for? Was he being unfair to her? Was this more than *he* had bargained for? But was a man not entitled to the comforts of the marriage bed?

He needed her tonight—ghastly admission. He needed the comfort of her in his arms. He was reminded of the times during the past four years when need had driven him to engage the services of a courtesan. Was this no different from that? But on those occasions it had been just physical need that had driven him—oh, and perhaps a touch of loneliness too. His need tonight was not just for sex and not just for a female companion. It was specifically for his wife. And it was not just sexual, though it was that too. It was not just loneliness either. How could he be lonely, surrounded as he was by his family and friends? It was . . .

It was grief.

Grief for his grandfather, who had been gone for almost a week, but to whom he would say a final goodbye tomorrow amid all the public pomp of a ducal funeral. Grief for his grandmother, who had become even more birdlike in the past days, brave and gracious and lost. Grief for Rowland and Max and Tom, all of them eighteen years old when they died in a shower of blood and dust and guts. And grief for their families, who had resisted their going to war. Grief for himself and all the wrongs it was too late to put right. Grief for the loss of innocence and dangerous idealism.

It would be so easy to let himself slide all the way back to those early days at Penderris, grief turning to depression turning to self-pity turning to self-hatred turning to despair turning to ... He had thought himself over the worst of this.

"Turn onto your stomach."

"What?" he said.

Chloe's voice had brought him back from the edge of some abyss.

"Turn onto your stomach," she said again, moving away from him. "I'll rub your back."

He almost laughed. *I'll rub your back.* That was one cure the physician at Penderris had never thought of. But he rolled obediently over onto his front, pushed his arms beneath the pillow, and turned his head toward Chloe. She was kneeling up on the bed beside him, her hair loose and tousled.

His own wakefulness had kept her awake too. He ought not to have held her. Her days this past week had been every bit as busy as his. Tomorrow would be both busy and stressful for her. She was going to have to meet some of the very highest sticklers of the *ton*, and she must be anticipating it with dread.

She rubbed his back lightly with one hand at first and then scratched it. Her touch felt exquisite. Then she leaned farther over him and worked both hands over his back, pressing and rubbing and kneading until he could feel knots loosening and muscles relaxing all the way down to his toes.

"Where did you learn to do this?" he asked her.

"I did not," she admitted. "But I can feel where you are tense. I am trying not to press on any of your old wounds. I hope I am not hurting you."

"I did not know," he said, "that a pair of magic hands

was being brought into our marriage along with the rest of you. I think I may have got the better half of our bargain."

"Not so," she said. "You brought a few titles and enormous wealth with the rest of *you*."

He heard himself laugh softly with genuine amusement and felt the strangeness of it. The heels of her hands moved hard over his shoulder blades and for a moment he moved with them. Then her touch softened and he relaxed even more deeply. He did not believe he had ever in his life felt so contented.

He closed his eyes and drifted off to sleep.

When he awoke, it was dawn. He was still lying on his stomach, his arms crossed beneath his pillow, and he was still warm and relaxed and comfortable. He lifted his head. It was almost half past six according to the clock on the mantel.

Chloe was on her side facing him, asleep. She looked very different from usual, without her cap, her hair in a riot all about her head and face and upper body. And now, in the early light of day, he was fully aware of its color. He felt an instant and quite intense desire for her and despised himself for it. It was not the necessary desire of a husband wishing to impregnate his wife. It was the raw desire of a man for a beautiful woman. It was without the respect he had promised her and given for the first week of their marriage.

He wanted her with a ravenous hunger—on the morning of his grandfather's funeral.

She opened her eyes. After a moment they focused upon him and she smiled.

"You slept," she said.

"I did."

He took her each morning before rising. It was necessary to do so, after all. He could see from the expression on her face that she expected it this morning too, that perhaps she would even welcome it. He set a hand on her shoulder, as he usually did, to turn her onto her back. But before she could move, his fingers tightened and then released her.

"It is going to be a busy day," he said curtly. "Have another hour of sleep. I am going out for a ride."

And he turned away from her and his own desire for her, swung his legs over the side of the bed, sat up, and reached down for his dressing gown.

He did not look back as he left her bedchamber.

The comforting thing about difficult days, Chloe had learned from experience, was that the sun rose at the start of them and set at the end just as it did on any other day. And there was always the assurance of better days ahead.

She faced the day of the late Duke of Worthingham's funeral with a determined courage. For it was not about herself. She was not to be a central player even though she was the wife of the new duke and must welcome an unknown number of members of the *ton* into her home during the course of the day. It would not be an ordeal impossible to face. She had greeted Ralph's mother and sisters and other members of his family during the last two days, after all, and in many ways that had been worse. She would get through today, and then everyone would go away again and she would be able to relax at last. She would begin her new life in earnest here at Manville Court.

A large number of outsiders did indeed attend the funeral in the village church during the morning and then followed the somber cortege on its slow procession to the family burial plot beside the chapel where Ralph and Chloe had married just the week before. Everyone then proceeded to the house to partake of refreshments and to express their sympathies.

Chloe did not have to face any of them directly until that last phase of the proceedings. She was introduced then to virtually everyone, including people with whom she had a previous acquaintance. Most nodded graciously but distantly to her. The occasion made that quite acceptable. Some regarded her with frosty, haughty stares and were only as civil as good manners dictated. But at least they *were* good mannered. A few—a small few—were amiable and even engaged her in conversation and congratulated her on her marriage. No one gave her the cut direct.

And there were, of course, those who had come purely for Chloe's sake—her father and brother and sister, and also Lord Easterly with Aunt Julia, Papa's sister. Her aunt and uncle hugged Chloe and congratulated her on her marriage and smiled at her with genuine warmth.

Sarah Toucher, Ralph's middle sister, and her husband arrived at the church only just in time for the service and had no opportunity to talk to anyone before it was over. Sarah made a point of seeking out Chloe at the graveside after the burial, though, and hugged her briefly.

"Amelia and Nora both wrote long letters to tell me all about you," she said. "I am *so* pleased Ralph had the good sense to marry you. I was very much afraid he would choose some insipid miss straight from the schoolroom, someone of whom my sisters would have approved with unqualified delight. If no one has yet told you, I am the rebel of the family and proved it when I rejected the very flattering offer of an earl three times my age during my first Season and married Andy instead. He was as rich as Croesus and I loved him to distraction, but to my family those details did not make up for the fact that he was a mere mister and that his maternal grandfather, the one from whom most of the money came, had been in trade." With that she hugged Chloe briefly again and then turned to leave. "Now, I must go to poor Grandmama. She will be feeling more than desolate today. She and Grandpapa adored each other, you know. Oh, you probably *do* know. You were living here, were you not, when Ralph met you?"

And she was gone in a whirl of black crepe and dark facial veil. But it was touches like her unexpectedly friendly greeting that sustained Chloe through the day. She did not dwell upon her own discomfort at being surrounded once more by members of the *ton*, however. Much of her attention was focused upon the dowager duchess, who bore herself with stoic dignity throughout the long day, but who must be inwardly reeling from grief and exhaustion. And most of the rest of her attention was upon Ralph, who wore his new ducal mantle with dignity and looked like a marble statue.

She tried not to remember the early morning. What was it that had sent him away from her bed so abruptly? His abandonment had felt like a slap across the face. Yet his words had suggested kindness. *It is going to be a busy day. Have another hour of sleep.*

There had been a fleeting expression on his face before he turned away and got up from the bed, but she had not been able to explain to herself what it had been. Disgust? But it had not been that definite. Revulsion? No, that was basically the same thing as disgust. Disapproval? But he was the one who had unpinned her hair last night and made her look like a wanton.

There had been *something* in that expression, something to explain why he had avoided the usual morning intimacy. He had said last night that he desired her, but this morning he had turned away even from what he normally considered his duty.

Her hair?

She did not have any time during the day to dwell upon the disturbing shifts in their relationship that had happened through the night, but the puzzle of it was there in the back of her mind all day, like a dull, heavy ache. Something *had* shifted. She knew him better, yes, understood him more fully after listening to at least part of his story last night. She had heard enough to understand that the three years he had spent in Cornwall had not really healed him at all. His physical hurts had been dealt with and perhaps the worst of his suicidal tendencies. But the blackness weighing upon his soul was still there and perhaps always would be.

For a while last night, with the telling and what had followed, they had seemed to grow closer. He had held her after they made love, and when she had felt his inability to relax and sleep, he had allowed her to rub his back and work upon his knotted muscles with untrained, instinctive hands and fingers to the extent that she had soothed herself as well as him. She had put him to sleep and had lain gazing at him for a while afterward before her own eyelids drooped and she slept too. It had felt as though they had crossed a barrier and drawn closer to being . . . married.

But she was no doctor for the soul, she realized today. Something had definitely changed and then changed again, but the changes were not necessarily for the better. Perhaps he resented her for forcing him to talk and remember. Perhaps he regretted allowing himself to relax and lower his guard under her ministrations. He had even laughed with her. But early this morning he had looked at her with her hair down and had seen someone different from the quiet, unemotional, undemanding wife he had bargained upon getting.

But it was not she who had let down her hair. It was not she who had been tense and unable to sleep.

The day drew to its inevitable end after all the outside guests had taken their leave. The worst of the ordeal was over. The houseguests drifted off to bed until Chloe felt herself able to withdraw too. She went up with Lady Ponsonby and Lady Trentham again, both of whom she liked. Ralph stayed downstairs with his fellow Survivors. It felt just like last night, except that the funeral was over and a certain emptiness had settled over the company during the evening.

She was not going to wait up tonight, she decided. She was so weary she hardly knew what to do with herself. And she did not want to see what look Ralph would have in his eyes when he came to her room—*if* he came and *if* there was any expression there at all. But she found herself lingering at her dressing table and gazing into the mirror, trying to decide whether to don her cap or not, whether to coil her braid about her head or leave it hanging down her back, whether to braid her hair at all. It was such a foolish indecision. Was she trying to decide which choice would better please her husband? What she ought to be asking herself instead was what *she* wanted to do. But she was too weary to think.

No, she *did* know what she wanted. She wanted hair as dark as Lucy's and her mother's and Graham's and her fath—

Which father?

She hated more than anything else these moments when such doubts got past her guard. Papa was her father.

Papa was her father.

Oh, her hair was to blame for *everything*.

And finally she decided.

She had nothing very large in the room with her. The best she could come up with was her sewing scissors, whose blades were not very long. But they were long enough. And they were sharp enough. She had sharpened them herself just before coming to Manville Court.

She cut off her hair to the bottom of her ears. She considered cutting it even shorter, hacking it off all over her head, but by that time her breathing was ragged with panic, and her hands were shaking and tingling with pins and needles. She turned on the stool and looked at the hair scattered along its length and heaped on the floor all about her. There was far more of it than she had expected. She felt suddenly sick to her stomach. She dared not lift her hands to feel the remaining hair. But she did not need hands. She could *feel* its absence. There was a lightness about her head, and the air felt cool on the back of her neck.

She was sitting facing out to the room, surrounded by hair, her scissors still dangling from the fingers of one hand, when a light tap on the door heralded the appearance of Ralph.

Good God!

Ralph came to an abrupt stop inside the door, looked at Chloe, looked at her scattered hair, and shut the door softly behind his back.

"Chloe?" he said.

She burst into noisy, gulping tears.

"I am not sorry," she gasped out. "I hated it. I *hated* it. I am not sorry."

All that glorious hair.

Gone.

He could do nothing but stare blankly for a few moments and gaze upon his wife's distress with incomprehension.

He had almost not come tonight—because he had been thinking of this moment all day. Despite all that had been going on, despite his genuine grief over seeing his grandfather finally carried out of the house, making the end of an era final, and despite the necessity of holding together his dignity in the face of all those who had come to pay their respects to one dead duke and to look with critical curiosity upon the successor, despite his concern for his grandmother and, to a lesser degree, for his sisters, despite his realization that this was a difficult day for his wife—despite everything, he had wanted only for the night to fall so that he could come to her again, bed her again, be with her again.

And his very longing for the night, for her body, for

her, had almost kept him away. For frankly he was a bit bewildered and more than a bit alarmed by his eagerness. He had to tell himself sternly that it was all because of the turmoil the death of his grandfather had caused in the past week, that soon now they would be able to settle into the routine of the marriage they had both bargained for.

More than anything else he wanted himself back to himself. He would share himself in marriage for all the essentials—the creation of children, the joint running of a home, though that would not be difficult since presumably she would run the house and he would run the estate. He did not want to share anything else of himself. Or of her. Such was not part of their bargain.

They must share a social life, of course.

He hated this confusion of mind, and the sooner he shook it off, the better he would like it. He had convinced himself finally that he was coming tonight because he had missed bedding her this morning and hoped very much to have her pregnant before her next courses were due. And, no, he had not asked her when that was.

And now this.

He had walked in on a crisis of monumental proportions. He understood that after those first few seconds. This was no simple matter with a simple explanation. And this was not the sensible, disciplined, dispassionate wife he had married.

What the devil? he thought. But even in those first moments he knew that thundering at her would achieve nothing. Neither would standing here and murmuring her name. It occurred to him briefly that he was in no way equipped to deal with female hysterics, but the thing was that she was not just any female. She was his wife.

She was Chloe.

Her hands had gone up to cover her face. She was still wailing. Her hair stuck out on either side of her head, coming to an abrupt end just above the tips of her earlobes. She was surrounded by a sea of red. A small pair of scissors had just clattered to the floor.

"Come, come, this will not do," he said, striding toward her, grasping her by both elbows, and lifting her onto her feet and clear of the hair before he wrapped one arm about her waist and held her face to his shoulder with the other hand spread over the back of her head. He crooned something unintelligible even to himself against her ear and rocked her, rather as if she were a child who had fallen and scraped her knee.

"I . . . hated . . . it," she said once more, gulping and gasping between words.

Presumably she was talking about her hair.

"Then you did the sensible thing," he told her. Though she might have waited until an accredited hairdresser could do the job for her.

"I l-look a f-fright," she gasped.

She probably did. He had not had a chance to properly assess the damages.

"Probably," he agreed.

The hysteria stopped, rather as if he had tipped a bucket of icy water over her. She drew back her head and looked up at him with her wet, reddened face, her shorn hair standing out to the sides, the right side slightly shorter than the left.

"Oh," she said, "there is no *probably* about it."

"No," he agreed. "I can see that."

Her teeth sank into her lower lip.

"I cannot stick it back on," she said.

"No," he agreed again, "you cannot. And I will not even add a *probably* this time."

And what now? He could hardly just take her to bed and extinguish the candles and proceed to business.

"We will go to my bedchamber," he said. "Come."

And he set an arm about her shoulders and led her there. Fortunately, they did not meet anyone on the way. He pulled on the bell rope in his room and went to the doorway of his dressing room when he heard his valet enter.

"Have someone sent up to clean Her Grace's room, Burroughs," he said. "She has been cutting her hair. And refrain from entering my bedchamber in the morning. I will summon you when I am ready to dress and be shaved."

"Yes, Your Grace." The valet disappeared.

"It is dreadfully late," Chloe said. "The cleanup could have waited until the morning."

He raised his eyebrows. "No," he said. "It could not."

She had given herself surely the worst haircut in the history of haircuts. She looked younger. She looked vulnerable.

She stood at the foot of the wide steps leading up to his canopied bed, dwarfed by the grandeur of it. It had always rather amused him to be given this room, originally designed for the duke with an equally ostentatious room for the duchess—it was now Chloe's room—on the far side of the dressing room. His grandfather had re-

fused to move into the apartments when he had succeeded to the title after his father's passing. They had
been kept for the convenience, or inconvenience, of the
heir when he visited.

What had happened in Chloe's room had been a ca-
lamity of monumental proportions, he had thought when
he walked in upon her. It was tempting now to ignore it,
to forget it with the sweeping up of her hair, to deal with
the mess of the haircut itself tomorrow, to go to bed now
and make love to her before falling asleep. He was weary
to the bone, God knew, and so must she be.

But . . . Well, *I hated it* was not really good enough as
a reason for doing such a thing, was it? But did he really
want to know more? To probe deeper?

There was no fire burning in the grate. It was not a
cold night, but there was a bit of a chill in the air. He
looked at the two leather armchairs that flanked the fireplace. He had never used either. There was a folded plaid
wool blanket over the back of one of them. He had never
used that either. Indeed, he did not recall ever having
noticed it before now.

"Come," he said, striding toward that particular chair
and shaking out the blanket.

When she came he wrapped it about her and looked
into her eyes. It had been his intention to seat her on the
chair, wrapped warmly, while he took the one opposite.
But she looked like a little bundle of misery in the blanket. He quelled a twinge of irritation and sat on the chair
himself before drawing her down onto his lap, guiding
her head to one shoulder and setting both arms about
her. She did not resist.

"It must have been called your crowning glory more

times than you could count," he said. "Why did you hate it?"

"The color stood out like a sore thumb," she said. "I heard my mother say just that to our housekeeper one day. She—my mother—used to dampen it down to darken the shade, and she used to braid it so tightly that my head hurt and my eyes slanted. She used to dress Lucy's hair in soft curls and ringlets."

He thought she was finished, but she drew breath, hesitated, shook her head, and continued.

"As a girl I looked like a freak," she said. "My second teeth grew in before my face grew to fit them, and my freckles were as big as pennies and covered my nose and my cheeks. A few of the other children in the neighborhood used to call me carrot top. When I was thirteen and painfully in love with the physician's boy, who was sixteen and wondrously handsome, he dashed my regard for him by telling me I looked like the rabbit and the carrot all in one package. But this talk is abject foolishness, and I would not indulge in it if the hour was not late and I was not tired and you had not asked."

Her mother must have been both horrified and embarrassed when her first child was born within nine months of her marriage with such undeniably red hair.

"Plain or even ugly children often grow into beautiful adults," he said. "It certainly seems to have been true of you."

"If it is true," she said, sounding cross rather than reassured, "then it is the wrong sort of beauty. When I went to London for my come-out Season, I had to stop looking at men. So many of them were looking back at me with—"

"Admiration?" he suggested. Had it been such an un-welcome surprise? Surely she had left behind her like-ness to a rabbit years before then?

"With *lust*," she said. "Though I hardly knew the meaning of the word then. There was no respect in those looks. It was not the admiring, even worshipful way they looked at the delicate, accredited beauties. One older lady, who had a great deal of influence in the *ton*, once told me there was a certain vulgarity about hair of so decided a red. As though I had chosen the shade. As though my hair defined my character."

A more confident young beauty would simply have smiled at such spite, knowing that she could take the *ton* by storm with such startling good looks if she chose—as Lady Angela Allandale had done last year.

"Lust is often a form of admiration," he told her. "Coupled with good manners it could be seen as flatter-ing."

"Not when one is told that one could be the most ex-pensive, sought-after courtesan in London if one wished to be," she said.

"If someone actually said that to you," he said, "I hope you slapped him very hard across the face."

"He apologized," she said, "when he saw that he had distressed me."

He felt a sudden suspicion.

"Was this the man who was paying court to you be-fore your sister ran off with Nelson?" he asked her.

"It does not matter." She sighed, her breath warm against his neck. "I had a fortunate escape from him. Sometimes it takes time and a bit of maturity to realize that."

She still had not named the man. Perhaps it was just as well. He realized he'd reached a point where he would want to do a great deal more than just slap the man's face.

"And then there was last year," she said. "If only I had been born with my mother's dark hair, none of that would have happened. No one would have thought of spreading such vicious gossip. And that was all it was— gossip. I am so sorry. I hate habitual complainers. They are a dead bore."

Yes. He should be bored. But in listing her complaints about her hair, she had told him a great deal about herself. He had not wanted to know. He still did not. It would be altogether more comfortable living through the marriage to which they had agreed if he knew her only by her day-to-day behavior. But he was beginning to realize that it had been naïve of him to expect such a shallow relationship.

Something occurred to him.

"Why tonight?" he asked her. "If you have hated your hair all your life, why was tonight the crisis point? Did something happen today? Did someone say something?"

"No." She sighed and did not continue. She was not relaxed, though. He could feel tension in her body, warm though it had become inside the blanket. He waited. "It was because of this morning."

"This morning?" He frowned.

"Last night you unbraided my hair," she said against his neck. "You spoke of the glory of it and of your desire for me. This morning you looked at me with distaste and left to go riding. And I knew that something in our marriage had been spoiled and that my hair was to blame.

Always my hair. Tonight I thought you probably would not come at all."

Good God!

He set his head against the high back of the chair and closed his eyes. He had not bargained for *this*. Why the devil had he taken off her nightcap last night? It had been a bit like opening Pandora's box.

How was he to explain to her?

"Chloe," he said, "I cannot love you. I cannot love."

"I have not asked it of you," she said. "I *do* not ask it. Did you think last night and this morning that I was—"

"No," he said, cutting her off. "I know—I knew that you were not trying to *lure* me, to use your own word from last night. Also, last night we agreed that desire is not a bad thing in a marriage such as ours, but I would not take advantage of your acquiescence. This morning I was afraid of taking advantage."

"So you went away out of *respect*?" she asked him, sitting up on his lap and frowning at him.

"It was most certainly not out of revulsion," he said. "Or out of any feeling that you were behaving like a . . . courtesan. The very idea is absurd, Chloe. *You?* So why the deuce did you cut your hair?"

She was still frowning. And then she was not. Her eyes smiled first, and then her mouth curved upward at the corners. Her hair, just as red as ever, stood around her face like a blunt-edged, flat-topped halo.

He heard himself laughing then and stopped abruptly. But she was laughing too.

"Does it look quite appalling?" she asked him.

"The truth?" Good God, had he actually laughed? Again?

"Does it?"

"It does," he said.

And she laughed once more and then bit her lower lip.

"I shall have to hide away until it grows back," she said.

"Or have it cut by someone who knows what she or he is doing," he suggested.

"Even shorter?"

"Well, it cannot be cut longer, can it?" he said. "I'll tell you something, though, Chloe. You are still beautiful. And I still desire you—with respect for our bargain."

Her laughter stopped, but she continued to gaze at him.

No, he could not love her. Not in *that* way. But perhaps he could come to love her as he loved his mother and sisters and grandmother. She was family, after all. She was his wife. She would be—he hoped—the mother of his children. He could love her in those capacities.

Perhaps there could be more for them than just what they had agreed upon. Perhaps there could be . . . friendship, affection.

Except that he did not want even that much, did he?

Perhaps he would have been better off after all choosing someone from the ballrooms of London. He was afraid that with Chloe he might come alive, and there was too much pain awaiting him if he was not very careful.

Without ever meaning to, he kissed her. And prolonged the kiss, drawing her down against him again, cupping her jaw with his free hand. He parted his lips, licked at hers, pressed a little way through to the warm flesh within. And, alarmingly, he felt as though he might weep.

He drew back his head and gazed into her face.

"You must be almost collapsing with exhaustion," he said.

"And you."

"We had better get to bed."

"Yes."

But something had changed between them. It had started last night and continued tonight. He was too tired to ponder what exactly it was, and what it would mean for him. For her. For them.

He was just too damned tired.

12

"It is high time you had a maid of your own, Chloe,"
Ralph said. "I know you have never had one and
say you would not know what to do with one if you did.
But you *do* need one, and this is a case in point. Besides,
you are the Duchess of Worthingham now, and the servants will soon be muttering with disapproval if you do
not behave like one. It is never wise to get on the wrong
side of one's servants."

He was fully dressed and looked elegant and rather
formidable in black. He also looked irritated. He was
standing at the foot of the steps leading up to his bed, his
feet slightly apart, his hands clasped at his back. In
Chloe's estimation he looked every inch the aristocrat he
was, and she marveled anew at how he could be two different men—the duke she saw now and the man who
had held her on his lap last night and then taken her to
bed and made love to her despite their exhaustion.

Secretly, that was what she called it now, since *having
marital relations* sounded far too stilted, even in her own
mind. Though *making love* was not at all accurate, of
course.

He had even kissed her last night while they were still seated on the chair. Really kissed her this time. Her first real kiss. Why had it seemed just as intimate as what had happened in his bed later, perhaps even more so? There were different types of intimacy, she supposed.

Chloe was not fully clothed. She was sitting bolt upright in the middle of the bed, covered to the waist with the blankets, wondering if there was anyone in the house from whom she could borrow a cap, since the only one she possessed was a nightcap and hardly suitable to wear down to breakfast or anywhere else beyond the confines of the bedchamber. She did not want to bother the dowager duchess with such a request.

"Am I to make your excuses to my grandmother and our guests?" Ralph asked her. "Tell everyone that you have the migraines and are likely to be incapacitated for the next . . . How long will it take for your hair to grow back?"

She glared at him with something bordering upon dislike. "I am not going to grow it back," she told him.

"Ah." He sawed the air with one hand. "Forever, then. I shall inform everyone that becoming a duchess has turned you into an eccentric recluse and that you intend to spend the rest of your natural life secluded in your own apartments, or rather"—he looked pointedly around—"mine."

She threw a pillow at him, and he caught it in one hand and set it on the bottom step.

"Chloe," he said, "I am not the one who cut your hair."

"Do you think you could have done a better job?" she asked him.

Surprisingly—very surprisingly—his lips twitched, though he did not actually smile. Or tell her that he could hardly have done worse.

She threw another pillow at him anyway.

"Let me go and fetch Bunker," he suggested. "She has been with Grandmama for at least a century and will undoubtedly be able to suggest something to help you avoid the fate of having to spend the rest of your life in my bed. Though, put that way, the prospect does have a certain appeal."

Had he *made a joke*? At such a time?

"Very well, then," she said. It would be horribly humiliating, though. Miss Bunker was a very superior person and sometimes made Chloe quail with a sense of inferiority. Chloe did not doubt that her hair looked even worse this morning after she had slept on it. But it suddenly occurred to her that *all* the servants must know already. Someone had been sent to her room last night to clean up the mess. That someone would certainly not have kept her mouth shut.

Even as she thought it there was a light knock on the door. Ralph strode over to it and opened it halfway while Chloe raised the bedcovers to her chin—though much good they did stopping there.

"Chloe is not in her room or anywhere downstairs, Ralph." It was Sarah, Mrs. Toucher's, voice. "Is she in here, by any chance?"

"Of course she is in here," he said. "She is my *wife*."

"Yes, we all know that," Sarah said. "You married her without any fuss or bluster, which, in my wayward opinion, was very sensible of you. Large weddings are an abomination. Is she . . . *all right*?"

"And why would she not be?" he asked. "I am not a monster. I have not been beating her."

"He is being deliberately obtuse, Sarah." Oh, goodness, Great-Aunt Mary was out there too. "Did she cut it off herself, Ralph? Made a mess of it, did she, and is ashamed to show her face—or, rather, her head? Oh, let us in, boy. That pirate's face of yours does not make *me* quake in my slippers."

"How did you know?" he asked, holding his ground while Chloe prepared to dive beneath the bedcovers.

"How did we *know*?" his great-aunt asked rhetorically. "I daresay the whole *world* knows. Who sent for a servant at close to midnight to sweep up the hair? If it was you, my boy, and you wished to keep the matter a secret, then you made a great tactical blunder. It is a good thing you were never promoted to general."

"Besides, Ralph," another voice said—the *dowager duchess's*—"it cannot be kept secret for long, can it? *Is* dear Chloe all right?"

Chloe flung back the covers, got out of bed, and stalked down the steps and over to the door, which she pulled from Ralph's hand and flung wide.

"I look a fright," she said.

And, oh dear, there were *six* of them outside the door. Lady Trentham and Lady Ponsonby were there too. So was a wide-eyed Lucy. And Great-Aunt Mary already had her lorgnette to her eyes.

"I cannot in all good conscience contradict you on that, girl," she said.

"Chlow, how *could* you!" Lucy cried. "All my life I would have given *anything* to have your hair instead of my own."

"Come, Chloe," the dowager said kindly, "we will take you to your own room and ring for Bunker. She will help you dress and make you feel a great deal better than you are feeling now. And we will discuss what is to be done about your hair. Seven of us plus Bunker will surely be able to solve one little problem."

Little.

"Run along, Ralph," Great-Aunt Mary said, waving her lorgnette dismissively in his direction. "You are not needed. Men rarely are when there are important matters under consideration."

And he ran along, or at least he did not argue or try to follow as Chloe was borne off on a tide of ladies.

At least they did not ask her why she had done it. They kept their minds upon finding a practical solution to the world's worst haircut. Miss Bunker was not much help except as a calming influence. She looked upon Chloe as though there were nothing different or unusual about her as she helped her into one of her black dresses and brushed what little hair she had left. She made no suggestions about repairing the damage, but that was hardly surprising since everyone else was making them instead.

Lady Trentham ended the discussion by offering up her own maid.

"I have a very good hairdresser in London," she explained, "but it would take several days to summon him here. When I am not in town, my maid trims my hair and really does just as good a job of it as Mr. Welland though she does not have his prestige. Will you trust your hair to her, Duchess?"

"Oh, call me Chloe, please," Chloe said. "I keep looking at Grandmama when I am addressed as *duchess*."

"Then you must call me Gwen," Lady Trentham said. "I will summon my maid, shall I?"

Gwen had short blond hair, very prettily curled. Chloe nodded.

"Please," she said.

"You are fortunate enough to have thick hair, Chloe," Viscountess Ponsonby observed. "And it has a natural wave. I believe it will look very becoming when it has been properly styled. And please call me Agnes."

"But it was so beautiful as it was, Chlow," Lucy said mournfully. "I can remember how all the gentlemen used to follow you with their eyes the few times I walked with you in Hyde Park during that Season when I was seventeen and Mama would not let me make my come-out with you. I was mortally jealous. Until I met Freddie, that is."

She said no more. Great-Aunt Mary had swung her lorgnette her way.

Gwen, Sarah, and Agnes remained with Chloe while the repairs were being made. Miss Bunker had left earlier, and the older ladies went down for their breakfast, taking Lucy with them. She actually looked rather gratified when Great-Aunt Mary took her arm and informed her that since she was young and strong she might as well make herself useful.

Gwen's maid looked critically at Chloe's hair and ran her fingers through it after she had been told that she had carte blanche to do with it what she thought best, provided it ended up looking better than it did now. Not that *that* would be a difficult task. Then she set to work with her scissors while the other ladies watched.

"Lady Darleigh has red hair too," Agnes said, "though

not as red as yours, Chloe. Hers is more auburn. She cut it off too, long ago when she was a girl. She has grown it back since she married Lord Darleigh last year. She was a thin, shorn little waif when I first met her shortly after their wedding. She is pretty and dainty now. They are very happy, I believe. No—I *know*."

"She has a new baby?" Chloe said.

"Thomas," Gwen said. "The first Survivor baby. I think mine will be the second." Her cheeks turned suddenly rosy as both Chloe and Sarah looked involuntarily in the direction of her stomach and Agnes smiled at her.

"How lovely for you!" Sarah said.

"Hugo did not want me to come here with him," Gwen said. "I have only just stopped feeling horribly bilious in the mornings. But I hate being apart from him, even for a few days, and I know he hates being away from me. I lost a child to a miscarriage once, a long time ago, during my first marriage. I am . . . ecstatic to be given another chance. And terrified. But not as frightened as Hugo is, poor thing."

"I am very happy for you, Gwen." Chloe smiled at her. "You do not resent them? The Survivors?"

"Resent them?" Gwen tipped her head to one side and looked rather curiously at her. "I met them all at once. I had trespassed unknowingly upon Penderris property. I was walking on the beach below the house and tried to climb to the top over a steep fall of loose stones. I slipped and sprained my bad ankle and Hugo found me and carried me up to the house. Meeting them all was a bit daunting, I must confess, especially as local gossip would have it that the Duke of Stanbrook had pushed his wife over a cliff, when in reality she jumped to her death. But they were all very kind to me and very courteous. I had to stay there for a few days until my brother came to fetch me. No, I do not resent them."

"They share an extraordinary bond with one another," Agnes added. "But they live their own separate lives too. And love is not a finite thing. They love one another, but they have plenty of love left over for their wives and families—or for a husband in Imogen's case, if she ever remarries. Did you know that one of the Survivors is a woman?"

Chloe nodded and then remembered that she must keep her head still.

"My mother and sisters," Sarah said, "have always been of the opinion that the three years Ralph spent in Cornwall did him more harm than good."

"The Duke of Worthingham," Gwen said, "was very badly hurt physically, but his wounds went far deeper than the worst of the saber cuts. And sometimes, Hugo has told me, the invisible wounds of war are far more deadly than the visible ones. Indeed, Hugo was not physically wounded at all. There is not a scratch upon his person. Yet he was brought home from the Peninsula in a straitjacket and spent three years in Cornwall with the others. He still suffers occasionally."

"I remember Ralph as he used to be," Sarah said with a sigh. "Perhaps he will be himself again now that he has married you, Chloe. Though that is an absurd thing to say. He will never be the same. None of us can be the same as we once were. Our lives and our very selves constantly change. But perhaps he will be happy again. Oh, *yes*!"

That final exclamation was for Chloe's hair. Gwen's maid had finished cutting and crimping it and had stood back so that everyone could view the finished effect. She handed Chloe a round mirror with a handle so that she could see too.

"Brilliant!" Sarah exclaimed, and she came hurrying across the room to hug her sister-in-law. "It looks *lovely*. It looks ... dashing. *You* look lovely and dashing. Oh, you will be all the rage, Chloe. Wait and see."

Chloe looked critically at her image. Her hair had been cut in short layers. It hugged her head in shiny, bouncy waves and made her face look heart shaped and her eyes look bigger. She scarcely recognized herself.

"It is very often assumed," Gwen said, "that all women look best with long hair. It is not so. I had mine cut many years ago and have never regretted it. You look more striking with short hair, Chloe. I would not have believed it, however, if I had not seen you both ways. And now you will surely have the courage to venture beyond your own room."

Chloe laughed and turned to thank the maid and commend her on her skill. She found her purse and pressed a generous vail into her hand.

"It is breakfast time," Sarah said. "Indeed, it is well past time, and I am ravenous even if no one else is."

"You do look pretty, Chloe," Agnes assured her, and she linked her arm through Chloe's as they all left the room.

"A minor crisis," Ralph explained to his mother and two of his sisters at breakfast. "Chloe decided to cut her hair last night and did not like the results. The matter has been taken to committee and will be resolved to everyone's satisfaction, I have no doubt."

He found himself having to repress a grin. It was not amusing for poor Chloe, especially when one considered *why* she had done it. But the memory of the rather large female delegation outside his bedchamber door and of Chloe inside it, her chopped hair standing out from the sides of her face and the back of her head, the cross look on her face turned to one of dismay, was worthy of any farce. He could not remember a time when he had been better entertained.

It was doubtless an inappropriate response.

And he had been happy enough to make his escape.

"Chloe has never liked her hair," Sir Kevin Muirhead said. "She has always been annoyed with the ancestor of mine who passed the bright color on to her. And the more it has been admired, the more she has hated it."

"Red hair does suggest a certain . . . flamboyance of character," Ralph's eldest sister, Amelia, observed.

"Then one can understand why the duchess is uncomfortable with it," Flavian said. "She is reserved and dignified and quite the opposite of f-flamboyant."

"She does you proud, Ralph," Hugo agreed. "Since you have persuaded us to stay another day, Vince and I are going to explore the park this morning, if we may. His dog will make sure we do not get lost in all the vastness. Is there any particular feature we ought to see?"

"I could hear what sounded like a waterfall yesterday when we were out at the chapel," Vincent said. "We will find that, Hugo."

"There is a lake, is there not?" George asked. "Lady Keilly, Lady Harrison, you must be familiar with the park. Would you care to show me the way while Hugo

and Vincent strike out on what sounds like a more strenuous search for the waterfall?"

Ralph looked with gratitude from one to the other of
his friends, who had deflected the conversation away
from Chloe and her red hair. He wished there was more
time to spend with them than just today and was tempted
to ignore his other responsibilities and lead the way to
the falls himself. But they were not the only ones who
would be gone tomorrow.

The gentlemen rose to their feet as his grandmother,
his great-aunt, and Mrs. Nelson came into the dining
room.

"Lady Trentham's maid is at work upon Chloe's hair,"
Great-Aunt Mary reported. "Lady Trentham swears that
she is competent with the scissors. The consolation is
that the girl certainly cannot make Chloe look worse
than she looked when we knocked upon your bedchamber door, Ralph. Someone fetch me coffee before I expire."

Ralph saw that his grandmother was looking wan but
composed this morning. He wondered if the worst was
behind her or ahead of her. He strongly suspected the
latter and hoped for the former.

"Sir," Ralph said, addressing Sir Kevin Muirhead,
"may I offer you another cup of coffee in the study?"

They discussed the marriage settlement, even though
the marriage had already been solemnized. Ralph wanted
to assure his father-in-law, and to commit it to writing,
that Chloe and any children of their marriage would be
well cared for while he lived and properly provided for
after his death.

"You have been more than generous, considering the fact that I am able to offer only a modest dowry," Sir Kevin said when all had been settled. "I have been worried about Chloe for the past several years. I was even more worried when I learned of her hasty marriage, but you have set my mind at ease. At least, I believe you have. Why did you marry her, Worthingham?"

The question took Ralph by surprise.

"I am the last of my line, sir," he explained. "One would have to climb quite high into the family tree to find a branch upon which there is another male heir. It was my duty to marry and set up my nursery, and my grandfather's deteriorating health imposed some urgency upon me even though I am only twenty-six. I met your daughter here a couple of weeks ago and . . ." No, he could not bring himself to say he had fallen violently in love with her. It would be a patent lie. "I considered her an eligible wife. She is a little older and more mature than any of the young ladies I had met in London. She is beautiful—not that looks were a primary concern with me. She is a lady of birth and breeding. I asked and she accepted."

"It all happened very quickly," her father said. "Did she tell you anything of her . . . past?"

Ralph leaned forward slightly over his desk. "All but the name of the bounder who jilted her so cruelly after your younger daughter eloped with Nelson," he said, "and who told her she could easily pass for a courtesan. Who was he, sir? Who *is* he?"

"Lord Cornell?" Sir Kevin raised his eyebrows. "I would have refused my permission anyway if he had asked to marry Chloe. I had already suggested to my

wife that she discourage the connection. He was a noto-
rious womanizer. I doubt he would have asked, however.
Marriage is too burdensome a leg shackle for gentlemen
such as he."

Ralph had a slight acquaintance with Baron Cornell.
A fine physical specimen of manhood, he was said to
delight in breaking female hearts and then boasting of
his conquests. Poor innocent twenty-one-year-old Chloe
had believed him to be a serious suitor for her hand.

"And she told me what happened last year." Ralph
watched the older man closely.

"Ah. That was all most unfortunate," Sir Kevin said
with affected unconcern. "She bore a certain resemblance to a nobly born young lady, I understand, and
tongues wagged as tongues will. It is a pity Chloe took
fright and ran home, though. Her actions merely fanned
the flames of baseless gossip. But she has always been
oversensitive to the opinions of others."

"Sir." Ralph fingered the edges of the desk blotter. "I
wish you will tell me whether there is any truth in those
rumors. Is there any possibility, or even a certainty, that
Chloe is the natural daughter of the Marquess of Hitching? I assure you your answer will go no farther than this
room unless you yourself choose to repeat it. I would
appreciate knowing the truth. It will make no difference
to my relationship with the duchess, but I would know
my heirs' forebears."

"Of course there is no truth in them." His father-in-
law sat abruptly back in his chair on the other side of the
desk and glared at Ralph for a long moment before his
shoulders slumped and he looked downward. There was
a rather lengthy silence. "I loved her mother from the

moment I first set eyes upon her, and she had a regard for me. But she was dazzled ... Well, what young lady would not have had her head turned by the determined attentions of a nobleman who was young and well favored? It was all over very soon. She loved me for the rest of her life. Anyone would tell you the truth of that. But she was honest with me when she came to sit beside me at a concert one evening after avoiding me for a few weeks. She feared she might be with child, she told me. We married a few days later by special license, and Chloe was born a little over seven months after that. She was a small baby. Her birth was premature—or so everyone was happy to believe, myself included, for my wife had not been *sure*. I loved that child when she was in the womb and after she was born. I have always loved her, just as I love Lucy and Graham. It makes no difference to me who provided the seed."

"Thank you." Ralph too leaned back in his chair. "You have not told the story quite this way to Chloe?"

"No!" Muirhead spoke quite emphatically. "She must not know that there is any doubt. *She is my daughter*. I do not love her any the less ..."

"But she knows there is a doubt," Ralph said. "She has known it since last year. She believes your denials and protestations because she wants to believe them. And yet part of her does not. And she is tortured by the necessity of believing what at heart she fears and suspects is not the truth."

"She has *told* you this?"

"No," Ralph said. He did not add more. He did not need to. Muirhead would have to be a fool not to know it himself.

Sir Kevin tipped back his head and covered his eyes with the heels of his hands. He exhaled audibly.

"I cannot tell her, Worthingham," he said. "It would destroy her."

"The not knowing is coming near to destroying her anyway," Ralph told him. "Are you afraid of losing her?"

"No." Sir Kevin's hands came down from his face and he looked wearily at Ralph. "*Yes*, of course I am afraid. Can you not see how unfair all of this is? I have been her father all her life and even before she was born. I have provided for her and loved her. I would die for her—for any of my children."

"Will you not trust her to understand that?" Ralph asked.

"It is better that she does not know," his father-in-law insisted. "And it is not certain, anyway. Perhaps I *am* her father. Perhaps she *was* prematurely born. Perhaps there *is* a red-haired ancestor in my past."

There was nothing more to say. But could the man not see that he was losing Chloe anyway? Why did he think she had left home to come and live here indefinitely with her mother's godmother?

Sir Kevin got to his feet. "You have given me your word, Worthingham . . ."

"I have, sir," Ralph told him. "And I will keep it."

"Thank you." The older man hesitated for a moment and then turned and left the room, closing the door quietly behind him.

Her father was the first person they ran into—almost literally. He was hurrying up the stairs as they were making their way down.

"Pardon me," he said, glancing up. Chloe stopped at the suddenly arrested look on his face. "Oh, your poor hair, Chloe. It looks very pretty, though, I must say. Very pretty indeed, in fact."

"You should have seen it an hour ago," Sarah said, and laughed gleefully.

"Papa." Chloe set both hands on his shoulders—he was standing two stairs below her—and kissed him on the cheek. He was looking strained, she thought. "You are leaving tomorrow? We must find time to spend together today."

"Yes, indeed," he said, "though I expect your new duties as duchess and hostess of a number of guests will keep you busy."

And he patted one of her hands on his shoulder, nodded to the other ladies, and continued on his way upstairs. Chloe gazed after him for a few moments before resuming her descent with the others. It had seemed almost as if he did not *want* to spend time with her after coming all this way because of her.

Viscount Ponsonby was standing down in the hall with Lord Trentham and Viscount Darleigh. Lord Darleigh's dog was seated alertly beside him.

"Gentlemen," Gwen said, laughter in her voice as she made a sweeping gesture with both hands, "allow me to present the new Duchess of Worthingham."

Chloe felt horribly self-conscious. She felt half naked without the weight of her hair.

"You look very dashing, Duchess, I must say," Viscount Ponsonby said, extending one hand and then carrying hers to his lips.

"Short hair suits you, lass," Lord Trentham said, "just

as it does Gwendoline." He beamed at his wife, lifted one arm as though to set it about her shoulders, looked suddenly sheepish, and patted her awkwardly on one shoulder instead before lowering his arm to his side.

"You look beautiful, ma'am," Lord Darleigh said, smiling sweetly and gazing almost directly into Chloe's eyes.

"And how would you know that, sir?" she asked him.

"I chose the wrong verb," he said. "You *are* beautiful, ma'am. I can tell by your voice. And I am glad. Ralph needs the very best. He has been unhappy."

Chloe gazed at him in some astonishment. Viscount Ponsonby clapped him on the shoulder.

"We are g-going out, the three of us," he said, "to find the waterfall. Vince could hear it yesterday from the graveyard. I cannot say I noticed it myself, but then I am handicapped. I do most of my noticing with my eyes. Vince will use his ears to find the f-falls, and Hugo and I will use our eyes to stop him from falling over them and getting wet. Together we make a perfect team."

"I do not need your protection, Flave," Lord Darleigh protested, "only your company. I have Shep to keep me safe. He has never let me down yet, have you, boy?"

The dog panted alertly up at him.

"You do not mind our going, Agnes?" Viscount Ponsonby asked his wife.

Chloe could feel any vestige of resentment melt away. She liked these men, her husband's dearest friends, along with the Duke of Stanbrook and the other two who were not here.

"Even so, Vince," Ralph said as he came out from the study, "let Hugo and Flave keep an eye on you, will you?

For my sake? The path beside the rapids and the falls is a rough one."

"What do you think, Ralph?" his sister asked, making the same flourishing gesture toward Chloe that Gwen had made a few moments before.

He stopped in his tracks and took his time about answering.

"It was an inspired decision of yours to cut it off, Chloe," he said at last. "It is perfect, and you look perfectly beautiful."

He had an audience, of course. He could hardly say she would have been better advised to cut her head off as well as her hair. But Chloe bit her lower lip and felt warmed through to the very heart. She blinked back tears.

How very idiotic of her!

. . . you look perfectly beautiful.

And then her heart—the very one that had just been warmed by his compliment—turned a complete somersault in her bosom, even if only figuratively.

For he smiled.

Right into her eyes.

13

ater in the afternoon Chloe found her brother out on the terrace with Mr. Nelson and her brothers-in-law, Sir Wendell Harrison and Viscount Keilly. She slid her hand through his arm and listened to the conversation for a while.

"Shall we stroll down to the river?" she suggested for his ears only after a few minutes. She did not want them all to come. She wanted him to herself for an hour or so.

She was dearly fond of Graham. He was a man of principle and integrity, both rare qualities among the gentlemen she knew. There were those who despised his lack of ambition or merely dismissed him as a failure and surely a disappointment to his family. There were those who accused him of being less than manly. He was never swayed by what others said of him. He would not allow hurt feelings to influence his actions, though he certainly did have feelings and could suffer hurt.

"Will you be happy, Chloe?" he asked her when they had walked beyond earshot of the other men. "As a duchess? With this grand place as your home? With Stockwood as your husband—Worthingham, that is? I really am happy that you are married at last, of course. I know you have longed for marriage and motherhood. I always thought, though, that you would thrive upon quiet domesticity with a husband of modest fortune with whom you enjoyed a mutual affection. I felt your pain when Lucy ruined the Season for which you had waited with such patience and your chance to find both love and an eligible mate. Last year I was hopeful that you might be given another chance. You were still young and still beautiful and you had Aunt Julia's influence behind you. That was most unfortunate. But there is no point in going back over that. *Will* you be happy? *Can* you be?"

"No one held a shotgun to my head," she told him. "Or to Ralph's. We married because we wanted to do so. We did not expect our lives to be turned so topsy-turvy within twenty-four hours of the wedding, it is true. But Ralph's grandfather was elderly and not in the best of health, and it was to be expected that sooner or later we would be facing all this. I do not regret our impulsiveness, though. I have passed the age of expecting that love and romance, marriage and happily-ever-after are all synonymous terms. I have marriage and I hope I will have motherhood. I expect a life of more or less quiet domesticity in the country. It is what Ralph has promised me."

Graham was frowning.

"But a spell in London will come first, surely," he said. "Everyone was agreed at luncheon that you must make an appearance there despite the fact that the old duke died so recently. Noble families, like royal families, are not allowed much time to be alone with their grief. How do you feel about going back to town, Chloe? I know you found all that foolish gossip rather distressing last year. And there were the events of six years ago."

The dowager countess, Ralph's mother, had brought up the subject at luncheon. It was Ralph's duty, now that the funeral was over, she had said, to present himself in London without delay, to make his bow at court and take his seat in the House of Lords as soon as he received his writ of summons. And it was no less his duty, having married hastily just before his grandfather's passing, to present his duchess to the *ton* at all the best social entertainments of the Season. She would help Chloe clothe herself suitably—not in mourning, but not in bright, flamboyant colors either. Her eyes had touched upon Chloe's hair, and she had looked slightly pained.

"Green," Great-Aunt Mary had said. "She should wear green. I never could wear it myself. It always made me look bilious. I always envied girls who could carry it off."

"There must be a grand reception at Stockwood House," the dowager duchess had added. "Perhaps even a ball, Chloe. I do not believe it would be considered disrespectful to my dear Worthingham's memory. Life must go on."

"Oh, will Freddie and I be invited?" Lucy had asked, looking wistful.

Ralph had let them all talk without responding, and Chloe had followed his lead. They would not go, of course. He had promised her. It must happen at some time in the future, she supposed. Next year, perhaps, or the year after.

"We will be staying here," she told Graham now as they came to the river and stepped onto the stone bridge.

"Ralph has said so. He does not allow himself to be ruled by his mother and sisters, and he is tired of London."

She stopped halfway across the bridge in order to gaze off into the shade of the trees, where she had walked with Ralph just a little over a week ago. It seemed far longer ago than that. What had impelled him to risk a dunking or worse by wading across the rapids to find her a perfect stone? And she would swear he had enjoyed those moments of boyish impulse. The stone was in the top left-hand drawer of her dressing table, on top of her handkerchiefs.

"Graham," she asked "how has he changed? How is he different from the way he was at school? What was he like there?"

She had heard stories about him at the time, of course, so many, in fact, that she had formed a decided and strongly negative opinion of Ralph Stockwood without ever having met him. But she had not known then that one day he would be her husband. She might have listened more attentively and questioned her brother more closely if she had known.

He rested his elbows on the parapet of the bridge as he squinted ahead.

"They are not easy questions to answer," he said. "Eight years have passed since we left school. It seems a lifetime. We were boys then and are men now. There are bound to be some pretty significant changes—in both of us. But really fundamental ones? I am not so sure there are any. He was . . . charismatic, Chloe. Quite remarkably so. He was good looking, an early developer physically. He was athletic, intelligent, good in most academic subjects, a reader and a thinker, a natural leader with strong convictions. But many of the same things could be said of other boys, including his three closest friends. One might have expected with those four that there would have been no real leader, that they would have been equal in stature and influence. But it was not so. The other three admired and deferred to him just as much as everyone else did. I would say they were dominated by him except that the word would not be quite accurate. He did not *dominate* anyone. He was never either a tyrant or a bully. He just . . . He had an energy, an *enthusiasm* that was infectious and quite irresistible to most people. He . . . sparkled. Ah, the English language is a woefully imperfect instrument for the expression of some ideas. Suffice it to say that I have never encountered anyone quite like Ralph Stockwood as he was at school."

"He *has* changed, then." Chloe turned away from the water and continued on her way over the bridge, and Graham followed and caught up with her. They walked into the longish grass of the meadow and were soon surrounded by clover and buttercups and daisies. It was sad to think that once her husband had sparkled with an enthusiasm and a fervor for life. She wished she had known the boy he had been.

"I am not sure he has changed all that much," Graham said. "I still sense a sort of leashed energy in him, though he is admittedly more subdued than he was. Perhaps a natural maturity will do that to any man, though. Perhaps grief is a part of it too. He was very close to his grandfather, was he?"

"Yes," she said. "I think more than he was to his father. And Graham, he blames himself for the deaths of those three friends of his."

"Does he?" He was silent for a few moments while Chloe bent to pick some daisies and weave them into the beginnings of a chain. "His passions swept all before him when he felt strongly about something. During our last year at school he had a fascination with Napoleon Bonaparte. At first he admired the man enormously, but the more he learned about him, the more he changed his mind, until he was obsessed by the idea that the man must be stopped if the world was to be saved from tyranny. He could never be content with passionate *ideas,* though. If Bonaparte must be stopped, then it was not enough to expect others to do the stopping. One must be prepared to do it oneself, or at least to do one's part. He could talk of nothing else for weeks on end. It was his duty to take up arms and an officer's commission as soon as school ended and to go off to fight in the wars. It was *everyone's* duty, even men, like himself, who had more reason to stay at home than to face the dangers of war. And if one's family was opposed to the idea, for whatever reason, then its members must be convinced of one's greater duty to save the world for freedom. Any reluctance those three might have felt at the start was quickly swept aside and they became as passionately eager as he was to ride into the glory of battle in a righteous cause."

"And you were accused of cowardice because you would not go too?" she asked him.

He turned his head to smile at her.

"I am not sure he ever pointed a finger directly at me and singled me out for the comment," he said. "But when I voiced opposing arguments, and eventually I seemed to be the only one who *did,* then he remarked that anyone who was unwilling to fight for the freedom of his own family and countrymen against a ruthless dictator like Bonaparte was a sniveling, lily-livered coward—or words to that effect. And maybe he was right. If Bonaparte had succeeded in conquering the whole of Europe, as he came perilously close to doing, then he would without a doubt have turned his attention to the invasion of Britain. Would I have held to my pacifist ideals if I had actually witnessed foreign soldiers committing atrocities against women and children, perhaps people I knew personally? It was all very well to hold those beliefs when the English Channel stood safely between me and the reality of ruthless aggression. But if the Channel had been breached? I am not sure, Chloe. I am still a pacifist by principle, but my convictions have never been put to the test. At least Stockwood put *his* to the test."

She gathered a few more daisies for her chain.

"Life seems so simple when one is very young, does it not?" she said. "Good and evil, black and white—they seem to be polar opposites with no shady areas between. But as one grows older, everything seems to be variously shaded. How can we know what is good and what is evil, Graham, and what is right and what is wrong? Your job must be very difficult. How do you do it?"

"I try not to make judgments," he said. "What is your good may be my evil. I try just to love—a simple enough concept, though even loving is not simple. Perhaps it merely means accepting people for who they are and respecting their choices and sympathizing with their pain."

"He *is* in pain, Graham," she said. And she knew it was true. He was not empty of emotion as she had thought at first. The emptiness sat upon a seething well of suffering and pain, mainly the agony of guilt.

"I know." He stopped walking and turned to gaze back toward the house. He spoke softly without looking at her. "So are you, Chloe."

Her mind denied it. She had been lonely and unhappy and insecure, that was all. Now she was married and she was happy. Well, *contented,* anyway.

"And you?" she asked.

"It is the human condition," he said. "No one who lives into adulthood can escape it. Even children cannot. It is what we do with the pain, though, how we allow it to shape our character and actions and relationships that matters. But life is not unalloyed gloom. One must absolutely not allow pessimism or cynicism to send one into a deep depression. There is much joy too. *Much* joy. *Can* you be happy with him, Chloe? *Will* you be?"

"We have come full circle." She laughed and completed her daisy chain before throwing it over his head—it was just long enough to clear the brim of his hat. "*Can* I be happy? Yes, of course. *Will* I be? Who knows? But if I am not, it will not be for lack of opportunity, or for lack of trying."

He held out one hand, and after looking at it for a moment, she set her own in it and they began the walk back to the house.

"Have you confronted Papa?" he asked her.

"Yes. At Christmas. Before I left home." She drew a slow breath.

"And?"

"He swore there was no truth in the rumors," she said.

"You believed him?"

They had crossed the bridge again before she answered.

"Maybe it does not matter what I believe," she said. "The past cannot be changed, whatever it was. He has always been Papa. If I had not gone to London last year, I would probably never have been given reason to suspect that perhaps he is not also my father. Perhaps the knowing or not knowing is of no importance whatsoever."

"Perhaps," he agreed. "Papa *has* always loved you, you know, Chloe, every bit as much as he has loved Lucy and me. And I have always loved you as dearly as I love Lucy."

"I know." She squeezed his hand.

Several people were gathered on the eastern terrace, Chloe could see, it being a pleasantly warm afternoon. It looked as if tea was being carried out. She had stolen enough time to be alone with her brother. It was time to take up her duties as hostess again.

Ralph was watching her approach, and unconsciously her footsteps quickened. Was it unnatural and a bit unkind of her to be looking forward to everyone's departure tomorrow so that they could be alone together at last? So that they could settle into the marriage they had agreed upon? Even his grandmother was leaving. She was going to London for an indefinite stay with Great-Aunt Mary.

It seemed unnaturally quiet in the drawing room on the evening of the following day despite the crackling of the fire. There were just the two of them, Chloe on one side of the hearth, seated in the chair that had always been

Ralph's grandmother's, he on the other side, seated in his grandfather's chair. It all felt . . . uncomfortable.

Her head was bent over a small embroidery frame. She looked elegant in her black dress. Pretty. Her short wavy hair seemed to have stripped several years off her age. And, heaven help him, she was his wife. Until death did them part.

For the first time it seemed fully, starkly real.

Ralph was tempted to get abruptly to his feet, hurry from the room and the house, saddle a horse, and gallop away into the night so that he could have himself to himself again. There was nothing to stop him from acting upon the impulse, of course, except that . . . Well, such a move would give merely the illusion of freedom, for he would have to come back.

He was the Duke of Worthingham—something he had hoped not to be for years and years yet. He had a wife, a duchess—something he would have liked to postpone for at least a decade.

Whoever had said that one was free to do what one wished with one's life? *Had* anyone said it? Or had no one ever been that foolish? Or that untruthful? Or that self-deluded? Yet he had thought it true in those long-ago days of his boyhood when he knew nothing about anything but thought he knew everything about everything. He had thought he was free to pursue his dreams and his convictions. And he had thought himself invincible. Youth was a dangerous time of life.

He closed his book without marking the page—he had not been concentrating upon what he read anyway—and set it aside. He got to his feet and crossed before the fireplace before moving past Chloe's chair to stand half behind it. She raised her head and smiled briefly at him before returning her attention to her embroidery.

She was the very picture of placid domesticity. He felt a purely unreasoned impatience and resentment toward her. Was he going to be looking across his own hearth at *embroidery* for the rest of his life?

"You must have been sorry to have to say goodbye to your family and friends so soon," she said.

"Yes," he agreed. "And you had all too short a visit with your father and your brother and sister."

Everyone had left this morning. Everyone except the two of them.

"Will your grandmother stay away, do you think?" she asked him.

"It is hard to say," he said. "Great-Aunt Mary has always been exceedingly fond of her, and she has been lonely since my great-uncle died a few years ago. And Grandmama has always been inordinately fond of *her*. But who knows whether she will decide to remain away from here or decide to return after a while? This has been her home for a very long time. It embodies most of the memories of her marriage, and that was, I believe, a happy one. But the choice is hers. We both assured her that this will always be her home. Thank you for joining your voice to mine on that."

Chloe had even shed tears over his grandmother this morning.

"But it *is* her home," she protested. "I have been sitting here feeling like a usurper although I know I am not. I miss her already—and your grandpapa."

"Your father is going to be staying in London too for a while," he said. "Did he *say* anything before he left?"

Chloe and her father had strolled out to the old oak tree together while the carriage was being loaded with baggage and Freddie Nelson was delivering himself of a bombastic speech to Hugo on the topic of his newest unfinished play.

"Only that he hopes we will be happy," she said.

Ah. He had not told her, then.

Ralph looked at the work she was doing. She was embroidering an exquisitely fancy *W* across one corner of a large handkerchief of fine linen. W for Worthingham?

"For me?" he asked her.

"Yes."

He felt immediate shame for his irritation with her.

"Thank you," he said, and briefly he squeezed her shoulder.

He wondered if he would ever feel perfectly at ease in her company—or she in his. Her hand, he noticed, was trembling ever so slightly as she tried to find the right place for her needle. He was making her self-conscious. He dropped his hand and made his way back to his chair. She had followed him with her eyes, he noticed after he sat down, her needle suspended above her work.

He sighed out loud.

"Tell me about you, Chloe," he said. Though he did not know why he had asked. He did not want to know any more about her than she had told him two nights ago. He did not want a relationship. But now the question had been asked—in the vaguest of vague terms and not even phrased quite as a question. "Tell me about your childhood. About your mother."

He both felt and heard her draw a slow breath. And he watched as she threaded her needle through the edge of the handkerchief and set her work down on top of a pile of colored silks in her workbag.

"Papa always told me he loved me," she said. "Always. And I never doubted him. He used to take me riding and fishing even when Graham and Lucy did not want to go. He taught me how to bounce stones across water—yes, with a special flick of the wrist. I used to think sometimes that I was his favorite, though it was a wicked thought because he loved us all equally."

It was interesting that she had chosen to begin with her father.

"And your mother?"

"She loved us too." Her eyes were directed downward to her fingers, which were pleating the fabric of her dress. "But I always worried—or *irritated*—her more than the other two did. Lucy was always perfect. I grew far too quickly and was thin and awkward among other things. I think Mama despaired of my ever looking even halfway pretty. I was not sunny-natured or sociable either and would always prefer to disappear into the barn to play with the baby animals when there *were* some or merely to read in the hayloft than to play with the neighborhood children who were sometimes brought to visit. When I *did* converse, I wanted to talk about fascinating things I had read in my books even though Mama kept drumming into my head that girls must never appear intelligent in company, especially male company. She was so beautiful herself, so vibrant, so sociable, so easy to love. I was a severe trial to her. She was, I know, afraid for my future. She so hoped to see me settled during that one Season I spent in London. *Half* a Season."

Ralph had tipped back his head and stretched out his

legs to the fire. He gazed across at her through half-closed eyelids and imagined her as she must have been as a girl—gawky and awkward and showing little promise of the beauty to come, while her mother and sister were both exquisite dark beauties. And riding and fishing with her father rather than playing with other girls. Bouncing stones. A bit unhappy, aware that she was a disappointment to her mother, that she could not compete with her younger sister in looks or charm. Playing with the farm animals. Reading. Losing herself in her own imaginative world. Being called a carrot top and even a rabbit and carrot all in one by the neighborhood children who ought to have been her friends.

And all this he did not want to know.

He did not *need* to know. For in the knowing he felt a sadness for that lonely girl and for the man who gave her a father's unconditional love despite the fact that she was not his own. And he felt a sharp anger against the dead woman who had not loved her firstborn as she ought, perhaps because that child reminded her of her own shame and embarrassment.

"Oh, she did love me," Chloe was saying as though she could read his thoughts—or perhaps merely to reassure herself. "I hope I have not suggested that she did not. She took me to London for a come-out Season when really she ought to have remained at home. She had been very ill, and she was ill again after we returned. I daresay she forced herself out of sheer willpower to appear healthy when we were there. And then she died. She wanted to see me well settled first. Married. She wanted to see me happy. It is all Papa has ever wanted for me too—that I be happy."

"What did you tell him earlier," he asked, "when he said just that—that he hoped you would be happy?"

She sank her teeth into her bottom lip for a moment, and her cheeks colored.

"I told him he must not worry," she said. "I told him I *was* happy."

"And are you?" he asked. It was a very unfair question. It was, moreover, another question he did not want answered. But it was too late now to recall it.

She was smoothing out the creases she had just made in her skirt.

"Happiness is just a word," she said. "It is like love in that way. There are many definitions, all of them accurate, but none of them all-encompassing. I am not sorry I married you."

"And that," he said, "is one definition of happiness, is it? That you are not sorry for something you have done?"

She raised her head and looked back at him—and laughed softly. It was a beguiling sight and sound.

"I am a married lady rather than a spinster," she said. "My present and my future are respectable and secure. I have experienced the marriage bed. Perhaps soon, within the next few months, I will be with child. Perhaps there will be more children after the first. You promised that you would show me respect and courtesy, and you have kept the promise. You promised me a quiet home in the country, and you have given me just that, even though this is a far larger home than the one I expected. Why would I *not* be happy?"

He closed his eyes. Did she realize that she had not answered his question—*are you happy*? After listing a number of reasons why she should be happy, she had summed up with a question of her own: *Why would I* not *be happy?*

But she was right in saying there was no satisfactory definition of the word *happiness.* All definitions, or all attempts to give the word meaning, merely revolved endlessly about an empty center, a core of indefinable nothingness. As a boy he had known what happiness was without any need of words, and he had forged his way toward it with confident, unfaltering strides. Happiness in those days was doing what was right against all the odds and all the naysayers. It was accomplishing a noble goal through the efforts of his own body and mind and will so that he could see the world set to rights forever after. Happiness was about certainties.

Foolish, idealistic boy. He had accomplished the exact opposite of what he had intended, and he had destroyed life and happiness and certainty in the process. He had destroyed innocence.

The light from the fire, low in the hearth, was flickering off her face when he opened his eyes. She was looking steadily back at him.

"Have I said something wrong?" she asked him. "I do not expect you to give me happiness. It is something I will draw for myself out of the conditions of my life. Any happiness I achieve will be my own, with no obligation upon you to provide it or to pretend to share it. Is it not better that I be contented than that I be miserable? We did not promise each other misery."

She made him sound like a coldhearted monster, though such was not her intent, he knew. She was not far wrong, though, was she? Could she possibly find any sort of happiness with him? And why could he not . . .

He got abruptly to his feet again. For a moment he stood gazing down into the dying fire, troubled by that familiar sense of yearning, the kind he could never explain to himself in words but only feel to the marrow of his bones.

She had risen too, he realized when he felt her hand light on his arm.

"I do not want to be miserable," she said. "I do not want you to be miserable either. Surely we are allowed—"

His arm came about her waist and drew her to him, and his mouth descended upon hers all in one swift movement, cutting off the rest of what she was saying. The fingers of his free hand threaded through her short curls, holding her head still.

And he allowed himself the full luxury of desire. Except, he realized after a while, that it was more than just a physical thing he was allowing. His yearning for something unnamable had just been multiplied tenfold until he was afraid—yet again—that if he lifted his head away from hers he would be sobbing.

He gentled the kiss, explored her lips and the inside of her mouth more lazily with his tongue, wondered if he was offending her, guessed he was not. For her arms were about him too, and she was leaning into him, and her mouth was open to welcome the invasion of his tongue.

Perhaps . . .

He raised his head and gazed into her face. Her lips were moist and slightly swollen. Her cheeks looked flushed in the semidarkness. Her eyes were both bright and heavy lidded.

His insides lurched uncomfortably.

"Sex," he said. "It is just sex, Chloe."

"Just?" Her voice was a whisper of sound that he felt against his lips. "That word suggests that it is a slight thing. I think it must be more than that."

He was amused despite himself. "It is," he agreed, opening his eyes. "But it is still *just* sex. It is not love. Or happiness."

"I understand that," she said. "But it always feels good anyway. Is it not meant to?"

For a long time after his return from the Peninsula he had refused to allow himself to feel any pleasure at all, for there were men who were dead and would never feel anything ever again. There were families who would never quite recover from their grief. He had worked through that particular phase, which had included the compulsion to end his life, with the help of the physician at Penderris and with the sympathetic understanding of his fellow Survivors. There was nothing to be gained by punishing himself forever, he had come to understand and accept. It was a kind of selfishness. Those men were beyond pain. He lived on. Those families could not be comforted by his suffering. Perhaps there was a reason he had not been killed too. Who was he to deny the unexpected, unwanted gift of life and a future?

But he had never returned fully, or even *nearly* fully, to his old self. He had instinctively shied away from pleasure, laughter, anything bordering upon happiness, illogical as he knew it was.

He was not alone in this marriage, however—the very reason for his reluctance to marry. He *did* owe his wife something despite the chilling terms of their bargain, to which she had agreed—which, in fact, she had suggested. She wanted happiness, though she would not demand that he provide it. She enjoyed sex, it seemed, as a momentary means to pleasure. Or perhaps it was just kisses she enjoyed. Perhaps she equated them with sex. Or perhaps it was the night and morning brief ritual of their joining.

Perhaps it was time to find out how much she enjoyed it.

"It could feel better if we went to bed," he said. "But it would have to be somewhat different from what we have been doing there since our wedding, Chloe."

She gazed at him.

"Perhaps," he said, "you would prefer to get back to your embroidery."

"That can wait," she told him.

He stood back and offered her his arm very formally.

Very formally, she took it.

He could not, it seemed, hold back change. But he had learned that lesson long ago. How foolish of him to have forgotten when he had come to marriage terms with her.

14

 $\mathcal{H}$ e took her to his own bed again, that vast monstrosity on its high pedestal that was nevertheless more comfortable than any other bed Chloe had ever encountered. He did not allow her to go to her own room first to change into her nightgown. When she protested, he informed her that she would not need it. And he proved his point as soon as the door was firmly shut behind them by unclothing her one garment at a time, including her stays and her shift and her garters and stockings, until she was standing naked before him, bathed in the light of what seemed like a million candles. He had a good look too while he was playing lady's maid, and he made no effort to stop his hands from brushing against her skin. Indeed, he was probably making an effort to see that they *did* touch her.

What surprised Chloe most was the fact that she hardly felt embarrassed at all. It would have been a bit silly to do so, of course, since she had been his wife for longer than a week and had already lost an exact count of the number of times he had had relations with her. But even so, standing naked before a fully clothed man with all her imperfections ought to have been more disconcerting than it was. Except that he did not look disappointed and her body was humming with what she could only guess was desire.

It occurred to her that perhaps she ought to unclothe him since he had done it for her, but she could not bring herself to be quite that bold. And he seemed to be doing well enough on his own. She noticed after his waistcoat and then his neckcloth had followed his evening coat to the floor that he really looked very attractive indeed in his shirt and tight pantaloons, but he was not wearing the former much longer. He peeled it off over his head and dropped it. His valet was going to be very cross with him in the morning. It was a good thing she had no maid yet to be cross with her.

He undid the buttons at his waist and opened the fall of his pantaloons, and in no time at all he was as naked as she. The difference was, of course, that she had seen him before. There were other scars in addition to the one about his shoulder and the one that slashed across the left side of his face. None of them—even the facial scar—marred his beauty. And he was beautiful.

His hands came to her shoulders then—they looked very dark-skinned against the paleness of her own flesh—and down behind to spread over her shoulder blades so that he could draw her against him until her nipples touched his chest, shocking her all the way down to her toes. He was rock solid—except that a rock was not warm and inviting and did not have a heartbeat. Her own hands found his shoulders as he lowered his head and kissed her openmouthed again.

Kisses were such an unexpected delight. And a shock

too, for she had never imagined that lips would part, that mouths would open, that tongues would explore and tangle and even simulate the marital act—or that such shocking activities would have a taste and a sound and would send sensations to which she could not put a name sizzling through her whole body until she yearned for the touch of him *there*.

Oh, she thought—and it was one of her last coherent thoughts for some time to come—she *must not* fall in love with him. It would be the most naïve and foolish thing she could possibly do.

Sex, he had said. *It is just sex, Chloe.*

She must, must, *must* remember that.

But *just sex* was glorious beyond imagining, she discovered during the hours after he took her up the steps and laid her on the bed. He followed her down onto it without extinguishing any of the candles. She was able to watch everything they did and to see that *he* watched too until at some time during the night the candles guttered out one at a time and there was darkness. By then, though, they were sated and exhausted.

His hands, his fingers, his lips, his tongue had touched every inch of her body on the outside and a good portion of her body on the inside too. And after the first round of . . . sex, her own hands and mouth had grown almost equally bold. He had been on top of her, she had been on top of him, and once he had even been on her but behind her. And none of it had been just the mildly pleasurable experience she had come to look forward to since her wedding night. Instead it had been . . .

But there were no words. Only feelings that built and built, time after time, to some pinnacle of glory, before exploding into something that made *glory* seem a paltry thing.

Oh, no, really there were no words.

It occurred to her once or twice—particularly when she heard herself cry out for no apparent reason—that perhaps she ought to be ashamed, that perhaps ladies did not behave with such wanton abandon. Undoubtedly ladies did not, in fact. But she always pushed the unwelcome thought aside. If ladies did not experience the wonders of *sex,* then they were to be pitied. They did not know what they were missing.

By the time the last of the candles wavered and went out he was sleeping, sprawled on his stomach beside her, his head turned toward her, his nose almost touching her shoulder, one of his arms flung heavily across her waist. He smelled of sweat and something else very male. It was surely one of the most enticing smells in the world—which was a *very* strange thought to be having. The bedcovers were down around their knees.

It had been sex, she told herself. And, because it had been just that, he had enjoyed it as much as she had. And it was enough. She would make it enough. But please, please let their relationship not revert now to the way it had been every other night. Let him not be satisfied simply to have proved a point to her. She had enjoyed every night and every early morning with him too, but from now she knew they would not be enough without *this* at least occasionally.

It was just sex, of course. But it was surely better than love, for there was too much turmoil, too much uncertainty, too much danger of heartbreak in love. There was only enjoyment to be had from sex.

She ignored a twinge of doubt as she closed her eyes and relaxed into the delicious languor that came after the exertions of sex.

This had been better than love.

When Chloe awoke sometime later, Ralph was gone from the bed though it was still full dark. He was not gone from the room, though. He was standing by the window with the curtains pulled back, and he was half dressed again in his shirt and pantaloons. His hands were on the windowsill, his shoulders slightly hunched.

"Ralph?" she said. It was chilling to see that he was dressed when there was still no sign of dawn.

He did not turn or say anything for a few moments. Then he sighed and spoke.

"We will be going to London next week, Chloe."

"What?" Chloe sat up abruptly and clutched the covers to her naked breasts. But she knew she had not misheard.

"Next week," he said, choosing the most trivial detail to repeat.

"You said we were to remain here," she told him. "You promised me . . ."

He turned, leaned back against the sill, and crossed his arms. She could see him only as a dark silhouette, but he looked both impatient and menacing.

"But they are right," he said. "My mother, my grandmother, all the rest of them. It is necessary that we go to town."

"But you promised—"

"Everything has changed, Chloe," he said harshly. "Can you not see that? It was naïve of us to plan our future as though we could go to Elmwood after our wedding and live in retired rural bliss there forever after. We knew my grandfather was well into his eighties. We knew he was infirm. We knew he was bound to die soon, even if we could not have predicted that it would be quite *so* soon. The whole reason for our marriage—on my part, anyway, and you were fully aware of it—was to secure the succession, and the whole point of doing *that* was that the dukedom matters. I would not have married otherwise—you or anyone else. The dukedom is more than an impressive title to attach to my name. It is an important office and brings with it duties and responsibilities. The Duke of Worthingham may not hide away in the country the way the Earl of Berwick with his courtesy title could have done. I ought to have taken that fact into consideration when I agreed that we would live in the country and ignore society and the London Season. I ought to have reminded you that we were free to live as we wished only until my grandfather died. The Duke of Worthingham will be expected to make his bow to the king and to be ready to take his place in the House when he is summoned. And, since he is a married man, he will be expected to make his appearance in society with his duchess at his side. Unfortunately the duke and duchess are not just impersonal entities. They are *us*. You and me."

"*You* married to secure the succession," she cried. "*I* married for other reasons. I married for a life of quiet domesticity, and you agreed that it would be so. It was a mutual bargain we made. You cannot change the rules now."

"Rules?" He leaned a little more toward her. "Have

you not heard a word I said? Are you quite as naïve as you sometimes seem? When have you ever known life to follow any *rules* we may try to impose upon the chaos? You knew whom you were marrying. You must have known that everything would change one day."

"Your grandparents lived here for years," she said. "They never seemed to believe it was their duty to spend the Season in London."

"They were *old*," he reminded her, "and they were thoroughly well established in their role. I am twenty-six years old. You are twenty-seven. We are novices. We have yet to establish ourselves, to prove ourselves worthy of the role for which fate has chosen us. There are duties associated with the privilege of rank and fortune, Chloe, and one of them is to mingle with our peers. I wish to God it were not so, but it is."

"You may break a promise you made me, then," she said, "in order to win the approval of people who mean nothing to you. Clearly *I* mean nothing to you."

Even to her own ears there seemed to be something a bit childishly petulant in her outburst.

"What promises *have* I made?" He pushed away from the windowsill and turned back to the window. "I made marriage vows, which I intend to keep. You made marriage vows too, Chloe."

"To *obey* you?" She scrambled up onto her knees and wrapped the top sheet about herself. She glared at his back. "You are going to enforce *that*, are you?"

She could hear his fingernails clicking on the sill.

"You made that vow, not me." His voice was cold. "I did not see anyone twisting your arm or otherwise coercing you."

"But you are going to coerce me into going to London."

He whirled about and strode toward her. He did not stop until he was up the steps and leaning across the bed, braced on his forearms. His face was a few inches from her own. She clutched the sheet tighter and held her ground.

"I will not whip you into submission," he told her. "Nor will I tie you hand and foot and toss you into the carriage and convey you to London as my prisoner. But I *do* say that we will be going there next week. I have duties and responsibilities. So do you. I was born for this. I was never particularly thrilled at the prospect. Indeed, I was even careless of the reality of it when I was eighteen and rode off to war with crusading zeal. My father still stood between me and the title at that time, and he seemed a firm enough bulwark. But he died of what seemed like a simple chill, and here I am. And there *you* are. You married me with your eyes wide open. You can cower here if you choose. I cannot—or, rather I *will* not—force you into accompanying me next week. But remember, Chloe, that in addition to being my duchess you will in all probability be the mother of a future duke. My son. How proud will he be of a mother who is afraid to show her nose to the beau monde lest someone bite it off? How happy will my daughters be with a mother who is afraid to take them to town when the time comes for them to seek husbands lest the *ton* dare find something in her about which to gossip?"

"I am not *afraid*," she protested.

"And besides," he said, "if you will not come with me to do your duty to society, you need to come to do your duty to me. You need to be *bred*."

Her hand was stinging suddenly, and she realized in some shock that she had slapped him across one cheek.

There was a heavy silence as he straightened up to stand beside the bed.

"I beg your pardon," he said, his voice tight. "That *was* crude."

"I am so sorry." Chloe spoke almost simultaneously. Her teeth were chattering. "Did I hurt you?"

Ridiculous question. She had hit him across the scarred side of his face.

"Yes," he said. "But I would have slapped me too if I had been you."

Chloe flexed her hand. It was hot and throbbing. She had never slapped anyone before.

He sat down on the edge of the bed and turned to look at her.

"Certain members of the *ton* once shunned you," he said, "because your sister had eloped with a married man. A known rake who had toyed with your affections cut your acquaintance with calculated disdain. Several years later—*last* year—it was discovered that you bore a passing resemblance to a lady who happened to be taking the *ton* by storm during her debut Season in London, and gossiping tongues began to wag with the salacious rumor that her father once paid court to your mother. So both those visits to London left you hurt. Understandably, you want nothing more to do with society. In retrospect, perhaps it was not wise of you to marry an earl who was an elderly duke's heir. But you did just that. And as a result you now find yourself being called upon to face society yet again—in the prominent role of a duchess this time. Are you going to do it, Chloe? Or are you going to allow fear to keep you here in hiding for the rest of your life?"

"I am not *afraid*."

"What do you call it, then?" he asked her.

She realized something suddenly. Graham had said he was not sure Ralph had changed fundamentally since his days in school. Now, she suddenly realized that in an important way, he was right. She could feel the power of his persuasiveness. Her will was being worn down by it.

"Is this how you did it when you were a boy?" she asked him. "Is this how you gathered other boys about you like slaves? Is this how you persuaded them to do whatever you wanted them to do, even against their will and their better judgment? Is this how you persuaded your friends to go to war with you?"

He shot to his feet as though she had slapped him again, and she realized too late the viciousness of what she had said.

He stood with his back to her for a few moments while her words seemed to hang in the air between them, like a physical presence. Then he went down the steps and across the room and out the door, all so abruptly that she could do nothing to stop him but stretch out one ineffectual arm.

"Ralph," she said. But the sound of her voice came at the same moment that the door clicked shut behind him.

She could not run after him. She was naked beneath the sheet. She bowed her head and set her forehead against her raised knees as she wrapped her arms about them.

It was full daylight by the time Chloe had pulled on her creased clothes and gone to her own room to wash and comb her hair and change into a freshly ironed dress. She made her way down to the breakfast parlor on slightly shaky legs. Early as it still was, Ralph had already eaten and was about to leave the room. He was fully, very correctly clothed, she saw.

Before she could say anything, he made her a slight, formal bow.

"I need to spend most of the day in the study with Lloyd and my steward," he told her. "Forgive me for leaving you to eat alone and to occupy yourself for the rest of the day."

She had come down with a head crammed full of things to say—apologies, explanations, questions. She had come down prepared to be calm and sensible, prepared to discuss, to come to some sort of agreement that would suit them both. Everything she had planned to say fled without a trace.

"Oh, you must not concern yourself about me," she assured him with bright cheerfulness. "I need to spend some time with Mrs. Loftus. I have much to learn. And she knows of someone who may be suitable as my lady's maid. I will need to meet the girl to see if I agree. And I really ought to call upon Mrs. Booth, who was not well enough to attend the funeral. I should make a courtesy call at the vicarage too. And I have my embroidery and . . ."

He was looking cold, remote, impatient to be gone, and her voice trailed away.

She wondered if she had dreamed up the man who had loved her with such hot intensity and such shocking intimacy last night. And the woman who had responded in kind. But of course she had not. It was only the word *loved* that was inaccurate.

Sex. It is just sex. . . .
Yes, it had been. Just sex.
He left the room without another word.

That ill-advised night of uninhibited sex was not re-
peated during the following week. Nor did Ralph take
Chloe to his room again. He went to hers instead and
resumed their marital relationship as it had been before.

That one night had been ill-advised for a number of
reasons, not the least of which was that he had known
even before it happened that he must break the unwelcome news to her that they would be going to London
after all. He had been too cowardly to speak up during
the evening. He had known she would be upset.

He had known years ago, when he finally abandoned
his attempts at suicide, that this time would come. After
the sudden death of his father, he had known too that it
would come in the foreseeable future. And he had made
the decision, reluctant though he had been, that he
would do his duty when the time came — and even before the time came in the matter of taking a bride and
setting up his nursery. It would perhaps be his penance,
he had thought, to accept that for which his life had been
saved. To do his best. To do his duty.

He had ignored one fact — or perhaps he could not
have expected to know it until now. His acceptance had
concerned himself. It had included a wife, but it had not
taken into account the fact that his wife would be a person in her own right.

Doing his duty now meant hurting Chloe, breaking
the promise he had undeniably made her. It meant forcing her into doing the very last thing on earth she wanted

to do—if, that was, he chose to assert his rights as her husband. He had had to decide between duty and a promise and had chosen duty. Though he had also chosen *not* to enforce obedience.

Had he done just that once before?

Is this how you persuaded your friends to go to war with you?

He had decided that they would leave for London one week after the funeral—or that he would, anyway. There was much to do in the interim. He was a bit sorry he had not spent more time at Manville Court during the past few years, learning something of the formidable task of running the many ducal estates. He had known this day was coming, after all, and ought to have been better prepared for it.

He spent the week consulting with his steward at Manville, studying reports from the other properties, dealing with the considerable amount of correspondence Arthur Lloyd drew to his attention every day, tramping about the home farm talking with foremen and laborers, calling upon tenant farmers and listening to their concerns. On the few occasions when he had some free time, he sat in the book room with a book open before him— it could hardly be said that he *read*—or out riding aimlessly about the countryside or walking down by the lake or up over the falls.

During much of that solitary time he grieved. It was incredibly difficult to be here in all the familiar surroundings, to know that it was all his now, to accept that his grandfather was gone. And he thought of his grandmother in London now with Great-Aunt Mary but surely feeling lost and homesick. He relived scenes from his boyhood and youth here. Once, when he explored a drawer in the desk in the book room, he found a little twist of paper lodged at the back and discovered three of the familiar sweetmeats welded together inside. Always three. And always twisted up in a piece of paper so that the sweets would not pick up lint in either his grandfather's pocket or that of the grandchild to whom he gave them. Ralph put the little bundle into his own pocket and left it there.

He would give anything in the world to bring back those days, to have the chance to take a different path into the future than the one he had actually taken. Sometimes he wondered what would have happened if he had not become so consumed with his grand idea of saving the world from tyranny or if his grandfather had put his foot down and refused to purchase his commission.

But such thoughts were pointless. Regrets were pointless. As was guilt.

Sometimes he found himself grieving too for his father, who had died almost unnoticed, by him at least. Ralph had still been very ill at Penderris at the time, too ill to return home for the funeral or even to comprehend fully what had happened. He had never been particularly close to his father, but he *had* loved him. There had been no goodbye, no chance to sit with relatives after his passing to relive half-forgotten memories. No real mourning. Just bruised feelings denied and pushed deep inside.

He *had* loved his father. He had hurt him too. He had been a disappointment to a man who took duty and responsibility very seriously. And it must have been a huge blow to his pride as a father to have his own father override his refusal to allow Ralph to go off to war.

Three times Ralph sat with Chloe in the evenings. Mostly he kept his eyes on his book when he did so while she just as firmly directed her attention to her embroidery or to her own book. She had not initiated any conversation since the night of their quarrel, but then neither had he.

He did not even know whether she was coming to London with him. And he would *not* assert his right to command her.

On the fifth evening, he set aside his book with more of a thump than he had intended, surged to his feet, and then had little choice but to cross the room to the sideboard to pour himself a drink since he could not think of any other reason to offer for getting up from his chair. Not that she had asked for any explanation. She had not even looked up. When he turned back to the room, glass in hand, however, she *was* looking at him, her needle suspended over her work. She looked down again without saying anything.

And he felt suddenly vicious. This was ridiculous. He wanted to stride toward her, haul her to her feet, and shake her. But good God, *why*? Because he was not comfortable in his own home? Did he imagine *she* was?

He swallowed a mouthful of port.

"I think your brother and I," he said, "might have been the closest of friends at school if we had not been so similar."

And where had *that* comment come from? Except that she always somehow reminded him of Graham. She irritated him in the same ways her brother had. As though even her silences—*especially* her silences— were accusatory. He had never thought of Graham and himself being *similar,* though. Quite the opposite, in fact.

She lifted her head from her work again, and he expected her to look skeptical, incredulous. She seemed exceedingly fond of her brother, after all. Instead she nodded.

"Yes," she said, "I have noticed."

What the devil? He frowned, swirled the liquor in his glass, and took another gulp of it.

"Pigheaded, both of us," he said. "Espousing untenable ideals. Both of us."

"Pacifism is untenable?" she asked.

"Of course it is," he said impatiently. "No man is going to stand by and watch his mother and his wife and his daughters raped before his eyes without wreaking murder and mayhem to prevent it."

"Graham said much the same thing when he was here," she said.

"Did he?"

"And is the ideal of fighting to end tyranny untenable?" she asked.

"Of course it is," he said again. "Tyranny will never be ended. Neither will violence nor aggression nor injustice nor cruelty nor any of the other evils humans are prone to."

"So we do away with soldiers and constables and magistrates and judges?" she asked him as he crossed the room to stand on one side of the hearth, his elbow on the mantel. "We allow tyranny and anarchy to spread unchecked because we can never stamp them out? *But* we lash out at anyone who threatens those nearest and dearest to us?"

He swirled what was left of his drink but did not raise the glass to his lips.

"I was a naïve fool," he told her. "I thought war in a righteous cause was a glorious thing—*dulce et decorum est pro patria mori* and all that nonsense. It is sweet and right to die for one's country. There is nothing sweet or right about war. Officers are vain and lazy and corrupt and often cruel. The common soldier is the spawn of the gutters and prisons of England. Battle is madness and chaos and blood and entrails and smoke and screaming. And when it is over, one shares a canteen of water or spirits and pleasantries with an enemy survivor of roughly equal rank while one sorts out one's own dead and wounded and he sorts out his—as though it had all been a pleasant day's game, like cricket."

It struck him that he ought not to be talking to a lady about such things. And why was he talking about them, anyway? Where had this conversation sprung from?

"And yet," she said, "it was through such chaos and such deadly games and with such frail, often undesirable human beings that the Duke of Wellington drove a wedge into the oppressive empire Napoleon Bonaparte had built and brought it tumbling down. It needed to be brought down."

"You do not support your brother's stand, then?" he asked.

"No," she said. "But I respect him for it. We are all entitled to our ideals. Most beliefs are neither right nor wrong in themselves. None of them ever contains the whole truth."

However had they got into this? He drained off the rest of his port in one mouthful and swirled it about his mouth before swallowing. She had lowered her head and was sewing again. It was still a man's handkerchief, he could see, though a different one from before. The colors were different.

"Graham's beliefs do not kill anyone," he said. "Mine do."

She put her work away after a tap on the door heralded the arrival of the evening tea tray. Ralph waited for the footman to set it down before her and leave. He watched her lift the teapot to pour.

"None for me," he told her.

"It was not your beliefs that killed men," she said. "It was not your beliefs that killed your three friends. It was war that did that—a terrible solution to a terrible problem, but perhaps the only one or at least the right one for that particular provocation. You participated because you believed in the cause. Your friends died because *they* believed in it, even if it was you who drew their attention to it."

And persuaded them into going with him.

Is this how you persuaded your friends to go to war with you?

"And you almost died," she said. She set the teapot down and looked up at him with troubled eyes. "How do you recover from such experiences, Ralph? How does *anyone* recover? How does anyone carry on with his life after he has been to war? And how does any man go on with life after *not* going to war?"

He frowned. "Graham?"

"In his own way," she said, "he feels as guilty as you—for the deaths of countless hundreds of men while he remained safely at home wondering how he would react if his pacifism was ever put to the test. For the deaths of your three friends, who were also his friends."

"He *told* you this?" he asked her.

"No," she said. "Not in so many words. And I did not even think about it until the last time I talked with him. We have lived through dreadful times, Ralph, and none of us has been exempt from suffering. But perhaps *every-one*, all down through the ages, lives through dreadful times. Perhaps it is the human condition. I used to think the only suffering war brought was the death of soldiers and the physical pain of the wounds of others. Those things are not even the half of it, are they?"

He stared at her bent head in silence as she drank her tea and kept her eyes lowered. He had thought of Chloe as an essentially placid woman who wanted only the seemingly simple things in life in order to be happy—marriage, home, motherhood. She had suffered disappointments and real pain in her life and had finally settled for a bloodless bargain that had nevertheless brought her the rudiments of contentment—until his announcement a few days ago, anyway. Now he was not so sure about her. She was beginning to seem to be very much more than the woman he had taken her for. And the more fool he for believing that anyone could be simply a few things and nothing else.

He had not expected to like her—*really* to like her. He had expected—and hoped—to be indifferent to her.

He opened his mouth to speak, but she spoke first as she set down her empty cup and saucer.

"I will be ready to go to London with you," she said. "The day after tomorrow, is it?"

"Yes."

He wanted to say more. He wanted to . . . apologize to her? For what? For the fact that his grandfather had died so soon? He wanted to . . . comfort her? But how? He wanted to . . .

He wanted. Always that longing, that nameless yearning.

"Thank you," he said. His voice sounded abrupt, even cold.

15

*C*hloe sat in an opulent carriage emblazoned with the ducal coat of arms and drawn by four magnificent black horses. It was driven by a stout coachman with a large footman at his side. Four hefty outriders rode beside it, two on each side. All six men were resplendent in the ducal livery. Everyone they passed on the road to London stopped in awe and stared, the men doffing hats and pulling on forelocks, the women dipping into curtsies. Ralph was out there riding too, most of the time well ahead of the carriage, just occasionally alongside it, perhaps to make sure Chloe had not taken fright and jumped out. He looked less conspicuously gorgeous than any of his servants. When he rode far enough ahead, he probably escaped any particular attention.

It seemed absurd to Chloe that as a result of that hurried wedding in the tiny chapel two weeks ago she was now a *duchess* and therefore worthy of all this pomp and excessive security—not to mention the services of a maid. Mavis, Mrs. Loftus's niece, was sitting inside the carriage with her new mistress, her back to the horses, and was looking fair to bursting with pride. Chloe had gone virtually unnoticed and unguarded and unattended on her journey to Manville Court just a few months ago.

Whenever they stopped at an inn for a change of horses, she was bowed and curtsied and flattered into the finest private parlor and plied with all the best refreshments the house had to offer, even though she suffered slightly from motion sickness and was never very hungry. Ralph remained outside in the inn yard each time to oversee the grooming of his horses. Even the fresh, new ones were his, sent ahead from the ducal stables so that the magnificent blacks would not have to be exchanged for inferior horseflesh. Sometimes Chloe wondered if anyone realized that he was the duke who owned the carriage and the horses and employed the servants and was married to the duchess then partaking of refreshments in the best parlor.

He never rode inside the carriage with her, even when it rained for a whole hour. And it was not just Mavis's presence that deterred him, Chloe believed. He never traveled inside any closed conveyance when it could be avoided, he had explained to her back at Manville when she had realized he intended to ride his horse the whole way. She wondered if it had anything to do with the time when he had been wounded and had been transported long distances in the close confines of various coaches. Or if it had something to do with her.

And she wondered if the whole of their married life would mirror the first two weeks. Occasionally they had talked, *really* talked, and she had felt they were drawing closer to each other, perhaps even becoming friends. And there had been that one night . . . But even at the time she had known it was only about sex—*his* word—

and not in any way about love or even affection. Even so, it had been pleasant—strange understatement—and it had seemed to bring them closer until it had been brought to an abrupt end by their quarrel in the middle of the night.

Most of the time he was withdrawn and treated her with a remote though courteous reserve of manner. His eyes were empty of any depth. He was, in fact, as he had been from the beginning of her acquaintance with him. Despite their marriage and the necessary intimacies of the marriage bed, despite the occasional conversation, the occasional kiss, the half a night of sex—to use his word again—nothing was different. And how could she complain? Their marriage was progressing much as they had agreed it would.

She could not even be angry with him any longer for the fact that they were on the way to London. He *had* said they would live quietly in the country after their marriage, but he could not have foreseen the change in their circumstances coming quite as soon as it had. And he was right about duty—both his and hers. Duty summoned them to London, where he must make appearances at court and in Parliament and where both of them must mingle socially with their peers.

And so here she was on the road to town in opulent splendor, with homage being paid to her as though she were someone of great importance, which, she gathered, she was. Would she ever grow accustomed to it all? She might have found some humor in the situation if she had not been so consumed with dread at the prospect of facing the beau monde yet again.

But face it she must. And face it she *would*.

And then at last through the window on one side of the carriage she could see water in the distance, a large body of it. The River Thames.

"We are close to London," she observed to Mavis, who pressed her face close to the window and looked eagerly for her first glimpse of a tower or church spire.

Chloe thought back to her own excitement as she approached London for the first time six years ago. Her long-ago self would not have been at all surprised to discover that the streets really were paved with gold.

His life had changed far more drastically than he had realized during the past two weeks, Ralph soon came to understand—and it was not just his marriage and his acquisition of the title and all the duties and responsibilities it had brought with it. It was . . .

Well, yes, actually it was just those things.

Getting himself from Manville Court to London was no longer a simple matter of mounting his horse or climbing up to the seat of his curricle and conveying himself along the king's highway at whatever pace he chose. Now there was a duchess to convey there with him, and somehow the duchess was a larger entity than just Chloe. She was a grand, precious, fragile commodity and had to be borne from one place to another in pomp and luxury and safety. Or so the servants decreed, and servants, Ralph was also discovering, could be quite tyrannical when it came to doing what they perceived to be their duty to ducal employers, for their own sense of consequence was at stake.

How Chloe enjoyed the very public procession through the countryside he did not ask. Though he almost did when it rained and he was half tempted to join her in the carriage. He was feeling amused despite the discomfort of the rain, and amusement was something that had been so rare with him for a long time that he had felt the urge to share it. He imagined them enjoying a good laugh together inside the carriage over the spectacle they were presenting as they moved across the countryside with minimum speed and maximum visibility.

He did *not* join her, however. He remembered just in time that whenever they had drawn closer to each other in the past two weeks than they had agreed upon, he had ended up feeling an inexplicable sort of panic and had taken a hasty step back. It would be best not to share his amusement with her. Besides, she had her new maid with her.

The rain soon blew over anyway, and he was glad he had remained out in the fresh air.

The fact that his life had changed almost beyond recognition was even more apparent after he had ridden into Portman Square and the ducal carriage and all its outriders as well as the laden baggage coach had come clattering and rumbling in behind him. Ralph would have been willing to wager a significant sum that windows about the square were suddenly bristling with spectators gathered to watch the show. He did not look to see if he was right.

Stockwood House had been basically his for a number of years now. He had come and gone as he pleased, always well served by the staff, but never obtrusively. Now the double doors were thrown back—both of them—and the butler stood in the doorway, stiff and stately in what was surely a new uniform. And behind him, if Ralph was not very much mistaken, the whole of the staff was lined up in formal rows. It was going to be his wedding day all over again, he thought, wincing inwardly.

He was not usually particularly observant when it came to servants, but he would have had to be blind not to see that every member of staff was also clad in a new uniform and that the hallway in which they were being paraded was positively gleaming with polish. If there was one speck of dust in the whole sizable entry hall, Ralph would be surprised.

He heard so many mutterings of "Your Grace" over the next few minutes that his head fairly buzzed. He could only imagine how Chloe must be feeling as he took her hand upon his sleeve and led her up the steps and through the doors. If she did not flee back to Manville without stopping to remove her bonnet, he would be a fortunate man.

But she surprised him. Instead of simply nodding graciously to left and right and continuing on her way up to the relative privacy of the drawing room or even all the way up to her own apartments, she stopped and smiled and spent well over half an hour working her way along the lines. She carefully spoke to everyone, moving from one side to the other, repeating the names the housekeeper murmured to her and occasionally asking a question of a servant—and stopping long enough to listen to the answer.

"Thank you, Mrs. Perkins," she said when they had come to the end of the line. "Would you have a tea tray sent up to the drawing room immediately, if you please?

And perhaps you and I could meet in the morning and become better acquainted. I will wish to go down to the kitchen too to speak further with Mrs. Mitchell. How splendid everyone is looking. And every*where* too."

Mrs. Mitchell, Ralph seemed to recall, was the cook.

"The house has always run perfectly smoothly without any effort on my part," he told Chloe when they were alone in the drawing room a few minutes later and she was removing her bonnet and fluffing up her short curls with both hands. "You must not feel obliged to exert yourself to any great degree."

She smiled at him, and there was something almost impish in her expression.

"Your grandparents have not been here for a number of years, have they?" she said. "And your mother has her own London home. There has been just you, then. Stockwood House has been a bachelor establishment. I daresay the staff has enjoyed fussing over you as though you were a child incapable of looking after himself. They would look less indulgently upon your wife, however, I do assure you, if it seemed that she was incapable of looking after *her*self and—more importantly—*you*."

Good God—*as though you were a child incapable of looking after himself.* There could not possibly be any truth in her words, could there? He clasped his hands behind his back and frowned.

She brushed her hands over the creases in her traveling dress.

"*This* is what I wanted, Ralph," she said. "Oh, not on quite as grand a scale, perhaps, and certainly not in London. But those are relatively minor concerns. I wanted a home of my own and a husband. I wanted to be able to run the one and care for the other. I will not be unhappy while I am at home here."

"Only when you have to move beyond its doors?" he asked her.

Her smile became more rueful.

"I have had the chance to listen to only one of Graham's sermons at church," she said. "But I will always remember it. He said that if we can only face our worst fears and move forward into them and through them instead of cowering or turning tail and running as far from them as we can, then we will never have to fear anything ever again. It seems an overly simplistic idea, it is true. What if we face up to a charging bull instead of running for safety as we ought? We would never have a *chance* to fear anything again. But I am sure he went on to explain the sort of thing he meant, and I understood without even having to be told. I have always been inspired by his words and thought it must be wonderful to be able to act upon them."

"Your worst fear is facing the beau monde again, I suppose," he said.

"Yes," she agreed, "it is, foolish as that may seem to you. By Graham's standard, I have already been a failure two separate times."

"Most of us have been," he told her, "at least two separate times."

She tipped her head to one side and regarded him in silence.

"It will be different for you this time," he said. "You will have me by your side, and you will find the courage to make a stand."

"And you will have me by yours," she said, sending

inexplicable shivers along his spine with her words. "And *you* will have courage."

A footman carried in the tea tray at that moment, and a maid followed behind him with a cake. In former times the manservant would have poured his tea, and the maid would have cut the cake and set a slice on a plate for him. Today, however, Chloe dismissed them with a smile and a word of thanks and performed those offices herself.

There was something undeniably disturbing about the changes in his life, Ralph thought. There was a very definite loss of independence, of privacy. He could ignore servants, though never with unkindness, he hoped. He could not ignore his wife. And this was what she had wanted, what she had made her bargain for—a home and a husband. Him, in other words. She intended to *care* for him.

And beyond the home, he could no longer go wherever he wanted whenever he wanted, with no one to please but himself. For one thing, he was no longer just the Earl of Berwick with his relatively meaningless courtesy title. He was an altogether grander being from whom much was expected. And for another, he was a married man with a wife's feelings and well-being to consider. And this particular wife had been brought to town against her will and dreaded having to set foot beyond their door. He could not simply abandon her.

It was one thing to accept responsibility for a role, an inanimate thing, a dukedom. It was quite another to feel responsible for another person—his wife, who was nervous and unhappy about what was facing her. It felt suspiciously like taking on an emotional bond, and he did not like it one little bit. Not liking it, however, would not make it go away.

"A little milk and one sugar," she said, setting his cup and saucer down at his elbow.

Exactly right. He was almost irritated by the fact. He did not have any idea how she liked her tea even though he had watched her pour it and drink it numerous times.

He had the uncomfortable feeling that Chloe really was going to make him comfortable.

"It will not be long before it is widely known that we are in town," he said as she seated herself and picked up her cup and saucer. "Invitations will start arriving in droves. People will be curious to see me in my new role and you in yours. And us as a married couple. We will need to decide which invitations to accept."

He expected her to make some sort of protest or at least to beg for time.

"Yes," she said.

"And we must start thinking about the grand reception or ball we will have here," he said. "It will be expected of us."

"Yes," she said again.

"Lloyd will help," he said. "And my mother."

She set her cup down in her saucer. "Help us, yes," she said. "But we will *do* the main work, Ralph."

Face your worst fears and walk into them and through them, she remembered Graham saying in one of his sermons. She had run from her fears twice, she had just told him. He could see that she was not going to do that again.

"Yes," he said, "we will do it."

Slowly, inexorably, he realized, he was being drawn back into life. So was she.

*   *   *

If Chloe had hoped to bury herself in domestic contentment at Stockwood House, she was soon to be disillu-
sioned. Not that she really had expected any such thing,
of course. She spent a busy, thoroughly happy morning
discussing household matters and menus with the housekeeper and the cook. The morning also brought a note
from her sister-in-law Sarah, who had persuaded Mr.
Toucher to spend a few weeks in town before returning
home, offering to take Chloe up in her carriage at four
o'clock on her way to visit her grandmother and great-
aunt. Chloe sent a note of acceptance, since Ralph had
gone out halfway through the morning and had not said
when he would return. But even before four o' clock the
quietness of the afternoon was dashed a number of times
by the sound of the door knocker and the arrival of visitors.

The Dowager Countess of Berwick, her mother-in-
law, came with Nora, Lady Keilly, to inform her that they
would take her with them the following afternoon to call
upon a number of ladies with whom it was imperative
she be on the best of terms. Those ladies were all, Chloe
guessed, the very highest sticklers.

Her father came with Lucy just after the two ladies
had left. Lucy suggested that Chloe join her for a walk in
Hyde Park the morning after next with the children and
their nurse — weather permitting, of course.

"The park is never as crowded in the morning as it is
during the fashionable hour of the afternoon," she said,
"but one sees a tolerable number of fashionable people
anyway, and some of them, both ladies and gentlemen,
are obliging enough to stop to converse. More people

will stop if *you* are with me, Chloe, for your name is on everyone's lips. How gratified you must be."

It was the last thing Chloe needed to hear, but it was inevitable, she knew. And there was no point in cowering at home. She had come to London because she had decided *not* to cower.

"I'll be delighted, Lucy," she said, and was warmed by her sister's bright and happy smile.

Lady Trentham called while Papa and Lucy were still with Chloe, bringing her young sister-in-law, Miss Emes, with her. She had come to ask if she might have the pleasure of introducing Chloe to a few of her lady relatives and friends one afternoon.

"They are curious about you and eager to meet you," she explained before laughing. "Oh, do not look so stricken, Chloe. They are very willing to like you and would be willing, I am sure, even if they did not know that you are my friend and married to one of Hugo's friends. Not *everyone* is swayed by all the wild and vicious gossip from last year."

"Thank you," Chloe said.

"That is very kind of you, Lady Trentham," her father added.

"You certainly will not need to run away this year, will you, Your Grace?" Miss Emes said. "You are the Duchess of Worthingham. And Gwen and Hugo's friend."

"Oh, I will not run," Chloe assured her.

And then, just before four, when Chloe had already donned her bonnet and gloves in anticipation of Sarah's arrival, Lady Easterly, Aunt Julia, arrived to offer to take Chloe shopping in the morning.

"For I daresay you will need some new and fashionable clothes, Chloe," she said. "I do not believe they will need to be black. What does Worthingham say? He will wish to wear a black armband for a while, I daresay, but he will probably not demand that you remain in mourning."

"My mama-in-law believes I may wear colors, provided they are not too flamboyant," Chloe told her. "And yes, I will need clothes, Aunt Julia. Plenty of them, I believe."

"I do not think we would persuade you into anything flamboyant even for a masquerade," her aunt said. "I am so glad you have come to London, Chloe. You ought not to have left in such haste last year. Gossip inevitably dies down when there is nothing to feed it. Had you carried on with the activities we had planned without showing any concern for the foolish things that were being hinted at, everyone would soon have lost interest. Well, now you are a duchess, and you have Worthingham to protect your name. I would not envy anyone who chose to cross him. He looks like a very formidable gentleman. There is something about his eyes. Or perhaps it is his facial scar."

"I will not run again," Chloe assured her. "And it is not just because I have Ralph to protect me, Aunt Julia. I am a lady, and I belong here."

Her aunt laughed and hugged her.

Sarah arrived on time to take Chloe to tea with Great-Aunt Mary and Ralph's grandmother. It was lovely to see the dowager duchess again, to hug her, to know that in a sense the old lady was now *her* grandmother too. And it was amusing to listen to Great-Aunt Mary's conversation. Both the older ladies were happy that Ralph and Chloe had come to London. Both were happy to see that neither she nor Sarah was wearing black.

"If we were all to wear black for a prolonged period for every relative who passes," Great-Aunt Mary said, "there would be no one left to wear colors."

"You must wear emerald green to the ball at Stockwood House," the dowager duchess said. "There will *be* one, Chloe?"

"There will," Chloe told her. "And I will wear emerald green, Grandmama."

Chloe arrived home just minutes before Ralph. They went upstairs together to change for dinner, and she was able to assure him that his grandmother was in tolerably good spirits though she still looked a bit lost. And *he* was able to inform *her* that their first appearance before the *ton* together as husband and wife would be that very evening. The Duke of Stanbrook had invited them to join him and a few other guests in his box at the theater.

Chloe had been rather pleased with her day and was looking forward to her dinner. But suddenly her appetite was gone despite all her words of bravado to several people.

"It will be a way," Ralph was explaining, "of being seen by the *ton* without having to mingle a great deal with its members, Chloe. And it is not as though you have never done it before, is it?"

"You could not have waited to tell me," she asked him, "until *after* dinner?"

He stopped outside her dressing room and raised her hand to his lips before opening the door for her and proceeding on his way to his own room.

"Just remember, Chloe," he said, "that you are *the Duchess of Worthingham.*"

"*That,*" she said, "is supposed to give me my appetite back?"

There was a suggestion of a smile about his lips as he turned away.

16

"*Who* are the Duke of Stanbrook's other guests?" Chloe asked as she sat beside Ralph in the carriage later, telling herself how silly it was to be nervous, as though she were about to be exposed to society for the first time. The very fact that it was *not* the first time was a large part of the problem, of course.

"Lady Trentham and Hugo," he told her. "The Earl and Countess of Kilbourne, Lady Trentham's brother and sister-in-law. And the Dowager Viscountess Lyngate, a widow of George's acquaintance. I have not met the lady, but George tells me she was born and raised in Greece, came to England when her father was an ambassador here, and stayed to marry an Englishman. I have met Kilbourne and his wife a time or two and have always found them amiable. They were married in the Peninsula and ambushed by the French the very next day. He was badly wounded and brought home, and she was assumed dead. A long time later he was about to marry someone else when his long-lost wife suddenly appeared to stop the wedding. And I do mean *wedding*. They were in the church with half the *ton* in attendance."

"Really?" she said. "She arrived only just in the nick of time? But how wonderfully romantic."

"Provided," he said, "he had not forgotten her and was not hopelessly in love with the other lady."

"Oh. *Had* he? And *was* he?" She turned her head to look at him, though she could not see his face clearly in the darkness.

"Apparently not, on both counts," he said.

"Then it *was* romantic," she said. "But was the other lady in love with *him*? Was she left brokenhearted?"

He clucked his tongue. "There is no satisfying hopelessly romantic sensibilities, is there?"

"But *was* she?" she asked again.

"I have never asked her, Chloe," he said. "It would seem presumptuous since she is virtually a stranger. Perhaps you might ask Kilbourne or his wife. But the lady concerned is now the Viscountess Ravensberg and does not look like a mere shadow of her former self. Not that I knew her former self, it is true."

She stared at his darkened profile and realized he was talking more and in a lighter vein than usual as a deliberate ruse to distract her. And he had succeeded.

"Ralph," she said, "never try your hand at writing a love story. You would leave your female audience howling with frustration and fury. A good love story needs a good ending, not just a well-they-look-happy-enough sort of ending."

"There go my aspirations to compete in the literary world with your brother-in-law," he said.

She stared at his profile in silence. Was this *Ralph*? She could not see his facial expression, but she would swear there was a smile in his voice.

"You would be doomed to disappointment if you tried," she said. "*No one* can outdo Lucy's Freddie."

The carriage slowed and she could see that they had arrived at the theater. The light from a number of torches revealed an area crowded with carriages and people on foot. Chloe had always enjoyed going to the theater. She was determined to enjoy it this evening too. No one, surely, had ever been driven from town *three* times.

The Duke of Stanbrook was an attentive host with flawless manners. He was outside the theater awaiting their arrival. He opened the carriage door and set down the steps himself instead of waiting for the coachman to descend from the box. He handed Chloe down and introduced both her and Ralph to the Dowager Viscountess Lyngate, a handsome older lady. The duke offered his arm to Chloe and escorted her upstairs to his box, talking to her the whole way while Ralph came behind with Lady Lyngate. Both the foyer and the stairs were crowded with people, to several of whom the duke nodded graciously without stopping.

It was all very smoothly and very deliberately done for her comfort, Chloe thought. Though really she was not feeling *very* uncomfortable. The *ton* would not frighten her away this year. And its members would not openly snub the Duchess of Worthingham, she kept reminding herself.

The other four guests were already in the Duke of Stanbrook's box, and Lord Trentham stepped forward, hand outstretched, as soon as they appeared in the doorway. His large frame almost completely hid the tiered galleries beyond the box and the people who filled them.

Chloe did not feel as much on display as she had expected. Again she felt that it had been a deliberate move on Lord Trentham's part to lessen her ordeal. Ralph's friends were very kind even if unnecessarily protective. Her fleeing last year had clearly given the impression that she was a fragile weakling.

Gwen greeted her with a warm hug after her husband had wrung her hand and turned to clap Ralph on the shoulder.

"I did not realize when I called on you this afternoon," Gwen said, "that I would be seeing you again this evening and that I would have the chance to introduce you to my other sister-in-law."

Chloe looked at the other couple with interest and curiosity as Gwen introduced them. The Earl of Kilbourne was a blond and handsome man, though coincidentally his face too was scarred, presumably from an old battle wound. His countess was small and pretty, with a face that looked as if it habitually smiled. Chloe decided almost immediately that they were a happy couple, though she had no acquaintance with them upon which to base her opinion. Perhaps it was just the romantic in her that wanted it to be true. But she *did* wonder about poor Viscountess Ravensberg, the lady Lord Kilbourne had been forced to abandon at the altar. She hoped there had been enough happy endings to go around.

Her eyes met Ralph's, and she was given the distinct impression that he could read her thoughts. There was surely a smile lurking in his eyes and at the corners of his lips, even if it *was* just a mocking smile.

The Duke of Stanbrook directed Chloe to a plushly

cushioned chair next to the balcony rail, and she took her seat—and felt suddenly as though she were in a fish bowl with a large crowd of spectators staring in at her. For the moment she found it impossible to look out, but with her peripheral vision she was aware of the lavishly draped tiers of boxes and galleries, of the myriad colors of silk and satin gowns, of waving fans and jewels glittering in the light of the chandeliers. And she knew without looking that the floor below would be crowded, mostly with men, most of them young and fashionable gentlemen, gossiping among themselves and perusing the occupants of the boxes above them through their quizzing glasses. Ogling the ladies. She remembered them well from six years ago. She remembered the mingled pleasure and indignation of being ogled herself.

Ralph was seated beside her, close enough that she could feel the reassurance of his body heat. She turned her head to smile at him. Soon she was going to have to find the courage to look beyond the box. How would she be able to watch the play otherwise?

"Attending the theater was my very favorite activity when I came to London for the first time," she told him.

"Not the balls?" he asked her. "Or the soirees and Venetian breakfasts? Or the picnics and evenings at Vauxhall Gardens? Or the masquerades and—"

She laughed and opened her fan. "Oh, all of it," she said. "I loved it all. I had waited twenty-one years, the last few of them in conscious, impatient anticipation, for my moment to come. And it all far exceeded my expectations and was wonderful beyond words."

"But the theater was especially wonderful."

She laughed again. "*Everything* was especially wonderful. Those were the days of my innocence, and may no one scoff at innocence."

She closed her fan without having used it and rested it on her lap.

"Do you realize," the Countess of Kilbourne said, turning her head to address Chloe and Ralph and Gwen and Lord Trentham beyond them, "that we enjoy double the value of the admission price whenever we come to the theater in that we get to view both the play and the rest of the audience? I sometimes think the audience provides more entertainment than the play."

"It certainly provides most of the food for drawing room conversations the day after," Gwen agreed. "One does not hear many people discussing the play itself, but the people who attended the play are a different matter."

"But without the play, Gwen," Lord Kilbourne said, "the *ton* would have to find another excuse to gather merely for the pleasure of observing one another and garnering fresh topics for gossip and speculation."

"Ah, but there is also the daily promenade in Hyde Park," Lady Lyngate said. "One could hardly say that the beau monde goes there for the mere benefit of riding or walking and taking the air."

"I see I have invited a party of cynics to share my box," the Duke of Stanbrook observed.

"*I* have come to watch the play even if no one else has, George," Lord Trentham assured him. "I never thought Shakespeare was worth all the fuss people— mostly teachers—make over him, until I saw one of his plays performed a few years ago. Not that I have ever warmed to the tragedies. There is too much gloom in the world as it is without having to watch actors deliver themselves of impassioned laments before stabbing themselves to the heart with their wooden daggers."

"Cynics *and* a philistine," the duke said with a sigh.

"When I attended my first play during my come-out Season six years ago," Chloe said, "I thought I had died and gone to heaven, though I was far too sophisticated at the time to say so aloud. I probably maintained an expression of bored ennui. And it was a comedy, Lord Trentham. I agree with you on that."

"It is marvelous, is it not," the Earl of Kilbourne said, "how one so often loses sophistication as one grows older? Just as one loses the conviction that one knows everything."

Chloe laughed and fanned her cheeks—and finally summoned up enough courage to turn her head to look out over the theater. The sight that met her eyes fairly took her breath away, as it always did. There was surely not an empty seat left in the whole of the theater— though even as she thought it she spotted one empty box across from their own though slightly farther back from the stage. At first it seemed that every single person in attendance was looking in the direction of their box and specifically at *her*. It was not so, of course. A more direct look on her part revealed that in fact everyone was scrutinizing everyone else. She remembered that the *ton* was particularly good at that. Some people were indeed looking toward their box. Many more, though, were not.

It was a reassuring observation, and Chloe felt herself begin to relax. She looked downward and immediately, by some unfortunate chance, saw a familiar and unwelcome figure. Baron Cornell, as handsome and elegant as ever, quizzing glass raised to his eye, lips pursed, was watching a young lady in one of the lower boxes whose bosom was fairly spilling out of her low-cut bodice. And *she* was watching *him*.

Chloe waited for the pang of hurt and humiliation that thoughts of Lord Cornell usually aroused in her even though she had known for a long time that he had never been worthy of her affections. But she felt . . . nothing.

She raised her eyes and looked along the galleries opposite, one tier at a time, to see how many people she recognized. There were a few. Two or three of them acknowledged her glance with an inclination of the head or a raised hand. No one glared or looked affronted. And then, just as she was about to turn her head away to ask Ralph if it was almost time for the play to begin, she saw movement in the box opposite—the one that had been empty until now. Two couples stepped inside, an older and a younger, and then a third couple a little way behind them.

There was a swell of sound from the audience, but Chloe did not even notice it. Her attention was riveted upon the third lady, who was dressed all in dazzling white and who even to Chloe's own eyes looked like a younger version of herself, complete with a head of piled bright red hair.

Chloe turned her head sharply toward Ralph. She smiled brightly and asked if it was almost time for the play to begin.

"Past time, I would think," he said curtly. He was looking pale and tense and grim. His eyes were fixed on the empty stage.

And then a buzz of shushing noises from a few members of the audience quelled the swell of conversation. The play—one of Shakespeare's comedies, *As You Like It*—was about to begin at last.

Was the older gentleman in the other box the Marquess of Hitching? But Chloe dared not look in that direction again. She would not recognize him anyway. But she felt no doubt whatsoever that the red-haired lady was Lady Angela Allandale.

It was not difficult to predict what the chief topic of conversation in the drawing rooms of polite society would be tomorrow.

The play was beginning, and Chloe set herself the difficult task of concentrating upon the action and enjoying herself. She was not the only one not succeeding, though, she realized after several minutes had passed. Although she did not turn her face away from the stage for a while, she could almost *feel* the silence of Ralph beside her. Well, of course he was silent. The whole audience was. But he was . . . silent.

Finally she turned her head to look at him. He was gazing at the stage, apparently intent upon what was happening there. But he felt her eyes on him and transferred his gaze to her face. Even in the near darkness she could see that his eyes were blank. He did not smile at her. She set the fingertips of one hand lightly upon his sleeve and leaned a little closer.

"Forget Lady Angela's presence," she murmured. "I am not upset about it."

He frowned at her. "She is *here*?"

She stared back at him. He had not noticed? He must be the only person in the theater who had not.

"What is the matter, then?" she asked him.

"Nothing," he said. "Watch the play. It is why we are here."

Lord Trentham was looking at them with some concern. Chloe smiled apologetically at him and turned her attention back to the stage. Or, rather, she turned her eyes toward it. Her mind did not follow suit. She had kept her hand on Ralph's sleeve. Beneath it his muscles were tense.

But he had not noticed the arrival of Lady Angela Allandale.

He was courteous, even charming, during the interval, when several people came to their box to commiserate with his loss and to congratulate him on both his new title and his marriage. He presented Chloe to those who were unknown to her, setting a hand that felt both warm and protective against the small of her back. She met, among others, Gwen's cousin, the Marquess of Attingsborough, and his wife, and Lady Lyngate's nephew, the Earl of Ainsley, and his countess.

No one mentioned Lady Angela, and Chloe did not look again in the direction of that particular box. It was impossible to know if the lady had seen *her*, though how could she not have done? What rotten bad luck it was that she was back in London this year. They were going to be dodging each other for the rest of the Season, yet it was inevitable that they would be invited to many of the same events.

As would the Marquess of Hitching.

By the time the play was over an hour or so later and all the thanks and good-night greetings had been said and Chloe and Ralph were on their way home in the carriage, she felt exhausted.

"It was a pleasant evening," she said.

"It was," Ralph agreed.

Gone, it seemed, was the light, almost teasing conversation in which he had engaged her earlier to relax her before they arrived at the theater. His curt response merely deepened the chill inside the carriage. Chloe listened to the rumble of the wheels, the rhythmic clopping of the horses' hooves. She watched as the interior of the coach was illuminated occasionally by the flare of torches in the streets outside.

"What is the matter?" she asked after a few minutes. "What happened?"

It was *not* the fact that Lady Angela Allandale had been at the theater.

"Why do you ask again?" His voice was cold and irritable. "I have already told you that nothing is the matter. If I am not forever smiling inanely and laughing mindlessly and chattering aimlessly, must something be the matter? That is not the way I am, Chloe. You must not expect it of me."

He was being grossly unfair. When had she ever suggested that she expected smiles and laughter and chatter from him? What had she done to incur this irritation?

"Oh, I do not expect any such thing," she said, her tone as careless as she could make it. "You made it very clear from the start that there would be no emotional bond between us, no friendship, no warmth, no confidences, no real communication. It was foolish of me to imagine that something had upset you merely because you were unnaturally quiet at the theater."

"One is not expected to chatter and disturb other audience members when a play is in progress," he told her as though she could not have guessed as much herself. "It is considered bad manners."

"I suppose," she said, "you refer to the whispered exchange that I initiated and to the fact that it disturbed Lord Trentham."

"If the glove fits, Chloe," he said, "then I would invite you to wear it."

"Is it ill-mannered, then," she asked him, "is it idle *chatter* to show concern for one's husband and question him when one can sense that he is upset?"

"When I am *upset*," he told her, "I shall burst into tears, and you may exercise all your tender sensibilities in devising a way to comfort me. When I am merely trying to enjoy a play, I would prefer not to have my concentration broken by an overimaginative female begging to know what is the matter with me."

Chloe stared at the dark outline of his profile for a few moments, her mouth open. He *should* have been joking. He should have turned to her, some sort of twinkle in his eye even if the darkness made it difficult to see.

He was not joking.

. . . an overimaginative female . . .

Not even an overimaginative *wife*.

She closed her mouth with a clicking of teeth and directed her attention to the darkness beyond the window on her side of the carriage.

"I am sorry I expressed concern," she said. "It was foolish of me. It will not happen again."

She half expected him to break the silence, to offer some sort of apology for his churlishness, or to show some sort of concern for the dismay and embarrassment she must have felt when she realized Lady Angela was also at the theater. But they rode the rest of the way in loud, injured silence. He did not break it and she would not. She would not break it ever again—not until *he* spoke to her first, anyway.

He handed her down from the carriage when they arrived home and offered his arm to escort her into the house. She took it simply because it would have been childish to refuse. Besides, the butler would have noticed and chances were the whole staff would know before morning that the duke and duchess had had a falling out.

She permitted herself to speak inside the hall since it was the butler who spoke to her. No, she told him, she did not wish for any refreshments. She was tired and intended to retire without further ado.

Fifteen or twenty minutes later, ignoring the fact that she was thirsty and a little hungry, she dismissed Mavis, climbed into bed, and burrowed beneath the covers, head and all. He was cold and unfeeling and unreasonable and bad-tempered, she decided, and a lot of other nasty things along the same lines. He was . . . no different from what he had said he would be. He had not promised any warmth, any intimacy, any real companionship in their marriage. In fact, he had promised the absence of those very things. And she had agreed quite readily. Indeed, she was the one who had first suggested their bloodless, emotionless bargain. There was no point whatsoever in being upset with him now because he had not wanted to share with her whatever it was that had disturbed him this evening—or because he had shown no concern for *her* upset feelings about being exposed to the one woman with whom she dreaded coming face to face.

There was no point in punishing him—and herself—
by never speaking to him again.

What if he did not come tonight? She felt a bit sick at
the thought—and then a bit sicker at the realization of
how much she had come to depend upon his nightly
lovemaking and presence in her bed all night. It was all
just a physical thing, of course. It was just *sex,* to use his
own stark, emotionless word. It was not *his* fault that it
had become a little bit emotional too for her.

But whatever had happened at the theater to make
him look so cold and remote and . . . empty? To make his
muscles tense and unyielding? *Something* had happened,
but she had promised not to ask again.

Well, she would not either. She would live her own
life and let him live his. Just as they had agreed to do.

He might go to hell as far as she was concerned, she
thought with shocking irreverence.

Something had happened to *her,* when Lady Angela
Allandale arrived. The whole audience at the theater
had reacted, but he had not even noticed or shown any
interest when she had told him. She might be suffering
dreadfully for all he cared.

She swallowed several times and willed herself not to
dissolve into self-pitying tears.

17

Ralph was lying on his wife's bed, one arm draped over his eyes, one leg bent at the knee, his foot flat on the mattress. He lay still and breathed deeply, hoping he would slip back into sleep, knowing he would not.

He had come here to apologize—for two separate wrongs he had done her. He had not noticed that Lady Angela Allandale was at the theater. He had not even been looking for her or Hitching. He had made some tentative inquiries during the day, but no one had seen either of them in town this year. They must have arrived within the last day or two—as had he and Chloe. He had not noticed when the woman had arrived at the theater tonight, and he had not noticed that Chloe was upset about it. And surely there had been some reaction from the audience at seeing Chloe and Lady Angela, in the same place. He had not noticed, and—worse—he had not shown any concern for his wife even when she had told him. He had been too wrapped up in himself.

She, on the contrary, had noticed *his* distress. She had asked about it and shown concern for him, both at the theater and in the carriage. And he had thanked her by biting off her head. He had offended her and hurt her. He had shut her out. But, damn it all, he wanted, he *needed* to be left alone. Marriage was a damnable institution.

He owed her a double apology and had come to make it.

She had been in bed when he arrived, however, facing away from him, all but the top of her head beneath the covers. It had been impossible to tell if she was awake or asleep. He had not wanted to wake her if she *was* sleeping. So, with a marvelous lack of logic, he had extinguished the candles, moved quietly around the bed, lain down beside her, and proceeded to have sex with her. He had even fallen asleep afterward.

Now he was wide-awake again, dealing with the dreaded sensation of having hit bottom with no further down to go. He had thought himself over such intensity of feeling. He had fought for years to level off his emotions, to avoid extremes. He had almost forgotten—until now—the needle-sharp regret he had felt at first that he was not dead, killed in battle, blown to bits with his friends, as he would have been if he had been in the front line of the cavalry charge with them. Instead, unusually, he had been in the second line and so had had a front-row view as they had disintegrated before his eyes in showers of red, just like the most spectacular of fireworks displays at Vauxhall.

He swallowed and kept his eyes closed and then clenched them even tighter in an attempt to blot out the visual memory. If only he had been killed then. If only he had been able to get at that medication here in this very house soon after he had been brought home. If only . . .

He had almost forgotten what this felt like. He had almost forgotten how to control his breathing when he *did* feel it, how to turn his thoughts from the blessed lure of death to the weary business of living on. He had almost forgotten how to claw his way out and up.

He had to think of life as a gift, however unwanted. Yes, that was it. For whatever reason, his life had been spared that day and restored to him over the months and years following it. There must be a reason. If, that was— and it was a very large *if*—one believed in some sort of divine plan.

He thought back unwillingly on the events of the evening.

The visit to the theater had been George's idea, though it had seemed a brilliant one. Chloe had not wanted to come to town. After her experiences last year and six years ago, she was skittish about mingling with the *ton* again. She would do it, of course. She had shown remarkable courage in the last few days. But here was a chance to ease her in gently, to allow her and the *ton* to see each other, but at arm's length, so to speak. And the guests George had suggested asking to join them seemed perfect for the occasion. Chloe already knew and liked Hugo and Lady Trentham, and Kilbourne was the latter's brother. His countess had always seemed like an amiable lady. George had described Lady Lyngate as reserved but charming.

It had promised to be a pleasant evening. Ralph had made a special effort during the carriage ride to the theater to help Chloe relax and had found himself relaxing too. He had been starting to feel more comfortable in his marriage than he had expected.

He had looked around the theater before the play began and acknowledged a few familiar figures with a nod. There was scarcely an empty seat apart from one box across and a little down from theirs. Shakespeare's comedies were always popular. Chloe was looking around too, he had noticed, after an initial tendency to restrict her attention to the occupants of their box as if she was afraid that everyone was looking at her—as everyone no doubt was for a while.

He had been about to transfer his attention to the stage, where the action must surely be about to begin, when his eyes alit upon one particular box opposite and one tier up from theirs and upon one of the two couples who occupied it.

His heart had turned over. Or stopped.

He had looked hastily away but had the feeling that the lady had turned her eyes upon him just as he turned his own away. He had not glanced that way again for the rest of the evening, and he had not suggested leaving the box during the interval, a decision made easier by the fact that a number of people called there, most of them with the purpose of shaking Ralph by the hand and meeting his duchess.

He was not certain he had been seen. Perhaps he had not. The theater was crowded, after all, and he had been half hidden behind Chloe. Or, even if he had been seen, he might not have been recognized. He had changed in eight years.

Nevertheless . . .

How long did they intend to remain in London? Were they here on a brief visit, or had they come for the whole Season? Could he avoid them that long?

There was no chance of getting back to sleep. Ralph pushed back the bedcovers on his side of the bed at last, got up as quietly as he could so as not to wake Chloe, whose soft breathing told him she was asleep, and looked down at his dressing gown. He should go to his own room, get dressed, go down to the library. Pour himself a drink. See if he could lose himself in a book. Or in a bottle, though drunkenness was a form of forgetting in which he had never indulged. But somehow, alarmingly, he could not bear the thought of being quite alone. The sound of Chloe's breathing was like a dose of some mild drug, just barely holding him back from the brink of a deep darkness that threatened to swallow him.

He left his dressing gown where it was and went to stand, naked, at the window, the curtains slightly parted. The square outside was in darkness. The night watchman must be elsewhere on his rounds. It was too early for any tradesmen. The room behind him was dark. No one would be able to see him standing here even if anyone were to look up. He braced his hands on the sill, bent his head, and closed his eyes.

It might have been ten minutes or half an hour later when he felt a slight warmth along his right side. She did not say a word. And she did not touch him with her hands. A blanket or a shawl came about his shoulders, making him instantly aware of the chill of the room, and her forehead came to rest against the edge of his shoulder.

God! Oh, God! He clenched his eyes more tightly closed and bent his head lower.

"I beg your pardon, Chloe," he said. "I *am* sorry. Forgive me if you can."

"It was just a silly quarrel," she said without lifting her forehead. "There is nothing to forgive."

"Yes, there is," he said. "You must have needed me, and I was selfishly unaware of your distress. And then I treated you abominably."

"You are forgiven."

The abyss yawned.

"It is beyond your power," he told her. "You cannot forgive me, Chloe. No one can."

Not even God. He had tried that, on the assumption that it was God who had given him the unwanted gift of his life on the battlefield, and that it was up to God to forgive him if he was to find the will to go on. But he was not sure he believed in God—though he was not sure he did *not*. Either way, though, how could a mere concept or spirit or life force or whatever it was God was supposed to be forgive him for doing irreparable harm to *people*? It made no sense. It was too easy. It was not fair to those people. Divine forgiveness could bring him no comfort.

"Ralph," she said, and he could hear the raw pain in her voice, "what *happened*?"

For a long while he said nothing, and she could feel all the tautness of his muscles through the blanket. She could feel the cold too now that she was out of bed. Her nightgown was too thin to warm her. She shivered.

He was not going to answer, and she had risked his renewed irritation by asking the same question yet again. She ought to have turned over in bed and gone back to sleep. Why had she not?

He must have felt her shiver. He opened the blanket and drew her inside it with him. He wrapped it about her, and she warmed her body against his, her head turned against his shoulder, her hands on his upper arms. She was more aware of his nakedness standing like this than she ever was in bed. She loved his body, so beautifully proportioned, so firmly muscled, so masculine. She even loved his scars because they were a part of him, because they had been dearly earned. Her left hand moved in to rest against the hard ridge of the one that circled his right shoulder.

He did not speak for another long while, though some of the rigidity had gone from his muscles. She realized something then—something she would really rather not have known, though it explained why she had left the warmth of the bed to bring him a blanket and to ask again the question he would not answer. She loved him. She scarcely knew him, of course. There were whole facets of his being that he carefully shielded from her knowing. But there were *some* things she knew. There was the intensely passionate, energetic, idealistic, charismatic boy he had been when he was at school with Graham. There was the young man with his broken body and shattered dreams who had been brought back to England from the Peninsula closer to death than to life, wanting death more than he wanted life. And there was the closed, disciplined, sometimes morose, very private man he was now with his empty eyes. Though they were not empty to her. The emptiness was like a curtain he had drawn across his soul to hide his pain from anyone who tried to look in.

It was not a romantic love she felt for him, for there were no illusions. She did not expect moonlight and music and roses. She did not even expect a return of her feelings. There was no euphoria and never would be. She was not *in* love. There were no stars in her eyes.

There was merely an acceptance of who he was, even the vast depths of him she did not know and perhaps never would. She loved the complexity of him, the pain of him, his sense of duty, his innate decency, even his difficult moods. She loved his body, the look and feel of him, the warmth and smell of him. She loved the weight of his body when it was on hers in bed, the hard thrust of his lovemaking, the sudden liquid heat of his seed.

She loved *him*, though she would rather she did not. For she would rather not be burdened with the one-sided failure of the bargain she had suggested and he had accepted. Keeping to the terms of it was going to be harder to do now that she had allowed an emotional bond after all.

On the other hand, she would rather the father of her children be a man she loved than one she did not. Her courses were due in a couple of days. They sometimes came early. Not this time, though. And perhaps—oh, please, please—they would not come on time either but would be late, nine months late. She desperately, desperately wanted to be with child. It was the one thing that would please him and please *her* and bind them into a closer tie.

Not that she would ever want to try to *bind* him.

He spoke at last.

"We very rarely spent school holidays alone," he said. "We spent them together at one another's homes. Their parents became like my parents, or at least like favored uncles and aunts, and mine became like theirs."

He was talking about his three friends. She did not need to ask.

"I did not fully realize at the time," he said, "how idyllic my boyhood was. Though I did know I was privileged, and I thought privilege brought obligation—to think, to form responsible opinions, to act upon my convictions even if doing so meant disappointing or even hurting those who loved me. As with many boys, my ideals were not tempered with realism or open to compromise. Youth can be a dangerous time of life."

Chloe said nothing. He was not seeking either approval or consolation.

"I was a leader," he said. "I do not really understand why, but it was so. Other boys listened to me and followed me, and because I was a boy and had not even entertained the idea that perhaps I might sometimes be wrong, I allowed them to do so, even encouraged it. And sometimes, to my shame, I felt impatience, even scorn, with those few who stood against me."

As with Graham?

"And so they came to war with me, those three boys," he said, "and they died. Ah, you might say that they came of their own free will, that they died for a righteous cause, one in which they believed. You might go on to say that countless thousands died in the course of those wars, including helpless civilians, even innocent women and children who happened to find themselves in the path of war. I cannot burden my conscience with the deaths of all those poor souls, though. And perhaps I would be able to let my friends go too if it were *only* they who had suffered, for, yes, each had a mind of his own and had made his decision to go with me. But each one had a family, people who loved them and lost them and have lived on, people for whom I have been the cause of endless suffering. People who took me into their homes and loved me. People I supposedly loved."

"They have surely forgiven you—if they ever blamed you in the first place," Chloe said. She could understand why he blamed himself. The whole experience had, after all, been unbearably distressing for him. But surely the families of his friends would not blame him. Those three boys had been leaders in their own right, according to Graham. They had not been helpless pawns in a reckless or ruthless game Ralph had been playing. "Have you seen or spoken with any of them since?"

"I saw Max Courtney's young sister a few times after I left Penderris," he said, reaching a hand beyond her shoulder to close the curtains as the flaming torch of the night watchman came bobbing into view in the square below. "And she wrote to me. She saw me as a final link to the brother she had adored and lost. She fancied herself, I believe, in love with me. I did all in my power to avoid her without being openly cruel. I even offered to fetch her a glass of lemonade at one ball but left the house instead and then London itself the next morning. She was the only one I saw, though. Her mother died a couple of years after Max did, and it was her aunt who was bringing her out into society. She—Miss Courtney— wrote to me earlier this spring when I was staying at Vince's home to inform me she was about to marry a clergyman. I let her down. I had a chance to comfort *someone,* for the pain I had caused, but I did not do it."

Miss Courtney, it seemed, had not blamed him for her

brother's death. Had he realized that? But something else occurred to Chloe.

"Was she at the theater tonight?" she asked.

"Miss Courtney?" he said. "No. But Viscount Harding and his wife were. Tom's parents. He was their only son, their only child. They doted on him."

His muscles had tightened again. Chloe set her hands on his shoulders and tipped back her head to look up at him. Her eyes were accustomed to the darkness, and she could see the hard, bleak emptiness of his expression as he gazed back.

"They begged and pleaded with him not to go," he said. "The viscountess, his mother, even wrote to me to beg me to use my influence with him. And I did."

Chloe tipped her head to one side. "And afterward?" she asked him.

He stared back. "There was no afterward."

"You did not hear from them?" she asked. "Or write to them?"

"No."

"Did they see you tonight?"

"Our eyes did not actually meet," he said. "But, yes, I believe they might have seen me."

Without stopping to think what she was doing, Chloe cupped his face between her hands.

"What are you going to do?" she asked him.

"Do?" He frowned. "Nothing. What is there for me to do? If they recognized me, I ruined their evening. I *know* I have ruined their lives. I owe it to them to stay out of their way. If they do not leave London, then I may have to—*we* may have to. That ought to please you."

He curled his fingers around hers and removed her

hands from his face. He held them clasped between their bodies, and the blanket slithered off his shoulders to the floor.

"We will run away?" she asked. "Because you saw the parents of one of your friends and I saw Lady Angela Allandale?"

"Run away." He laughed softly, but there was no amusement in the sound. "Did you not know, Chloe, that that is an impossibility? You ought to know. You have tried it a few times. The trouble with running away is that you must always take yourself with you."

"You must face them, then," she said. "You must call on them. Perhaps, as with Miss Courtney, they will see you as a link with their son and be delighted to see you."

He dropped her hands in order to brush her hair back from her face, to cup her cheeks as she had done his, to tip her face closer to his own.

"No," he said softly.

"You are content, then," she said, "to live out the rest of your life in hell?"

She had not planned those exact words. She heard their echo as though someone else had spoken them. His eyes looked like large pools of darkness.

"Content?" He laughed again. "It is as good a word as any, I suppose. A wife is a troublesome thing to have, Chloe."

"An interfering baggage, do you mean?"

"As I recall saying once before quite recently," he said, "if the glove fits . . ." But he did not speak with irritation this time.

"I cannot help caring just a little bit, you know," she told him. "I care that you are unhappy."

"And you?" He moved his head a little closer. "How could I not have known Lady Angela Allandale was at the theater? You are sure it was she?"

"Yes," she said. "And even if I could not be sure, the reaction of the audience would have told me I had not mistaken."

"And I missed it all," he said, "selfish brute that I am. I am sorry, Chloe."

"It does not matter," she said. "We bear a coincidental likeness to each other. People will soon grow tired of remarking upon it."

"Yes. They will." He closed the distance between their mouths and kissed her.

It was not a sexual kiss. Or, rather, it *was,* but it was more than just that. There was warmth in it and something else. Need, perhaps. Yearning, perhaps. Or perhaps something that went deeper than feelings and therefore deeper than words.

Her arms went about him and his came about her, and the kiss deepened as his tongue sought the inside of her mouth and she felt his hardening erection against her abdomen.

Even when he took her back to bed and stripped off her nightgown and laid her down and came directly on top of her and into her—even then, as he moved in her and she twined her legs about his and moved with him, it was not really a sexual coupling. Or not just, or not primarily. Nor was it only about the begetting of a child.

It was . . .

Ah, no. There were no words.

But he needed her. He did not just *want* her. He needed her. As she needed him. She had been more upset by the events of the evening than she had realized at the time.

And so she opened to him as she had not done before, even during that one night of unbridled passion. She opened everything that was herself and gave. She gave her heart and her love, without speaking a word. And she received too. For when he finally stilled and spilled his seed in her, the warmth and the wonder of it spread to fill her whole being.

Or so it seemed. Neither of them spoke.

But though he disengaged from her and moved off her, he stayed within her arms, his head nestled against her bosom, his legs entwined with hers. And she heard him sigh and felt him relax into sleep.

She nestled her cheek against the top of his head and closed her eyes and felt a strange, seductive happiness.

18

"$\mathscr{A}$unt Julia is coming in the carriage for me at ten," Chloe explained at breakfast when Ralph asked about her plans for the day. "We are going shopping. I need new clothes. I hope you do not mind."

"Of course not," he said. "You have carte blanche."

"Oh." She smiled at him. "You may regret that."

"I think not." He did not actually smile in return, but there was a certain warmth in his eyes. They had woken at the same moment early this morning. He had still been in her arms, his head pillowed on her shoulder. He had sighed with what had sounded like contentment, kissed her breast, and proceeded to make lingering, almost tender love to her.

It had *seemed* like tenderness. It had seemed like lovemaking.

"Perhaps," she said, "I have wildly expensive buying habits. And perhaps I have a quite uncontrollable attraction to the gaming tables. Perhaps I adore glittering objects, especially if they are made of diamonds."

He leaned back in his chair, his coffee cup in one hand, and actually *did* smile.

"And that puts me in mind of all the family jewels locked away at Manville," he said. "They are ancient and priceless, and no modern woman would be caught this side of the grave wearing any of them. I have not bought you anything except your wedding ring, which we really must have made a little smaller for you. I will buy you jewels for our reception and ball."

"Oh," she said, "there is no need."

"On the contrary." He raised his eyebrows. "There is every need. Besides, it will give me pleasure. I hope it will give *you* pleasure to wear them."

Chloe was sure her cheeks were flushing. "It will," she said. "But there is still no *need*."

"I looked in at the study on my way here," he said. "Lloyd was not there yet, but there was a formidable pile of mail on his desk. Mostly invitations, I would imagine. He should be there by now. Shall we go and look? And I asked him yesterday to start compiling one of his famous lists of what must be done in preparation for our ball. It would be strange indeed if the list is not already as long as my arm. Shall we see it?"

It felt lovely, she thought as she took his arm, doing things together, planning together, being part of each other's lives. It was more than she had expected.

There were indeed invitations. Mr. Lloyd had already divided them into three neat piles, one for probables, another for possibles, and a third for improbables. Chloe read every one, as did Ralph, and discovered that the secretary's judgment was nearly faultless. They decided to accept all but one from the first pile, only one from the second, and none from the third.

"And the ball, Lloyd?" Ralph asked.

Mr. Lloyd produced two lists. One was for all the preparations he could think of. Chloe looked it over and added a few more points. The second list, a very long one, was of prospective guests. It was divided into the same three categories as the invitations: probable, possible, improbable.

One set of names on the improbable list caught Chloe's attention.

"The Marquess and Marchioness of Hitching and family?" She looked inquiringly at Mr. Lloyd.

He looked downward in apparent confusion. "I thought it possible, Your Grace—" he said. "That is—"

Ralph came to his rescue. "I would have put the names on that section of the list too," he said, "if I had put them anywhere at all."

"You will be sure to send an invitation to the marquess and his family, Mr. Lloyd," Chloe said.

"Are you quite sure?" Ralph was frowning at her.

"Yes," she said, though her legs felt distinctly unsteady. "I will not allow a little mischievous gossip from last year to cause me—or you—to slight perfectly innocent people by excluding them from our guest list."

"Very well, then, Lloyd," Ralph said. He tapped his finger on another name, one on the main list. "But here is someone you may exclude."

Chloe leaned forward to read the name. "Lord Cornell?" she said. Did Ralph *know*, then?

"He is not welcome in my home," Ralph said. "Or within half a mile of my wife."

Ah, he *did* know.

They spent a few minutes longer discussing both lists. But Chloe could not delay long. Her aunt would be coming soon.

She went about the rest of the day with something of a spring in her step. Her marriage was progressing far better than she had expected when she suggested it, even if it would never be the stuff of which dreams were made. This morning she was going shopping with her aunt, something she always enjoyed. And this afternoon she would go visiting with her mother-in-law and Nora, who may not like her yet but would go out of their way to smooth her entry into society as the Duchess of Worthingham. And she would hold her head high. She had nothing of which to be ashamed, after all.

Ralph could not take his seat in the House of Lords before he received a Writ of Summons from the Lord Chancellor's office. It had not come yet. He was to attend one of the formal levees at court next week. George, Duke of Stanbrook, had arranged it and had agreed to accompany him. In the meantime, Ralph carried on with his life much as he had before the death of his grandfather, grateful that he was not expected to accompany his wife either to Bond Street or on the round of visits his mother had planned for the afternoon.

He was looking through the morning papers in the reading room at White's Club when his father-in-law stepped into the room. Sir Kevin Muirhead looked about him until his eyes alit on Ralph, and then came toward him with purposeful strides. Ralph stood and they shook hands.

"Your butler thought you had come here," Sir Kevin said, his voice hushed so as not to disturb the other readers. "I am glad he was right. I need to have a word with you."

"Perhaps you would care for some luncheon, sir." Ralph gestured toward the dining room.

"Graham is busy with parish work," Sir Kevin explained when they were seated. "And Lucy is walking in the park with a lady friend of hers and their children and nurses. Nelson is deeply immersed in the writing of one of his plays, or rather in sawing the air with one arm while he proclaims each speech before he writes it. He is ever hopeful of penning the masterpiece that will immortalize him. Julia has gone shopping with Chloe, and Easterly is at the House for what he considers an important debate. You were the only one left to keep me company, Worthingham."

"It is my pleasure, sir," Ralph said as a waiter arrived to take their order.

"Hitching is in town," Sir Kevin said abruptly when they were alone again, "with his whole family. They came a day or two ago."

"Yes," Ralph said. "Lady Angela Allandale was at the theater last evening."

"And you . . . ?" His father-in-law looked appalled.

"We were there too," Ralph said. "There was no unpleasantness. Chloe behaved with great fortitude. So, I suppose, did the other lady. They did not come face to face."

Sir Kevin closed his eyes briefly and exhaled audibly.

"I once informed Hitching," he said, "that he might retire to his estates in the north of England and live out his life there with my blessing, but that if he should ever dare show his face in London again, he could expect me to rearrange the features on it. Or words to that effect. I was young and foolish enough to believe that he would heed the warning and live forever after in fear and trembling of my wrath."

He had to pause while the waiter set their food before them.

"That was twenty-eight years ago," Muirhead continued, frowning down at his plate as if in disbelief that he could have ordered such a hearty feast. "If he was ever afraid of me, clearly he is afraid no longer. Though I daresay he never was. Now he is here with his wife and daughter and one of his sons."

"It *was* all a long time ago," Ralph said. "There may be no need of any unpleasantness, sir. We are to host a ball at Stockwood House. My secretary presented us with a list of prospective guests this morning, and Chloe insisted that Hitching and his whole family be included on it. She seems determined to prove to everyone that last year's gossip was so much nonsense."

His father-in-law had eaten only one mouthful of his roast beef. He set his knife and fork down across his plate with something of a clatter. He closed his eyes and rubbed two fingers up over his forehead from a point between his eyebrows. Ralph held his peace, and the silence between them stretched for what seemed a long time. There was a hum of conversation from the tables around them.

"I suppose," Muirhead said at last, lowering his hand and looking across the table at Ralph, "she ought to know the truth. Do you think?"

"I answered that question at Manville, sir," Ralph reminded him.

"Does *she* know, I wonder?" Muirhead said. "Hitching's daughter, I mean? Has he ever told her? Or his wife? It has not occurred to me until this moment that they too must have been affected by the gossip last year. Yet they have returned this year."

Sir Kevin was still not eating. He was rubbing his temples with a thumb and middle finger as though he had a headache.

"Perhaps, sir," Ralph said, "you would care to come for dinner this evening. Bring Graham too. I am sure Chloe would be delighted."

Muirhead lowered his hand and looked steadily at him.

"Thank you," he said. "I think that would be best."

"I think it would," Ralph agreed, and hoped he spoke the truth.

Sometimes sleeping dogs were best left lying. And sometimes not. How was one to know which choice was better in a certain situation? And, unbidden, a memory returned from last night.

You must face them, then. You must call on them, Chloe had said, referring to Viscount Harding and his wife. And, when he had said he would not, *You are content, then, to live out the rest of your life in hell?*

Chloe was feeling tired when she arrived home late in the afternoon. The shopping trip had gone well. Her aunt had both a good eye for color and design and a knowledge of what was fashionable and would suit her niece. Chloe had her opinions too, most of which coincided with her aunt's. Most of the clothes she ordered for all occasions were in muted shades of her favorite greens, browns, and creams. The gown that was to be made for the ball at Stockwood House, however, was emerald green. Grandmama would be pleased.

The afternoon had been more daunting than the morning, but without unpleasant incident. The Dowager Countess of Berwick had arrived promptly with Nora to take Chloe visiting, and they had called upon three ladies and stayed for a very correct half hour at each house. There were other visitors too, all ladies, with some of whom Chloe had a prior acquaintance from her earlier stays in London. A few of the others she had met at Manville Court on the day of the funeral. Several she had not met before. Some were more friendly than others, but all were polite. Chloe wondered if Mrs. Barrington-Hayes, who welcomed them to her home with almost obsequious deference and presented them to her other guests with open pride, remembered the time six years ago when her butler had informed Lady Muirhead and Miss Muirhead that she was not at home.

Ralph was already home when Chloe returned. He came out of the study as she was removing her gloves.

"Your mother and Nora took me to pay three afternoon calls," she told him, "and I have arrived home all in one piece."

"As I see." His eyes swept over her best green outfit— the one she had worn to her wedding. "I hope you have not tired yourself out. We have guests coming for dinner."

"Oh?" Her spirits fell.

"Your father and your brother," he told her. "I ran into your father at White's."

She smiled with relief. "That will be lovely."

"I hope so." He inclined his head to her and turned back to the study.

There had been not a glimmering of a smile on his face or lurking in his eyes, she thought as she climbed the stairs to her room. But then she supposed having her father and Graham to dinner would be no great pleasure for him. He had invited them for *her* sake. She warmed herself with the thought.

Ralph did not need to make any great effort to keep the conversation going during dinner. Graham, when asked, was quite willing to recount some of his experiences in the London slums, where he did most of his work. None of the stories redounded to his glory or made the poor and the destitute sound like inferior beings, Ralph was interested to note. There was real affection in Graham's voice when he talked of people Ralph himself would pass in the street without so much as a glance. It was a humbling realization and filled him with that old mingling of admiration and irritation.

Sir Kevin, when prompted, spoke of the time when his daughters and his son were children, and Chloe and Graham chimed in with memories of their own, sometimes conflicting ones. All of them were careful not to exclude Ralph from the conversation, however. They explained things to him that might have been puzzling and identified people he did not know. They must have been a happy family, he concluded.

Chloe described her afternoon visits when her father asked about them and amused them all with her keen observations on various ladies she had met. She was obviously enjoying herself enormously, Ralph thought, noticing her sparkling eyes and somewhat flushed cheeks. Whatever had driven her from home a few months ago seemed to have resolved itself, and all of them appeared to be having a merry time.

Perhaps Sir Kevin was going to be content to leave it thus.

"But all the conversation has been about *us*," Chloe said at last, looking apologetically across the table at Ralph. "How dreadfully ill-mannered we have been. We will talk of nothing but *you*, Ralph, when you join me in the drawing room with Papa and Graham. It is a promise. I shall leave you to your port now."

Muirhead spoke up as she got to her feet.

"Chloe." He glanced Ralph's way and set his napkin down on the table. "I will come with you if I may."

"Of course." She raised her eyebrows in surprise but smiled with obvious pleasure. "You do not want any port, Papa?"

"Not tonight," he said, taking her by the elbow. "I would prefer to have a word with my daughter."

His voice and his manner were grave, and her smile faltered before she left the room with him.

Graham, Ralph was interested to note, made no move to follow them. He was looking steadily at Ralph instead. With a brief nod Ralph dismissed the footman who remained in the room.

"You know?" he asked when the two of them were alone.

"He told me a few hours ago," Graham said. "I suspected, of course. Well, I suppose I knew. But sometimes it is preferable to cling to illusion than to admit an unpalatable truth. I loved my mother. I still do. But all through life, it seems, we have to learn and relearn the lesson of loving people unconditionally, no matter what. It is not always easy to do with our parents. We grow up believing them to be perfect."

Ralph poured them each a glass of port. "And will this knowledge change your feelings for Chloe?" he asked.

"If I were not a peaceable man," Graham said, "I might feel obliged to plant you a facer for asking that question, Stockwood. Chloe is my *sister*. Does the reality of her birth make *you* think any less of her?"

"Not at all. But I had little doubt of the truth even before I married her," Ralph told him.

"Does *she* know?" Graham asked.

"In the same way you did—and did not," Ralph told him. "Having the matter put beyond all doubt will be a blow to her. But ultimately it will surely be better for her to know."

He hoped he was right.

Graham toyed with his glass, twirling it by the stem.

"Why did you marry her?" he asked.

"I needed a wife," Ralph said after a small hesitation. "More specifically, I needed—I need—a son, an heir. Chloe wanted a husband and children but thought all her chances had passed her by. She knew—she overheard me tell my grandmother—that I was reluctant to marry, that I had nothing beyond material goods to offer any prospective bride. So *she* made *me* an offer. We could both have what we wanted, but there would be no illusions, no sentiment, no pretense of any emotional attachment."

"And you agreed?" Graham said. "No sentiment, Ralph? No emotional attachment? Nothing to offer? *You?*"

"I will look after her," Ralph assured him. "You need not fear that I will not."

Graham pushed his glass away, the port untouched.

"Why have you never been able to let them go, those three?" he asked. "You had so much more to give to the world than any of them. You had ideas, ideals, *passion*. Sometimes—often—I disagreed with you, but I always respected you, except perhaps when you called me a coward. But even then you were speaking out of the depths of your convictions. The others just wanted adventure, action, glory. I liked them—and I mourned them. But you have not been able to recover from their deaths, have you?"

Ralph took a drink from his glass.

"They would not have been there in the Peninsula if it had not been for me and my dangerous *ideals,*" he said.

"You do not know that." Graham frowned. "To what degree are we our brother's keeper? I did not go with you, though I heard your arguments as often and as clearly as they did. I disagreed and made other plans for my future. They did *not* disagree. It was their right and they acted upon it."

"But they always agreed with me," Ralph said.

"That did not make you *responsible* for them," Graham said. "One cannot always keep one's opinions, one's *passions*, to oneself, Ralph, for fear one might influence others and they might suffer, even die, as a result. Provided we do not try to coerce others in any way, that is. You never did."

"I called you a coward," Ralph reminded him.

"But did I turn my back on all my beliefs and follow you to war just to win your approval?" Graham asked.

"Don't be absurd, Ralph. Boys call one another names all the time. They oughtn't to do it—it causes pain. But no one is perfect, least of all a growing boy. You do not *still* call people names, do you?"

Ralph's smile was a bit twisted. "Why did you agree to a duel and then refuse to take up a pistol, you idiot?" he asked.

"Well, I could hardly refuse," Graham said. "It was an affair of honor, and I *am* a gentleman. But violence is abhorrent to me. I cannot stop others using it, but I *can* stop myself. And you *do* still call people names."

They looked at each other and smiled slowly—and then laughed.

"And so you ended up as a clergyman, working in parts of London most people would never dare go," Ralph said. "And I daresay you walk about the streets without even a club with which to protect yourself. Coward? Never. Idiot? Maybe."

"And you ended up married to my sister," Graham said. "Who would have thought it?"

"I *will* look after her, Gray," Ralph told him.

"Yes," Graham said, nodding slowly, "I believe you will. And I believe *she* will look after *you*."

19

"I am so glad you came to London again, Papa," Chloe said, her hand still linked through his arm as they entered the drawing room. "You have not been back here since—well, since Lucy married Mr. Nelson, have you? It is really not so bad, is it? Although I would have preferred to remain in the country, I am not sorry Ralph persuaded me to come here and face the *ton*. We have accepted a number of invitations for the coming weeks, and we have begun to organize our own ball, which everyone seems to believe will be one of the grandest squeezes of the Season. You *must* stay long enough to attend that."

It was hard to recall all the conflicting emotions that had compelled her to leave home after Christmas, to put some distance between herself and her father at least for a while. But one of the happiest moments of the past few weeks had been seeing him descend unexpectedly from Graham's carriage at Manville and realizing that he was *Papa* no matter what.

He patted her hand before releasing it and stepping

closer to the fire. He held both his hands to the blaze while she took a seat.

"The Marquess of Hitching is in town again this year with his family," he told her.

"Oh," she said. "Is this why you left the dining room with me, Papa? To warn me? But I knew. Lady Angela Allandale was at the theater last evening. I know it was she though no one actually said so. She really does resemble me a little—even I can see that. And there was a swell of sound when she entered her box across from ours. I did not mind so very much, though, you know. Indeed, it will be a relief to meet her face to face one of these days, to be civil to her, to let the *ton* know that all those rumors are pure nonsense. We will be sending them an invitation to our ball. There is no reason *not* to. Indeed, it would be remarked upon if we did not, and then the gossip might be revived. You must not worry for me, Papa. Truly you must not. I do not—"

"Chloe."

He did not turn away from the fire or speak her name loudly, but there was a sharpness to his tone that silenced her.

And she knew what was coming, as surely as though the words had already been spoken. She held up a hand to stop him, but he was not looking at her.

"No father ever loved his child more than I love you," he said. "I was there with your mother five minutes after your birth, though the midwife protested that neither of you was ready to be seen. I had never seen anything more beautiful in my life than the two of you. I named you. Did you know that? You were a tiny ball of precious humanity, and I immediately thought of a small and precious name for you. I did everything a father can do, Chloe, except provide the spark that gave you life. It was . . . Hitching who did that."

And there was a world of difference, Chloe thought, between knowing deep down that something was true and knowing it beyond all doubt and denial. A universe of difference.

The air felt sharp and cold in her nostrils. Her hands and feet tingled with pins and needles. There was a faint roaring in her ears. And she felt the sudden impulse to jump to her feet and run—and to keep on running and running.

The trouble with running away is that you must always take yourself with you. Ralph had said that last night. She *had* run away once—twice—and it had not worked.

Papa was not her father, then. She could no longer even cling to the illusion that he was.

The Marquess of Hitching was her father. Lady Angela Allandale was . . . her half sister. And had she heard that there were sons too? Her half brothers.

Just as Graham was. Just as Lucy was her half sister.

Her papa was still looking into the fire.

"You discovered the truth after you married Mama?" she asked.

"No, before." He turned to her then, his face wan. "She was perfectly frank with me. I had been in love with her from the start of that Season, from my first sight of her. And she had liked me too. But there was a dazzle about . . . *him*. He had looks and charm and rank and boundless wealth—or so it seemed. I thought I had lost her until she sought me out at a concert one evening and told me he was very close to financial ruin and must therefore marry into money. She told me too that she feared she was with child. When I offered to marry her without delay, I also promised never again to refer to the secret she had confided in me. And she in turn promised to love me steadfastly for the rest of her life. We both kept our promise. I was more blessed in my marriage than I ever deserved to be. I had a wife with whom I shared a mutual love and three children we both adored. It has always been my dearest hope that you would never have to learn the truth. I warned him never to return to London. But he came last year and again this year, his family with him. And you have married a nobleman and will inevitably move in the same social circles he does. I have no choice but to tell you the truth now, at last. I wronged you at Christmas time when you asked and I lied. I was afraid of losing you, but I almost did anyway."

. . . three children we both adored.

Chloe gazed down at her hands, which she had spread across her lap, palms down. *Had* her mother adored her? Or had Chloe's existence been an irritant, a constant reminder of her shame and of the man who had jilted her for a rich wife and of the man she had been forced to marry in order to avoid ruin?

Had her mother loved her? Had she loved Papa?

But the question here was not about her mother. Her mother was dead. Her father—Papa—was not. Chloe got to her feet and closed the distance between them. She stood in front of him, twined her arms about his waist, and buried her face against his neckcloth, inhaling as she did so the familiar, snuffy scent of him.

"I am sorry I ran away and hurt you," she said.

His arms closed about her, and she was a little girl again, safe from all harm. A memory surfaced from nowhere—perhaps their reminiscences over dinner had shaken it free—of climbing a steep slope of loose pebbles somewhere until she froze with terror. Papa, who had been climbing ahead of her with Lucy, came back down and took her hand, and she scrambled upward, all fear gone, hardly dependent upon his help at all, but knowing that never in a million years would she be unsafe as long as her papa was holding her hand.

A minute or two later the drawing room door opened and her father released her. Ralph and Graham had come to join them. Both were looking a bit uncertain of themselves.

"Yes," Chloe said, "Papa has told me."

Graham strode across the room toward them.

"Did you always know?" she asked him.

He shook his head. "Not for sure until today," he said, "and not at all before last year. It makes no real difference, though, Chloe. We are still your family. Love does not diminish just because a minor fact changes. And it has not even changed really, has it? It has always been so. It is just that we did not know it until today."

. . . a minor fact.

"I ought not to have married you," she said, looking beyond her brother to Ralph.

His eyebrows rose. "If it is any consolation to you, Chloe," he said, strolling past Graham to take her hand in his and lead her back to her chair, "I had no doubt of the truth before I married you. I married you anyway. Because I wanted to. And because I was led to believe that *you* wanted to marry me. I hope I was not mistaken in that?"

She shook her head.

"Because if I *am*," he said, "then I am sorry, but there is nothing I can do now to release you. I believe you are stuck with me."

He had turned the tables on her. *She* was stuck with him, not the other way around. He was looking steadily down at her. His face did not smile, but, oh goodness, his *eyes* did. He had set out to make her feel better, and he had succeeded. How very kind he was.

Ralph? Kind?

She learned something new about him every day. What a delightful thing marriage was.

"I wanted to marry you," she said, "and I am not sorry I did."

And for a mere moment something else happened to his eyes. Something . . . intense. And then it was gone even before she was sure it was there. And like so many things these days, it was beyond her ability to put into words.

"It might be wise, Worthingham," Papa was saying, "to stay away from any entertainment you might expect Hitching and his family to attend. Chloe must be protected from unnecessary embarrassment."

Ralph was still standing before her chair, looking down at her.

"I believe my wife may have something to say on that subject, Muirhead," he said. "I am hers to command. Chloe?"

"We will not avoid anyone or anything," she said, lifting her chin. "And I do not need to be *protected*. I am the acknowledged daughter of Sir Kevin Muirhead and the wife of the Duke of Worthingham."

"Good girl," Graham said.

Ralph merely nodded slowly.

"Graham," she said, "would you pull on the bell rope, if you please? It is time the tea tray was brought in. Do sit down, Papa. Am I such a shockingly poor hostess that I have not even thought to offer you a chair? Mama taught me better than that."

Graham did as he was asked and then took a seat. "It is your turn, I believe, Ralph," he said, "to entertain us with childhood memories of your own, since we entertained you so royally with ours during dinner."

"Unlike you, though, Gray," Ralph said, looking away from Chloe at last and taking a chair close to her brother's, "I had *three* sisters to plague the life out of me. I built a fort deep in the woods at Elmwood and high up in the branches of a tree for good measure. I was well prepared to hold it against all female comers, but no one ever did come there except imaginary pirates and highwaymen and dragons—tree-climbing dragons, of course. I was a solitary boy, though a vivid imagination saved me from ever feeling lonely. I was very happy to find company of my own age and gender when I was sent off to school."

Chloe looked from her husband to her brother and back as they recalled some humorous and hair-raising incidents from their school days. They were not excluding either her or Papa, but they were focused upon each other and upon a budding friendship that had never come to full fruition during their school years. Perhaps it would now, though they seemed poles apart in the way of life each led.

She glanced at her father and smiled at him when their eyes met. Her *father*!

The Marquess of Hitching was her father.

Her stomach lurched with a nausea she willed away.

Their visitors did not stay late. Graham's work got him out of bed early in the mornings, Ralph guessed. And Muirhead had looked strained even while he smiled and joined halfheartedly in the conversation after dinner. But poor man, he had finally had to divulge a secret he had hoped to take to the grave and had risked losing his daughter as a result.

The drawing room seemed very quiet when Ralph and Chloe were left on their own. They found themselves at opposite sides of the hearth again. Chloe reached down for her workbag and her embroidery, apparently changed her mind, and sat up again, her hands folded in her lap.

"When I said I was at your command," he told her, "I meant it, Chloe. Do you wish to go home?"

She raised her eyes to his. "To Manville?" she asked him. "Alone?"

"I would come with you," he said, "and stay with you." And to hell with what was expected of him as the new Duke of Worthingham here in town.

"You are very kind," she said. "*Very* kind. But, no. Nothing has changed really, has it? You knew the truth. I did too, though I chose not to believe it. Now I have no choice. But I will not run away."

He rested one elbow on the arm of the chair and propped his jaw against one balled fist. "None of the invitations to our ball have gone out," he said. "If you wish, I will have Lloyd—"

"No," she said. "They will remain on the list."

When had he first realized, he wondered, that he cared for her? But of course he cared. She was his wife. He would protect her and care for her needs for the rest of his life. He bedded her nightly. They would share children. Of course he cared.

But why hide truth from himself, as she had done since last year on a far larger issue? He *cared,* though he did not wish to analyze what exactly that meant.

He cared about her happiness.

What must it feel like to discover right out of nowhere that one's father was not one's father after all? He felt a sick jolt to the stomach at the very thought. To discover that one's mother had conceived one with another man. To know that one's apparent father had lived with the lie all one's life.

"I suppose," she said, "this whole situation is as awkward for them as it is for me."

He watched as she opened her fingers, gazed down at her palms, and then clasped her hands in her lap again. He supposed she was talking about Hitching and his family.

"After I fled last year," she said, "they must have assumed that I would not return. But here I am, the Duchess of Worthingham, and likely to be wherever they plan to go. Does she know, do you think?"

"The marchioness?" he said. "I daresay she suspects."

"I meant Lady Angela," she said. "But, yes, there is the marchioness too. I have hated Lady Angela since last year. But she is quite innocent. I suppose she hates me. Yet we are half sisters." She shivered even though the fire had been built up while they were downstairs seeing her father and Graham on their way. "She is as much my sister as Lucy is. And she has brothers, does she not? My half brothers."

Her fingers had curled into her palms. Her head had dropped. Her eyes were closed. He wondered if she would faint—or vomit.

"What you *could* do," he said, "is call upon Hitching at his home. Tomorrow is Saturday. He will not be at the House."

"What?" She looked up at him with startled, incredulous eyes. Her face had turned even paler, if that was possible.

"At least all the eyes of the *ton* would not be upon you there," he said. "The inevitable meeting would come at a time and place of your own choosing. You would have some control over it."

"But it would be utter madness." Her eyes were wide and fixed upon his. "To walk up to the door of his *home,* Ralph? To ask for him by name? To come face to face with him? To speak to him? To speak the truth openly? It would be madness."

"I would come with you," he said.

She was shaking her head from side to side.

"No," she said. "I will face them all in public. I will be civil, as I daresay they will be too. They will be as anxious as I not to initiate any closer contact than that. But go deliberately to call upon him? No, Ralph. Do not ask it of me."

"I do not," he assured her. "I merely made the suggestion. Did you not tell me of a sermon Graham once gave about confronting your worst fear, walking into it and through it, and thus conquering it? Or something to that effect?"

"But *you* will not do it," she said.

He froze.

"You will not go to call upon Viscount and Lady Harding," she said.

"That is altogether different," he told her.

"Is it?" She was gripping the edges of her chair arms. "How?"

"Forget that I made the suggestion." He wished to God he had not. "It probably *was* madness. And Graham was right and you were right, nothing really has changed. And there is no reason why you on the one hand and the Marquess of Hitching and his family on the other cannot coexist with civility during the times when you are in the same place at the same time. The *ton* will tire of speculating. Forget that I spoke."

Her fingers were playing the edges of her chair arms like a pianoforte. Her face was still pale. She was gazing fixedly at the carpet between them. After a minute or two of silence, during which he tried to think of something to say that would distract her and relieve the tension, she looked up at him.

"You will come with me?" she asked.

Not *would* come, but *will* come.

"Yes." He nodded.

Ah, Chloe.

She said no more for a while but returned her gaze to the floor. Then abruptly she got to her feet and came hurrying toward him. He got up quickly from his chair and opened his arms just before she collided with him and wrapped her arms about his waist and burrowed her head into the hollow between his neck and his shoulder. His arms closed about her and held her tight.

"How many sons are there?" she asked after a while, her voice muffled against his shoulder.

It took him a moment to understand what she was talking about. Hitching's sons. Her half brothers.

"Two or three. I am not quite sure," he told her. The eldest is Gilly—Viscount Gilly. He is my age, I believe, or perhaps a little younger."

"And just the one daughter?" she asked.

"I believe so."

He really did not know the family. Until last year they had never been in town when he was there, and last year he had avoided them. Or at least he had avoided Lady Angela Allandale for fear someone would try a bit of matchmaking.

She pressed even more tightly against him.

"I have you close," he told her.

"Have you?" He heard her inhale slowly and release the breath again on a sigh. "You cannot know how I longed to have someone to hold me close last year and again at Christmastime. Forgive me for clinging. I thought I could be brave."

"Pardon me," he said, raising one hand to cup the back of her head and turning his own to murmur the words into her ear, "but I think you *are* being brave. Do you or do you not intend to call upon the Marquess of Hitching in his own home?"

"I do." She laughed softly, though he did not believe she was amused.

You cannot know how I have longed to have someone to hold me close . . .

A wave of the familiar yearning swept over him as he held her through a lengthy silence.

She drew back her head to look into his face.

"You must not fear," she said, "that I will make a habit of leaning heavily upon you. I beg your pardon for doing so now. It is silly really. I *knew*, after all. And the Marquess of Hitching is just a man. After tomorrow I can cheerfully meet him anywhere and nod courteously in his direction when we cannot avoid being in the same place. I will not burden you, Ralph. I promised I would not, and I will keep my promise."

She smiled at him.

He should have been relieved. He wanted no emotional involvement after all. Except that . . . Well, it was already too late.

"You misconstrued my silence," he told her. "I am your husband. When you feel lonely or afraid or unhappy, it is to me you must come, Chloe. My arms are here for you, and my strength too for whatever it is worth. You will never be a burden to me."

Her teeth were biting down on her bottom lip. And then her eyes warmed with a smile and what looked to be genuine amusement.

"I will remind you of that," she said, "the next time we quarrel."

"Will we?" he said. "And will you?"

"Yes and yes," she told him.

He took her face between his hands and wondered when the walls about his heart had been breached. For they *had* been.

He kissed her.

20

$\mathcal{I}$t *was* a mad idea. Chloe had thought so last night when Ralph suggested it, and she thought so now as Mavis put the finishing touches to her hair and then fitted one of her new bonnets carefully over it so as not to disorder the curls she had created.

Actually, it felt even madder this morning. Her stomach was churning and she was not sorry she had been unable to eat much breakfast.

She had had to send a note off to Lucy to postpone the proposed walk in the park until tomorrow. She hated having to do that. She had not seen her niece and nephew, Lucy's children, since Christmas.

Had the Marquess of Hitching known of her existence before last year? The question had plagued Chloe half the night, as well as all the questions associated with it. He must have heard the rumors last year, of course. Did he believe them? *Would* he believe them when she called on him if he did not already? But he must have known of the possibility twenty-eight years ago when Papa warned him to leave London and never return. Did the marchioness know? Did Lady Angela? And her brothers? But how could they not?

"The duke is taking you somewhere this morning, is he, Your Grace?" Mavis asked. "Somewhere nice?"

"Visiting friends." Chloe smiled at her in the mirror and wished desperately that she could switch places with Mavis. How tranquil and uncomplicated a maid's life must be. Which was an absurdly foolish thought, of course. No one's life was all unrelieved tranquility and ease.

How on earth was she going to be able to knock on the Marquess of Hitching's door and announce that she had come to see him? She must tell Ralph before it was too late that she simply could not do it.

But it was precisely what she *was* doing half an hour later—or rather what Ralph was doing for her. Chloe had to use all her willpower not to take a step back and duck sideways so that she would be half hidden behind him when the great oak door opened. She thought yearningly of the carriage mere feet behind her.

"Inform the Marquess of Hitching that I would have a word with him if he is at home," Ralph told the servant who opened the door.

The man looked from one to the other of them, glanced beyond them to the carriage with its ducal crest, briefly consulted the card Ralph had handed him, and stepped aside to admit them, bowing respectfully as he did so. He directed them to a salon that led off the hall and informed them that he would see if his lordship was at home.

"What if he is not?" Chloe said hopefully as the door closed quietly and she was left alone with Ralph. "What if—"

"He obviously *is* at home," Ralph told her, "or his footman would not have gone looking to see if he is."

Ah, the logic of polite society.

It was a visitors' salon into which they had been shown, Chloe could see, a magnificent apartment with a high, coved ceiling painted with a scene from mythology, gilded friezes, and wine-colored brocaded walls hung with dark landscapes in heavy, ornate frames. Gilded, intricately carved chairs were arranged about the perimeter of the room. There was a wine-colored carpet underfoot and heavy curtains of a slightly lighter shade half drawn across the single window.

It was a room meant to reduce the visitor to size, to intimidate him. Or her. It was certainly having its effect upon Chloe, who came to a stop not far inside the door, her hands clasped tightly over the top of her reticule. Ralph had strolled over to the window and stood looking out.

Neither of them spoke again.

There was a nasty buzzing in Chloe's ears. Her hands felt damp, even inside her gloves.

Perhaps they should assume the marquess was not at home and leave without further delay. She opened her mouth to suggest it, but she was too late. The door of the salon opened and a man stepped inside. An invisible someone closed the door silently behind him.

He was an older man of medium height and solid build. He was quietly, tastefully dressed. He had a pleasant, though not outstandingly handsome face and thinning hair that was turning to gray, though it must have been red in his youth. If Chloe had expected a towering, sneering monster on the one hand or a handsome, austere, thin-lipped aristocrat on the other, she was proved wrong on both counts. Not that she had tried to picture what he would look like. How did one picture in one's mind the father one had never seen or even known about with any certainty until yesterday?

He ignored Ralph, who had turned from the window though he did not move away from it. He—presumably the marquis—stood looking at *her*, his lips pursed, a slight frown between his brows, his arms clasped behind his back. If he planned to feign ignorance, he was not making a good start.

It did not occur to Chloe to break the silence.

"Despite all that I have heard about you," he said at last, "I expected that you would bear some resemblance to your mother. You do not. Not at first glance, anyway."

"I wish I did," she said. "Then I might have gone through life without ever learning the truth."

"You did not know it?" He looked surprised. "You were not told?"

"Not until last evening," she said.

"Last evening?" His eyebrows rose higher.

"My *papa* told me," she said, laying slight emphasis on the one word.

"Yet last year's gossip sent you scurrying home," he said.

"The gossip was my first inkling," she told him, "though I refused to believe it, and Papa denied it."

He nodded his head slowly.

"I was sorry," he said, "to hear last year of your mother's passing—*Chloe,* is it not?"

"That happened more than three years ago," she told him.

"For years I did not leave the north of England," he said, shrugging apologetically. "I did not hear. I am sorry. I hope she did not suffer unduly."

Chloe felt suddenly light-headed. Could this man, this polite stranger, possibly be her *father*? She could feel no connection to him.

"Your papa," he continued when she said nothing, "made it very clear to me when he married your mother that he would consider it a personal insult if I should ever try to offer any ... assistance or support for your upbringing or if I should ever try to see you or her. I respected his wishes."

He *had* known, then. But he had never tried to see her—because he had respected Papa's wishes. Or perhaps because he did not care. He had not even known until last year that Mama was dead. Or, presumably, that she was still alive. Had he even known that she herself was a girl, not a boy?

"You have recently made a brilliant match," he said, glancing briefly and for the first time at Ralph. "I am happy for you."

Chloe's chin came up. By what right was he *happy* for her?

"I did not come for your congratulations," she said. "Or for your approval."

"No," he said with a faint smile. "I do not suppose you did."

Dizziness threatened again. Without this man, she thought, she would not even have life. He was her *father*.

"I came," she said, "because we move in the same social circles and will almost certainly find ourselves at many of the same functions. Your ... daughter was at the theater two evenings ago when we were there too, though we did not come face to face. I imagine she was as aware of my presence as I was of hers. It would be just too absurd if we were all going out of our way to avoid one another for the rest of the Season and pretending that there was nothing between us when we failed. There *is* something. I am your daughter."

She felt her cheeks grow warm as she put the relationship into words, and she did not believe she imagined the way he flinched slightly.

"Yes," he said. "You are. You came to confront me in private, then, so that in public we may acknowledge each other with apparent ease and unconcern for what everyone knows to be the truth? It may very well prove to have been a wise course of action. You are far more courageous than I, Chloe. I would feel proud of you if I had a right to such a feeling."

She raised her chin again.

He opened his mouth to continue but hesitated before doing so.

"Allow me to say this, if you will," he said. "Your mother was *not* a woman of loose morals, Chloe. I had assured her of my enduring affections and of my firm intention to marry her. I even believed at the time that I *would* defy all the factors that dictated I do otherwise. Perhaps I would even have done so if I had known in time that she was . . . Well, if I had known that there would be you. Though perhaps not. None of us is ever as free to follow inclination as we would like to believe ourselves to be. Please be assured, though, that any and all blame for what happened between your mother and me was entirely mine. I would not have your newly acquired knowledge sully your memories of her."

She clenched her teeth hard as she stared at him. How dare he tell her how to remember her mother. She turned her head to look at Ralph.

"I have said what I came to say," she said. "We may leave now. I daresay I will be seeing you again . . . sir. And you may expect an invitation to attend the ball we will be hosting within the next few weeks."

Ralph looked gravely back at her with eyes that were no longer empty, she half realized. He had made no attempt to say anything and still did not, but his very presence was full of reassurance.

When you feel lonely or afraid or unhappy, it is to me you must come, Chloe. My arms are here for you, and my strength too for whatever it is worth. You will never be a burden to me.

"My wife and daughter are upstairs in the morning room," the Marquess of Hitching said. "I was with them when Worthingham's card was brought up and my footman informed me that the duchess had come with him. I have not been the most popular of husbands or fathers since last year, I must confess. I doubt my wife and daughter would have returned this year if they had not felt confident that after your hasty retreat last year you would certainly not be back. Word of your marriage did not reach us until after we arrived here and my daughter saw you in Stanbrook's box. She was severely shaken. You are quite correct, though, Chloe. If we are all to remain in town without any of us fleeing and stirring up a renewed storm of gossip, it will be as well if we can all come to a point at which we are able to meet with some ... civility at least. Will you and Worthingham come up to the morning room with me?"

Chloe gazed at him in dismay. How could she possibly ... ? But seeing and speaking with the marquess—her father—alone like this was dealing with only half the task she had set herself. She had hoped that perhaps *he* would undertake the other half and explain to his family.

She looked at Ralph again, but though he was frowning, he did not intervene. He was there to support her, his silence seemed to say, but not to act for her. And then, quite unexpectedly, he smiled.

You can do it.

Though how could she possibly know what that smile meant?

"Very well," she said, looking back at the marquess.

He offered her his arm, but she did not take it or move closer to him. Instead she turned to Ralph, and he came toward her with firm steps and drew her arm through his. His free hand came up to cover hers and pat it a couple of times.

The marquess led the way up a broad staircase.

Ralph had mentally castigated himself all night. His suggestion had been an impulsive one. It might also have been a disastrous one. He had had no idea how Hitching would react to having his by-blow turn up at his door while the rest of his family was in residence there. And he had had no idea how Chloe would stand up to the ordeal. He had half expected, half hoped that she would change her mind when morning came. But she had not done so.

She had acquitted herself magnificently. He had been poised to intervene from the moment Hitching set foot inside the salon but had not needed to do so. He had watched her with admiration and pride—and an uneasy feeling that she was far more courageous than he would ever be. She had run in the past, it was true, most notably last year when she had first got wind of the possibility that Muirhead was not her real father. And she would have avoided coming back to London if she could this year. But she *had* come. And now she had come here.

Ralph had not thought beyond the meeting with Hitching, however. He had assumed that the marquess would himself undertake to speak with his wife and daughter and sons. Yet here they were, on their way to meet the women of the family.

Hitching opened a door at the head of the stairs.

Three people—not two—looked toward the doorway, and all three looked suddenly startled to see that the marquess was not alone. One was a plump, square-faced older lady with florid complexion and dark hair turned mostly to gray. Behind her chair stood a young man who had her dark coloring while in features and build he resembled Hitching. The young lady who sat on a love seat was fashionably dressed in russet brown, a color that emphasized the vivid redness of her hair and the green of her eyes.

She did not really look like Chloe after all, Ralph thought. Her face was narrower, her mouth smaller, her eyebrows straighter. She was not as beautiful despite the fact that last year, according to George, she had been known as the Incomparable. He was partial, of course. And she was noticeably younger than his wife. There was enough of a resemblance, however, to account for the rumors that had sprung to life last year.

"My dear," Hitching said, stepping to one side and addressing the older lady first, "Angela, Gilly, allow me to present the Duke and Duchess of Worthingham. My wife, my daughter, and my eldest son," he added, turning to his visitors.

Viscount Gilly's fingers closed about the handle of a quizzing glass though he did not raise it all the way to his eyes. His mother sat very still. Lady Angela Allandale tipped back her head and fixed Chloe with an arctic stare along the length of her nose.

"How do you do, ma'am." Ralph bowed to the marchioness as he advanced farther into the room, one hand firm beneath Chloe's elbow. "Lady Angela? Gilly? I hope we have not interrupted you at an inconvenient moment. It seemed to my wife and me, however, that we really ought to call on you privately, and the sooner the better, since it is almost inevitable that we will meet in public very soon."

"How do you do, ma'am," Chloe said. "I do assure you that I intend you no harm or embarrassment. Quite the contrary, in fact. I have a family of whose members I am dearly fond and have no intention of making any claim on another. My only wish is that we can all agree to meet in public without stirring the gossip mill again. It is what we must *all* wish."

Ralph did not release her elbow. They were not offered seats, for which fact he was relieved.

"I will *never* be able to meet this woman in public, Mama," Lady Angela said, not taking her eyes off Chloe.

"How could she dare set foot in this house? Why would any servant admit her? And how could Papa bring her up here?"

Lady Hitching ignored her daughter.

"How do you do, Duchess, Duke?" she said with awful civility. "I am quite sure I will always treat any member of polite society I may meet outside my own home with the good manners expected of a well-bred lady. And within my own home too when such persons are presented to me by my husband. I have raised my daughter to do likewise. You will forgive her, I trust, for the uncharacteristic outburst occasioned by your unexpected appearance in such a private apartment of our home. As for my sons, the younger two as well as Gilly have been raised by their father to behave as gentlemen under all circumstances."

She was, Ralph thought with not a little admiration, a formidable lady. This must be a dreadful moment for her, but she had somehow taken command of it with a great deal of dignity.

Viscount Gilly, with little choice but to live up to her description, inclined his head stiffly and let his glass fall on its ribbon.

"Perhaps, my dear," the marquess suggested to his wife, "you would ring for a tea tray? Perhaps our guests—"

"Oh. No. Thank you," Chloe said hastily.

"We will bid you a good morning, then," the marchioness said. "Duke? Duchess?"

The marquess led the way back downstairs. He nodded to the footman who had admitted them earlier, and the man opened the front doors. The marquess accompanied them down the steps to their waiting carriage and touched Chloe for the first time. He took her right hand in his and raised it to his lips.

"He has been good to you?" he asked her. "Muirhead? Your papa?"

She stared at him until he released her hand and smiled ruefully.

"But of course he has," he said. "I remember him from all those years ago as a decent sort. I am sorry you inherited my coloring, Chloe. It would have been better for you if you had never known the truth. Better for me too, perhaps. Now that I have met you, I wish I might know you better. But it will not happen, will it? I wish you well. I will *always* wish you well."

She nodded briefly and turned toward Ralph. He handed her into the carriage, turned impulsively to shake Hitching by the hand, and followed her up the steps. He took her hand in his as the coachman shut the door and climbed back to his box.

"I hoped that I would dislike him quite intensely," she said as the carriage moved forward—she did not look toward the window, though Hitching raised a hand in farewell.

"But you did not?" he asked her.

She shook her head. "Perhaps I ought to be glad," she said. "I was not, I think, the result of a . . . sordid encounter."

"No," he agreed.

She did not say any more, for which fact he was glad. He kept hold of her hand, but he moved a little away from her and settled his shoulders across the corner of the seat. She had been incredibly courageous and dignified. Going upstairs to meet a family that surely hated and despised her must have been particularly difficult, but she had acquitted herself admirably. And she had made it possible for them all to meet socially without unpleasantness or undue embarrassment.

Part of him wanted to gather her into his arms. Another part of him wished there were not this carriage ride to be made together before they were home and he could be alone. She had stirred him to the very root of his being. He had not wanted to be stirred. He still did not. He wanted his life to be as it had been for the past seven years.

Safe.

Almost safe.

Unstirred.

He wanted desperately to be alone.

She had spoken words to him last night that he could not shift from his mind today. *But* you *will not do it. You will not go to call upon Viscount and Lady Harding.* And when he had protested that that situation was entirely different from hers, she had said, *Is it? How?*

The difference was that she had not done anything to shatter Hitching's life. The difference was that she was not responsible for the death of any of his children, let alone his only child. The difference was that she was not so loaded down with guilt that sometimes even the mythical Atlas was enviable because he had had only the earthly globe to support on his shoulders. The difference was ...

The difference was that she had the courage to do what she found almost impossible to do, and to do it all alone. Although he had come with her for moral support and support of a more physical sort too if she had needed it, she had *not* needed him for either. How she had done it, he did not know.

She put him to shame. And he almost disliked her for it. Certainly he resented her. For there *was* a difference. And if there was not, what business was it of hers?

You are content, then, to live out the rest of your life in hell?

She had said that to him too. What did it matter to her how he chose to live? Heaven was out of his reach anyway.

And such a wave of longing washed over him that involuntarily his hand closed more tightly about hers and he set his head back against the cushions and closed his eyes.

"Ralph," she said, "thank you for coming with me. I could not have done it without you—or without your encouraging me to do it. But it *was* the right thing, was it not? I am glad I have met him, and I think he was glad to have met me. His family did not like my going there, and I cannot blame them, but I still think it was necessary and that they will think so too once they have recovered from the shock of seeing me. Thank you."

He opened his eyes. Her face was turned his way and she was looking directly at him with a glow of happiness. Or perhaps it was only relief. But—could this possibly be the same woman he had dismissed just a few weeks ago as a sort of nondescript unpaid servant of his grandmother's? She was incredibly, vividly beautiful.

"You belittle yourself," he said. "You did it all alone without any help from me."

"But you were there with me," she said, "and I kept remembering what you said last night."

He looked blankly at her.

"My arms are here for you," she reminded him.

He had spouted more such nonsense too, he remembered. He wished he had not.

"Did you mean it?" she asked him.

"Of course," he said. "I am your husband."

Her eyes searched his before she turned her head away and her face was hidden behind the brim of her bonnet. He stared at it in silence until they arrived home.

He would go to White's for luncheon. He could hardly wait to get away.

21

$\mathcal{T}$he following couple of weeks were in many ways happy ones for Chloe. They were certainly busy ones. Scarcely an evening passed when she and Ralph did not attend some evening function—a concert or dinner or soiree or the theater or opera. They avoided balls as perhaps a little too frivolous so soon after the death of Ralph's grandfather, though they would host their own soon enough at Stockwood House.

No one gave Chloe the cut direct. Of course no one did—she was the Duchess of Worthingham. It was a great relief, though, to find that she was not being shunned in company or excluded from any of the more glittering events of the Season. Indeed, she and Ralph had to decline far more invitations than they could possibly accept.

They saw the Marquess of Hitching's family for the first time at Mrs. Chandler's crowded soiree. Guests filled the drawing room and the music room beside it and the salon beyond that where refreshments had been laid out. The marchioness was entering the music room from the drawing room at the same moment as Chloe was coming into it from the salon with Gwen and the Countess of Kilbourne. It was the marchioness who chose to approach Chloe, while the general volume of conversation decreased quite noticeably.

"Ah, Lady Kilbourne, Lady Trentham, Duchess," she said, deliberately not lowering her voice—or so it seemed to Chloe. "Good to see you. A pleasant entertainment, is it not? Elsie Chandler can always be depended upon to attract the very best company to her soirees."

"Lady Hitching," the countess said while Gwen smiled. "How do you do? Yes indeed, and we look forward to the pianoforte recital later."

"Good evening, ma'am," Chloe said. "How delightful. I hoped when we met a few days ago that I would see you again soon."

"Ah, Duchess." The voice came from beyond the marchioness. The marquess had followed her into the room. He came closer, took Chloe's hand in his, and raised it to his lips. "You look quite charming in blue. Ladies?" He bowed to the other two as he released Chloe's hand and then offered his arm to his wife. "Shall we find you that lemonade, my dear?"

And that was all, apart from a distant bow from Viscount Gilly and a frosty stare and a slight inclination of the head from Lady Angela Allandale across the room during the music recital later.

It was all, but Chloe was more grateful to the Marchioness of Hitching than she could say. She was in no doubt that the woman detested her, but she had obviously made the decision to squash gossip by observing the strictest of civilities toward the daughter her husband had fathered only a very short while before he married her. And she had clearly imposed her will upon her eldest son and her daughter, who, if they could not be quite polite, were at least civil.

The onlookers had no doubt been fascinated by the exchange yet were probably frustrated by it too. Had it or had it not settled the burning question of whether the new Duchess of Worthingham was or was not the natural daughter of the Marquess of Hitching?

Even at those evening entertainments, Chloe did not spend much time with Ralph. It was not good etiquette, of course, for husbands and wives to cling to each other's company when there were so many other people with whom to mingle, but Chloe sometimes found his almost constant absence from her side a little depressing. She tried not to do so. Theirs was not a marriage that had promised any closeness, after all. Perhaps it would have been better, though, if there had never been any at all. But there had been some—or so it had seemed at the time. Perhaps she had just misunderstood. Even those most cherished words of his were capable of a different interpretation from the one she had given them at the time.

I am your husband. When you feel lonely or afraid or unhappy, it is to me you must come, Chloe. My arms are here for you, and my strength too for whatever it is worth. You will never be a burden to me.

She could still feel what seemed like a lump in her throat when she remembered those words. They had sounded so very tender. They had seemed almost like a declaration of love or at least of deep caring. But perhaps all they had expressed was duty. He was her husband. He would care for her needs as any husband ought. He would not consider her a burden because he had made vows to her.

She must not care that he did *not* care. He *did* support her emotionally as well as materially. He had accompanied her to the Marquess of Hitching's house and had seemed like a rock of dependability. But in the carriage on the way home, when there was no more need to bolster her confidence, he had withdrawn. She had felt it. It had been more than just the fact that he had moved his position, sitting across the corner of the carriage seat, as far from her as he could get.

She must not feel depressed.

Their days were spent almost totally apart except for the time they spent in the study together with Mr. Lloyd, going through the pile of invitations each morning's post brought and working on the plans for their own ball. They stayed home one morning writing invitations. And they did go together one afternoon to call upon his grandmother and Great-Aunt Mary and stayed all of two hours. But those instances were the exception to the general rule.

Chloe was not idle—or alone. She went shopping with Sarah and to a garden party in Richmond with Nora and her mother-in-law. She went with her father to the library and to a church bazaar in which Graham was involved. She went driving in Hyde Park with the Duke of Stanbrook and walking there with Gwen and her young sister-in-law. She went to Gunter's for ices with Lucy and the children one afternoon. She went walking with them in the park too.

In fact, that was just what she was doing on one particularly bright morning when the sunshine seemed to have brought out half the fashionable world to stroll or ride close to the Serpentine. Several children played beside the water, including Lucy's two. Jasper Nelson was sailing the wooden boat his father had made for him, pulling it along parallel to the bank by the attached string. He was pretending to be Lord Nelson and was fiercely resisting his sister Sukie's attempt to seat her doll in the vessel. There were no females on the *Victory,* he told her crossly. Did she not know *anything*? And no, not even Mrs. Lord Nelson.

"*Lady* Nelson," Sukie cried scornfully. "There is no such thing as a *Mrs.* Lord So-and-So. Is there, Mama?"

Thus appealed to, Lucy stepped forward to settle the dispute and stop Sukie from capsizing the boat and Jasper from drowning the doll. Chloe stayed back on the footpath, a smile on her face. Sometimes there were definite advantages to not being a parent, especially when the children's nurse had a cold and had been persuaded to remain at home in bed. She rested the handle of her parasol against one shoulder and twirled it above her head.

She would not be a parent herself just yet. Not within the next nine months, anyway. The discovery had been a terrible disappointment, but . . . Well, perhaps next month . . .

"Ah." The clopping of horses' hooves close behind her stopped. The voice was male and sounded bored. "The delectable duchess. And the scandalous sister."

"Never tell me, Corny," another voice said as Chloe spun about, wide-eyed. "It is there in the old memory box somewhere. Eton. English class. Boredom supreme. *Alliteration.* Yes, that's it. Alliteration. Hadn't thought of the word in years. Well done, old chap. Aspiring to be a poet, are you?"

Lord Cornell, handsome and elegantly dressed for riding, looked down upon Chloe from horseback. A second gentleman, who bore a distinct resemblance to his horse, rode beside him.

"You may observe, Cedric," Lord Cornell said, "that when two ladies are sufficiently lovely and sufficiently determined, they may steal husbands and flout scandal and even decency to win their way to the very top. Though a prince would have been a more brilliant catch than a duke, I daresay. *Close* to the very top, then. But what can one expect when one considers the mother? And one wonders if the delectable duchess won her duke in the same way as the mother tried to win a marquess and the scandalous sister won her—ah, playwright."

Chloe stared up at him in disbelief. She had not realized that Lucy had turned away from the water and her children until she spoke.

"*One* of them," Lucy said, "was fortunate enough to escape the clutches of a cad and a villain. But what can one expect when one considers that the man is not a gentleman?"

The horsy gentleman guffawed.

"Hoisted with your own petard, Corny," he said. "I remember that from English class too. The Bard himself, if I am not mistaken. I had no idea I had paid that much attention."

Lord Cornell grinned appreciatively at Lucy, touched the brim of his hat with his whip, and looked Chloe over from head to toe before riding onward along the path.

"You were quite right, Lucy," Chloe said. Her voice

was shaking, she could hear. And her knees felt decidedly unsteady. "He *is* a cad and a villain. And no gentleman."

"Freddie said so even before I ran off with him," Lucy told her. "But I could not tell you at the time, Chlow. You would have wanted to know who had told *me*. Besides, you would not have believed me. You were terribly enamored of him."

She turned back toward the lake to keep an eye on the children.

"Chlow," she said after a few moments, "what did he mean about Mama? Do some people still believe those rumors?"

Chloe closed her eyes briefly and gathered together her scattered thoughts. It was all very well to know with her rational mind that the purely uncalled-for spite of her former beau was not worth getting upset over. It was another thing to convince her emotions. And now here came another crisis. She had hoped Lucy might never have to know the truth. Presumably, so did Papa and Graham. But Lucy had a right to know.

"They are true, Luce," she said. And she told her sister about their father's confession and about her visit to the Marquess of Hitching's home.

Lucy was openmouthed and wide-eyed by the time she had finished.

"You are my *half* sister, Lucy," Chloe said, "just as Lady Angela Allandale is. Graham is my half brother, just as Viscount Gilly and his two brothers are. I have not met those two. I do not believe they are in London."

Lucy flung herself into Chloe's arms, drawing a few curious glances from the people around them.

"Oh, no," she cried. "There is all the difference in the

world, Chlow. He may be your father, and his children may be your half sister and half brothers, but Papa is your *papa*, and Gray and I are your *brother* and your *sister*. And do not ask me to hate Mama, Chlow. It cannot be done. I did exactly what she did but even worse, for Freddie was still married at the time, and Jasper would have been a ba— He would not have had a proper father if Freddie's wife had not been obliging enough to die. Though that sounds callous, does it not? I am sorry, but I cannot feel really sorry for her. She *despised* him, you know. She did not understand him at all or appreciate his great talent. And she did not love him."

The children were squabbling again. The doll lay forgotten on the grass while Sukie tried to wrest the string of the boat from her brother's grasp, loudly admonishing him for refusing to *share*. Lucy hurried off to adjudicate.

It was only later, as they were walking home, the children ahead of them, that Lucy referred again to the incident on the path.

"That *man*," she said, "ought not to be allowed to get away with insulting you so, Chlow. Will you tell His Grace?"

"Oh," Chloe said. "No, such silliness is best forgotten, Lucy. No, I will not say anything."

She and Ralph did not say a great deal to each other. Oh, no, that was not quite correct. They conversed at the dinner table each evening and at the breakfast table when they took the meal together. They spoke to each other on the way to and from the various evening functions they attended. There was rarely silence between them.

But they rarely if ever *talked*. Not since her visit to the

Marquess of Hitching, anyway. And his eyes, if not quite empty again, had become inscrutable. Chloe remembered her first impression of him as a man who was unknown and unknowable. He had become that man again. But she could not complain. It was that man she had married, after all, quite deliberately.

And he was never cold with her or unkind or neglectful.

She tried to be happy with what she had. It was not *his* fault that she loved him.

Ralph could not seem to move ten yards from his own front door without feeling the compulsion to look over his shoulder. But any hope he had entertained after that evening at the theater that Viscount Harding and his wife had been making a brief stay in town was soon dashed. He saw them from the carriage window on the afternoon he went with Chloe to visit his grandmother. They were walking arm in arm along Oxford Street. They did not see him.

He had liked them, just as he had liked Max's parents and Rowland's. But these two in particular, because they had liked him. Lady Harding had laughed at all his silly boy's jokes as though they were really amusing and had commiserated with him whenever he complained about having three sisters to plague him but no brothers to offer companionship. Viscount Harding had listened patiently to all his impassioned ideas upon any and all topics that had captured his boy's imagination and had told him that he would be a great leader one day. They had liked Max and Rowland too, of course. It was not that they had singled *him* out as their favorite. And Tom, their own son, was obviously the apple of their eye, the light of their very existence.

Ralph said nothing to Chloe about having seen them.

He said nothing at all of any significance to Chloe, in fact, during the few weeks following their visit to Hitching. They conversed—there were never awkward or strained silences between them. But they talked to each other more like polite strangers than anything else.

Oh, it was true that he had held her briefly to comfort her the night she broke the news to him that she was not with child. He had assured her that of course he was not annoyed with her.

"Annoyed?" he had said, setting her a little away from him and frowning down at her. "But why would I be? It takes two, you know. I assume you *did* know."

She had smiled wanly at his weak attempt at a joke.

"I was so hoping I *would* be," she had said.

"Well, let us not be too disappointed," he had told her. "Now I have an excuse to keep on visiting you here nightly."

He had intended that too as a kind of joke. But as he spoke the words, he had realized that they were true. He might have felt obliged to keep his distance from her if he had impregnated her. He did not want to keep his distance. And it was not just the sex, though that was admittedly a large part of it. He liked sex with Chloe. It was also, however, about being in bed with her all night, about being close to her even if they did not touch, about feeling her warmth, hearing her breathing, smelling her soap and the essence of her. On the whole he had been sleeping better since his marriage.

He had, however, felt obliged to quit her bed and her room for the five nights of her courses. He had hated it. His bed had felt as big as a small country. He had found it difficult to get warm despite the fact that spring was turning to summer. He had kept waking up and reaching out one arm—or reaching out one arm and waking up. He was not sure which provoked which. He *did* know that he had not slept well during those nights and had returned to his wife's bed with an almost embarrassing eagerness when the five days were over.

But during those five days he had withdrawn into himself a little further. If he had wanted to tell her the night he held her that he would miss her for the next little while, that she meant more to him than he had expected, that she was crucial to his comfort and well-being, he was very glad afterward that he had held his tongue and not made such an ass of himself.

He was not really worthy of Chloe. She was his superior. And he had *certainly* not expected that. He had thought her a nondescript, shadowy mouse of a woman when he first met her. Good God, he had not even noticed that she was in the drawing room that evening when he and his grandmother talked about the need for him to find a bride as soon as possible.

He was not worthy of her—or of anyone.

Sometimes he almost hated her. And he had started to hate himself again, something he had worked hard at Penderris to *stop* doing. Perhaps he never had stopped anything except feeling. He had been tempted to feel again since his marriage. He had even given in to that temptation a time or two. But allowing himself to feel meant allowing excruciating pain back into his life, and that was merely self-destructive.

Sometimes he wished he had chosen one of those girls from the ballrooms of London as his wife. And sometimes the thought of not having Chloe in his life brought him to the edge of tears before he froze the thought and turned his mind elsewhere.

He kept busy. He escorted Chloe to the very best social events each evening. Introducing her to the *ton* as his duchess was one of the main reasons for this stay in London, after all. He kept up his usual activities during the day and helped his wife and Lloyd plan the ball, which was already being talked about and was expected to be the grandest squeeze of the Season. He wrote a long letter to Imogen, Lady Barclay, the one woman member of the Survivors' Club, after she wrote from Cornwall to congratulate him on his marriage and newly acquired title and to commiserate with him over the death of his grandfather. He wrote another to Ben—Sir Benedict Harper— who had written a far briefer letter from Wales on the same themes. He wrote his regular biweekly letters to his maternal grandmother. He called a few times on his mother.

He went with George to attend one of the king's formal levees and accepted His Majesty's condolences and congratulations.

"I understand, Worthingham," the king said, "that there is to be a celebratory ball at Stockwood House in the next week or two."

"There is, indeed, Your Majesty," Ralph said. Good Lord, did the whole world know, though the invitations had not even gone out yet?

"I shall think of honoring it with my presence," the king informed him. "Provided neither you nor the duchess is of a modern turn of mind and likes to keep windows open on the assumption that night air is good for the constitution?" His eyebrows were raised. He was awaiting an answer.

The king's own entertainments were famous for their fainting ladies and stiflingly hot and stuffy rooms.

"All windows will remain tightly closed, Your Majesty," Ralph assured the great mountain of a man before him.

"And so," he told George in the carriage a short time later, "we will all boil in the heat that evening on the faint chance that Prinny will take it into his head to show his face at the ball for all of five minutes."

"Not Prinny any longer," George reminded him. "The king—George the Fourth. And yes, we all will, Ralph. But if he comes, you know, even for five minutes, yours will indeed be pronounced the entertainment of the Season. That will be gratifying for your wife."

Ralph laughed. "She will die of terror when I tell her," he said. "No. No, she will not. She will carry it off with cool dignity even if her knees are knocking."

George turned his head to smile at him.

"You made a good choice, Ralph," he said. "I am not sure you are fully aware of that fact yet. But it *was* a good choice."

They were on their way to Hugo's house for a late luncheon, just for the men. Lady Trentham was out somewhere with family members and had taken Hugo's young sister with her.

"Well, you two look grand enough to stop a few female hearts," Hugo said, looking over their court dress when they arrived. "Come and tell this poor commoner all about it."

Hugo *was* a commoner, or had been. His father had been a wealthy businessman of solidly middle-class background. Hugo's title had been awarded him after he had led a bloody and successful attack in Spain.

George had to leave after they had eaten. He had asked Chloe earlier when he had brought his carriage to take Ralph to court if he might have the honor of driving her in the park later in the afternoon.

"If I know your husband, Duchess," he had said, "and I believe I do know him a little, he will answer all your questions about the levee with monosyllables. I, on the other hand, will tell you everything."

"I would be delighted to be seen in the park with you even without that incentive," she had said, laughing. "Everything?"

"Every sordid detail." George had even winked at her. Ralph did not believe he had ever before seen George wink.

After they left, Hugo and Ralph settled back at the table with a pot of coffee between them, Ralph having declined anything stronger.

"Well, lad," Hugo said.

Ralph poured them both a cup and added some cream to his own. Those words had not been meaningless. Hugo had always had a way of indicating that he was ready to allow the conversation to become serious. Big and seemingly gruff though he was, he had always been a sensitive listener, though sometimes he had been the one needing to talk. That was what had made their group so close knit. They all took from it. And they all gave back to it in equal measure.

Another thing about Hugo was that he was not intimidated by silence. He never rushed to fill it when he knew his companion needed time.

"Do you feel that Lady Trentham is your superior, Hugo?" Ralph asked him at last.

Hugo pursed his lips and considered.

"My grampa dropped his aitches more often than not," he said, "and ate his food with his knife and both elbows on the table. He had a Yorkshire accent so thick you could have cut it with his own knife. My pa's accent was only slightly thinner. They made their money the hard way, the vulgar way, if you like. Gwen's blood is blue to the very heart. There is hardly a member of her family that does not have a title attached to his name—or hers. And most of them are titles that go back for generations. Is Gwen my superior? No, she is not. Nor am I hers. She is not up there on a pedestal with stars about her head for a tiara while I grovel down here worshiping and adoring. And I am not up there, the great military hero, while she bats her eyelashes with adoration from down here. It just would not work either way, Ralph. We are equal. We are together. We are one. I do sound more than a bit daft, don't I? But you did ask."

Ralph gazed into the cup he held in one hand.

"You think the duchess is your superior?" Hugo asked.

Ralph looked up at him and set down his cup.

"That evening when we were at the theater with George," he said. "Viscount Harding and his wife were there."

"Harding?" Hugo clearly did not know whom he was talking about.

"Their son was with me in the Peninsula," Ralph explained. "Tom."

"Ah." Hugo understood. He knew about Tom and Max and Rowland. "Did *they* see you?"

"I looked away before our eyes met," Ralph told him. "But, yes, I think so."

"Ah, lad." Hugo sighed. "I am *not* going to tell you that you ought to have gone to see them long ago, or written to them at the very least. I am *not* going to tell you that you are not as responsible for their son's death as you believe you are. I am *not* going to suggest that they may not hate you as much as you believe they do. I am not going to tell you anything. I have been where you are, even if my case was a bit different from yours. I still find myself in that place occasionally, and a deep, dark place it is. I know getting over it is not a simple matter of willing it away. Most people would not understand. I do. What is the connection between the Hardings and your duchess being your superior?"

Ralph pushed his cup and saucer away, his coffee untouched.

"She went to call on Hitching," he said, "the morning after Muirhead told her the truth about her birth. It was the very last thing she wanted to do. But what else *was* there when she is likely to meet him and his family innumerable times this spring and in the coming years? I went with her, Hugo. She was terrified. She even went with Hitching to meet his wife and his daughter and son. They did not greet her warmly. I can only imagine what

it must all have felt like for Chloe. Good God, Hugo,
Hitching is her *father*. But she did it. I thought she might
need to lean on me a bit, but she did not. She did it all
herself. I am not fit to kiss the hem of her dress. That
sounds theatrical. But I am not."

"Because you cannot get up the courage to call on
Harding and his wife?" Hugo said.

"I would probably do more harm than good if I did,"
Ralph said.

"To whom, lad?" Hugo asked quietly.

Ralph closed his eyes and clenched one hand on the
tabletop.

22

"*You* have plans for this afternoon?" Ralph asked. They were eating luncheon together at home, an unusual occurrence. Usually he was gone from the middle of the morning until late afternoon.

"Sarah has invited me to tea," Chloe told him. "Your grandmother and Great-Aunt Mary are going too. And Lucy. And Gwen will be there with her cousin, Viscountess Ravensberg, who has just recently come to town with her husband. She is the abandoned bride, Ralph, the one the Earl of Kilbourne was about to marry when the countess arrived at the church just in time to stop the ceremony. I cannot wait to meet her. Oh, and the countess herself will be with them."

"Ah," he said.

Chloe looked more closely at him, her knife and fork suspended above her plate. She had expected a bit more of a reaction from him.

"What is the matter?" she asked.

"Nothing." He looked back at her with raised eyebrows—and blank eyes. "Nothing at all. I hope you enjoy yourself."

"What did you *want* me to do this afternoon?" she asked him.

"Nothing." He frowned.

"What are *you* going to do?"

He set his knife and fork down across his plate with a clatter.

"Sometimes you can be the most pestilential of females," he said.

Chloe recoiled but did not stop staring at him.

"I beg your pardon." There was a dull flush in his cheeks. "I *do* beg your pardon, Chloe. That was quite uncalled for. I will be paying a call of my own this afternoon."

She did not ask. She waited instead.

"Viscount Harding and his wife are leasing a house on Curzon Street," he explained when she did not break the silence. "I thought I would call on them. Apparently they are at home most afternoons. Today may be the exception, of course."

He was doing a lamentable job of sounding casual. Chloe had not forgotten who the viscount and his wife were.

"You wanted me to come with you?" she asked.

"No," he said, "there is no need. You have other plans. You may tell me this evening if your curiosity over Viscountess Ravensberg has been satisfied." He picked up his knife and fork as though he intended to resume eating, then merely frowned at his food.

"I shall come with you," she said. "I'll send a note to Sarah excusing myself."

"There is no need," he said again.

"Yes, there is," she insisted. "I'll come. You came with me."

"Did I ever tell you," he asked, his eyes inscrutable as they lifted to meet hers, "that sometimes you can be the most pestilential of females?"

"Yes, a time or two," she said. "But I am coming anyway."

And then she bit down hard on her lower lip. Before he turned his head sharply away and got abruptly to his feet, his eyes had glistened with what she would swear were tears.

Ralph wondered fleetingly if this was how Chloe had felt when they stood outside Hitching's door, waiting for it to open. And he wondered if this was the most selfish thing he had ever done. Was he trying to make himself feel a little better at the expense of people who must wish he were buried in the deepest point of the world's oceans and consigned to the farthest corner of hell?

Would he feel better?

Or ten times worse?

Was there any worse to feel? Or was there only *feeling* to feel? He had cut it off more than four years ago as a technique of survival. If he did not feel, then there was nothing to drive him back to the brink of suicide. He had allowed himself to become fond of six friends and to love his family, it was true, provided he kept himself at some emotional distance from them all. And he had allowed himself in the last month or so to grow fond of his wife. It had seemed only right and fair. He had tried, though, to keep her far enough from his heart that he could survive.

He had tried . . .

The door opened and a thin young man in an ill-fitting footman's uniform looked out at them.

"The Duke and Duchess of Worthingham to see Viscount and Viscountess Harding, if they are at home," Ralph said, handing the young man his card.

"Oh, they are at home, right enough, Your Lordship, Your Worship," the footman said, still blocking the doorway. "But I'll have to go and ask. That is, I do not know if they are at home or not, but I'll find out for you."

"New on the job?" Ralph asked.

"Just promoted yesterday from kitchen help," the young man said, flushing scarlet. "Jerry was dismissed on account of he was light fingered and got caught with a silver spoon down his stocking, and Mr. Broom said as how I could have a chance before they went looking for someone else, Your Worship, Your—"

"*Your Grace* is the term you are looking for," Ralph said. "I am a duke. And I believe you ought to admit us and perhaps offer Her Grace a chair while you run off to see if your master and mistress are at home and willing to receive us."

"Right you are, guv," the footman said, stepping to one side. "I daresay it's a bit nippy standing out there. Come on in, then."

"Thank you," Chloe said, smiling at the young man as he dragged a chair close to the door for her to sit on. "And congratulations on your promotion. You are learning your new duties quickly."

"Yes, Your Highness. Thank you, ma'am," he said and hurried away up the stairs, waving Ralph's card before his face like a fan.

Ralph exchanged a glance with Chloe and clasped his hands at his back.

"Well, that was diverting," he said. Strangely, it had been too. Though now he felt sick to the stomach again.

They were not kept waiting long. It was not the thin footman who came back down the stairs, though, but Harding himself, his wife on his heels.

"Worthingham," Harding said, reaching out his right hand. "*Ralph*. Good God, man, *you* have come to *us* when we ought to have come to you. You *did* see us at the theater, then. We ought to have waited on you at your box during the interval. Or we ought to have called at Stanbrook House the very next morning. Instead, we have made *you* come to *us*."

He was wringing Ralph's right hand as though he would break every bone in it. Then he stepped aside while his wife took both of Ralph's hands in her own and held them tightly to her bosom.

"Ralph," she said, her eyes filling with tears. "Ralph Stockwood. Oh, my dear boy. We neglected you quite shamefully when you were brought home to England, and ever since then we have been too ashamed to seek you out or even to write. How do things like that happen? And now you have come to us. And you have brought your new wife?"

"Yes." He stood back, more than a bit bewildered. "Chloe, the Duchess of Worthingham. Viscount and Viscountess Harding, Chloe."

"*Chloe,*" the viscountess said, beaming. "What a pretty name. And what a very pretty lady. And you grew into a very handsome man, Ralph, as of course I knew you would. But, oh, your poor, poor face. It was cut when—?"

"Yes," he said.

"I am so glad you came," the viscountess told him. "Though you have put us to shame. We have been feeling more and more guilty every day and keep on saying that we really *must* call upon you. It is not so easy, though, when so much time has passed. We thought you must be disappointed with us, even angry with us. We thought perhaps you thought we did not care. But now you have come to us. Oh, do come upstairs to the drawing room. What are we thinking to keep you standing down here? Duchess, do come up. Or may I call you Chloe? Ralph was almost like a son to us, you know."

And she linked an arm through Chloe's and drew her in the direction of the stairs.

Harding gestured with one arm so that Ralph would follow them.

"How are you *doing,* Ralph, my boy?" he asked. "We heard that you hovered near death for a long time, and then you went off to somewhere in Cornwall and were there for years. We feared you must be permanently incapacitated. But then Courtney's girl saw you in London and reported that you seemed fine apart from a nasty scar. How *are* you?"

Ralph had no opportunity to answer. They had arrived in the drawing room, and Lady Harding was directing them to a couple of chairs. Ralph did not sit down. When he did not, they all turned to stare at him. For a moment, there was silence.

"You do not . . . *hate* me?" he finally asked, looking from one beaming face to the other.

"*Hate* you, Ralph?" Lady Harding looked puzzled.

"Because you lived and Thomas died?" Harding's

smile had faded. "And Max and Rowland too? But you did not kill them, Ralph. The French did."

"Did you think we resented the fact that you lived while our son died?" Lady Harding had tears in her eyes again. "Oh, Ralph, my dear boy, is that what you have thought all these years because we did not come to see you? We did not come at first because we were prostrated with grief and you were not allowed any visitors. And then you went off to Cornwall and we did not know exactly where. We could have found out, I suppose. We *should* have found out. We should have written to you at the very least. But what was there to say? And so much time had passed before we thought of it that we felt awkward and guilty. We ought to have done it sooner. You were one of Thomas's dearest friends. You had been a frequent guest in our home and we had loved you. We were embarrassed about neglecting you. We were always going to write but never actually did. And then we saw you a couple of weeks ago and *still* could not make ourselves go and talk to you. How dreadful you must have thought us."

"But Tom would not have been in the Peninsula if it had not been for me," Ralph said. "I talked all three of them into it. You did not want Tom to go. Max and Rowland's parents did not want them to go. They came because I persuaded them."

"Sit down, Ralph," Harding said and waited until he had seated himself on the chair the viscountess had indicated. Harding stayed on his feet. "We raised our boy to have a mind of his own. We were pleased with the friends he made at school. You were all good lads, you and Max and Rowland, and there were a few others too. You were the leader, of course. That was clear. But we did not mind. You had a good heart and a good head on your shoulders, and none of them followed you slavishly. If they disagreed with you, they said so. If you disagreed with them, *you* said so. We were dismayed when Thomas begged me to purchase a commission for him when he left school. We argued with him for a while, and I was determined to keep on refusing. But he was a young man more than a boy. I *talked* with him at last, man to man— took him fishing for a whole day and just talked. And he convinced me that he could not be happy unless he did what he conceived to be his duty and went to fight. I knew you had planted the idea in his head. But I knew too by the time I gave in and let him go that he was following his own firmly held convictions, not yours. He would have gone even if you had changed your mind."

"I wrote to you to beg you to talk him out of going, Ralph," Lady Harding said. "I ought not to have done that. You were not responsible for what our son did or did not do. We let Thomas go—we *both* did. We sent him to war with our blessing, with dreadful consequences. But we were proud of him. We *are* proud of him. And we were and are terribly sorry for you. Not sorry that you survived. We were both very, very glad that at least one of you did. But we were sorry for what losing your three closest friends right before your own eyes must have done to you at such a young age. I think *that* is why we never got around to writing. We thought you did not need the reminder. Though that was foolish. You could not forget anyway, could you? But you thought *we* blamed *you*? Oh, my poor, dear boy."

Ralph stared at her and then at Harding.

"I think, my boy," Harding said sadly, "we had all better start assigning blame where blame is due. I have blamed myself for permitting Thomas to have his commission, and you have blamed yourself for putting the idea into his head. It was war that killed him, though. We must not blame even the French. They were trying to kill you just as you were trying to kill them. They were just ordinary boys, like you and Thomas and Max and Rowland. It was war that was to blame, or rather the human condition that leads us to believe that we must fight to the death to settle our differences."

"You are extraordinarily kind," Ralph said. "Sir Marvin Courtney and Lord and Lady Janes may see things differently, however. They may—"

"Oh, no," Lady Harding said. "The deaths of our sons drew us close in our grief. And we all felt the same way about you. Lord Janes went to call on you after you were brought home, but he was turned away at the door. You were not receiving visitors. Neither were your mother and father, who were distraught over your condition, I daresay. He did not go back. Lady Courtney wrote a letter of commiseration to your mother but did not receive any reply. Your mother, I suppose, was too busy watching over you to read her letters, or at least to answer them."

She fumbled for a handkerchief, and Harding handed her one of his.

"Lady Courtney died a few years later," she continued after she had dried her eyes. "I think her heart was broken, though she still had her daughter left, and a sweet young lady she was too. But I never heard Lady Courtney breathe one word that would suggest she blamed you, Ralph. Or any of the others either. Quite the contrary. We all felt dreadfully sad for you. You had lost your three best school friends all at once, and it seemed very possible that you had seen them ... die. Did you?"

"Yes," he said. "Ma'am, they were cheerful and brave. They were —"

"Yes," Harding said. "We knew our son."

"Chloe," Lady Harding said, getting to her feet and pulling on the bell rope, "you have not said a word. You have not had a chance to say a word. We have been depressing you with all this talk about our sad history. We have been told that your name was Muirhead before you married Ralph. Thomas had an earnest young friend of that name at school. Is he related to you?"

"Graham," Chloe said. "He is my brother, ma'am."

"Ah," Lady Harding said. "He was a likable boy. Our son was very fortunate in all his friends. He enjoyed his school years. It is a comfort to remember that. What has become of your brother?"

And, incredibly, for the next half hour they all drank tea and nibbled on cakes and conversed on a variety of subjects. Viscount Harding told them about his twin brother with whom he had always enjoyed an extraordinarily close relationship. The brother had married late and had a growing family of three boys and two girls. It was very clear to Ralph that both Harding and his wife doted upon their nieces and nephews and saw them frequently. The eldest boy was, of course, Harding's heir after the boy's own father. The nephews and nieces would never replace the Hardings' own son, of course, but it was clear that they *were* a consolation.

Lady Harding told Chloe that Miss Courtney, the

young sister of Ralph's friend Max, had just married a clergyman from the north of England.

"We were at the wedding," she said, "and a very pretty one it was too. The bride glowed. It was understandable, I must say. Her husband is a well-set-up young gentleman and more handsome than any clergyman has a right to be. It was very clearly a love match—the very best sort, would you not agree, Chloe?"

"I would, ma'am," Chloe said and smiled.

"You must not be strangers," Harding said when Ralph got to his feet a short while later. "Now that we have seen one another again and got over the awkwardness of a long silence, we must keep in touch."

"We will send you an invitation to our ball at Stockwood House," Chloe said. "Please come. Graham will be there. He will be delighted to see you."

Five minutes later they were walking home, Chloe's arm drawn through Ralph's. He had dismissed the carriage when she had assured him she would enjoy some fresh air. They walked in silence for several minutes.

"I like them," Chloe said eventually.

"What?" He paused to toss a coin to a young crossing sweeper who had cleared some horse droppings from their path. "Oh. Yes. They are very pleasant. They always were."

"I hope they come to the ball," she said.

"Mmm."

They did not speak again until they reached the house. He could not seem to unfreeze his brain.

"Chloe," he said when her foot was on the bottom stair.

She turned to look back at him.

"Thank you," he said, "for changing your plans and coming with me."

She smiled. "It was my pleasure."

"I could not have done it without you," he said.

She smiled again and continued on her way.

Ralph let himself into the library and shut the door behind him. He had something to think about, though he could not at the moment imagine what it was exactly. But whatever it was, it was something he needed to do in private.

Ralph had not gone out. The butler reported that he had shut himself in the library upon his return with Her Grace and had not come out again—or rung for any service. He had not gone up to his room to change for dinner. Burroughs reported that he had waited with His Grace's shaving water and evening clothes, but he had waited in vain.

Ralph did not come to the dining room for dinner, and Chloe decided not to have him summoned. She ate alone and then sent off a short note to Nora explaining that they would not be going to a private concert at which they had arranged to meet Nora and Lord Keilly. She spent the rest of the evening alone in the drawing room. She tried reading but gave up the attempt when she realized she had turned perhaps three pages in half an hour but had no idea what she had read. She worked doggedly but without enjoyment at her embroidery.

And she wondered for surely the dozenth time if this afternoon's visit had made any difference at all to Ralph. Was his sense of guilt so deep-seated that he would never be able to let it go? Was he willing to accept forgiveness even though it would seem none was necessary? Would he be willing now to live again? And if so, what about her? Where would she fit in his life? Would he be forever sorry he had married her? And if he was *not* willing to be forgiven, or, more to the point, to forgive himself, what then? Could she go on like this? But she did not have much choice, did she?

She put away her embroidery eventually and got to her feet though it was early to go to bed. What else was there to do? She was feeling horribly depressed though she ought not to be. This afternoon's visit had really gone very well indeed. And surely it had gone a long way toward setting Ralph free.

She paused when her foot was on the bottom stair leading up to her bedchamber and looked toward the stairs going down. Was he *still* there? Or had he gone out some time during the evening without her hearing him? She hesitated for several moments longer and then took the stairs down. The footman on duty in the hall scurried ahead of her to the library and opened the door. He closed it behind her after she had stepped inside.

A branch of candles had been lit. There was no fire burning, but it was not a cold night. He was slumped in a chair beside the fireplace. He had removed his neckcloth and opened the neck of his shirt. But he was still in his coat and waistcoat and pantaloons and Hessian boots from this afternoon. His hair was disheveled as though he had run his fingers through it a time or two. A half-empty glass stood on the table beside him, though he did not look drunk. A glance toward the sideboard assured Chloe that all but one of the decanters there were still full, and even that one was not depleted by more than a glass or two.

He looked across the room at her.

"Where do memories live?" he asked. "Have you ever thought about it, Chloe? Suddenly we remember things that happened years ago, things we have not thought about since, yet they are as vivid as the events were when they were happening. Where have they been in the meanwhile? You would think we would need heads the size of a continent just to store them all."

He did not *sound* drunk.

"What have you been remembering?" she asked him.

"Mostly school days," he said. "People tell boys, and maybe girls too, that those are the best days of their lives, but *as* boys we scoff at them and hurl ourselves headlong at adulthood. I hate to perpetuate a cliché, but they *were* the best days."

She walked toward him. There was no stool beside his chair. The chair on the other side of the hearth seemed too far away. She lowered herself to her knees before and to one side of him, set a hand on his knee and rubbed it slightly before setting her cheek there instead, her face turned away. His hand came to rest on her head, and his fingers played gently through her curls.

"What time is it?" he asked.

"Ten o' clock."

"Ten?" He sounded surprised. "I missed dinner, did I? Were we not supposed to go somewhere with Nora and Keilly this evening?"

"I sent our excuses," she told him.

"I am sorry," he said. "Was it something you were particularly looking forward to? And you gave up your afternoon visit for me too."

"It was no great sacrifice," she told him.

"I have been remembering every scrape and antic I got up to with those three," he said, "and every debate and quarrel. Every laugh we had. Every holiday we enjoyed together. And those early days in the Peninsula. There were not many of them. They were cut down far too soon. The reality of war was shocking, you know, to four boys fresh out of school, with only idealism and high spirits and energy to buoy us. But there were good times. There was laughter. We were laughing over something at breakfast that morning even though we knew what was coming, and I suppose the laughter was tinged with fear. I wish I could remember what had amused us, though I suppose it was something quite trivial. And then, just an hour or so later, I watched them die."

His hand smoothed lightly over her hair and fell still. Chloe gazed into the unlit coals. And then she heard a slight sound. Muffled laughter? Another memory? It sounded less like laughter the next time, though. She heard him swallow.

She raised her head and scrambled to her feet, and both his hands went up to cover his face.

"The devil!" he said. "Go away, Chloe. Get out of here."

She turned and sat on his lap instead. She burrowed her head against him and slipped her arms as best she could about his waist. And she held him while sobs wracked him until he could no longer hold them in but wept and wept for three dead friends and the end of youth.

She held him for long minutes after he had finished and found a handkerchief and blown his nose and presumably dried his eyes.

"I never wept for them," he said at last. "I never felt I had the right."

"Until now," she said.

"Is it possible," he asked, "that they really do not blame me? That they never have?"

"I think," she said, "that they want to believe, quite correctly, that their son acted on the strength of his own convictions, that he insisted upon going because it was what *he* wanted to do. I think the other parents believe the same thing about their sons."

"It was a strange sort of vanity, then," he said, "to believe that I had so much influence over them?"

Chloe hesitated.

"Yes," she said. "I think if you search your memories, Ralph, it is quite possible you will remember that the idea came from you but that the decision was individually made by four friends."

They lapsed into silence. One of his hands came to the back of her head again, and she felt him lower his head to kiss her.

"I do not suppose," he said, "you will ever be an obedient wife, will you?"

"It is not unmanly to weep," she told him.

"The devil it is not." He nudged her away from his chest and gazed into her face. His own was a bit blotchy. His scar was more pronounced than usual."

"I hope you do not mind too much that I stayed," she said. "Sometimes we need company while we weep, especially when we are mourning a loss."

"They have been dead for more than seven years," he said.

"No," she said. "For you they have just died."

"What did I do to deserve you?" he asked her.

"Oh. Nothing." She sat up abruptly and got to her feet. "*I* asked *you,* if you will remember. It was very brazen of me." She brushed her hands over nonexistent creases in her skirt.

"I am very glad you did," he said.

She looked down a little uncertainly at him. He was looking more disheveled than ever, quite rumpled, in fact. And almost irresistibly gorgeous.

"Are *you* glad?" he asked her.

"Of course I am," she said. "I did not want to go through life a spinster."

"And that is all this is?" He was half smiling at her. "A convenient marriage?"

She did not know how to reply.

"You tell *me,"* she said.

He got to his feet, took her right hand in his, and drew it through his arm.

"I think we had better go to bed," he said, "and make love. We still have an heir to create, remember? Or perhaps a daughter first. I would like a daughter. Do you think she would have your hair? Let's go create. And have some pleasure too. It *is* enjoyable, is it not?"

He turned his head and raised his eyebrows when she did not reply.

"Yes," she said, "it is."

His hand was on the doorknob. Before he turned it, he lowered his head and kissed her briefly and open-mouthed.

23

Ralph could remember only one occasion when the ballroom at Stockwood House had been used as such. He must have been somewhere between the ages of eight and ten. It had been his grandparents' ball, though it was his mother and father who had acted as hosts through most of the evening. Ralph and his sisters had watched the revelries from an upper gallery for half an hour or so under the supervision of a nurse, but while the girls had been enraptured by absolutely everything and everybody and could not *wait* until they were old enough to attend such a ball themselves, he had watched the men bow and scrape to the ladies and mince gracefully about the dance floor like idiots and wondered in horror if *he* would ever be expected to behave in such an asinine way.

He smiled at the memory now as he looked about the ballroom. The floor gleamed with fresh polish. The three chandeliers still rested on it, but soon the candles would be lit and they would be hoisted up close to the ceiling, which was ornately coved and gilded and painted with angels and cherubs and harps and trumpets floating in a blue sky among fluffy, pinkish clouds in a scene that came from no classical myth or Bible story that Ralph had ever encountered. The wall mirrors had been polished until not a speck of dust or a single fingerprint remained. Vines had been twined about the pillars down the length of the room. Banks of flowers and greenery surrounded them and filled the air with their mingled scents. Several instruments were propped on the orchestra dais.

Through the wide double doorway at the far end of the room, Ralph could see long tables covered with white linen cloths that would soon be piled with platters of fruit and dainties and drinks to refresh the guests before supper.

His mother had come and fussed. So had Nora. Great-Aunt Mary had come and made free with her lorgnette and advice. Grandmama had asked a thousand anxious questions. Ralph had made it clear to all of them that he and Chloe needed no assistance, that they had organized the ball themselves and did not anticipate any major catastrophe—or any minor one for that matter.

It was a bit unfair to claim all the credit, of course, since Arthur Lloyd had done a great deal of the planning and most of the work had been undertaken by the housekeeper and the cook and all the household staff.

When his mother had come to offer her services, Chloe had been from home and Ralph had been about to go out. She had sat down in the drawing room after he had thanked her for coming but declined her help and gazed at him for a long moment.

"Ralph," she had said then, "you are back? You are really *back*?"

He might have been forgiven if he had not known what on earth she was talking about. But he *did* know.

"Yes," he had said. "I am, Mama."

She had closed her eyes and drawn a slow breath. "Chloe did this?" she had asked. "It is a good marriage after all, then, is it?"

"It is very good," he had assured her. "I called upon Viscount Harding and his wife. Chloe came with me. And I wrote to Sir Marvin Courtney and to Lord and Lady Janes."

"You were not responsible for what happened to their sons, Ralph," she had said. "Your father and I told you that again and again."

"It seems their parents agree with you," he had told her. "I am so sorry, Mama. I must have given you years of heartache—and Papa too. I wish I could make it up to him. I wish—"

But she had surged to her feet.

"Ralph," she had said with the severity he could remember from his childhood when he had been up to some mischief. "You must not *do* this. Yes, your father was unhappy because *you* were unhappy and there was nothing he could do or say to comfort you. But you had nothing whatsoever to do with his brief illness and passing. He loved you always, and he *always* understood, even when he felt at his most helpless. I will *not* have you feel guilty over your father or over me. You will have children of your own one day, soon, I hope, and then you will understand how parents ache to see their children happy and would never, ever want to see their children unhappy over *them*."

Her words, and the passion with which she had spoken them, had startled Ralph. How little he had known his parents, he had realized a little sadly. It *was* sad in his father's case because he could do nothing now to cultivate a closer relationship with him. It was not too late with his mother, though. And it was time he looked at her, not through the selfish eyes of a boy, but through the more mature eyes of a man so that he could see her as a person with all her imperfections—and his own.

He had hugged her warmly before she left. He had not been able to remember the last time he had done so.

He looked across the ballroom now and smiled when he saw the partially opened French windows leading out onto the balcony. They would have to be closed soon, pleasant as the cool outside air felt. For the king might come. Chloe had reacted with near hysteria when he had told her, but she had soon recovered and squared her shoulders and lifted her chin.

"Well, then," she had said, a martial gleam in her eye.

That was all. She had not needed to say more. Chloe, he believed, would always confront her fears and march straight through the middle of them. Whether he had had something to do with making her that way, he did not know, but certainly she had not been like it last year when she had fled London at the first whisper of gossip. Perhaps he *had* had a positive influence on her, as she had had on him. He doubted he would ever have approached Harding if it had not been for his wife.

His wife!

It was time he went up to see if she was ready for the ball. The first of their guests would be arriving in the next half hour or so. And there would be many of them. Of all the invitations they had sent out, they had received only four refusals, and each of those had come with a personal note of regret. They could expect almost everyone, then, as well as a few people who would inevitably slip in without having been invited. This ball was going to be one of the grandest squeezes of the Season, a prospect that would have horrified him just a couple of months ago.

His mother had been quite right, he thought as he made his way upstairs. He *was* back. He felt as though he had shed a great burden and was physically lighter. He felt years younger. He felt his age, in fact—he was only twenty-six.

The strange thing was, of course, that his grief—for his friends, for all the men of his regiment who had died while he was in the Peninsula, for his father, for his grandfather—had sharpened to a painful degree during the past few weeks even as his sense of guilt had ebbed away. But then *all* his feelings had sharpened.

He was in love with Chloe.

Yes, he was—madly, passionately in love, though he had tried hard not to make an idiot of himself by showing it. But his feelings went deeper than the merely romantic or sexual—though neither of those two felt like a *mere* anything.

He *loved* her.

There was no language for that particular state, however. It merely *was*. He loved her. He supposed he had shown it or at least a glimmering of it during the past weeks. He certainly had not tried to hide it. But one day soon he was going to have to say something, even if only the inadequate cliché *I love you*. Words, he understood, especially words that expressed emotion, were important to women. He wished it were not so, but it was.

One day soon he would tell her.

Despite all the stress of hosting a ball for the *ton* during the London Season and even the expectation that the king might make one of his rare appearances there, and despite the fact that some of the guests and combination of guests made her feel a little as though her head were spinning on her shoulders, and despite the fact that the evening was less than half over and disaster might still strike before it ended—despite it all, Chloe was feeling happy.

Quite consciously *happy*.

She had confronted her worst fear a few weeks ago, and really it had not been so dreadful after all. Her papa had looked apprehensive and had even shed a tear when she told him about her visit to the Marquess of Hitching. But when she had hugged him tightly and told him that he would always, *always* be her beloved papa, he had shed a few more tears and hugged her back and told her she was a good girl and had done the right thing. And he was here at the ball tonight with Graham and Lucy and Mr. Nelson even though she had warned him that the marquess had been invited and had accepted.

The marquess had arrived fairly early with his family. He had squeezed Chloe's hand as they passed along the receiving line and smiled at her. The marchioness had inclined her head, setting her hair plumes to nodding, and murmured something cool and gracious. Lady Angela had looked slightly disdainful but had bidden Chloe a polite good evening. Viscount Gilly had taken her hand in his, raised it to his lips, and called her sister, a mocking though not noticeably malicious gleam in his eye.

A few minutes later Chloe had seen her papa actually shake the marquess by the hand and introduce Graham.

Ralph's grandmother, wearing heavy mourning, had come with Great-Aunt Mary, who looked resplendent in purple with an enormous turban on her head and a jewel-encrusted lorgnette. The two of them were sitting in the small salon close to the ballroom, holding court to a number of the more elderly guests.

The Duke of Stanbrook had come, as had Lord and Lady Trentham. And several of Gwen's family and lady friends, to whom Chloe had been introduced at an afternoon tea, were there with their husbands—the Earl and Countess of Kilbourne, the Marquess and Marchioness of Attingsborough, Viscount and Viscountess Ravensberg, Lord and Lady Aidan Bedwyn, the Duke and Duchess of Bewcastle. The ladies felt like personal friends, Chloe thought, even though she had met a few of them only on that one occasion.

She belonged.

She was wearing the emerald green evening gown she had had made especially to please the dowager duchess. She had had her hair trimmed again, and Mavis had done wonders with the curling tongs. And she wore the emerald pendant necklace and earrings with which Ralph had gifted her earlier today. She believed she looked her best and no longer felt the need to fade into the background and hide the vividness of her coloring. Whether the *ton* believed the Marquess of Hitching really was her father she neither knew nor cared.

She was happy. She had thought she would be contented just to be married, and indeed she would have been if the bargain she had agreed to with Ralph had been kept strictly according to its original terms. But there was so much more. Oh, she must never expect more than she already had, but it was enough to make her happy.

Ralph was a changed man. His eyes were no longer blank or shuttered. He had been forgiven—or at least he had been assured that no forgiveness was necessary because no offense had been committed. More important—of infinitely greater importance, in fact—he had forgiven himself. He had recognized too, perhaps, that he had never been as much to blame for his friends' presence in the Peninsula and in the line of fire as he had always insisted upon believing.

He was at peace with himself. That did not mean that he had stopped mourning those three men or ever would. Nor did it mean that he would not continue suffering the aftereffects of having been at war, of having killed and been gravely wounded, of having witnessed unspeakable atrocities, all at the age of eighteen. But at least he was fully in the land of the living again.

He was fond of her, she believed. They still carried on with their nearly separate lives during the daytime, as was the way of the *ton* during the months of spring, and attended social functions together in the evenings. They still made love each night. Ah, but the nature of that lovemaking had changed. Some of their encounters were brief, some more prolonged. Some were quiet, others more tumultuous. Sometimes they spoke, sometimes not. Sometimes—most times, in fact—he stripped her night-

gown up and off her body before he started or soon after
he started. Almost always he slept with one arm beneath
her neck or an arm flung across her waist, or one leg
hooked over hers. He seemed to need to touch her. The
lovemaking no longer seemed to be *just* about getting
her with child.

It was not love. She must not and would not make the
mistake of thinking it was. She would only invite heartbreak if she did. But it was . . . something. There was
some affection there. She was sure of it. There was, after
all, some emotional bond between them. And it was
enough. She would make it enough.

She was happy.

Chloe and Ralph had led off the dancing together
with a quadrille. Then she had danced a stately country
dance with her papa. She had been standing with Graham and the Duke of Stanbrook before the third set,
having just greeted a couple of late arrivals, and had expected that one of them would solicit her hand. But before either could speak up, the Marquess of Hitching was
bowing to her and asking if he might claim the set.

"I suppose," she said when the figures of the dance
brought them together and allowed them a few moments
for private speech, "we are the object of much curiosity."

"Does that upset you?" he asked her.

"No." She shook her head. "Not at all. I am glad you
came."

The figures took them apart again.

"I am glad you came back to London after last year,"
he said the next time they had a chance to speak, "and
that you are well married. *Happily* married, if I am not

mistaken. Your mother must have been very proud of you, Chloe. She would be especially proud tonight."

She smiled but did not tell him that her mother had been embarrassed by her more than she had been proud.

She danced with Lord Aidan Bedwyn and was dancing with Lord Keilly, her brother-in-law, when a bit of a commotion near the door heralded the appearance in the hall below of the large entourage that preceded the arrival of the king. Chloe hurried toward the ballroom door while the music stopped abruptly and everyone moved back to the sidelines, buzzing with eager anticipation.

The poor king had been generally unpopular when he was merely the Prince Regent, irreverently known as Prinny, prior to his father's death. He was no more popular now. Nevertheless, he *was* the King of England, and it was a huge coup to have one's entertainment graced with his company.

Despite herself, Chloe's knees felt decidedly unsteady as she made her way downstairs on Ralph's arm.

The king was a huge man, blown up by excessive eating and drinking and self-importance and vanity. He was also, Chloe thought after she had sunk into a deep curtsy and he had taken one of her hands in both of his and patted it and commended her on her looks and her home and her husband, capable of a boyish charm that made him irresistibly likable.

He escorted her upstairs, wheezing every slow step of the way, stood inside the ballroom with her hand on his, acknowledging the homage of his subjects as he inclined his head in all directions and gentlemen bowed and ladies sank into curtsies, commented that the ballroom looked like a particularly lovely garden, declined the glass of wine Ralph offered him, gestured to the orchestra to resume its playing, and took his leave, his whole entourage turning with him.

It was all over in ten minutes. By the time Chloe and Ralph arrived back in the ballroom, having bowed and curtsied the royal procession on its way, the dancing was in progress again and someone had thrown all the French windows open.

"Well, that," Ralph said, laughing down into her eyes, "is an event with which we may inspire awe and admiration in our grandchildren when we describe it in minute detail every time they come to visit us."

She laughed back up at him, and something wordless and warm and wonderful passed between them. And this, surely, she thought just a moment before she looked beyond his shoulder, was beyond all doubt the happiest night of her life.

What she saw beyond his shoulder was a group of very late arrivals, all gentlemen, all but one of them invited guests.

The exception was Lord Cornell.

Ralph noticed Cornell a few minutes later after Chloe had gone off to introduce a thin, pimply young man to a plump, mousy young lady whose mother was too busy gossiping with a group of older ladies. The banns for those two would probably be being called within a month, he thought in some amusement as he watched the young man blush and the young lady make herself look quite pretty by smiling in obvious relief. And Chloe could claim all the credit.

Then he spotted Cornell and raised his quizzing glass. The man looked inebriated, though he was not making a spectacle of himself. He was merely laughing rather too loudly with his all-male group. He ought to be asked to leave, since Ralph had personally vetoed his name from the prospective guest list Lloyd had drawn up. However, one hated to make a scene in such a public setting. It might do more harm than good. He would keep an eye on Cornell, though, and make sure he did not get close enough to Chloe to upset her. Damn his impudence!

The one person Ralph did not think of keeping an eye upon, however, was Lucy Nelson.

During the supper hour everyone had feasted sumptuously and lingered for a few speeches and toasts since the ball was in the nature of being a wedding reception too. Most people were moving back to the ballroom, and the members of the orchestra were tuning their instruments, when Ralph became aware of a muffled scream coming from the direction of the French windows.

By the time he reached the balcony, a few other people had gathered there and Hugo and the Duke of Bewcastle were on their way down the steps to the garden below. Someone down there — someone female — sounded very cross. It was Lucy, Ralph soon realized as he followed the other two men down.

"The lady," a male voice was saying, "appears to be afraid of the dark."

The garden was not in total darkness. A few lamps had been lit for the convenience of anyone who wished to escape the heat of the ballroom for a few minutes.

"I came down here when the speeches began," Lucy said, addressing herself rather tearfully to the new arrivals. "It has been the most wonderful, most exciting night of my life, and I needed a few minutes just to catch my breath. But then *he* came down after me and tried to make me to do some very improper things."

"The lady misunderstood." It was Cornell's voice, sounding amused. "I was strolling here too. She must not have seen me in the dark and was startled when I bade her a good evening."

"*And* he said horrid things in the park one day when Chloe was with me," Lucy said, looking at Ralph now. "He called her the delectable duchess and me the scandalous sister. And he accused Chloe of getting you to marry her by doing what M-Mama did with the M-Marquess of Hitching. He is . . . He is not *nice*."

"The lady takes a little teasing humor too literally," Cornell said.

Hugo rumbled. It was the only word to describe the sound he made in his throat.

"Hugo," Ralph said, his eyes on Cornell, whom he could see quite clearly despite the dimness of the light down here, "escort my sister-in-law back to the ballroom if you will be so good."

But Bewcastle was already speaking to her, his voice sounding almost bored, though it was slightly raised to carry quite clearly to those ball guests who had gathered on the balcony above.

"It was a particularly large spider, I suppose, Mrs., ah Nelson?" he said. "No, you need not feel foolish. I would not have enjoyed an encounter with it myself. Perhaps you will allow me to escort you back indoors and will do me the honor of dancing the next set with me."

"Oh." Her voice sounded breathless. "You are the

Duke of Bewcastle. Oh. Yes. Thank you. I *am* a bit afraid of spiders, especially the really big ones with long legs."

Bewcastle led her away.

"You have outstayed your welcome, Cornell," Ralph said, "in my home and in my life. And most certainly in the lives of my wife and my sister-in-law."

"It was all a misunderstanding, Worthingham," Cornell said.

"Yes, so you have suggested more than once," Ralph said. "I was not responsible for my wife's honor six years ago, Cornell, or even last year. I was prepared to allow your mistreatment of her then to go unavenged provided you kept your distance this year and every year in the future. It seems you have *not* kept your distance, either from my wife or from Mrs. Nelson."

Cornell laughed. "You want satisfaction, Worthingham?" he asked. "You wish to name your seconds?"

"You can count on me, Ralph," Hugo said from behind him.

"But I fight only with gentlemen, Hugo," Ralph said. "On the other hand, I *punish* vermin."

"No, you don't," another voice said, and Ralph very briefly closed his eyes. Graham Muirhead! He had come to throw himself between the combatants and urge them to kiss and make up, no doubt.

"Stay out of this, Graham," Ralph said.

"Not a chance." Graham strode past him. "The ladies are *my sisters*, and I protect what is my own."

With which words, worthy of Freddie Nelson for bad theatrics, he knocked Cornell down with a blow to the chin that would surely have felled an oak.

"Neatly done, lad." Hugo's voice was full of admiration.

Ralph looked at his brother-in-law in some astonishment. He could not see his face clearly in the darkness, but his voice sounded a bit sheepish when he spoke again.

"Well," he said, "I suppose that answers *one* question. Did I kill him?"

Ralph looked down at Cornell.

"I do not believe dead men moan," he said. "But it was not for lack of trying, Gray. I should resent you. I wanted the satisfaction of doing that for myself."

"You had better return to your guests, Ralph, and put to rest any nasty speculation that is going on," Hugo said. "Though I do not imagine anyone would care to contradict Bewcastle's explanation about spiders. Have you ever noticed his eyes? Pure silver and straight out of the wilderness. I doubt anyone has *ever* contradicted him. You go on up too, Muirhead. You do not want murder on your conscience. Not when you are a clergyman. Come on, then, lad. You cannot moan down there all night. Show some backbone. Take my hand and I'll help you up. I'll show you off the premises. There will be a door here somewhere, I daresay, leading straight out to the street. It will save you some embarrassment."

"A word of advice, Cornell," Ralph said before following Hugo's advice. "Stay far away from both the Duchess of Worthingham and Mrs. Nelson for the rest of your natural lifetime. I am not sure I will be able to keep the Reverend Muirhead on his leash if you do not."

Freddie Nelson, he discovered a short time later, was still in the supper room, talking with great animation and flamboyant arm gestures to a small group of captives who looked as though they would far rather be in the ballroom.

Lucy was dancing with Bewcastle and managing to look both triumphant and terrified. Chloe was dancing with George and was smiling brightly and looking across the room at *him* with anxious eyes.

Ralph winked at her and grinned—and suddenly her smile was so dazzling that it almost knocked him off his feet.

"Graham did?" Chloe stared at Ralph in disbelief. *"Graham?"*

She had had no opportunity for the last hour to ask him what had happened, though clearly *something* had. It had been whispered about the ballroom that Lord Cornell had insulted Lucy in the garden. But the whisperings had not grown into full-blown gossip and perhaps would not. The Duke of Bewcastle, who had escorted Lucy back to the ballroom and then danced with her, had confronted those who were gathered on the balcony with his exquisitely jeweled quizzing glass half raised to his eye, and apparently that glass wielded by that particular nobleman was considered one of the most lethal weapons in the *ton*. Or so Gwen had whispered in Chloe's ear, and Chloe could believe it. How the sunny-natured duchess could live with him, Chloe did not know. One well-placed glance from those silver eyes was surely capable of freezing grapes on the vine. Though he *had* gone to Lucy's rescue and made up a story about a spider. He was holding one of the duchess's hands in both his own at the moment, his head bent toward hers while she smiled and talked.

"It was as neat and deadly a blow as I have ever seen," Ralph said in answer to Chloe's question. "It was a privilege to witness it, though I must confess I would rather have dealt it myself. Hugo escorted Cornell off the premises. I do not believe he will be troubling either you or your sister again."

"Thank you," she said. "But *Graham*?"

He grinned at her. "Have I told you how lovely you are looking?"

"Am I?" she asked him. "I am not . . . too vivid? Some people might believe I ought to be still in black."

"My mother is not," he said, "or my sisters. And you are wearing this particularly bright shade of green at the specific request of my grandmother. I must compliment her on her good taste, by the way. It is perfect. And as for your hair . . . Well, it would seem you are stuck with that color and I am stuck with having to look at it until you turn old and gray."

"Ouch," she said.

"I look forward to growing old with you, Chloe," he said. "In the fullness of time, that is. I look forward to being young with you first and then middle-aged. I look forward to living all my life with you. Promise not to die before me?"

She did not know whether to laugh or cry.

"Only if *you* promise not to die before *me*," she said.

He laughed softly. "We will do all things together, then, will we?" he asked and raised his head to look about the ballroom.

It was very late—or very early, depending upon one's perspective. Grandmama and Great-Aunt Mary had gone home after supper, and a number of the more elderly guests had left at the same time. But most remained. There was one set left — a waltz. There had been two others during the evening. Chloe had danced the first with Lord Easterly, her uncle, and the second with Viscount Gilly, who had been perfectly agreeable without making any further reference to the relationship between them. And she had watched Ralph dance the first waltz with the Marchioness of Attingsborough and the second with Lucy.

There was one set left.

One waltz.

Then they would see all their guests on their way, send all the servants off to bed rather than insist that they clear up first, pronounce their ball to have been a resounding success despite the unpleasantness with Lord Cornell, and go up to bed themselves. And tomorrow their normal, everyday lives would resume. Ralph had received his Letter of Summons from the Lord Chancellor's office and would take his seat in the House of Lords next week. At the end of the Season they would go back home to Manville Court and . . .

But she was too weary to think beyond that point. And she was feeling unexpectedly and unaccountably depressed. She was tired, she supposed.

A gentleman whose name had slipped her memory stopped in front of them, exchanged a few remarks with Ralph, and then asked Chloe if she would honor him with her hand for the waltz. Couples were already gathering on the floor.

"Too late, Fotheringham," Ralph said. "I have already laid claim to the duchess's hand myself and am not to be persuaded to relinquish it."

Chloe turned her head to smile at him, her tiredness and her low spirits—and Lord Fotheringham—forgotten.

"The last waltz," she said.

"At last." He looked back at her with half-closed eyes. "It is the very devil to be the host of a ball, Chloe, when there is only one lady present with whom one wishes to dance and she happens to be one's wife. Am I fated to become a dull dog, uninterested in any female company except that of my duchess? It is enough to give anyone the shudders."

"*Are* you?" She licked her lips. She was unaccustomed to him in this mood.

"I fear I am." He smiled slowly at her. "And I fear I will find the last waltz at an end if I do not stop babbling. Come."

And he took her hand, set it half across his silken cuff, half across the back of his hand, and led her onto the floor to join the other dancers. Lucy, bright eyed and chattering, was gazing up at a lazy-eyed, half-smiling Freddie Nelson, who was giving her his undivided attention. Gwen, one hand on Lord Trentham's shoulder, the other in his, was laughing at something he was saying. And she managed to *dance,* Chloe had noticed all evening, despite her heavy limp. Viscountess Ravensberg, her husband's hand already at her waist was saying something to the Earl of Kilbourne, who had his countess on his arm—the first wife and the jilted bride and the bridegroom all together on the dance floor, clearly comfortable in one another's company. Lady Angela Allandale had taken to the floor with the most handsome of the considerable court of admirers who had clustered about her all evening.

And then the orchestra struck a chord and the music began.

Chloe had felt consciously happy earlier in the evening. She recaptured that mood again as Ralph twirled her into the dance and she followed his lead as though they had always been meant to waltz together. Except that it was not just happiness she felt now. This was . . . oh, this was the happiest moment of her life. Nothing could or would ever be more perfect than this.

Nothing could ever be more perfect than perfect.

She smiled at the thought as she listened to the music, to the slight thumping of feet and swish of silks, as she watched the colors of gowns swirl past and the glitter of jewels and the sparkle of candles. The smell of flowers and greenery was heavy on the air. There was a welcome suggestion of coolness from the French windows as they danced past.

No, not quite past.

He danced her out through one set of doors and halfway along the blessed coolness of the deserted balcony. And he stopped and stood looking down into her upturned face without releasing his hold on her.

"I was a debater at school," he said. "A good one. A persuasive one. I could always find the right words."

She smiled up at him a little uncertainly. What . . . ?

"I always spoke from the heart rather than from a script as the other boys did," he said. "It worked for me. I spoke with passion."

She raised her eyebrows. Was she supposed to know . . . ?

"I cannot think of a blessed word to say," he said.

And she understood. Oh, yes, in a great upsurge of joy, she understood.

"Except *I love you,*" he said. "Ridiculous, meaningless words. Clichéd. Inadequate. Embarrassing. The trouble is, Chloe—"

She raised one hand and set her fingertips over his lips.

"But they are the most beautiful words in the English language when strung together," she said. "Listen to them. I love you. I love you, Ralph."

He frowned. "If you think I was angling—"

She replaced her fingers.

"I do not," she said. "You perhaps think I am still clinging to the terms of our bargain—no emotional bond, or something like that. I was an idiot. So were you. I love you. And now you have to say it to me or I will dash off into the darkness in my embarrassment and never reemerge. Oh, don't stand there staring at me as though I had grown an extra head. Now I feel *such* a prize—mmmm."

His mouth had stopped her.

And then he was gazing down at her again in the near darkness.

"You are the most precious thing that has ever happened to me," he said.

She feathered her fingers lightly along his facial scar and smiled.

"I think," she said, "we had better return to our guests. Besides, I have longed all evening to waltz with you. I would hate now to waste the chance."

He looked boyish and handsome and altogether gorgeous when he smiled full on. She would never tire of that expression, she thought, as he kissed her swiftly once more and twirled her along the rest of the balcony and through the other set of French windows to join their family and friends and peers.

She would never tire of *him*. Of *this*. Of this marriage and this life and this love that by some miracle they shared.

He was still smiling at her as though there were no one else but her in the ballroom.

"I will waltz with you all my life, Chloe," he said. "I promise."

"A foolish admission." Chloe laughed. "I shall hold you to it."

Read on for a look at the next book in
the Survivors' Club series by Mary Balogh,

ONLY A KISS

Available from Signet in September 2015.

*I*mogen Hayes, Lady Barclay, was on her way home to Hardford Hall from the village of Porthdare two miles away. Usually she rode the distance or drove herself in the gig, but today she had decided she needed exercise. She had walked down to the village along the side of the road, but she had chosen to take the cliff path on the return. It would add an extra half mile or so to the distance, and the climb up from the river valley in which the village was situated was considerably steeper than the more gradual slope of the road. But she actually enjoyed the pull on her leg muscles and the unobstructed views out over the sea to her right and back behind her to the lower village with its fishermen's cottages clustered about the estuary and the boats bobbing on its waters.

She enjoyed the mournful cry of the seagulls, which weaved and dipped both above and below her. She loved the wildness of the gorse bushes that grew in profusion all around her. The wind was cold and cut into her even though it was at her back, but she loved the wild sound and the salt smell of it and the deepened sense of solitude it brought. She held on to the edges of her winter cloak with gloved hands. Her nose and her cheeks were probably scarlet and shining like beacons.

She had been visiting her friend Tilly Wenzel, whom she had not seen since before Christmas, which she had spent along with January at her brother's house, her childhood home, twenty miles to the northeast. There had been a new niece to admire as well as three nephews to fuss over. She had enjoyed those weeks, but she was unaccustomed to noise and bustle and the incessant obligation to be sociable. She was used to living alone, though she had never allowed herself to be a hermit.

Mr. Wenzel, Tilly's brother, had offered to convey her home, pointing out that the return journey was all uphill and rather steeply uphill in parts. She had declined, using as an excuse that she really ought to call in upon elderly Mrs. Park, who was confined to her house since she had recently fallen and badly bruised her hip. Making that call, of course, had meant sitting for all of forty minutes, listening to every grisly detail of the mishap. But elderly people were sometimes lonely, Imogen understood, and forty minutes of her time was not any really great sacrifice. And if she had allowed Mr. Wenzel to drive her home, he would have reminisced as he always did about his boyhood days with Dicky, Imogen's late husband, and then he would have edged his way into the usual awkward gallantries to her.

Imogen stopped to catch her breath when she was above the valley and the cliff path leveled off a bit along the plateau above it, though it still sloped gradually upward in the direction of the stone wall that surrounded the park about Hardford Hall on three sides—the cliffs and the sea formed the fourth side. She turned to look downward while the wind whipped at the brim of her bonnet and fairly snatched her breath away. Her fingers tingled inside her gloves. Gray sky stretched overhead, and the gray foam-flecked sea stretched below. Gray rocky cliffs fell steeply from just beyond the edge of the path. Grayness was everywhere. Even her cloak was gray.

For a moment her mood threatened to follow suit. But she shook her head firmly and continued on her way. She would not give in to depression. It was a battle she often fought, and she had not lost yet.

Besides, there was the annual visit to Penderris Hall, thirty-five miles away on the eastern side of Cornwall, to look forward to next month, really quite soon now. It was owned by George Crabbe, Duke of Stanbrook, a second cousin of her mother's and one of her dearest friends in this world—one of six such friends. Together, the seven of them formed the self-styled Survivors' Club. They had once spent three years together at Penderris, all of them suffering the effects of various wounds sustained during the Napoleonic Wars, though not all those wounds had been physical. Her own had not been. Her husband had been killed while in captivity and under torture in Portugal, and she had been there and witnessed his suffering. She had been released from captivity after his death, actually returned to the regiment with full pomp and courtesy by a French colonel under a flag of truce. But she had not been spared.

After the three years at Penderris, they had gone their separate ways, the seven of them, except George, of course, who had already been at home. But they had agreed to gather again each year for three weeks in the early spring. Last year they had gone to Middlebury Park in Gloucestershire, which was Vincent, Viscount Darleigh's home, because his wife had just delivered their first child and he was unwilling to leave either of them. This year, for the fifth such reunion, they were going back to Penderris. But those weeks, wherever they were spent, were by far Imogen's favorite of the whole year. She always hated to leave, though she never showed the others quite how much. She loved them totally and unconditionally, those six men. There was no sexual component to her love, attractive as they all were, without exception. She had met them at a time when the idea of such attraction was out of the question. So instead she had grown to adore them. They were her friends, her comrades, her brothers, her very heart and soul.

She brushed a tear from one cheek with an impatient hand as she walked on. Just a few more weeks to wait . . .

She climbed over the stile that separated the public path from its private continuation within the park. There it forked into two branches and by sheer habit she took the one to the right, the one that led to her house rather than to the main hall. It was the dower house in the southwest corner of the park, close to the cliffs but in a dip of land and sheltered from the worst of the winds by high, jutting rocks that more than half surrounded it, like a horseshoe. She had asked if she might live there after she came back from those three years at Penderris. She had been fond of Dicky's father, the Earl of Hardford, indolent though he was, and very fond of Aunt Lavinia, his spinster sister, who had lived at Hardford all her life. But Imogen had been unable to face the prospect of living in the hall with them.

Her father-in-law had not been at all happy with her request. The dower house had been neglected for a long time, he had protested, and was barely habitable. But there was nothing wrong with it as far as Imogen could see that a good scrub and airing would not put right, though even then the roof had not been at its best. It was only after the earl was all out of excuses and gave in to her pleadings that Imogen learned the true reason for his reluctance. The cellar at the dower house had been in regular use as a storage place for smuggled goods. The earl was partial to his French brandy and presumably was kept well supplied at a very low cost, or perhaps no cost at all, by a gang of smugglers grateful to him for allowing their operations in the area.

It had been upsetting to discover that her father-in-law was still involved in that clandestine, sometimes vicious business, just as he had been when Dicky was still at home. His involvement had been a bone of serious contention between father and son and a large factor in her husband's decision to join the military rather than stay and wage war against his own father.

The earl had agreed to empty out the cellar of any remaining contraband and to have the door leading into it from the outside sealed up. He had had the lock on the front door changed and all the keys to the new one given to Imogen. He had even voluntarily assured her that he would put an end to the smuggling trade on the particular stretch of the coast that bordered the Hardford estate, though Imogen had never put much faith in his word. She had never made any mention of smuggling to anyone afterward, on the theory that what she did not know would not hurt her. It was a bit of a morally weak attitude to have, but . . . Well, she did not think much about it.

She had moved into the dower house and had been happy there ever since, or as happy as she ever could be, anyway.

She stopped now at the garden gate and looked upward. But no, no miracle had happened since yesterday. The house was still roofless.

The roof had been leaking as long as Imogen had lived in the house, but last year so many pails had had to be set out to catch the drips when it rained that moving about upstairs had begun to resemble an obstacle course. Clearly, sporadic patching would no longer suffice. The whole roof needed to be replaced, and she had fully intended to have the job done in the spring. During one particularly dreadful storm in December, however, a large portion of the roof had been ripped off despite the sheltered position of the house, and she had had no choice but to make arrangements to have the job done at the very worst time of the year. Fortunately there was a roofer in the village of Meirion, eight miles upriver. He had promised to have the new roof in place before she returned from her brother's, and the weather had cooperated. January had been unusually dry.

When she had returned just a week ago, however, it was to the discovery that the work had not even begun. The roofer, when confronted, had explained that he had been waiting for her to come back so that he would know exactly what she wanted—apparently a new roof had not been clear enough. His workers were supposed to be here this week, but so far they had been conspicuous in their absence. She was going to have to send one of the grooms with another letter of complaint.

It was very frustrating, for she had been forced to move into Hardford Hall until the job was done. It was no particular hardship, she kept telling herself. At least she had somewhere to go. And she had always loved Aunt Lavinia. During the first year following her brother's death, however, it had occurred to Aunt Lavinia that for sheer gentility's sake she ought to have a female companion. The lady she had chosen was Mrs. Ferby, Cousin Adelaide, an elderly widow, who was fond of explaining in her deep, penetrating voice to anyone who had no choice but to listen that she had been married for seven months when she was seventeen, had been widowed before she turned eighteen and thus made a fortunate escape from the slavery of matrimony.

For years after her bereavement Cousin Adelaide had paid supposedly short visits to her hapless relatives since she had been left poorly provided for, and she had stayed until someone else in the family could be prevailed upon to invite her to pay a short visit elsewhere. Aunt Lavinia had voluntarily invited her to come and live indefinitely at Hardford, and Cousin Adelaide had arrived promptly and settled in. Aunt Lavinia had collected one more stray. She collected them as other people might collect seashells or snuffboxes.

No, it was no great hardship to be forced to stay at the main house, Imogen told herself with a sigh as she turned away from the depressing sight of her roofless house. Except that now, soon, being there was going to become a lot worse, for the Earl of Hardford was coming to Hardford Hall.

That roofer deserved to be horsewhipped.

The new earl was coming for an indeterminate length

of time. His title was really not so very new, though. He had been in possession of it since the death of Imogen's father-in-law two years ago, but he had neither written at the time nor put in an appearance since nor shown any other interest in his inheritance. There had been no letter of condolence to Aunt Lavinia, no anything. It had been easy to forget all about him, in fact, to pretend he did not exist, to hope that he had forgotten all about them.

They knew nothing about him, strange as it seemed. He might be any age from ten to ninety, though ninety seemed unlikely and so did ten since the letter that had been delivered to Hardford's steward this morning had apparently been written by the earl himself. Imogen had seen it. It had been scrawled in a rather untidy, though unmistakably adult, hand, and it had been brief. It had informed Mr. Ratchett that his lordship intended to wander down to the tip of Cornwall since he had nothing much else to do for the moment and that he would be obliged if he could find Hardford Hall in reasonably habitable condition. And in possession of a broom.

It was an extraordinary letter. Imogen suspected that the man who had penned it, presumably the earl himself since it bore his signature in the same hand as the letter itself, was drunk when he wrote it.

It was not a reassuring prospect.

In possession of a broom?

They did not know if he was married or single, if he was coming alone or with a wife and ten children, if he would be willing to share the hall with three female relatives or would expect them to take themselves off to the dower house, roof or no roof. They did not know if he was amiable or crotchety, fat or thin, handsome or ugly. Or a drunkard. But he was coming. Wandering suggested a slow progress. They almost certainly had a week to prepare for his arrival, probably longer.

Wandering down to the tip of Cornwall, indeed. In February.

Nothing much else to do for the moment, indeed.

Whatever sort of man was he?

And what did a broom have to do with anything?

Imogen made her way toward the main house with lagging steps despite the cold. Poor Aunt Lavinia had been in a flutter when Imogen left earlier. So had Mrs. Attlee, the housekeeper, and Mrs. Evans, the cook. Cousin Adelaide, quite unruffled and firmly ensconced in her usual chair by the drawing room fire, had been firmly declaring that hell would freeze over before she would get excited about the impending arrival of a mere man. Though that man was unwittingly providing her with a home at that very moment. Imogen had decided it was a good time to walk to the village to pay a call upon Tilly.

But she could delay her return no longer. Oh, how she longed for the solitude of the dower house.

One of the grooms was leading a horse in the direction of the stables, she could see as she approached across the lawn. It was an unfamiliar horse, a magnificent chestnut that she would certainly have recognized if it had belonged to any of their neighbors.

Who . . . ?

Perhaps . . .

But no, it was far too soon. Perhaps it was another messenger he had sent on ahead. But . . . on that splendid mount? She approached the front doors with a sense of foreboding. She opened one of them and stepped inside.

The butler was there, looking his usual impassive self. And a strange gentleman was there too.

Imogen's first impression of him was of an almost overwhelming masculine energy. He was tall and well-formed. He was dressed for riding in a long drab coat with at least a dozen shoulder capes and in black leather boots that looked supple and expensive despite the layer of dust with which they were coated. He wore a tall hat and tan leather gloves. In one hand he held a riding crop. His hair, she could see, was very dark, his eyes very blue. And he was absolutely, knee-weakeningly handsome.

Her second impression, following hard upon the heels of the first, was that he thought a great deal of himself and a small deal of everyone else. He looked both impatient and insufferably arrogant. He turned, looked at her, looked pointedly at the door behind her, which she had shut, and looked back at her with raised, perfectly arched eyebrows.

"And who the devil might you be?" he asked.